Passions of the Heart

Book II of the Passion Series

By Sheri Chapman

Cover by Veronique Poirier

COPYRIGHT

Trient Press
3375 S Rainbow
Blvd
#81710, SMB
13135
Las Vegas,NV
89180

Ordering Information:
Quantity sales. Special discounts are available
on quantity purchases by corporations,
associations, and others. For details, contact
the publisher at the address above.
Orders by U.S. trade bookstores and
wholesalers. Please contact Trient Press: Tel:
(775) 996-3844; or visit
www.trientpress.com.
Printed in the United States of America
Publisher's Cataloging-in-
Publication data Chapman,
Sheri
A title of a book :Passions of the Heart
ISBN Hard Cover:9781953975-058
        Paperback: 9781-953975065
        E-book: 9781953975072

Dedications

<u>**Key to symbols:**</u>

***   indicates   passage of time
(symbols appear before and after)

+++   indicates   Flash back
(symbols appear before and after)

= = =   indicates   switch in perspective   (symbols appear before and after)

<u>**Dictionary of Lakota terms**</u> found at the back of this book

CHAPTER ONE

Betrothal

Kaitlin Farley stared at the back of the legendary war chief as he addressed the very large gathering thronged around him. Her legs shook with nerves, but her heart sang with ecstatic joy. The leader had just announced to his Lakota band of the Sioux tribe that she was his betrothed!

The white woman looked down at his mark of ownership around her neck. The *wanapin* was designed from a centerpiece of a single bear claw flanked by opalescent stones that were joined by reddish sparkly sandstone, midnight onyx, golden flecked Formica pebbles, and more of the tiny gleaming iridescence nuggets. It stood for her induction into Indian society, a denouncement of her *wasicu* ways and beliefs, and her accepted proposal to become the *thawicu*, or wife, of a renowned leader.

The golden beauty looked upon his powerful bronze frame with love as *Woniya*

Mato addressed his people. His body rippled with muscular strength, and his commanding voice resonated over the crowd as he accepted her into the Bear Claw Clan branch of the intrepid Oglala. The three other members of the tribal council lent their voices in support. The crowd cheered madly.

As Chief Spirit Bear turned his six-foot frame toward her, his bear claw and teeth *wanapin* bounced on his hard chest. He was dressed in buckskin finery. The prominent man's fringed shirt was decorated with colorfully dyed porcupine quills in intricate patterns. His leggings were also fringed but did not have the quill adornments. The breechcloth, however, displayed a similar pattern with no fringing. The warrior's stealthy feet were clad in the softest moccasins with the same complicated quill design.

Woniya Mato's shiny black hair hung feely. His chieftain war bonnet of many eagle and hawk feathers marked his countless coups. Red feathers with black tips along with bear teeth and claw streamers adorned his head. The feathered ensemble cascaded along with his hair down his back.

The war chief captured Kaitlin's attention with his obsidian eyes. He held out his hand in her direction. In his warm tenor voice, the man of war commanded her to come. With trembling legs, Kaitlin did as he bid.

Spirit Bear's handsome face smiled upon the young woman as she approached. His eyes twinkled with pride. The honey-haired girl reached her hand toward his outstretched one. He clasped his warming comfort around hers and drew her into his strong embrace. In front of the whole tribe, the warrior lowered his lips to hers and sealed their fate with a passionate kiss from his heart.

It was the only thing the stalwart male could've done to take the blonde's mind off of being the center of attention of every person in the community. When *Woniya Mato*, or Spirit Bear as the whites would call him, touched her, she forgot all but him. The leader's tender kiss erased all of Kaitlin's worries and unease.

When her betrothed's full lips withdrew, the white woman sighed with happiness. Spirit Bear smiled with reciprocated joy. Both were winners in this union.

"Soon, *mita wastelaka,* but not soon enough, *nimitawa ktelo*, you will be mine, joined for all time under Indian law, blessed by *Wakantanka* himself!" his voice, deep with passion, confided in her.

They turned and the crowd surged to congratulate them. Arms touched, patted, and caressed her hair and arms. Many friends surrounded them and smiled in happiness for the couple.

After the multitude began to resume the celebration, Kaitlin sighed in relief. Spirit Bear looked upon her with amusement.

"You will endure many of these celebrations in the years to come," he confessed with humor warming his voice.

"*Tos*, my chief. I will do many things with joy in my heart, for I am full of pride that I am the one to tame the mighty Spirit Bear!" she teased.

They sat back down with the others. The tribal council's seating was reserved in the center of the celebration grounds. The huge bonfire burned brightly behind them while the dancing of the people occurred in front of them, and the instruments played to the side of the congregation. Her close friends, Apple Blossom, Playful Otter, and Desert Rose were the dates of the other leaders.

Sky Warrior, or *Wawakte Towanjila,* was the second ranking chief of the village. He was the main man in charge of village affairs. If the matter was a minor affair, he settled the problem. Larger issues were brought before the council (made up of the four chieftains) to decide a fair and just settlement. He was a fierce warrior, but unless it was a major raid, he usually stayed behind in the village to protect it.

The third leader was Wonder Worker, or *Wawakankan.* He was the spiritual leader and healer of the tribe. His shaman knowledge of spiritual incantations was distinguished above most. He had a vast wisdom of herbs and medicinal plants that saved the lives of many. A blushing and shy Playful Otter sat near him.

The final member of the council was Lone Wolf, or *Isnala Sungmanitu*. He was the chief in charge of major hunting expeditions. His stealth and tracking abilities were comparable only with those of the war chief and ultimate leader of the band. Lone Wolf's strategies for large game hunting were illustrious. His date was Desert Rose.

Wawat'ecaka, Wonder Worker's mother, brought forth more fine foods for the tribal council and their guests. There was roasted duck, elk, deer, and rabbit. *Tinpsila*, or sweet prairie turnips, accompanied fresh carrots, asparagus, poke, and cress. Indian bread, *aguyapi*, sweetened with fresh fruits accompanied every dish.

Chokecherries, blackberries, buffalo berries, and apples were in bone plates easily accessible. Drinks of flavored berry beverages filled every cup constructed from animal horn. Women and men ate together, an unusual practice with Indian customs, but this was a special occasion.

Kaitlin was known as *Mazaska Zi Ista* to the Indians. The chief had named her that after her unusual coloring of her eyes: they were golden with green flecks.

She was a delicate golden flower blooming among the dark forest of plants. Hers was the only light-colored skin present. The white woman's silky hair was honey-colored, kissed by the sun. It curled in loose spirals around her face.

"Congratulations, *Mazaska Zi Ista!*" Desert Rose said with a smile. "You, too, my chief," the maiden said teasingly when he lifted a brow in her direction.

"Yes, thank you for letting me know how I captured the mighty bear where others failed before me," Kaitlin answered, very nearly using fluent Lakota. She loved to jest the vibrant male beside her.

"I will have to show you who tamed who," Spirit Bear growled though his smile.

Lone Wolf was a man who valued privacy, but this intimate group of friends expanded his range of comfort to include them. Never before had he wished for company, especially for more than two or three at a time. Large hunts were the exception. He added to the taunting.

"*Tos, Woniya Mato.* I believe it was you who captured her and enslaved *Mazaska Zi Ista,* but really just the opposite has occurred," he informed. The only evidence of his jest was the tiny crinkling of the edges of his eyes.

"The fall of the mighty warrior occurred at last. Let us chant to *Wakantanka,*" Wonder Worker added to the merriment. He was the closest friend Spirit Bear had. All four men on the tribal council were exceptionally close, but none could take the place of *Wawakankan.*

Sky Warrior had to join the teasing of the intimidating man as well. His deep voice added, "Your enemies, *toka,* will praise the Great Spirit for many moons. It was believed that the war chief of the Bear Claw Clan would never succumb to defeat."

"To my enemies, *hiya,* I will never accept defeat, my *kolas,* but to *Mazaska Zi Ista, tos*," Spirit Bear acquiesced. His mischievous smirk twitched the edge of his sensuous mouth as he eyed Kaitlin's reaction to the light banter.

"Praise to *Mazaska Zi Ista*!" Apple Blossom said softly. "Tell us of this magic you weave that can tame a ferocious bear!"

"*Tos*, we must know this secret," said Playful Otter shyly. She'd had a crush on the man beside her for eons, it seemed. She was nervous around *Wawakankan*, but thrilled as well. He'd know every way to entice the spirits to aid in his plight, whatever that may be, and she couldn't resist dropping a subtle hint to her true feelings as she teased her friend.

Out of her peripheral vision, Playful Otter caught the gleam in Wonder Worker's eye and the smile that tugged on the corner of his sexy lips. She blushed and would make sure to avoid eye contact with him for a few moments.

"Gentlemen of council, where is my coup feather?" Kaitlin demanded playfully. Her jest was met with four wide grins. "I want my coup chanted before the next communal meeting of the village," she continued.

"Oh, your coup will be chanted all right," Spirit Bear said. "You'll be vowing to obey me in every way," he warned.

The distinctive group's conversation died away as a special dance was performed by a couple. The dance was meant as a tribute to signify the impending joining of the chief and his chosen one. It was a dance of lovers and of happiness. All four couples watched, enthralled, for each one felt something special for the one whose mats were placed close by.

CHAPTER TWO

Reminiscing…

When the dance died away, Kaitlin thought about the day she'd met the impending man of her life. Never would she have dreamed of falling in love with him. Never would she have believed that she was more accepted in the Indian community than among her own people!

+++

Kaitlin had been living with her father and brother in the first house built outside of the small village surrounded by supportive wooden walls. They were bereft of money and possessions. Even so, her father and brother drank the days away and gambled possessions they didn't have. Finally, her father sold her to the highest offer: Jed Coldwater.

Jed was an evil man. He'd committed many vile and atrocious crimes against the Sioux people and herself. The two oldest Coldwater boys had raped and killed three Oglala maidens as well as sacrificed a young brave not yet in manhood.

Kaitlin had run away from her fate, hoping to make a life of her own inside the walls of the settlement rather than be the payment for her father's debts. Unfortunately, Jed found her before she reached safety. While trying to escape his evil clutches, Kaitlin was knocked unconscious.

When she awoke, the white girl was cradled in the strong, domineering arms of the bronze war chief. His eyes had caressed her body and made her experience feelings that had never been born in her before. Fear and desire warred within her for many days. During the time of healing, the enchanting blonde didn't realize that she now belonged to the prominent leader…

+++

Kaitlin looked up into *Woniya Mato's* mesmerizing eyes. There was a question in them. She shook her head, ridding herself of the last of the hazy memories she'd momentarily lapsed into.

"Are you tired, *mita wastelaka*, my love?" his spirited voice asked softly.

"Not excessively," she replied. He drew her into his warm embrace. The gentle woman leaned her supple shape against his hard body and watched more festivities.

It was an hour later when Spirit Bear pulled her to her feet and took her to their tipi. She still obeyed him without protest. Today was her first full day of freedom from her shackles of bondage.

Was it really only the day before that he'd asked her to marry him? Kaitlin had been a slave then, escorted by a male wherever she went. She'd earned the leader's mistrust with her attempted escape the prior month.

How had the captive gone, in one month's time, from a fully escorted slave into the status of betrothed to *Woniya Mato*? It seemed impossible. If it weren't for the black she-bear, it wouldn't ever have happened.

The Indians seemed to worship the strength of the bear above most animals. Other animals they favored included the eagle, hawk, wolf, and fox, but the bear was the most mighty and fearsome of all. Warriors never killed them unless the Great Spirit instructed them to or if it was to save a life.

If the bear's essence had to be sacrificed, it was mourned and praised like a fallen warrior. Only men who had slain a bear were allowed to wear its claws and teeth. Kaitlin was allowed the bear claw *wanapin* because the she-bear had given it to her of her own free will.

Kaitlin had run into the large black mother bear at least three times, and three times, she had walked away unscathed. The superstitious Indian community took it as a sign from *Wakantanka* that she was an Oglala at heart, and it was the will of the Great Spirit for her to join with the famous chief.

Before yesterday, Kaitlin had no rights and no power of choice. She was at the chief's beck and call. The blonde woman had fulfilled every whim at the moment he desired it. Even with that being the case, the man of war had always treated her with warmth and respect.

+++

Kaitlin had fought against the love building for the chief in her heart. She'd vowed to escape the leader's wild passions. As a slave, she couldn't stand being denied the freedom of choice. Slightly more than a month back, the white woman had taken advantage of the warrior's absence and stole away into the night along with the other village slave, Apple Blossom.

A few days after the getaway, Apple Blossom miscarried Snake Strike's baby. While Kaitlin was bathing the other woman and trying to soothe her pain, the escapee looked up into the war-painted face of the very handsome man she'd just agreed to wed.

Spirit Bear had been indomitable, terrifying, and had nearly killed her. He'd believed her to be Jed's party of whites on a mission to slay him. Kaitlin had looked into his red and black striped fierce face, mouth opened in victory, with a lethal tomahawk prepared to strike death upon her. Only his power of love for the golden one had stayed his hand.

Before heading back to the village, Spirit Bear and his warriors overcame and defeated the enemy party of whites. Jed had been granted a one-on-one fight with Spirit Bear. The war chief had not easily taken the *wasicun* life. The white dog had to pay for the lives he had stolen from the Oglala. After eleven grueling hours of torture that Kaitlin had to witness, Spirit Bear ended Jed's life and scalped him.

Kaitlin didn't understand the depth of Jed's evil or the retaliation of the chief. It caused a swift fear of the leader to form in her heart. She'd never viewed this terrifying, cruel side of *Woniya Mato* before.

Just when she was getting back into the swing
of Indian life, the mighty chief left once again.
He was gone for several days. During this time,
many berries were ripening that the tribe dried
in preparation for winter. Along with her
friends, Kaitlin had left the village to gather the
luscious fruits.

In her search for the berries Kaitlin wandered
away from the group and became disoriented.
A storm materialized and separated her from the
society, wiping out traces of anyone's passage.
Snake Strike took the opportunity to retaliate
against the tribal council who'd robbed him of
being a man: he intended to murder *Mazaska Zi
Ista*. An injured Brave Elk intervened in an
attempt to save her.

 Just when the shaman and war chief arrived on
the scene, a black she-bear had resolved the
issue with the small, resentful man. Both
leaders took it as a major sign from *Wakantanka*
that the lives saved, both Golden Eyes and
Brave Elk (then Young Elk) were destined for
greater things.

+++

"This is why I was allowed to break the chains of servitude," Kaitlin thought. *"This is how I got inducted into Oglala society. And this,"* a wondrous gift she would never forget, *"is the reason I will soon marry the only man to ever tempt my heart."*

The former slave undressed when she entered the tipi. Spirit Bear's eyes caressed her womanly curves, but he knew she was very tired. He forced his desire to calm so that she could rest her recovering body.

= = =

Mazaska Zi Ista was not ill, Spirit Bear noted, but the Golden One sustained several significant bruises from Snake Strike's swift foot. Luckily, the spunky blonde had managed to only significantly welt her hamstring and derriere. The chief fixed a drink for the woman of his heart. He added a pinch of yarrow powder to help her relax and sleep without dreams.

= = =

Kaitlin slept better than she had in a long time. The many bruises didn't hamper her, nor did her mind fly with excitement over her new status: the release from slavery and impending marriage to her true love. The blonde couldn't imagine her life better!

Morning birds were beginning to sing when Kaitlin stretched languidly. She looked at the chief. His polished, midnight eyes watched her intensely. He'd such depth to his every look. It was as if the man could see into the very soul of who he targeted with those black orbs.

A smile transformed *Woniya Mato's* striking face into one of unbelievable male beauty. It made her heart beat faster with just a look. Kaitlin ripped her gaze from his and brazenly

traced a hungry path down his enticing body
with her eyes.

The blonde noted how his masculine neck
blended into his shoulders, joined together by
bulging trapezius muscles. His chest was hard,
and his pectorals were pronounced above his
clearly defined abdominals. Spirit Bear's eight
pack stretched and contracted with his every
breath.

Her eyes slid lower. The war chief wore a
breechcloth. He didn't wear one to sleep in
often, and today, it seemed to have risen on its
own accord. Without meaning to, Kaitlin drew
in a quick breath. Quickly, the golden eyes
reclaimed him.

= = =

Spirit Bear wore a broad smile brought on by
her shock at finding what state he was in and
also because she'd initiated sexual interest with

her bold perusal of him. The chief cocked an
eyebrow at her.

= = =

The white woman could only stare an invitation
at her soon-to-be husband. Kaitlin was still
fairly new to the ways of love though he'd
shown her much in their short time together.
However, she was still not quite ready to initiate
physical contact.

The smile on the man's sensual mouth did not
fade as he slowly lowered his head to hers. The
contact of lip on lip was electrifying. *Woniya
Mato's* mouth worked on hers, gently, teasingly.
Kaitlin gasped with desire.

Spirit Bear chuckled at her lust and happily
deepened the kiss. The blonde parted her lips in
willing invitation. His hot tongue found hers,
and they circled one another for a time. Slowly,
Kaitlin's hand sneaked behind his neck and
lightly caressed his nape as she moaned his
name.

= = =

This golden goddess could drive him wild in a moment's notice. Spirit Bear was quickly reaching the point of no return. His manhood already ached with longing for release. His hands boldly stroked and fondled her willing body. *Mazaska Zi Ista* arched under his administration.

"You are *gopeca, mita wastelaka.*"

There was a question in her amber eyes, for she was still learning the Lakota language; however, he preferred not to explain it to her right now. He'd honor her by his next actions…

In the aftermath of lovemaking, the chief's strong arms circled the womanly form and snuggled her into his powerful frame. *Woniya Mato* looked down into her face that still reflected awe at the pleasure such a joining could create.

"*Gopeca* is the light of *wi* shining on the land.
It is the flower as she opens up her petals for the
first time." As he usually did when
communicating with her, Spirit Bear included
gestures to help her comprehend.

= = =

A dawning of understanding crept over the
blonde. "*Gopeca* must mean 'pretty'. Or
maybe 'beautiful' when translated into English."

"Which is better?"

"*Beautiful* is more breath-taking."

"*Gopeca* is buftal," he smiled at his attempt to
form the word that his mouth was not used to
uttering.

"Thank you, my love. You are kind."

"*Hiya*, just truthful." His eyes twinkled at her.

Finally, they began to dress, for the day was full of work that needed to be done. Every day, food was gathered and stored for the severe winters that struck the lands. The cold season was never easy to survive.

When *Woniya Mato* opened the flap on their tipi, he laughed. It was a deep, masculine sound that Kaitlin loved to hear.

"There is a surprise waiting for you, *Mazaska Zi Ista*."

Kaitlin came to the opening to see what he was talking about. To her surprise, there were gifts left by the tipi. There was a necklace made of bone and carved beads with a matching bracelet. Three colorfully woven mats were piled on top of one another as well as a set of fire-hardened wooden bowls. In the bowls, someone had prepared their breakfast.

"Wow! This sure is nice! I wonder who…?"

"The wedding gifts are beginning already."

"Wedding gifts?"

"Do you not realize what a time it is in our people's lives to get to see the wedding of one of their leaders? There will be many gifts in the next moon. We will have many visitors, some from other bands. Enjoy it *mita wastelaka*, for it will end soon enough. This is the time in your life to find delight!"

He smiled at her then said, "I am going to work on bow shooting with my *kolas*. We need to perfect our technique before we hunt bison."

Kaitlin nodded at him and watched as he took his bow and disappeared. This was also a major difference in how she was treated. Before, with slave status, the man merely disappeared with no explanation to her. She slaved away and never knew when he'd reappear.

CHAPTER THREE

Freedom?

Just when the blonde completed her mint tea sweetened with raspberries, *Wawat'ecaka* entered.

"Come. Drink tea with me," Kaitlin invited the mother-like figure.

"*Tos*, I would enjoy that. When we finish, let us work with the sacred white elk hide."

Mazaska Zi Ista nodded in agreement. After filling *mniapahta* with fresh water and stacking newly gathered firewood, the women went to the place where they tanned leather. The location was well-shaded by oak and other trees. A small stagnant pool was nearly separated from the main branch of the river. Further back from the pool, a rock wall bordered its side.

Under the shade by the tepid pool sat a wooden rack in which a great white elk hide was stretched. *Wawat'ecaka* walked to the rock wall and followed it back about twenty-five feet. She grabbed two fire-hardened wooden bowls from a shallow cave etched into the side of stone.

Handing one to Kaitlin, they walked together to the hide. Each woman stood at opposite ends of the pelt and began to smear the mixture of brain and fat from the bowls onto the leather. Kaitlin worked the goop into the elk until it would no longer absorb into the surface.

The procedure was repeated with the opposite side. When both sides had been completely oiled, the women stretched and pulled on the leather to create the supple flow of the someday fabric in which *Wawat'ecaka* was famous for. Then they tacked it back to the wooden frame, stretching it as much as possible.

"This will make the best leather. It is my… our masterpiece! *Wawat'ecaka* claimed with pride. "It belongs to your betrothed. He made the killing strike."

"He will be pleased, I am sure!" Kaitlin agreed.

The women took the yucca root soaking in a rock indented with a natural shallow place. They pounded the root until soapy froth was produced. Each woman washed hands, arms, and face. Then each returned to their tipi for a quick lunch and rest during the heat of the day.

Working the leather was hard work. As always, Kaitlin welcomed resting her tired muscles. She was thankful that her body was responding to the more intense rigors of Indian life in the past month. The adopted woman still slept when she rested, but not so deeply.

When *Mazaska Zi Ista* awoke, she grabbed the two newest baskets she'd woven and a sharp digging stick. She wanted to collect tubers and yams that grew wild in a nearby field. The blonde planned on sharing her find with *Wawat'ecaka*.

Gentle Rabbit took care of her tipi and that of her son's. The elder woman's husband had been killed in a raid several years back. Normally, her son would reside with her until he took a mate, as was Indian custom, but her son already achieved important status in the tribe. A medicine man, especially one in so much demand, needed a private lodge to treat illness and to practice ritual incantations.

The same was said of all four tribal council members. All four lived in their own tipi. Men did not own tipis, but these leaders were granted one until they took a woman. Then the woman would own the structure.

When each young man attained leadership status early in his life before he'd selected a mate, all were honored with a tipi for taking so much responsibility onto their shoulders. No higher honor could be bestowed upon these leading men by the band. Most men in the tribe resided in the structure of his parents' until he married.

Upon her marriage to the chief, Kaitlin would become owner of the dwelling, but she was unaware of this custom. She still had much to learn about the Indian community.

When the single woman had a basketful of tubers and another of yams, she headed for the village. Kaitlin spied some sassafras on the edge of the field and collected that as well. *Wawat'ecaka* enjoyed the tea made from the root of the plant.

Suddenly, a pair of legging-clad powerful legs materialized in front of her crouched position.

"*Woniya Mato*, you startled me!" she breathed.

He stood tall and proud as he looked down at her. His features didn't soften. "You wandered off alone. I just wanted to check on you."

"I do not need an escort," she informed him. "You do not fear me running from you, do you, my mighty chief?"

"*Hiya*, I know you would not do that. But it is not wise for a female to wander off alone, *Mazaska Zi Ista*."

"It's just… I have not been *alone* – able to go anywhere – by myself for at least a month!" she paused, then mumbled, "…more like two!"

"*Tos*, I know. I understand. But do not go alone far from the village. There are many dangers for one such as you. You are *gopeca*. You inflame desire within a man without knowing you do so." He stepped nearer to her and grasped her upper arms. "It is important for you to understand this, *mita wastelaka.* I could not bear for something to happen to you."

"*Tos*, my chief. I will do as you ask."

He nodded once then dropped his hands from her. Spirit Bear didn't want to alert his *winyan* that she faced more dangers than just from a man. There was evidence of their *toka*, the Crow, on the prowl near their camp. They would not dare cross into the camp, but the chief had stepped up the security as a precaution. A Crow warrior could count many coups if he captured the heart of *Woniya Mato.* The dominant leader couldn't bear to ever lose this golden angel he'd stumbled onto.

"*Uwa yo, Mazaska Zi Ista.*" He reached a bronze hand to her.

Kaitlin smiled up into his stoic expression and placed her small hand into his larger one. He picked up one of her baskets and let her carry the other so that they could walk with hands clasped as lovers were prone to do.

Before they reached the village, the chief handed her the second basket and walked a little ahead, as was the tradition. He headed back to the bow range.

Kaitlin went to *Wawat'ecaka's* tipi and smiled with pleasure at the thought of her surprise. The other woman had given her much. Kaitlin had offered little in return.

"Wawat'ecaka, uwa yo. I have something for you."

Gentle Rabbit came forth from her tipi. Her mouth formed an O-shape as she looked in wonder at the two brimming baskets.

"We share!" the young white woman exclaimed.

"Mazaska Zi Ista! You sneaky girl! When did you do this?"

"Just now!"

"Did you go alone?"

Kaitlin looked down. *"Tos*, but *Woniya Mato* said I cannot go by myself again."

"He is wise, *Mazaska Zi Ista*. The young *winyan* promised to the chief would be a tempting target for any *toka*."

"*Tos*, he explained this to me."

"You are gracious and generous, Golden Eyes. I am honored that you include me in you bounty."

Kaitlin looked up in surprise. "It is *you* who is generous, *Wawat'ecaka*! You always give to me, and I never give to you in return!"

"Child, how can you say that? I could not do all the leather tanning or women chores for three tipis without your help!

Kaitlin knew this wasn't true, for Gentle Rabbit had done this and much more before she'd come onto the scene. Kaitlin's heart warmed at the woman's attempt to make her feel worthy, and perhaps she did help to lighten the elder woman's load.

They selected four yams to roast that night. They would also eat fresh *Tinpsila* and buffalo berries. *Wawat'ecaka* had managed to capture four wild grouse for their supper.

Gentle Rabbit and Golden Eyes hung the grouse from a tree and began to pluck the feathers from their bodies. The feathers were stacked neatly into a leather bag for storage.

Kaitlin started a fire in the outside hearth in front of the chief's tipi. She burned it hot and then let the outside embers smolder. When only ash was left, she placed the four yams in the cooling embers.

Wawat'ecaka skewered the grouse and placed them around the flames. She used the skillet Kaitlin had brought with her from her other life to catch the meat drippings for *aguyapi*, Indian bread.

Kaitlin crushed wild onion and garlic and added a little water. She added a stick of salt brush and boiled the mixture. With a small brush made from stiff horse tail hair, she painted the grouse with the solution.

In another fire-hardened wooden bowl, Kaitlin crushed plums. She added water and then strained the pulp out. She placed the juice into the *mniapahta.*

The white girl kept the base of fruit pulp, added a few buffalo berries, the meat drippings, and then placed the pulverized grain powder into the bowl with water. She mixed it and began to cook it on the flat rocks near the fire.

When the meat was nearly cooked, Kaitlin retrieved the yams from the ash. They were cooked to perfection! The outside skin was crisp, but she knew the inside would be a creamy texture.

The mouth-watering aromas filled the air. Kaitlin's stomach rumbled in response. She looked up to see *Woniya Mato* and *Wawakankan* approaching.

The women fixed the men's plates and sat on the logs to wait for them to eat. The two leaders easily conversed in relaxed camaraderie, but Kaitlin knew the chief watched her unobtrusively. She couldn't catch him, but she felt the weight of his stare.

When they finished, *Wawat'ecaka* and she ate.
The golden skinned one nearly sighed in
pleasure at the steaming hot meat filled her
mouth and burst forth flavor. The yams were
good as well, but she loved the meat best.

Kaitlin looked at Wonder Worker in interest.
He was carving a flute from a slender section of
wood. She'd never seen someone shape wood
before. *Wawakankan* glanced up to see her
watching him. He smiled.

"Are you the one who carved the designs on
Wawat'ecaka's plates?" the blonde inquired,
remembering the wooden dishes with the carrot
and onion designs meticulously carved as border.

"*Tos,* I did that. You like it?"

"*Tos,* you have much talent."

He smiled at her but did not entertain her with
his attention for long. The chief was not known
for jealousy, but what man wouldn't feel a little
insecure when another man lavished too much
attention on his chosen one? Out of respect for
his *kola*, the medicine man returned his attention
to the woodwind and continued designing.

The two women collected the dishes and clean garments. They washed the dishes first and went to the women's area to bathe. Kaitlin preferred to wash her soiled clothing upon donning fresh ones so that the clean items would be dry for wearing on the following night.

She looked down at the robe-like dress she wore, a gift from *Wawat'ecaka*. The other woman had made all of her clothing from the softest leather that the blonde had ever encountered. This robe creation, however, was not typical in the Indian community.

+++

Jed had caused severe bruising and nearly separated her ribs when he'd forced her to accompany him when he escaped from Spirit Bear's plan of returning him to the band so the mourning parents could have justice in front of the tribe. Kaitlin had no memory of how she'd been returned to the war chief's arms. When she'd first arrived in the native encampment, she'd been unconscious. Upon awakening, the golden girl couldn't raise her hand without severe pain. *Wawat'ecaka* had ingeniously constructed a poncho-like dress so that she wouldn't have to raise her arm when attempting to dress and cover her nudity. Kaitlin would forever be thankful to the other woman!

---+++

Because of *Wawat'ecaka*, she now owned three female breechcloths, a robe that she wore for a night dress, two supple work dresses, and a finely decorated creation for ceremonial wear. She'd also have a work pair of moccasins and an exquisite pair that matched her special dress.

Each woman bid the other good night and returned to her tipi. In the time before night claimed the lands, each usually spent doing what they enjoyed after the labor-intensive day. Kaitlin usually worked on drilling holes in pretty stones she'd found to use in decorations someday, or she wove colorful baskets. *Wawat'ecaka* sewed.

Sometimes, they shared the same fire. The two men, *Woniya Mato* and *Wawakankan* were raised as brothers. Each enjoyed the other's company a great deal. Both looked upon Gentle Rabbit as their mother.

The chief's parents had disappeared before he was ten winters. Because *Wawat'ecaka* had only been blessed with one son, she and her husband took in *Woniya Mato* as their own. With the two boys' close alliance with Sky Warrior, the three had been nearly inseparable in their early years. Little had changed.

CHAPTER FOUR

Precautionary Measures

Kaitlin retrieved the waterproof basket she was constructing. Her other one was in constant use to soak the soap roots used to bathe and clean with daily. Another finely woven basket to hold water would be welcomed and well-used.

On this night, Spirit Bear took flint pieces to shape into arrowheads. He'd told Kaitlin he was working on preparing for the buffalo hunt that the tribe usually did before the winter months, but he also was preparing for war. It was an untimely thing to do before his wedding in about a month, but war never chose well. The Crow could not be permitted to prowl Sioux lands. They would be driven forth!

Kaitlin watched him as she prepared her weaving materials. He seemed so intense on his work. Usually the former captive could not look at him for a moment before he turned his stygian eyes upon her. The leader's power was focused as he shaped the sharp tips for arrows.

The blonde worked on her basket slowly. It was precise work, and she was more interested in watching her fiancé zero his vast power into such precision as to make the delicate-looking arrowheads. She admired his sleek and graceful moves. For such a big man to hold such composure astounded her.

The bronze man's body was honed to physical perfection. Even his forearm muscles rippled with unbound strength that he mastered in the art of knapping. Kaitlin watched as he struck the flint onto a conical structure in his lap, and another sliver of sharp flaking broke free.

Woniya Mato held the new sliver up to examine. It was thin and sharp. When sharpened and shaped onto the end of a light shaft, it would sink deeply into the tough hide of a bison… or a deadly enemy, *toka*.

Kaitlin watched the warrior as he began to work on shaping the stone tip. He had a very thick piece of rawhide in his lap. He held the flint in place with his thumb while he placed an antler

tine onto the spot he wanted to whittle. Then
the knapper placed a stone tool on top of the
antler and applied pressure until a sliver from
the opposite side broke free. He repeated this
procedure until slowly, and the arrow head took
shape.

Next, the war leader took a core of obsidian. He
repeated the entire process with the shiny black
stone. When he was finished, two very sharp
instruments of death were ready to be united
with a light shaft with feather guides.

Light was waning when Kaitlin stood to take her
basket weaving supplies back into their home.
Her day had been long, and she was weary. The
chief stayed outside a little longer to clean up
his sharp flakes so that none would damage feet
or shoes on the needle-like shavings.

= = =

When the warrior entered the tipi, Kaitlin was
already asleep. Spirit Bear stripped and lay

down beside her. He loved to watch her relaxed features.

The *winyan's* honeyed hair spilled around the top of her head, for she did not like it against her neck while she rested. The blonde's finely arched brows flitted delicately above her thickly fringed eyes. Those golden orbs were now resting behind fragile pinkish lids.

The white woman's nose was straight with a hint of being pert. Her lips were just right. They could not be called full, but neither were they thin.

Kaitlin's cheekbones were fairly high, and shallow hollows underneath them added to her beauty. The chin was feminine, and her forehead was of medium height. The Oglala warrior had never seen a finer specimen of womanhood.

Spirit Bear wished he could break her habit of wearing the robe-garment to bed. His *winyan* was so modest! Slowly, as not to disturb her, he unlaced the braided leather ties and removed the garment. His body would be all the heat she would need this night.

In the morning, there would be a warrior's meeting in the ceremonial lodge. The tribal council would be present as well. A decision would be made on what to do about the imposing Crow. Spirit Bear's mind kept straying to his *toka* as he tried to relax.

Many hours passed before sleep claimed the mighty warrior. His arm was possessively draped over the woman of his heart. His sleep was light, and the leader awoke well before the first morning bird.

When the first bird's song broke the stillness before dawn, *Woniya Mato* could wait no longer. Slowly he untied the laces of Kaitlin's breechcloth. He inhaled as her fully uninhibited beauty struck him yet again. He loved this *ska winyan* more than life itself.

The war chief's hands began to lightly explore and stroke her body. Golden Eyes smiled in her sleep and muttered his name. His seductive mouth perked in pleasure at her response.

Spirit Bear increased the pressure of his hands as they rubbed up and down the full length of her body. He gently rolled her to her back and focused on her beautiful and shapely breasts. With a groan, he bent his head down.

Kaitlin stirred to passionate arousal. When she opened her indolent golden eyes, they met the hot blackness of his. Her lips parted, and she licked them; it was almost more than the war chief could bear…

= = =

Immediately upon completion of their lovemaking, Spirit Bear propped himself up.

"I was not too rough, was I, *Mazaska Zi Ista?*" he asked sheepishly.

"*Hiya*, my chief. It was welcomed if you could not guess," she smiled at him.

"You are sure that I did not hurt you? I am not usually so… harsh when I take a woman."

"*Hiya*, my chief," she repeated. "I enjoyed this coupling."

Woniya Mato hugged her to him, still feeling a little guilty for losing control over his stringent restraint. The beauty present, not only of her body but also of her soul, caused him to be weak with her. Spirit Bear knew he might be facing war and absence by her side for a time. It made his taking of her more insistent. They lay, still as one, until time finally receded that part of him. He kissed her again before he rose.

"I have an important meeting in the tribal council lodge this morning," he told her. "I should be back by the time you come to eat your mid-day meal."

She nodded her understanding.

"If you leave to gather food, take a group with you. If only one will come, see if a young man will accompany you."

She turned her head to meet his look of serious concern.

"Why, *Woniya Mato*? Have I displeased you in some way?"

He met her question with a heated look that made her blood boil afresh. "You need to ask me that, *Wastelaka*? You please me much. This is why I must enforce this precaution. You have not witnessed this since your stay with us, but the Sioux have many *toka*. Many seek to destroy our strong band. We must always stay wary and vigilant so that we can meet and destroy all threats."

"*Tos*, my chief. I will do as you ask."

He nodded and turned. The warrior headed to the entrance flap.

"Do you not wish to eat first, *Woniya Mato*?"

"*Hiya*, but I will eat if you make something at mid-day." He could not tell her that his adrenaline was already brimming with the excitement of gathering a troop to drive the Crow from their lands. With one last look from his dark eyes, he was gone.

= = =

Kaitlin sighed and grabbed her *mniapahta*. She might as well begin her normal chores since she was up. As the fire began to blaze, she placed a pot over the flames and dumped in the remaining water for her morning tea. When the water began to boil, she sprinkled mint leaves over the top of the water.

After it boiled for about five minutes, she removed the pot from the flames to let the tea steep. The blonde went to the place of privacy and refilled the *mniapahtas* while she waited for the water to cool.

Kaitlin added crushed raspberry and strained the leaves from the beverage and poured it into a horn cup. Then she drank the concoction she'd grown to love.

The young woman gathered wood for herself and the tipis of *Wawat'ecaka* and *Wawakankan*. She wanted to help the other woman as much as she helped her. The former slave also wanted to repay her kindness and loving friendship. Gentle Rabbit emerged from her tipi when Kaitlin began stacking the dry wood.

"Thank you, *Mazaska Zi Ista*! You rise early this day!"

"*Tos, Woniya Mato* had a council meeting."

The older woman's eyebrow shot up. She did not voice any words, but Kaitlin could sense unease in her friend.

"What is it, *Wawat'ecaka*? Is there something to worry about?"

"*Hiya, Mazaska Zi Ista*. The chief will tell us all we need to know." Kaitlin stacked the last stick of wood and said, "*Uwa yo,* let us work the sacred hide once more. In four more suns, the hide will be finished."

The exhausted women returned before noon to the camp. Kaitlin wanted to prepare her man a good meal because he'd missed breakfast. She took the net she'd woven from grasses that grew by the river. The young woman would return to the banks to try to capture a fish.

Kaitlin knew the perfect place. Upstream, the river water spilled over a rock ledge. The backwaters swirled into a pool carved into the bank over time. The pool reminded the blonde of a pond, but the only difference was that it was never separated from the main body.

The betrothed woman could enter the pond where the water swirled in, always alternating fresh water with old. Then she could drive the bigger more cautious fish forward and net one.

Heeding *Woniya Mato's* warning about going alone, she asked Desert Rose, Playful Otter, Morning Dove, and Moon Eyes to come with her. The four women gladly accompanied her. In fact, they all wanted to help in the fun. They laughed and joked as they entered the waterway together.

"Oh, look! There are six nice ones!" Playful Otter pointed out.

"If we can catch them all, you each will get one to take back to your tipi," Kaitlin offered, "and one left over for *Wawat'ecaka*!"

"*Mita hingnaku* would be pleased," Morning Dove said happily.

The women slowly moved in on the wary fish. They darted to and fro and then regrouped. The aquatic animals sensed the trap but one broke forward and the rest followed. The women, each grasping the net, surged forward and surrounded the panicked fish.

Collectively, the women lifted the net upwards and six fat, shiny fish flipped their tails in the bright light. All appeared to be big-mouth bass. When they hauled the animals onto the bank, the women fell over, laughing.

"That was fun! Anytime you need assistance catching fish, we'd love to help you," Moon Eyes exclaimed.

When she arrived back at the village, Kaitlin took one of the two fish to *Wawat'ecaka*. Then she returned to prepare her own for lunch. She used her deep skillet to prepare a fish stew. She boiled the whole fish. She placed chopped tubers, onion, carrot and *tinpsila* into the boiling water. She mixed a batch of *aguyapi*. She used wild grain and acorn powder with bigger pieces of the nut.

The meal was complete upon *Woniya Mato's* arrival. He smiled at her when he entered. He was so handsome she nearly swooned!

Kaitlin dipped out the stew into a bowl and brought him it with the *aguyapi*. She poured water from the *mniapahta*.

"Eat with me, *Mazaska Zi Ista.* Within our own tipi, I would like to share your company while I eat. I will close the entrance flap to ensure our privacy."

The young woman's eyes widened. The chief wanted to break the age-old custom and eat with a woman? She was very surprised but didn't question his request. Kaitlin didn't like the tradition and was only too glad to bend the rules. Besides, she was hungry.

"Um, this is good," Spirit Bear said in praise.

"Thank you," she responded.

Spirit Bear's future wife wanted to ask him about the council meeting, but she didn't think he'd confide that much in her. Besides, Kaitlin wasn't sure if she really wanted to know. She'd learned her lesson about men matters when she watched her chief extract vengeance upon Jed!

CHAPTER FIVE

Lovers

"I will be leaving in the morning before you arise, *Mazaska Zi Ista*. I will be gone for three suns."

"Why, *Woniya Mato*?"

"We have enemies on our land. The *toka* must be forced from our territory before they strike. The Sioux will make the first move against the Crow!"

She bowed her head in acknowledgement. "I understand, my chief. Please, be careful."

"None will defeat me, *mita wastelaka*. Do not fear for me. Before you know it, I will return to your side."

They laid together in the heat of the day, spoke words of love, and shared tender embraces and passions a second time.

"Let us go to our spot, *Mazaska Zi Ista*. We can cool our bodies in the icy waters."

"I love the blue pond. *Tos*, let us go."

The lovers walked to their special place. Instead of walking down the hill from the village as they did to reach the river, the couple walked up. The blue pond was exactly that. Spring fed icy waters accumulated into blue depths before spilling over and continuing down to flow with the mother river. The pond was sheltered by a grove of trees including the medicinal white willow. Kaitlin loved the simple beauty of the place. It also held many memories of the man who lovingly held her hand.

They stripped and dove into the invigorating waters. Kaitlin was the first to break the surface. She looked around for the brawny form of her promised. Suddenly, something captured her ankles and lifted her upright. The blonde squealed as he dunked her.

"Why you!" she breathed with a smile. "You'll pay for that one."

Spirit Bear lifted a mocking brow. He captured her against his smooth, hard chest. "And how will you manage that, my sweet?"

"Put me down, and I will show you."

He arched his head back and laughed at her! He actually *laughed* at her! Kaitlin might not possess six feet of raw muscle and sheer male strength, but she knew how to give a shot.

She pounded her small fists against him in feigned anger. When that didn't work, she grabbed his head and brought his sexy face towards hers. She captured his lips on a searing kiss. Instantly, everything changed.

The preeminent man lowered his body down in the coolness so that she was cradled above him in the water, but both of their shoulders were out of the wet environment. Suddenly, the white woman jumped from his arms and pushed with all her might against him. His eyes were large as he toppled back into the water.

Immediately, the warrior gave her chase. Kaitlin didn't escape from the water before the supreme athlete captured her. This time, Spirit

Bear didn't give her freedom to move. She was
a prisoner trapped against his heated body.

"You will pay for that deception, *mita wastelaka*.
If you do not play fair, I will not either."

With a devilish glint in his eye, he took a breast
in his mouth. He feasted hungrily upon the taut
peak. All playfulness aside, she groaned and
caressed the back of his head.

Woniya Mato captured her hands in one of his
larger ones. He smiled as he roguishly tortured
her with his sensuality and attention to her chest.
Kaitlin tossed her honeyed tresses back and
forth in tortured agony. Her breath gasped with
tiny mewling noises.

= = =

Then the war chief put her down. It killed him
to do it, but the warrior still had pride. He
turned to walk away. Teaching her a lesson was
nearly unbearable for him. If Spirit Bear hadn't

turned when he did, she'd have seen the evidence of her power over him.

"Oh, no you don't!" suddenly erupted from behind him. A nude female jumped on his back like a rabid she-cat. The *ska winyan* nibbled on his ears. Her breasts were flattened on his back and hard nipples protruded into his skin. They made a statement as she hung on. Kaitlin purposefully rubbed her body against the smooth texture of his skin.

The warrior couldn't take the torture. He was only a man! Spirit Bear groaned and turned toward her. "You asked for it now," he growled.

The masterful man had a dangerous look in his eye, but his smile twitched the edges of those luscious lips. Kaitlin needed no encouragement; she was hot for him. With a frenzied need, their bodies met and joined…

"I love you, *Mazaska Zi Ista*," he said seriously as he gazed upon her. His features were relaxed in satisfaction.

= = =

"And I love you, my mighty warrior. I will await your safe return to my side."

They rinsed off once more before dressing. Kaitlin smiled to herself. She couldn't believe what a crazed affect this man had on her. The blonde would never have thought she could do what she did with this man of her heart!

Woniya Mato beamed as he listened to her hum as she dressed. It was a sound of happiness. The war chief was thankful that he was the one to give her this emotion. They walked back to the village with light hearts.

When Kaitlin arrived back at the tipi, two Indian women waited for her. They were shy and weren't well-known to her. The betrothed woman smiled at them to ease their discomfort. They were from a smaller tipi from the outskirts of the community.

"We want to honor the bride and groom on their approaching wedding. We bring gifts."

Kaitlin glanced at the chief, and he nodded subtly in her direction. "*Tos*, thank you," she managed.

The first girl brought forth a cutting tool for slicing hide into shapes to sew. It had an antler handle and a very sharp obsidian blade. Kaitlin gently hugged the girl. The other became embarrassed and looked down.

The second woman gave Golden Eyes a stiff rawhide in which three bone needles protruded. There was a wrapped ball of sewing sinew as well as a second ball of the softer suppler rawhide-type thread. Again, Kaitlin gave the woman a loose hug to show her thanks. They were fine gifts.

"I have much honor for these fine gifts. I will treasure and use these gifts for many moons!"

The first girl's quiet voice trembled, "Perhaps you can sew clothes for a child soon."

Golden Eyes was taken off guard, but quickly recovered and agreed with the girl. A woman's worth in the Indian community was placed on her ability to bear children, male in particular.

The more children a woman could bring forth into a tipi, the more *Wakantanka* smiled upon her.

Both women nodded to Kaitlin and then returned to their tipi. Kaitlin walked past *Woniya Mato* to place her new supplies in their tipi. He wore a small smirk on his full lips.

Kaitlin wondered if it was because of the comment about making clothes for a child. Well, that would have to wait. That was not the most pressing thing on her mind!

The engaged woman bustled around the tepee when she noticed the war chief was attaching his new arrowheads on the tips of light shafts. His feather guides would send their barb wherever the big man wanted it to go. A concerned line appeared on her forehead.

Spirit Bear had just completed perfecting a new technique on his bow that increased his yardage by a minimum of thirty feet. The Crow would know no wrath like that of *Woniya Mato*! And he'd shared his secret with his warrior and hunting brothers in his band.

The day passed quickly with gathering more food items and placing them on drying racks. *Wawakankan* provided three rabbits for the evening meal. The spiritual man did not mind to hunt especially when the chief was preparing for a confrontation!

The women ate after the men, as custom demanded. When Kaitlin and Gentle Rabbit went to clean up the dishes, they noticed the men were joined by Sky Warrior and Yellow Feather. Soon, Brave Elk also joined the fire. It would be his first mission as a *Cante Tinza,* Brave Heart Warrior Society. The young fighter was eager to prove himself!

Kaitlin retrieved her basket supplies and worked on the waterproof weave while the men talked about the possibility of *toka.* She was half-way finished with the container when her eyes had trouble focusing on the task. The blonde sighed and retired to the tipi.

It wasn't long before her betrothed followed her lead. He stripped to his breechcloth and lay beside her on the supple furs. She rolled to face him.

They just looked into each other's eyes, the gaze
saying all that needed to be said to each other.
Finally, Kaitlin's golden almond-shaped eyes
closed and her breathing deepened. Spirit Bear
knew he would have great difficulty sleeping.
He was able to will his body to relax so that at
least his reflexes would be quick. At last, sleep
took him as well.

He was gone before Kaitlin awoke. She sent up
a silent prayer for his safe return. This would be
the worst part of being married to a war chief!
The blonde would always worry about his life
and his return to her side.

The next three days passed very slowly for
Golden Eyes. She worried nonstop. A party of
about fifteen men rode out of the village in
pursuit of the Crow. She nearly swooned when
the cloud of dust alerted the village to their
return.

The adolescent boys took the war horses off to
care for them while the men were greeted by the
community. Kaitlin's eyes were for *Woniya
Mato* only. His face was noble as his eyes
found hers in the crowd.

The bride-to-be quickly went to her fiance's side. Kaitlin was dying to bombard her man with questions but held herself back. An over emotional female upon return of her warrior man would indicate no faith in his prowess.

When the crowd assembled, the chief announced to his curious people that they didn't find any Crow warriors on their land, but they did find evidence of their presence. The trail was cold, and it appeared they'd left several days before the Sioux hunted for them. The village members were to maintain safety in numbers for the next week or two. The warriors would be on cautious alert to ensure the health of the community.

The village cooked the deer, rabbit, and antelope that Lone Wolf and a hunting party had secured for the arrival of the war chief and his band. The people were fed with the slain animals. All wanted to show appreciation for the protection the leaders provided to their people.

Near evening, Kaitlin entered the tipi. *Woniya Mato* had just returned from taking a bath.

"I have missed you, *Mazaska Zi Ista*," he stated in a deep voice full of emotion as he turned to face her.

"Oh, my chief! It is I that missed you! I know I am not to worry about such a fierce man, but my heart cannot ignore the fact that I cannot live without you!"

They were finally able to greet one another as they had longed to do many hours ago. They passionately hugged and exchanged tender embraces. They retired early so that the chief could rest his body that had lived off adrenaline for several days.

When her bronze warrior made a passionate overture towards her, Kaitlin looked him in the eyes. "I want you to rest your body this night, my chief. The morning will be soon enough for us to join our bodies." It was the first time she'd ever been able to tell him no and get by with it.

The fierce war chief looked into her face for a few moments, his face displaying no emotion. She almost felt the familiar quaking brought forth by his domineering gaze, for such an intense stare could wither the iciest mound. *Woniya Mato* had defeated many enemies with it. Kaitlin wondered if he would press her. She was honestly only thinking of him.

"My body yearns for yours, as well, my love. I do not mean to hurt you," she hastily added.

Finally, he grinned at her.

"I will do as you ask, *mita wastelaka*. My body could use reviving so that I can pleasure you longer."

In the morning, his made his promise ring true. He kept her busy until most other villagers had greeted the day. Kaitlin always felt uncomfortable when others could guess what kept their entrance flap closed, but yet she was joyful that her man desired her so.

When Spirit Bear left to do his many chores, she went to *Wawat'ecaka's* tipi. She motioned for Kaitlin to follow her. She also collected Apple Blossom, Desert Rose, and Playful Otter.

"What are we doing this day, *Wawat'ecaka*?" Kaitlin asked.

"We gather new poles for guest tipis."

"Guest tipis?"

"*Tos*, *Mazaska Zi Ista*. Wedding guests will be arriving in the next few weeks. Your joining is coming up quickly. Your guests will want to settle in and celebrate with others before the big event."

The knowledge of her marriage was overwhelming. Kaitlin was nervous getting married in front of the village as it was. She still didn't know many of the inhabitants. There were so many people!

The prospect of visitors coming that she would have to entertain was unsettling to the sole white woman. It made her nervous and jumpy. However, she realized it was all in honor of the chief and his chosen one.

The women went several miles from the camp to select many young pine saplings. They were about four inches in diameter. They chopped branches off and debarked the poles before taking them back to camp. The women worked all day carrying the twenty-four-foot pine bases.

After a quick dinner of dried meat, watercress and poke salad, berries, and the *aguyapi*, Katlin quickly cleaned the dishes. She washed and turned in for the night early. The young woman was asleep almost as soon as she lay down her head.

CHAPTER SIX

Tipi Construction

= = =

Woniya Mato looked over her sleeping form and smiled. He was so proud of his *winyan*. She worked harder than many of the maidens in the community. The leader had much to thank *Wakantanka* for. As was his ritual every night, Spirit Bear sat before the fire spot and chanted a prayer to his god.

The chief removed his clothing and lay beside the sleeping form of his golden bird. The *ska winyan* was like an angel. She worked hard, never complained, and was every man's dream. Her body was *gopeca*.

The silent warrior removed the sleeping robe the blonde was so fond of. He would not wake her but would enjoy viewing her body's perfection.

Mazaska Zi Ista had a muscular but very feminine build. Her shapely legs were delicious; the muscles gave them a distinctive outline. Her derriere was taut and firm yet had enough meat to command a man's attention when she swayed by him.

The *winyan* skin was kissed by the sun. The white color had deepened to a golden hue that accentuated her honeyed hair and amber eyes. This unusual coloring alone would have a man or woman turn in her direction to admire her unique and exotic beauty!

Kaitlin had a slender build with luscious curves. Her breasts were full but firm. Her hips flared out enough to give her figure an hour-glass shape.

Woniya Mato made himself stop gazing at her body. He was ensnaring himself in a wave of desire. The chief would have to awaken her exhausted body or force his mind to end its torture.

= = =

In the morning, Kaitlin awoke to fiery touches
and passionate caresses. The young woman
loved waking up to the bronzed god-like warrior.
He was a perfect specimen of manhood. Spirit
Bear brought her to fulfillment many times
during each love-making session.

After their ardor was spent, Kaitlin relaxed into
his arms. The blonde loved the raw power that
radiated from his body. It was a strong magnet
that always made her want to run her hands over
his bulging muscles.

After a few moments of silence, Kaitlin asked,
"*Woniya Mato*, how many visitors will we
have?"

        "Are you worried, *Wastelaka*? Do not
be nervous. They come to honor us."

"*Tos*, I understand. I just do not like so many
eyes on me."

He laughed to ease her tension. "All eyes will
be on you, *Mazaska Zi Ista*. You are a very
gopeca winyan. All men will wish you were by

their sides… or that they could steal you from mine.”

“And all women will wish they were saying vows with you, as well. I am fortunate that I am the one who is promised to you!” Kaitlin said with fervor.

“*Uwa yo, Wastelaka.* Let us share a breakfast. If you work as hard as you did yesterday, you will need all your energy.” He chuckled then added mischievously, “Especially since you already used some up!”

Kaitlin flushed slightly and stood. She donned a work dress and began to prepare a simple breakfast of wild cooked oats and honey along with the Indian bread and fruit. They ate together, and it became their manner in privacy. Then the blonde left to meet her friends to resume the construction work with *Wawat’ecaka.*

“Look at who finally comes!” pointed out Desert Rose in a playful tone.

Blushing furiously, Kaitlin tried to defend herself. “I made breakfast for the chief.”

"Did you also kill the animal before cooking it? That would explain the time factor," Desert Rose continued with a smile.

The other women were glad Golden Eyes received the brunt of the teasing. She was the one betrothed. Each of them would have a turn at the teasing banter in the future.

Gentle Rabbit came forth and handed each woman a sanding tool. It was sandstone worn smooth on one side from oils saturating the stone by their hands. The other side was flat and rough from the sanding of wood.

Each woman took a pole and began to rub the coarse edges away. It was tiresome work, but not so difficult as scrubbing the hides clean of hair in the heat of the day.

"We will need a new tipi just to hold the gifts of *Mazaska Zi Ista*," Playful Otter jested. "Look, already more gifts are piling up in the yard by her tipi."

Indeed, it was true. Kaitlin saw three more women bringing hides, utensils, and other things.

They piled it neatly close to her outside fire hearth.

Apple Blossom added, "Maybe our guests won't mind sharing a sleeping place with her gifts."

Embarrassed beyond words, Kaitlin could only bow her head and continue to press on the pole.

"*Mazaska Zi Ista*, you know we only joke…" began Desert Rose.

"*Tos*, I love my friends. But I shake with fear when I think of all the people coming to see me. They give me gifts. I will have to walk before them. I wish I could just marry *Woniya Mato* without all the hype."

Wawat'ecaka said, "Do not worry, *Mazaska Zi Ista*. On your joining day, your eyes will only be for your *hingnaku*. No other will enter your sight."

Kaitlin's worried golden eyes met with *Wawat'ecaka's*.

"*Tos*, I know what you say is true. I still cannot help but to feel overwhelmed by all the generosity amongst our people."

"You are a very special *winyan* to have captured the heart of the greatest warrior. Do not doubt your worth. None will find you lacking."

= = =

At noon time, Spirit Bear watched his woman collect her booty and bring it into their lodge. He secretly smiled at her vexation. They did not need the gifts.

Woniya Mato was rich as far as Indian standards went. He was a good provider. They always had fresh meat and plenty of hides. The warrior had many horses and could trade for anything desired.

Still, the leader liked for his promised to have many fine womanly things as well. *Mazaska Zi Ista* had learned a great deal from the people but still had much to learn. It would be good for her to collect the tools and materials needed for sewing and other chores until she learned or had time to make them herself.

With her basket and the leather making skills,
the young woman would also be able to trade
for many items she desired as well. They were
a good match! Both were highly skilled in their
chosen areas!

= = =

In the next few days, the women continued to
prepare the lodge poles for use. When the
sanding was completed, they used flaxseed oil
to polish and preserve the wood. Most of the
time the wood would be dried more before use,
but time did not permit this usual practice.

Kaitlin helped the other women prepare the
lodge poles for the hide covering. According to
Gentle Rabbit, she would be responsible for the
disassembly of her tipi when their camp moved
location. Most likely, she and her friends would
pair up and help each other, but because the
woman owned the dwelling, it was ultimately
the female's responsibility for home
preparations. Kaitlin sighed in relief at the

many women she called friends who made much work seem light.

The first thing the women did on the lodge construction was to take three poles and bind them together to form a tripod. *Wawat'ecaka* brought forth a sewn canvas from previous guest tipis. They placed it on the horizontal tripod with the tripod binding sticking above the leather by about a foot.

Next, the women used many more poles to form a cone shape within the structure with only a small circle around the tip that stuck above the material. The top was lashed together with the extra ropes hanging free. With these ropes, they erected the structure.

The women draped the leather fabric secured at the top around the skeletal frame and gathered the overlapping sections with lacing pins. The poles were stretched taunt against the cloth walls and tacked down to the ground. Vent poles were placed at each flap to encourage air to flow into the dwelling.

A fire pit was dug in the center of the tipi and lined with rock. A stout stake was secured

inside as the anchor rope was attached to it.
Last, the flap was secured with more lacing pins.
Guests would have one temporary home for use.

The women continued to repeat this process
until a total of six tipis stood waiting on guests
to fill them. The visitors would be highly
honored by the placement of the tipis on the
fringe of the ceremonial grounds near the big
tipi of the dominant chief's.

Kaitlin dusted her hands on the skirt of her dress,
noting a new blister on her palm. Then she
turned toward her own tipi and began to prepare
lunch. For once, Kaitlin was glad to see a
woman approach with a large mixing bowl full
of a soup. She smiled warmly at the woman and
thanked her genuinely.

"It is my privilege to present you with squirrel
soup. I hope you enjoy it and the bowl and
serving spoon. They come with the gift."

"Thank you so much, Kind Breeze! This gift
could not have come at a better time!"

The other woman smiled, for it was no secret
that the friends of *Mazaska Zi Ista* slaved along

with the golden-eyed woman in preparation for wedding guests. She then dropped more of the surprise on her.

"In this leather bag you will find many pones of sweet bread. I heard you favor strawberry. Many are of this variety."

As was Kaitlin's custom to show her thanks, she hugged the other woman loosely so as to not cause unease. Then each went to their tipi to consume their meal and rest.

Kaitlin poured two bowls of the soup and laid out three pones of bread. She filled two cups of water. Just as the meal was readied, *Woniya Mato* entered the tipi. She smiled warmly upon his handsome features.

"Sit, my chief. Our meal is prepared."

She secured their tipi flap and settled down to share her meal with him.

"Is this a new recipe?" he asked.

"It is a wedding gift from Kind Breeze. The pones also came from her."

He nodded once in understanding.

"Have you perfected your bow and arrow technique?" Kaitlin asked tentatively. She knew that it was an area that men discussed and wasn't sure he would confer about it with her, but the blonde wanted to show interest by asking.

"I have, *tos*, but some still struggle with it. Some may choose to use their old bows made in the customary way. I believe most will be ready for the bison hunt."

"When is the bison hunt, *Woniya Mato*?"

"Usually we go now, but with our wedding, we will hunt in a handful of suns after our joining ceremony."

"We hold off the hunt because of us?" she squeaked.

The chief placed his bowl aside and drew her into his powerful embrace. "*Mita wastelaka*, the bison will not lose enough fat in one cycle of the moon to make a difference to us. The calves will be weaned and the females will gain back weight lost while nursing. It is a good thing.

 "B-b-but to h-hold off the whole hunt for us!?" she wailed. "I just can't believe it!"

He smiled and smoothed her silky hair. "It is a great honor our people wish to bestow upon us. Surely you do not wish to wait?"

"*Hiya*, my chief. I want to join with you quickly."

With a devilish twinkle in his eye and a roguish grin, he said, "That, my sweet, can be arranged." He swept her back onto their mats to do as requested.

***

Four more days passed before the first visitors began to appear in the village of the Bear Claw Clan of the Oglala. The chief and wife along with five other couples from a Cheyenne tribe appeared. They filled one tipi.

The next day, more Oglala men and women appeared from other bands. Arapaho tribe members came, and last, Yankton Sioux filled all the guest tipis. More hunting and gathering were required to feed the increased population. Kaitlin welcomed the extra work. It kept her mind from focusing on the sixty or so guests they had housed in the newly constructed tipis.

The wedding was now nine days away. Kaitlin went to *Wawat'ecaka*. "Gentle Rabbit, what do I need to do to prepare for this day?" she asked in a worried tone. The white girl had never seen a Native marriage.

"You do not need to do anything. Others are making preparations to show they care. You will be a *gopeca* bride."

Lone Wolf brought in several more deer and smaller animals for the evening meal. Several women helped to prepare, including the guests.

After the meal was served, Spirit Bear came to Kaitlin. "Let the other women clean up the dishes. I want you to come with me and meet our guests."

"May I bathe first?" she breathed, for the work had been hot and grueling all day. She tasted sweat on her lip and her hair was tangled.

"Of course. Do you want to bathe at the woman's place, or do you want me to escort you to the blue pond?"

"I will just go to the woman's area this night."

The chief grinned at her, for he knew she didn't want to be teased by strangers disappearing together alone. "I will watch for your return. Then I will walk you around so I can show off my treasured *winyan*."

Woniya Mato hadn't seen the other leaders for quite some time! Each night the skilled entertainers were generous in sharing tales and coup stories by the light of the fire. It was a time to celebrate and catch up with friends!

Kaitlin returned smelling of fresh strawberries. She'd put on a fresh dress, and her hair had been combed. Already, a few tendrils curled around her exquisite face.

"Uwa yo, Mazaska Zi Ista. Let us formally meet our guests."

CHAPTER SEVEN

Wedding Guests

The first man they approached was about twenty-five years their senior. Obviously a warrior, the male was powerfully built. Gray strands worked themselves through the crisp blackness of his thick hair. He was attractive and commanded respect.

"Chief Hawk Eyes, this is *Mazaska Zi Ista*." The war chief paused then said, "*Mazaska Zi Ista*, this is the chief of the Cheyenne band just to the southeast of us."

The older man's eyes studied her thoughtfully for a moment. Then a smile broke his serious face. He grasped her hand with his on top.

"You have chosen splendidly, *Woniya Mato*. She is a rare rose in the forest of trees. Guard her well!"

Spirit Bear clasped the older man's forearms in acknowledgement of such high praise. Kaitlin blushed and looked down. She had some difficulty understanding what the other man said. He attempted to speak Lakota, the language of her band of the Sioux, but it was heavily accented as if he didn't normally speak it.

For her benefit, all visitors spoke Lakota. Kaitlin still didn't fully understand the complex language, but because she knew many words, she could usually get the gist of the conversation.

The Yankton tribe was the last group Spirit Bear introduced her to, one of the seven distinctions of the mighty Sioux Nation. The first man to stand presented himself to the couple.

"I am *Sunmanitu Wacitusni*, Sly Coyote," he began by clasping forearms with the chief. "I share mothers with Eagle Talon, husband of Opossum Eyes. He sends his regrets that he was not able to make your wedding. Under current circumstances with his wife… he thought it best."

Spirit Bear chuckled. "Tell my friend that I understand and agree with his decision!"

+++

Kaitlin recalled the unfriendly girl, Opossum Eyes. She was an Oglala woman who desired *Woniya Mato* for herself and went out of her way to antagonize Kaitlin. The chief had arranged for the girl's marriage to Eagle Talon of the Yankton Sioux to further unite their tribes as well as to take care of the problems she presented. Spirit Bear saw to it that she would no longer cause misery to his betrothed.

+++

The chief, Wise Owl, wishes me to tell you he will arrive a few suns before the marriage. There are some things in the village he needs to tend to first." *Sunmanitu Wacitusni* informed.

"*Tos,* I understand," he paused for an appropriate moment of time and then introduced his *winyan:* "This is *Mazaska Zi Ista,* my promised."

Kaitlin felt the power of the man's intense stare. She shifted uncomfortably under the weight of his scrutiny. The white woman felt like a prized horse being analyzed by a potential buyer.

"She is *gopeca, Woniya Mato.*"

"*Tos.* I agree. Thank you."

The leader then took Kaitlin's arm and introduced her to the rest of the group. Because all the guests had now met his beautiful golden bird, the couple joined the last group to visit. Kaitlin sat with the three women in the assembly who were situated a little apart from the men. The chief remained to visit with the other important company.

"Hopping Robin, I am pleased to meet you," Kaitlin began. "And you, Soft Touch, and you also, Little Foot."

The women smiled in welcome at her. They began to speak of the skills each had developed as they aged. Little Foot got up and went to her guest tipi. She returned with a bag.

She poured its contents into her hand and held up each one to show Kaitlin. Inside were fine jewelry items. An amber necklace and bracelet gleamed in the lowering sun. A leather band with more amber beads would circle her upper arm. There were places for her husband's feathers to be attached to show who she belonged to.

There was also a pastel necklace of lightly colored crystals. The subtle hints of color would make any woman breathe in pleasure. Kaitlin wanted to show she understood about the work involved, but also the talent in making such eye-catching combinations.

"You are very skilled, Little Foot! They are very *gopeca*!"

"I brought them for you," she confided with a smile.

"Oh, thank you!" Kaitlin shyly smiled. "They are truly magnificent!"

While she smiled in pleasure, she hugged the items to her chest. She felt eyes upon her. The engaged woman looked up expecting *Woniya Mato's* eye, but instead, it was the black weight of Sly Coyote.

His face was devoid of emotion. His eyes lingered upon her and engulfed her even when she caught him looking. Kaitlin's face flushed, and she shifted uncomfortably.

Sunmanitu Wacitusni was slightly shorter than her betrothed and very muscular as well. His obsidian eyes were sheltered under distinctive brows. His nose was large, but not overly so. His mouth was outlined by lips that were neither too thin nor full. He was handsome, but not devastatingly so as her man.

When Kaitlin sneaked a peak back at him, he was engaged in conversation with the other men. The two remaining women went to retrieve their gifts for the promised couple. Hopping Robin presented Kaitlin with a nearly black leather hide of moose. She also placed a wooden box containing many dyed porcupine quills for decoration into the golden skinned woman's lap.

Soft Touch also placed a wooden box onto Kaitlin's lap. It held many bone beads of different sizes and shapes. Much work had gone into shaping the items. She provided a core of tough rawhide used for the bottoms of moccasins to Kaitlin.

"Thank you so much, my new *kolas*! These are lovely gifts! I am much honored!" and she hugged each woman.

The women conversed for a time. Finally, *Woniya Mato* stood and held his hand out to Golden Eyes. She stood and approached him. As they left, she saw Sly Coyote's eyes upon her once more. She shuddered slightly.

"What is it, *Mazaska Zi Ista*?" asked the muscular man softly.

"It is nothing, my chief."

When they lay down on the sleeping mats, the leader could sense something was weighing on Golden Eye's mind. She seemed distracted and uneasy.

"Come, *mita wastelaka*. Tell me what troubles you," his warm, masculine voice persuaded her.

"It is probably nothing, but I do not like the way Sly Coyote looks upon me."

The chief chuckled and stated, "You are every man's dream, *mita gopeca winyan*. It is only natural for a male to stare upon you when seeing you for the first time. You are the golden light of *Wi* taken shape."

"Still, *Woniya Mato*. I know I am not a warrior, but there is something about him that I cannot put my finger on."

"He would not be so stupid to try something when you are the chosen one of the war chief of the Oglala!" Spirit Bear exclaimed. "Neither would it be wise of him to make an overture to you during our pre-ceremonial days. I would claim his life for such a deed!"

"*Hiya*, my chief. I did not mean to imply he has less-than-honorable intentions, but I just feel… strange around him."

"Put the matter from your mind, *Wastelaka. Istinma* now," he commanded. He brought her feminine outline against his rock-hard one. His strong arms circled her possessively. "I will permit no harm to befall you, my love," he whispered into her hair.

The next morning, Kaitlin and many women left to gather vegetables and fruit for the numerous people in the camp of the Bear Claw Clan. Kaitlin provided various baskets; both of her own construction and some from the many gifts she'd received to carry the booty back to the camp.

Although fairly new to Native culture, the white woman was aware of the subtle eyes that followed her. Sly Coyote allowed her to see that he watched her but was less obtrusive when others were around. She didn't like it at all. Still, Kaitlin didn't verbalize any more unease to her beloved.

When the golden-skinned woman filled her *mniapahta* at midday, she felt as if the unsettling gaze were still upon her. Kaitlin stood to look around but didn't detect anyone near. The blonde shook her head and continued the chore.

When the water skins were full, she stooped to collect the watercress and fill a basket she'd brought along for that purpose. The young woman had always loved watercress salad flavored with fat drippings from roasted meat mixed with onion and carrots; it was one of her preferred greens.

Kaitlin waded into the water further, her bare feet delighting in the delicious coolness of the stream. She picked and filled her basket as she wandered. Just as the young woman was reaching for more of the freshwater plant, a masculine hand swam into her vision. The hand was full of rich green cress.

"Oh!" the soon-to-be-married woman gasped in startled surprise. "You scared me!" She looked up into the deeply probing eyes of Sly Coyote.

A slightly mocking smile lit up his face. He raked her body with his eyes before he refocused on her face. The heat radiated from him, making her very much aware of her femininity. Slowly, the commanding man placed the greens into her basket.

"I-I must be getting back," she stammered.

"Do you fear being alone with me?" the Yankton man's deep tone asked, slightly teasing the blonde to rile her so that she would stay longer with him.

"N-no, but I…" Kaitlin searched for a plausible excuse, "I just don't think it's proper."

"Why? Do you feel more for me than what a stranger should feel for another?" *Sunmanitu Wacitusni* took a step closer to her. "There is no reason to feel uncomfortable around me."

Her foot chose that moment to slip on a slick stone. Kaitin flailed slightly and tried to stabilize herself. Sly Coyote reached out and grabbed her to help support, his arm in a half hug behind her. The startled blonde could feel his warm fingers on her waist through the cool fabric of her dress.

"We are not on the well-used path…" she began.

The Yankton man's fingers began to circle her side ever so slightly and he pulled her a little toward him. Kaitlin found herself facing the muscular stranger in the water. Only inches separated her chest from his! The golden girl could feel her respiration accelerate from her nervousness. When she looked up, Kaitlin noticed that the bronzed warrior's breathing rate had increased as well. Apprehensively, the stunning woman looked hurriedly over her shoulder. Escape was imperative!

To regain the blonde's attention, Sly Coyote took his free hand and gently touched her shoulder and trailed his hand down her arm. He grasped her elbow. Kaitlin trembled under his touch but refused to show the man how unsettled she was in his presence.

"I know," Sly Coyote said huskily.

Kaitlin then heard *Wawat'ecaka* call for her. Her timing couldn't have been better!

"I must go, *Sunmanitu Wacitusni*" the attractive girl said and turned from him without a backward glance. The betrothed woman couldn't help that her spine stiffened as she

quickly retreated.   Sly Coyote's eyes burned
into her back until she disappeared from his line
of vision.

CHAPTER EIGHT

Pursuit

That evening as the women prepared for supper, Kaitlin made sure she placed a friend's body between hers and that of the unsettling stranger. Her unease had increased since the meeting in the woods. The blonde dared not tell *Woniya Mato*, for the warrior had already said he would kill a man that made moves toward her. Kaitlin couldn't have a death shadowing her wedding, especially of one of the guests! It was supposed to be the most joyous occasion in her life!

After cleaning up the dishes, the chieftain called her to him. Spirit Bear drew her against his body and continued to converse to the other men. Women joined their men in the evening visits.

In the group surrounding Spirit Bear was the chief of the Cheyenne. Kaitlin immediately liked the commanding man. He spoke to her with respect. Chief Hawk Eyes did not treat her as if her skin was of another color. No one did, really, but the solidary white always wondered when one would.

"Have the Crow been wandering near your lands?" *Woniya Mato* asked Hawk Eyes.

"*Hiya*. I have not seen signs of this."

"If war is what they want…" growled the Oglala war chief.

"It would be foolish to attack a camp this full," agreed the other powerful man. "*Woniya Mato* and the Bear Claw Clan have many *kolas* that would be more than happy to help!"

A new person joined their group. Sly Coyote seemed interested in the conversation. Spirit Bear felt Kaitlin stiffen in his embrace. He rubbed his hands up and down her arms possessively to relax her once more.

I will watch this stranger, Spirit Bear thought. I will see if Mazaska Zi Ista's worries are founded. If they are, may the Great Spirit help this man, brother of my friend. I do not make war with those I try to unite bands with, especially other Sioux, but no man will approach my winyan, the golden bird of my heart!

Kaitlin noticed a difference in the Yankton man who made her so uneasy. He didn't watch her as closely as previously. Still, the blonde couldn't trust the attentive male after her meeting with him in the woods. The young woman shrank closer into *Woniya Mato's* potent frame. Only he drove away her insecurities, this man of her soul.

Perhaps because Kaitlin was snuggled within the secure arms of the domineering man, the other didn't pursue her with his intense eyes. For whatever the reason, Kaitlin was grateful. The dazzling blonde turned her attention to her attractive betrothed.

Kaitlin loved how her chief spoke with gestures. His biceps bulged and rippled beneath the bronze skin in his arms. Golden Eyes loved the feel of his hard, muscular chest against her back.

Just leaning against this perfect specimen of manhood started her blood boiling. The *ska winyan* shifted uncomfortably while Spirit Bear

continued to speak of the Crow. She could feel
his flat abdomen and slim hips against her
bottom. Without meaning to, her breathing
increased.

"My chief, I think I will meet you in our tipi,"
she stated breathlessly. Kaitlin couldn't
continue to torture herself in front of an
audience of men.

= = =

Woniya Mato smiled at her, noting her flushed
cheeks and heightened senses. She couldn't be
aware of how her hardened nipples showed
themselves against the fabric of her dress.

*You will not have to wait long, mita wastelaka.
I will follow you shortly and take care of your
burning needs. You please me greatly in your
desire for me.*

= = =

It was not only Spirit Bear who noticed the golden-eyed beauty's discomfort. The older chief smiled, teasing the husband-to-be with his secret knowledge. Both men's knowing eyes met. One other man had noticed as well, and he'd also been affected by the golden girl's arousal.

"You are a lucky man, *Woniya Mato*," Chief Hawk Eyes announced. "Had you not first found *Mazaska Zi Ista*, I would challenge you for her!" Both men laughed genially. The Cheyenne chief received a playful punch from his wife. The men chatted a while longer and then, as soon as it was cordial, Spirit Bear excused himself.

Kaitlin lay wide-eyed upon the sleeping mats. She'd finally calmed herself but was still too aroused to sleep. She grinned broadly at *Woniya Mato* when he entered their tipi.

He smiled widely back, for he knew the reward waiting for him. The chief quickly stripped and came to her. Expertly, Spirit Bear slowly and sensually removed her clothing.

"You about drove me crazy out there," he stated matter-of-factly as he rolled her onto her back.

"Why?"

"I knew you burned with the mating fever."

"Oh!" Kaitlin exclaimed, immediately wondering who else might have detected her state.

"I came as quickly as I could, *mita wastelaka*. But I tried to be discrete because of your modesty," the leader added with rumbling amusement.

"Don't you laugh at me!" the blonde squealed.

"You make me wild wanting you, *Mazaska Zi Ista*!"

"If you weren't so darn sexy!" she squirmed under his body. He'd trapped her with his superior strength.

Spirit Bear began to fondle her breasts with his hands. His mouth seared hers with lustful fury. He intoxicated her senses and left her drunk with longing…

***

Afterwards, Spirit Bear looked down at Golden Eye's glowing features. They were still connected in love. "I love you, *mita wastelaka. Nimitawa ktelo.*"

"*Tos,* and you are mine!" Kaitlin claimed huskily.

When morning came, they still lay cradled in each other's arms. Two hearts beat as one while the gentle morning light slowly accentuated their features. Each wore a warm smile for the other.

***

One week prior to the date of their wedding, one of the sentinels sent up a warning. A band of Crow warriors had been sighted near Oglala land. A war party, headed by *Woniya Mato*, left immediately to pursue the *toka*; they headed out at the break of dawn.

Kaitlin didn't want to worry, but all she could think about was war before the wedding. What kind of an omen could it be? She chided herself on being as superstitious as the Native she now proclaimed to be.

Woniya Mato was the greatest warrior alive. His skills were surpassed by none. The war chief was a living legend. No evil *could* befall him. However, the blonde could not stop from worrying.

When Kaitlin worried, she worked. It was the only way to keep from driving herself insane. Her mind always imagined the worst, and the young woman couldn't bear to think about that.

Tubers were always one of her favorite meals. The blonde knew many guests would find them delectable as well. She'd try to find enough to fill a basket of tubers and one of yams, for both were popular in the tribe.

Kaitlin went to the guest tipi of the Cheyenne. She softly called to Wild Flower, the chief's wife. She exited her tipi.

"*Tos*?" she said in a heavy accent.

"Would you like to gather tubers and yams with me this day?"

"*Tos*. I would enjoy the outing."

"Others may come, also, or I will need to find a male escort." Kaitlin remembered what Spirit Bear had said.

The Yankton women, Hopping Robin, Soft Touch, and Little Foot also joined them. Kaitlin provided enough baskets for each of them.

"Did you make this basket?" Little Foot asked.

"*Tos*."

"This is very good work."

"I can make many. You each keep your basket to remember me by."

"You should not be giving us gifts," Hopping Robin said.

"I want to," Kaitlin confided, "besides, I have too many in my tipi!"

Each woman laughed and accepted her gift.

Before noon, Kaitlin began to feel the hair stand on the back of her neck. *Someone was watching them. Was it the Crow that her betrothed hunted, or was it someone else? Was it possible Sunmanitu Wacitusni had followed them to spy on them?* The solitary white knew the man had to have been watching her on the day he handed her the water cress.

The baskets were brimming, so the women returned to the village. Kaitlin's sense of discomfort didn't lessen. Surely no danger would present itself in the village. Kaitlin took a deep, calming breath and ducked into her tipi.

Did she just have an overactive imagination? Did she imagine the eyes she felt upon her? Perhaps she was being paranoid. Kaitlin had worked herself up over Sly Coyote's persistence.

She took more calming breaths and sloshed a
little water on her face to refresh herself.

Golden Eyes ate a light lunch and lay down in
the heat of the day. However, she didn't sleep.
The blonde couldn't stop the sense of
foreboding that was beginning to consume her.
Was Woniya Mato okay? Kaitlin couldn't seem
to stop worrying about him. *How would she
ever endure a life of always worrying about him?*
Still, the white woman knew if she were to be a
part of his life, bear it she must.

After rest time, Lone Wolf and Sky Warrior
provided meat for the evening meal. The
women began preparing the many carcasses for
cooking. This time they made roasts with tubers,
carrots, and onions. They made stews. The
meat would stretch further this way and would
fill many bellies. There would be enough for
the next day as well.

Near evening, Kaitlin walked with her newly
established friends to the bathing area.

"When do you think the men will return?"
Apple Blossom asked. She didn't have to worry

about her man, for *Wawakte Towanjila* stayed to protect the village.

"I don't know, but I wish they'd come home!" Kaitlin revealed her anxiety.

"Do not worry, *Mazaska Zi Ista*. *Woniya Mato* is blessed by *Wakantanka* himself! A Crow arrow could never touch him!" Desert Rose exclaimed with confidence.

"I know this is true, but I cannot help but to worry. My marriage occurs in only six more suns!"

The women soothed Kaitlin the best they could. None had doubts about the prowess of the war party, but they could understand Golden Eye's worries. She had enough to be concerned about without her promised pursuing *toka*!

Kaitlin washed her clothes and went to the area of privacy. Her friends returned to the village to give her a few moments of solitude. While the blonde finished up, she felt an overwhelming sense of premonition engulf her once more. The chief's betrothed nearly swooned with it.

Woniya Mato, please be safe! Kaitlin prayed and pleaded with his essence. *I love you more than life itself! Return to my side this night!*

The young woman picked up her wet dress and began the walk up the hill toward the village.

"*Mazaska Zi Ista,*" a rich male voice called her name from the nearby woods.

She couldn't see who uttered her name, but it rang with minute familiarity. She answered hesitantly, "*Tos?*"

"*Uwa yo.* I have some news of great importance. It concerns *Woniya Mato.*"

Her heartbeat quickened and beat erratically. *Could her deepest fear be true? Could her beloved be injured somewhere?*

Kaitlin walked toward the wood and came face to face with Sly Coyote. He had two horses with him.

"What news of *Woniya Mato, Sunmanitu Wacitusni*? Do not tease me about my betrothed!"

His deep voice was somber as he replied, "I would never jest about the fall of a mighty war chief, *Mazaska Zi Ista*. I was asked to fetch you to bring you to his side. His injury is severe. He gasped your name. You better come quickly!"

CHAPTEr NINE

Sly, Sly Coyote

Kaitlin paled and lost all strength when she heard that her beloved was critically injured! Staggering under her heavy limbs, the blonde nearly went down. Sly Coyote's arm snaked out and crushed her body against his. He looked down at her upturned face.

"*Uwa yo*," he stated gruffly. "I will assist you on your horse."

He led the golden girl to the side of a slender built horse of medium size. It was a liver chestnut with a blaze and four socks. It danced eagerly under her weight as *Sunmanitu Wacitusni* placed her on its back. The horse had a rope around its neck. Sly Coyote held the end in his hands.

The stealthy man jumped nimbly onto the back of a deep blue roan stallion that stood nearly five inches larger than the other animal. He tapped the steed's side, and they turned and picked their way back through the woods.

Kaitlin grasped the hair on her horse's mane. She'd ridden horses before, but not in the unrestricted way that the Indians chose. Normally, the white woman needed reins to guide her animal as well as the saddle to remain secure. *Maybe that was why Sunmanitu Wacitusni guided her horse for her with the rope.*

When they broke free of the woods, they galloped northwest. The sun was setting and the light quickly dimmed. Kaitlin clung madly to the animal's back. It was difficult to stabilize herself on the smooth width of the creature; the young woman used muscles she didn't think she had. Most of the night passed as they maintained this staggering canter.

"How much longer until we reach *Woniya Mato's* side, *Sunmanitu Wacitusni*?" she yelled so he would hear her.

"We ride another sun and night. Do not talk, or you could alert the Crow to our presence," his

deep voice warned. Kaitlin nodded her
understanding against the dark sky.

When the sun shattered the blackness of the
night, *Mazaska Zi Ista* needed to stretch her
weary muscles, but she dared not. It would be a
matter of life and death where her love was
concerned! The war chief's wife-to-be had to
reach him as quickly as possible!

*Please, my love, do not desert me! I cannot face
a life without you! I will pray for my own death
so that I can join your side if you are taken from
me!* Kaitlin promised herself.

Near midday, Sly Coyote stopped by the banks
of a stream. He wiped the horses down and
made sure they were sound. After cooling them
by walking the equine, he allowed the animals
to eat and drink.

Kaitlin walked behind a tree to relieve herself
and then returned to the bank of the river. She
washed her face and arms, then drank from the
refreshing waters. Finally, the young woman
succumbed to her shaking, weak limbs. She lay
under a shady tree and did not move.

Sly Coyote gave her some pemmican and a peach. He refilled the *mniapahta* while he allowed her to relax. The determined man crouched a short way away from her and studied her exhausted form.

Normally, his stare made Kaitlin uneasy, but her fatigued state didn't even alert her to the weight of his eyes. The golden one merely tried to rebuild her depleted strength.

Without realizing she'd dozed off, the firm grip of Sly Coyote broke her confines of sleep. Kaitlin stretched and then was hoisted back onto her chestnut horse. They resumed the pace they'd maintained the entire time they'd been traveling.

Quickly, the blonde's muscles lost their power. She managed to hang on, but her tiring body could not sustain the grueling pace without dire consequences. Kaitlin made it until evening.

"*Sunmanitu Wacitusni?*" she called softly.

He looked back at her. His expression was stern.

"I do not think I can hang on any longer."

"Then you will ride with me."

Kaitlin didn't like this idea, but if she could tolerate it, she'd reach the side of her ailing man's sooner! Because it was a matter of life and death, she acquiesced.

Sly Coyote signaled to his horse, and it slowed immediately. He pulled the mount she was perched on and drew her form to his on the back of the big stallion.

The white woman didn't care for the familiar way his hands lingered on her slender sides, but she would tolerate almost anything to be by her love's side! Sly Coyote placed her body in front of his and draped an arm around her waist. His hand rested against her taut abdomen.

Kaitlin drew in a sharp breath, but she realized she needed this support to avoid crashing to the hard earth on the way to her beloved. Still, the *ska winyan* was uncomfortable with another man's athletic form pressed intimately against her back side. The golden girl gritted her teeth and tried to lean forward some. As time passed, her fatigued body grew wearier; she gave up and sagged against his hard frame.

As the grueling pace continued, Kaitlin's vision blurred. Her head began to bob. She hadn't slept except for the few minutes at noon for the past thirty-five hours. Before she knew what happened, the blonde slumped against Sly Coyote's frame and remembered no more of the night.

Just before dawn, Kaitlin began to stir. It felt as if her legs had been rubbed raw against the constant sliding against the horse's hair. A strong band still encircled her waist to keep her from falling.

"*Woniya Mato...*" she murmured huskily against the manly form. She caressed his arm in her sleep. That same arm suddenly tightened and brought her to full awareness.

"What...?" the blonde said. It took a few minutes for her to recall where she was and why *Sunmanitu Wacitusni* was holding her.

Sly Coyote slowed his steed and walked it toward a clump of trees. He dismounted gracefully. When Kaitlin slid down the stallion's side, she landed in his arms.

The muscular Native held her a moment longer than necessary, perusing her. His nostrils flared a miniscule amount, and the blackness of his eyes deepened. Kaitlin looked down and saw that a good portion of her thigh was exposed from her dismounting. Blushing, she tugged at the dress hem. The Yankton man gently set her on the ground.

Clearing his throat, Sly Coyote announced, "We will rest here for an hour or two. Then we continue. We should reach our destination by noon."

"Can we not continue?" she asked.

"The horses need to rest, drink, and feed. I, also, need to rest."

Suddenly, Kaitlin chastised herself. She realized she'd rested, and he'd had to keep her on his horse as well as himself. The blonde's cheeks pinked.

"I am sorry. It's just that I worry. I cannot bear for something to happen to *Woniya Mato*!"

The Sioux man looked upon her with his heavy black stare until she looked away. Finally, Kaitlin went into the grove of trees to relieve herself. When she returned, Sly Coyote provided her with more pemmican and another peach. She gratefully ate the items.

When he lay down to rest, she did the same. Kaitlin lay in some long grasses away from him to relax. She still felt exhausted. In an hour or two, she would be able to ride her own horse again. For that, she was very thankful. *Mazaska Zi Ista* didn't like being so close to another male, especially one who disturbed her so.

In no time, it seemed, Sly Coyote shook her awake again. Kaitlin drank more, relieved herself on additional time, and then allowed the other to help her back on her horse. The golden skinned woman took in a shallow breath as she felt the man's hand on her bottom as he hoisted her up.

After an hour of riding, Kaitlin softly called to Sly Coyote. "Are we not coming to the edge of Oglala territory? I do not believe we claim more than this area to protect."

"Your promised pursued the Crow past your boundaries. When he rode several hours away, he was ambushed along with his party. This is where I take you. Prepare yourself. What you will see will shock you, *Mazaska Zi Ista*."

She fell silent once more, her heart beating frantically under his new warning. *What if Woniya Mato had passed on to walk with Wakantanka? What would she do? How could she live with it?*

Kaitlin thought about Spirit Bear's easy smiles. He'd always had one ready for her. She called his arresting features to mind. It was a talent that he could strike desire in her soul simply with a look while imposing fear in his enemies, his *toka,* with those same eyes…

Could it really be true? The Great Woniya Mato, struck down by the Crow? She nearly scuffed. But then… if that *wasn't* true… what could all this mean?

Kaitlin didn't mean to, but now that she was rested and not panicked, she began to think more clearly and logically. *Why hadn't Sunmanitu Wacitusni brought Wawakankan with them?* No man had more skill with medicine and spiritual power to save a life, and no man cared more than he for the war chief to live.

Drawing in a deep breath, Kaitlin kicked her horse a little. It drew alongside the big roan. "Why did you not bring *Wawakankan* to treat *Woniya Mato*?"

Sly Coyote did not respond to her question. He only looked ahead and rode his mount. She tried again, louder. "*Sunmanitu Wacitusni*! Why did you not bring *Wawakankan*?"

Finally, he turned to look at her. This time, his look was frigid. As always, his eyes drilled into her very soul. "I could not find him in camp," he finally said. Then he looked forward once more.

Kaitlin was beginning to feel very suspicious, and she berated herself for blindly trusting this man whom she'd always felt was untrustworthy. In a way, her heart sang, for it he'd lied to her, then *Woniya Mato* was not on his death scaffold. On the other hand, if he *did* lie, then her life could be endangered!

*What could his plans be for her? What purpose
would he have for stealing her? It would be a
very fool-hearty thing to do!* The chief of Sly
Coyote's own village was planning on attending
their joining ceremony! There was also a chief
of the Cheyenne present, not to mention *Woniya
Mato* himself! His rage would know no bounds
if the man she followed had dared to steal the
betrothed of the legendary war chief!

Kaitlin wondered what she should do. She had
no control over the horse that was still roped
and bound to Sly Coyote. If she jumped off, it
would only be a second before the man and
beast would catch up to her. The blonde would
just have to sit tight and see if the Yankton man
spoke the truth; there was no other choice.

The next several hours passed very slowly for
Kaitlin. Her heart mourned: one way or another,
the blonde felt that her beloved was lost to her.
Either he lay, near death himself, or she was
ripped from his side. The golden bird knew
she'd be lost to him forever! What evil plot
Sunmanitu Wacitusni planned, she didn't know,
but she knew it involved separating her from
Spirit Bear.

How could she be at another man's mercy when she had first known Woniya Mato? Sly Coyote could not have honorable intentions for her! Either she rode to her death, or she was obviously another man's slave. *And she knew what that meant.*

The horses' pace slowed. Maybe she would soon discover his intentions. They were headed down a valley toward a grove of trees that probably surrounded a water source.

Kaitlin's eyes widened in shocked misery when she found herself surrounded by a small band of male Indians. She didn't recognize any of them, but they seemed to know Sly Coyote; they greeted him by name. He received many slaps on his back and wide grins. She, on the other hand, received leering eyes that raked her as if she wore no clothing.

They spoke in a strange, guttural tongue she was not familiar with. The solitary woman shook with alarm and swallowed the bile that had risen threateningly into her throat. Terror as she'd never known overtook her.

CHAPTER TEN

The Crow's Coup

"*Sunmanitu Wacitusni*! I never believed you could actually succeed with your brazen plan! You did what you claimed!" Black Bird praised him.

"It was easy," Sly Coyote claimed nonchalantly.

One warrior, Falling Rock, laughed so hard, he arched his head back. "Not only did you steal this *winyan* out from under the war chief's nose, but also the shaman's nose, the other two chiefs, and countless other leaders from different tribes!" He took a breath and wiped the tears from his eyes. "I'd have never thought it possible."

Sly Coyote nodded with a grin.

"Your coups will take all night to chant!" congratulated Falling Rock. "You will jump to the top of the warrior ranks!"

Sunmanitu Wacitusni acknowledged with one nod.

"You did not tell me she was so pleasing to the eye!" Black Bird noted as his heated gaze stroked the white woman's body again.

"She has great power. Never before has *Woniya Mato* failed to see a strike by the enemy. She clouds his vision," Sly Coyote revealed, but he wisely withheld her effect on him.

"Let me cloud her vision," Black Bird sneered. "Then the mighty *Woniya Mato* will snarl no more." He licked his lips meaningfully toward Kaitlin and smiled evilly.

Sneaky Weasel agreed, "With this, his spirit would truly break!" He took a step nearer to the terrified woman.

"*Woniya Mato* will be one angry man. I hope this plot works out as you predicted, *Sunmanitu Wacitusni*," rang the concerned voice of Raven's Wing. He continued, "Otherwise, it will not be the end of the mighty bear, but our demise instead!"

"You worry too much," Dark Horse scoffed. "You act as though you doubt the prowess of the mighty Crow!"

"No, but I know of the ruthlessness of *Woniya Mato*. We have met before."

"Do not forget that he stole my right from me," Sly Coyote stated. "His betrothed is my ticket back into my true heritage!"

Black Bird said, "We do not forget our father, Sly Coyote. You, also, are your father's son! You will have your many coups chanted upon our return to the village! Night Hawk is avenged! You have proven your loyalty to the Crow and denounced your slave Sioux mother's heritage! At our celebration, you will be inducted into our warrior society!"

"Yes, because of *Woniya Mato's* interference, I was raised by the Sioux, but this is good, for I know many strengths and weaknesses of our foe!" *Sunmanitu Wacitusni* bragged.

"*Woniya Mato* did not know when he killed one mighty Crow, Night Hawk, two replaced him.

Twice the prowess, twice the power!" raved Black Bird.

"Let us dismount and rest a few minutes," Falling Rock said.

The men dismounted. Sly Coyote came to Kaitlin's side and held his hand out to her. She trembled and spoke. "I do not require your assistance."

"You will come to me. Now. You would not like the consequences if you do not obey," he spoke Lakota to her.

Slowly, the now-reserved woman allowed him to help her off the horse. Sly Coyote led her into the circle of men. Five Crow warriors surrounded her.

"*Woniya Mato* knows how to choose a woman!" admired Falling Rock.

"I have never seen one such as she!" breathed Dark Horse.

"Who gets her first?" Sneaky Weasel asked hopefully.

"The sons of Night Hawk, of course!" shouted Black Bird gleefully, making Kaitlin jump in fear.

He prowled up to her and grabbed her hands roughly in one of his. The dark man yanked her arms up and pulled her back against his body. With his other hand, he rubbed her breasts through her dress. Kaitlin struggled vainly under his advance.

"Stop!" *Sunmanitu Wacitusni* commanded, his voice growled with meaning. The others stopped and turned to stare at the proclaimed Crow man.

"Technically, she is mine. I captured her. I say we do not rape her."

"Why?" Black Bird asked. "She is beautiful. I desire her, and she belongs to our greatest enemy. What way could be better to extract our revenge than to slowly torture our exquisite captive into submission?" he paused and added, "Surely you do not save her for yourself?"

"No. She has much power. Think of *Woniya Mato*. His downfall stands before you. His death will be because his heart is gone. She stands there," he pointed to Kaitlin dramatically. "Do you want the same to happen to you? Do not underestimate her power on a man. Already, she has tempted me. I stand strong. I will not succumb to the same downfall as *Woniya Mato*. We keep her alive to capture him. That is all."

The other men looked disappointed, but they saw the truth and wisdom behind Sly Coyote's words.

"You speak true," Dark Horse admitted. "*Sunmanitu Wacitusni*, you are right. She tempts a man greatly with only her looks. You are wise to advise us to stay away from the depths of her power."

Black Bird released the golden woman abruptly. Kaitlin crumpled to the ground, tears leaking from her eyes. She kept her head drooped to avoid the gazes of the men.

***

Mazaska Zi Ista didn't know what the six men planned on doing with her. She'd thought the worst with all the lustful stares at her, especially when the aggressive warrior fondled her so intimately. The captured woman feared they'd all take her right there!

Kaitlin had slumped to the ground on shaky limbs when Sly Coyote allowed her to sit to the side of the group of men. They continued to speak in the strange language. She heard Spirit Bear's name mentioned frequently. The men also stared at her a lot, especially the man who'd dared to touch her.

Please, Woniya Mato! Come for me. I cannot take it if they treat me as a captive! I only want you! I will not be able to endure the touches of other men! Save me, my love!

Kaitlin turned her back on the men. Silently, she cried for her dire future. It was so bleak! How could she ever escape six men unscathed? It seemed she'd never know happiness again!

The beautiful blonde placed her head on her knees as the crystal tears continued to leak from her golden eyes. Slowly, she rocked back and

forth to console herself. Many eyes witnessed
her misery.

"If only *Woniya Mato* had a spiritual connection
with his woman. He would understand the
circumstances she now faces," Black Bird said.
"Of course, if you would allow me to find
pleasure with her, he would lose all hope!" he
added wistfully.

"My brother, it is your fate I care about when I
deny you this request."

"I know. She *is* so tempting!"

"This I realize!" *Sunmanitu Wacitusni*
responded and laughed. His spirits could not be
higher. He'd swiped a very tempting morsel
from beneath the great twitching black nose of
the Oglala war chief! His sense of euphoria
would take some time to wear off.

The men talked and celebrated a while longer.
Then they decided to ride for the Crow camp.
Sly Coyote had not slept much in the past day
and two nights, but he was invigorated at the
high coup that would be bestowed on him once
in the Crow camp. He would attain a high

incoming status with his daring feat. The proclaimed Crow warrior would ride another week if it called for, but he knew the camp was only two days and night's ride from their meeting spot.

The men mounted back up and rode in a northwesterly direction. Kaitlin stared forlornly at her horse's mane. She clung on for dear life. The shattered woman refused to look at the party of men surrounding her. The golden girl was aware that Sly Coyote continued to hold the rope to her steed in his hand.

Just before nightfall, the team stopped to rest the horses for an hour or so. The men cared for the animals and let them eat and drink. Kaitlin wandered behind a tree to have a little privacy. When she came out, the mean Indian who'd grabbed her stood only five feet away.

He smiled wickedly and sneered at her. His eyes were narrowed as they stared at her chest. His appreciation brazenly lingered there before casually trailing back up to her face. The menace ran his tongue slowly over his lips to deepen her terror.

Kaitlin's face flamed in embarrassment and fear. She stood, frozen to her spot, unable to walk toward him. Her golden eyes were the size of sauces in her dainty face.

Black Bird relished the fright and intimidation he held over the woman of Spirit Bear. He would find a way to take her sometime when they were back in the village. His brother could not watch her every moment. Then the warrior-up-to-no-good would break her spirit and in doing so, count a coup on his enemy.

+++

Black Bird was very glad to have his older brother back in the village with him. They were actually only six months apart in age. When the Sioux slave became large with his brother, Night Hawk had claimed his right and wed a Crow maiden. She'd conceived a short time after consummating their vows. The two brothers were born in the same tipi.

Years later, Night Hawk was on a hunting trip.
Sly Coyote, eight winters old at the time, had
asked to accompany his father. Because he
would be facing manhood in a handful of years,
Night Hawk agreed. However, the hunting
party had turned into a war party when they
happened upon an Oglala band of warriors. The
Crow had lost the skirmish; *Woniya Mato* had
killed Night Hawk, his first major coup as a
warrior at the age of twelve winters.

This band of Oglala warriors had taken Sly
Coyote back to join his mother who'd been
reunited with her Yankton family group years
ago when she'd been recaptured during a raid on
the Crow village.

When Sly Coyote's mother, Touch of Wind, had
rejoined the Yankton, Hunter of the Skies had
taken her as a *thawicu*. A year later, Eagle
Talon was born. When Sly Coyote was rejoined
with his mother, the half-brothers were three
winters apart in age.

+++

Faith and honor had been given to Sly Coyote. He'd betrayed them all. He'd proven where his true roots lay: with the Crow.

"Come," Black Bird commanded the golden-eyed one. She didn't move. The white woman continued to stand and stare at him with wide eyes.

The Crow man loomed over her in three quick steps. He grasped her arm and pulled her into his chest. The stranger looked down at her with gritted teeth. He wanted her to feel his total power over her; he wanted her to feel disheartened.

Black Bird felt her tremble against his body. Her fear encouraged him; it aroused him. To further terrorize her, he pushed his hips forward. She tore away from his grasp, turned, and ran a few steps toward the group of men.

He caught her arm almost as soon as she'd broken free and held it in a painful grasp. He jerked her back, nearly knocking her off her feet; Kaitlin was recaptured in his strong arms.

Black Bird forced her head back with a brutal assault on her mouth.

The betrothed of Spirit Bear squirmed and writhed to escape his overpowering strength. Kaitlin gagged and tried to scream, but his mouth continued to sear hers in unwelcome invasion. Her breath came in ragged spurts, and she let the power go out of her legs.

He released her when she collapsed on the ground. The blonde could not control the sobs that racked her body. The solitary woman was totally alone and at the mercy of the enemy! She was devoid of hope. Spasms shook her as she wept out her misery.

The pair of masculine legs did not move during her crying spree. The horrid man stood and waited for her to empty herself of emotion. When she finally dared to look up, Black Bird wore a malicious smirk.

"You're an evil, evil man! I hate you," she whispered.

Dark Horse yelled toward them, "Come, Black Bird. Bring the girl. We ride!"

Sly Coyote had not witnessed the kissing scene, but he knew Black Bird watched over the girl as she cried in dejection of her future. The new Crow warrior knew *Mazaska Zi Ista* needed to expend her emotional energy, so he allowed his brother to oversee her. However, the kidnapper didn't know of his sibling's plan to appease himself with his captive.

Kaitlin heard the man command her to rise. She didn't understand his words, but she knew he meant for her to return to the group. The men were mounting up, so the dejected blonde dragged herself to her chestnut. She didn't resist when masculine hands grasped her body and purposefully felt her slender waist and bottom when they hoisted her onto her mount. Raucous laughter followed.

Kaitlin was more morose than Sly Coyote had ever seen her. The warrior knew he must distance himself from her. He couldn't allow the seed of warmth for her to grow. The golden woman's power over *Woniya Mato* was strong. The now-Crow man couldn't allow her power to overcome his as well.

The horses thundered on into the night. Raven's
Wing led the party through the darkness. He
knew the land in any form: dark, light, winter
ice, or summer drought. He was sure of the path.

CHAPTER ELEVEN

The Path of Losing Hope

The wear on Kaitlin's body and her emotions were great. The blonde no longer cared if she fell from the horse into the sharp thundering oblivion. She almost welcomed the blackness over the fate that surely awaited her upon the arrival into the enemy camp!

Sly Coyote didn't share her feelings. He watched her like a hungry wolf. When he noticed her form weaving from weariness, the warrior pulled the chestnut to his roan and scooped her from its back.

The subdued woman didn't resist Sly Coyote. Kaitlin almost felt as if he were the closest thing to a friend in a camp of evil. Although the man was responsible for her presence, she knew that he alone had prevented the other man from taking her in front of the others. Still, the blonde couldn't find gratitude within her.

Wearily, the golden-skinned woman lay weakly against his chest.

= = =

Warm electrodes sparked through *Sunmanitu Wacitusni's* body at her trust. He angrily pushed his feelings away, but they returned a short while later when he looked down at the woman's sleeping form. The attractive girl's innocence was ensnared within her soul and radiated out. Without his permission, it caused tendrils of protection to begin winding around Sly Coyote's heart.

= = =

Ribbons of light seared through the sky. Kaitlin awoke still nestled against the stalwart man. She looked up at Sly Coyote. He felt her gaze and met it. The claimed Crow man drilled holes into her resolve until she looked away.

The golden one shifted, uncomfortable with stiff and sore muscles. *Mazaska Zi Ista* also needed to relieve herself, but she was determined not to ask for a thing. She cared not for her life now that *Woniya Mato* had been taken from her.

Bringing the striking and imposing man to her mind made Kaitlin mourn afresh. *Oh, Woniya Mato, what have I done?* She thought in agony. *What do they plan for me? Do they think you will come for me? Do they set a trap for you? Oh, if I could only take back that day! I knew not to trust Sunmanitu Wacitusni! But my fear for you overrode my caution. Now it is too late to save myself, let alone protect you!*

Kaitlin bowed her head as tears dripped once more, uncontrolled, from her eyes. Her miserable spirit had no pride left. If it pleased these men to see her gloom, then let them rejoice!

Finally at midmorning, the party stopped their grueling pace. Sly Coyote jumped from his steed and caught her limp form as she slid from

the animal's height. The others ribbed one
another as he placed her gently on her feet.

"Falling under her spell so quickly?" taunted
Dark Horse.

"No, but I do not want her to harm herself. She
needs to be healthy and strong should we need
her in the future."

"What if we need her now?" needled Black Bird.
"I can think of one use I have for her!" He
laughed derisively.

Through her misery, Kaitlin was able to produce
a shudder. She knew without comprehending
their guttural language that they spoke of her.
The terrified young woman finally muscled up
the courage to point to the trees fifteen feet
away and looked at Sly Coyote. He nodded.

"Brother, give it a rest. Her magic is strong,"
chided Sly Coyote. "Let us see what comes of
Woniya Mato. Then we decide what will be
done with her."

Raven's Wing said, "I think this is a good plan."
He really did not agree with torture of women,

even one belonging to the ultimate enemy: the Oglala war chief.

When Kaitlin returned, Falling Rock handed her his empty water skin. He pointed to the water. It was clear that she was assuming the role of slave and had to fill all the drinking containers. She filled seven bags. Each man made her hand it to him. Four men made her feel uncomfortable. Only Sly Coyote and Raven's Wing treated her decently.

Kaitlin was unsure of Falling Rock and Dark Horse. They certainly leered at her womanly curves, but they didn't make sexual overtures toward her. Sneaky Weasel and Black Bird, however, were different. They made her feel as if she were a lowly whore to sate lusts upon. The white girl had no doubt they would try to do just that the first opportunity presented to them.

Both men had grasped her hand when she handed them their water skin. They wouldn't let go of her until she looked at them. Each had stared with narrowed eyes upon her womanly form and smiled sardonically at her despair.

Kaitlin lay down a short way from the men. She scooted as far from them as they would allow her and presented her back. Dark Horse passed out pemmican to each person. He tossed one to Kaitlin as well. It landed in the grass directly to the front side of her. Although she was hungry, the white girl did not reach for the flavorful traveling food. Instead, she closed her eyes.

Sly Coyote came before her and picked up the rounded food. "Eat, *Mazaska Zi Ista*. You will need your strength to hold on to the horse when we move again."

"I do not care. I do not want anything from you or… *them*," she scoffed.

"Perhaps you enjoy riding with me, then. If you do not eat, I will see you ride the entire time in my arms. I find it rather… entertaining," he said softly.

Sly Coyote knew that would be the fastest way to convince her to eat. If he had to, he would force her, but he would try to outwit her first. Kaitlin glared at him, but she took the meal he offered and ate it.

"Why, *Sunmanitu Wacitusni*? Why do you
betray me to our enemies? What offense have I
committed against you?" she asked gently.
"Why do you hate me so?"

"I do not hate you," he said. He stood abruptly
and returned to the men.

Kaitlin could only look at his retreating back.
She drank from the water skin and collapsed
onto the ground. If the Golden One belonging
to Spirit Bear hoped to ride alone, then she
needed to rest as much as possible.

***

 "Will we be ready to move on with our plan? If
I know *Woniya Mato*, he will move to strike
within seven suns of our return. We'd best be
prepared," Sly Coyote told his comrades.

"Yes. During your visit to the Oglala camp, we
had several Crow bands agree to unite to entrap
the mighty legend. He has made too many

enemies among the Crow. We all desire to see him defeated!" Falling Rock responded.

"We will have many sentinels watching for his arrival. He will try to surround the camp, but we will surround him! Then we attack from both sides. He'll be trapped in the middle with nowhere to run!" Black Bird cried compassionately.

"But what of our women and children?" Raven's Wing asked. "You know that even when we succeed, there will be casualties!" He did not want his wife or child injured.

"We move them before the time comes," Dark Horse snorted.

"It is about time Spirit Bear loses his teeth and claws. I hope we can capture him! Then we can prolong his torture!" Sneaky Weasel cackled.

"He will have the same idea about us!" Raven's Wing stated huskily.

"Why did you join this group if you are so concerned?" Black Bird asked pointedly.

"I want revenge as well as any of you," he admitted. "Most Crow in our village have had some loss because of that solitary man. I, too, want *Woniya Mato's* reign to end, but I am a realist."

All knew Raven's Wing spoke true. None could stand before their reputable enemy and not feel a quiver of fear. He'd earned respect on the war field. His name alone commanded reverence. Spirit Bear's anger would know no bounds when he discovered Sly Coyote's betrayal.

"Where will we move the women, elderly, and young?" Raven's Wing persisted.

"There is a cave about a mile from the village. They can seek refuge there," Falling Rock suggested.

"Oh, I cannot wait to capture the bear who has snapped at our heels for far too long!" Sneaky Weasel said in glee. "I would gladly give the killing strike!"

***

Kaitlin slumbered and was trapped in a bizarre dream:

The tiny golden bird flew before the large white bear. The bird's flight was labored as if it was weighed down by an unseen heavy load. As it beat its fragile golden wings, it became trapped in a bramble of dark, thorny bushes.

The bear charged forward, somehow seeking to aid the bird. As it did, a blanket of black fell upon it. The mighty creature roared and stood on his hind legs, but no matter how much the claws shred the cloth, more covers replaced the one before it.

A massive roar of frustrated anger came forth from the prodigious jaws of the enraged animal. It never could free the bird that'd been ensnared in the wicked thorns of undergrowth. Both animals called out, one in fear, the other in rage. Somewhere in the distance, a coyote howled. The cry rang of mockery and betrayal, even to the bird beating its helpless wings...

===

"*Mazaska Zi Ista,* it is time to wake," Sly Coyote tried to rouse the sleeping beauty. She turned her head on the ground and moved her arms in a strange manner.

"*Mazaska Zi Ista!*" he commanded more intently.

Finally, her golden eyes opened. They were looking at him, yet they didn't seem to see him. Sly Coyote watched as they slowly appeared to focus on his features followed by the realization of what he was doing as he crouched over her.

"*Uwa yo.* It is time to travel. Are you able to ride on your own?"

Kaitlin couldn't answer. Her mind was still on the dream. Taking that as a reply, he placed her before him on his steed. He was slightly concerned about her strange behavior. The captured woman hadn't issued a word.

What was *Mazaska Zi Ista* thinking? Did she know that he would allow none to harm her?

Sly Coyote desired her as he never had any other women, but he had to keep her power over him at bay. The now-Crow man would not succumb to the same defeat as *Woniya Mato*!

Perhaps when the enemy had been conquered, Sly Coyote would allow his body to seek release upon hers. Never would he allow his tribe to call her equal and take her to wife. She would always remain an attractive slave, for none could forget that she was once betrothed to their greatest enemy! The golden goddess was and always would be his greatest living and breathing coup!

If the white girl's power ever became too great for him, Sly Coyote would trade her away. The warrior knew his brother wished to couple with her, but he didn't think he could bear to see her treated as degraded as his brother surely would. Therefore, the Crow man would trade her to another tribe for items they didn't have access to. In this way, he would be justified for getting her out of his sight.

= = =

The horses rode on. The sun began to grow sleepy in the sky. When night claimed the lands once more, Kaitlin succumbed to sleep. Her body wasn't used to the rigor of the pace. The only other time she'd forced her body beyond its means was when she escaped the Sioux camp as a slave. Even that was nothing to what she was going through now! Her emotional turmoil kindled the fire of exhaustion. The white woman couldn't bear to think of the plan they were forming for her beloved.

= = =

Sly Coyote cradled the curvy sleeping form to his possessiveness. He'd sneak peeks down at the golden relaxed features, thinking how very like a princess *Mazaska Zi Ista* was. He couldn't imagine how another female would react if she'd found herself in this woman's moccasins. Despite his oath not to fall under her power, the warrior slid a little further.

The men did not stop through the night. When they rested just before dawn, all men relaxed except Falling Rock. He kept vigilance on the group. They were not expecting trouble, but they'd learned that it was a fatal mistake to underestimate their enemy.

According to Sly Coyote, *Woniya Mato* preferred to strike quickly before allowing his *toka* time to group and plan. Falling Rock was sure their path was being tracked even as they rested, but no man could travel for four days and four nights nonstop without rest breaks and hope to defeat a powerful enemy.

= = =

And the Crow would be a forceful opponent. Falling Rock smiled when he pictured the demise of the Oglala legend. This daring group of Crow men would go down in history! Their coups would be chanted for years after they walked with the Great Spirit.

Falling Rock assisted with the kidnapping of *Woniya Mato's* promised for glory, and he did it for the women. Falling Rock planned on taking two women to wife. Both had rejected his advances recently, but once his daring was known, their fathers would beg him to accept them.

The Crow man loved women, and his hand was well-known. This is probably why the girls had rejected his interest. They probably believed they would fall into the category of his other loves: discarded. However, he was ready to settle down. He wanted a son to follow in his path. These two girls were delectable! He smiled as he dreamed.

= = =

Three hours later, Falling Rock awoke the men and the golden girl. They prepared for another long day of travel. Kaitlin wished she had the will to attempt to escape, but she had no energy

even if she dared. The white girl went to stand
by the chestnut horse.

Sly Coyote lifted her up and leapt nimbly onto
his stallion. How could these men stay so
strong with less sleep than she? Kaitlin was so
tired… even after sleeping most of the night
during travel in *Sunmanitu Wacitusni's* arms
and the three hours she'd just slept, she still had
no energy.

Sly Coyote handed her a ball of the pemmican
and a strip of dried meat. Maybe she just
needed to nourish her fatigued body. Kaitlin
began to eat. The blonde moved mechanically,
for she no longer wished to think about the dark
bleakness of her future.

The men moved quietly this day. They didn't
talk, but each focused on their path to success.
The closer they approached the village, the more
glory thoughts each harbored. All the men's
eyes would wander throughout the trip to their
prize. It had been ingenious! Never before had
any dared to walk right into the Oglala village
and swipe such a tasty morsel from under the
nose of the great man himself!

When Kaitlin happened to see a smile on one of
the men that surrounded her, she knew it
couldn't be a good thing. The golden one could
worry no more over what they'd planned for her.
Never would she have guessed the amount of
planning that had gone into her abduction and
the true reason for it.

CHAPTER TWELVE

Induction into Crow Society

Kaitlin knew *Woniya Mato* was a legend among his people. How else had he achieved such high status at such an early age? Nevertheless, the men didn't share war stories with the women unless it was at a celebration. Even though the white woman had witnessed his prowess first hand with Jed, the golden girl had no idea what he was truly capable of in war.

But the Crow did. And when they held his heart in their power, there was no way the beating organ of the bear would continue to supply his life's blood! They would see to it!

The party continued the journey. It was difficult for the men not to increase the pace as they grew closer, but their mounts had traveled far. They didn't wish to destroy such magnificent steeds just to arrive an hour sooner.

Kaitlin could tell a greater air of confidence claimed the men. Only Sly Coyote appeared to grow more nervous. The attractive female merely hung on to her horse, void of emotion.

As dark claimed the lands, they slowed the animals but didn't stop. Kaitlin was glad for she was going to have to ride with Sly Coyote again if they continued the gallop. However, the blonde could hold on by herself at a walk.

The big roan approached and Sly Coyote handed her a water skin. When Kaitlin finished drinking, he asked if she needed to take a small break. The captive nodded.

The daring Crow man stopped his horse and caught Kaitlin in his arms before setting her on the ground. He allowed her privacy behind some bushes. The others waited in a group. When she returned, Sly Coyote lifted her back onto the chestnut. His eyes lingered on her face while he mounted and pulled the rope on her steed. Her morose golden eyes haunted him as they rode on.

Two and a half hours after light had hidden from the lands, they saw a glowing camp ahead.

Fires burned brightly. Kaitlin had felt as if she was devoid of emotion, but new feelings surged through her; her body tingled with electric awareness, and she shivered in the night. Sly Coyote pulled the rope of her horse closer to his.

As they approached the blazing village, Black Bird led the entourage. He was followed by his half-brother, Sly Coyote, and his slave, the betrothed of *Woniya Mato*. Raven's Wing, flanked by Falling Rock and Dark Horse, walked before Sneaky Weasel. Without realizing it, they entered the camp according to their current rank.

Much of the community slept, but a great number had waited with anticipation on the return of the daring group. People surged forward. Most of them were men, but a few women present.

Kaitlin noticed a vast difference between the two Indian Nations immediately. The Crow men resembled the Sioux as far as appearances went. Both wore long flowing hair and elaborate dress. They walked with noble pride and hunter's stealth. Both distinctions lived in bison-hide tipis. The real difference was the women.

Crow women dressed very plainly and wore their hair in a cropped fashion. They also carried weapons like the men! They commanded respect as much as the men in their community. Kaitlin was rather shocked.

The people closed in on the men and beasts. Kaitlin shrank against Sly Coyote's side. She had the distinct feeling that he, too, was nervous.

Two men and a woman approached the group. The crowd cleared a path in front of them, alerting Kaitlin to their importance. The warriors dismounted, and Sly Coyote held out his arms to her. She was placed on her feet to face the crowd.

"I see our plan worked, Night Hawk brothers! Congratulations to you both! *Sunmanitu Wacitusni*, you will be inducted with the rise of the sun into full Crow warrior status!" the man slapped both men on the back.

Black Bird's voice reflected his pride under the honor, "Thank you Chief Midnight Star."

Sly Coyote smiled and hit his chest once in the acknowledgement of such high praise.

"It is a job well done, men!" the husky woman's voice joined in on the praise. "Introduce your woman to me."

Sly Coyote stepped forward, his arm guiding Kaitlin's.

"This is *Mazaska Zi Ista,* Bight Sky. She is the promised one of *Woniya Mato.*"

The Crow leader assessed the other female. She noted every detail on Kaitlin from head to foot. She was several inches shorter than the white girl and not so slender in build.

"I can see why this yellow eyes has held his interest. It is good that you caught her without having to harm her. This is a greater coup for you!" commended Bright Sky.

The high chief also perused Kaitlin. The terrified girl shook with nerves, but she stood tall and proud. Her shoulders were back, and her spine was straight. The betrothed woman would honor Spirit Bear until her death! Her chin jutted forward in renewed determination.

"She is a fine specimen of womanhood. She can definitely find a place in our village!" Chief Midnight Star breathed.

The war chief, Bloody Knife, stepped forward to more closely observe the girl with golden eyes and honeyed hair. He, like most, had never seen a yellow eyes up close. However, he'd heard stories. "This girl is the heart of *Woniya Mato*?" he asked.

"Yes, Chief Bloody Knife. She owns his life. I have seen it myself!" *Sunmanitu Wacitusni* revealed. A collective gasp came up from the crowd.

Kaitlin turned her golden gaze upon the man beside her. What had he said about *Woniya Mato*? She was curious, but her interest was quickly forgotten. The crowd kept inching closer and closer.

The chief turned and said something to the crowd. They backed off and allowed the men and white woman to go to their tipis. Sly

Coyote and Kaitlin followed Black Bird to a tipi just beyond the center few.

When they entered, a man and woman rested on one mat. A girl child of about two rested on one, and another girl about eight rested on another. Three more mats were laid out in the tipi along the walls. Black Bird took the one by the entrance flap, Kaitlin the next one up, and then Sly Coyote.

Kaitlin immediately reclined upon hers as well as did the men. All were asleep a short while later. The night was gone in a flash. When Kaitlin awoke, she was greeted by the insolent stares of the young female and the mother of Black Bird. The child tooled around the tipi, and the unknown man had left.

***

"So this is the woman of *Woniya Mato*?" Wild Flower asked.

"Yes, mother, she is," answered Black Bird.

"Her mate stole the life's breath from the father of my brother?" screeched the eight-year old Fire Fly.

"She is promised to him. They have not yet joined," *Sunmanitu Wacitusni* stated.

"Hungry," stated the little girl, Dancing on Air.

"Just one minute, darling," Wild Flower spoke soothingly to her youngest daughter. Her fiery eyes never left Kaitlin's.

***

A drum beat filled the air. It announced that in one hour, the chief would address the community. Fire Fly collected wood and stacked it in the hearth. Her mother began a fire. Then Wild Flower cooked wheat with molasses and pones of fruit bread for breakfast.

Kaitlin was taken with the two resentful females to the place used for privacy by the women of the village. Next, she was given six water skins to fill. The mother and daughter waited on her to do their chores and did not offer to help her carry the filled skins back to the tipi.

Sly Coyote and Black Bird awaited the return of the women. When the females returned, the brothers took Kaitlin with them and left the tipi. The man of the home, Arrow Head, joined his wife and daughters. The littlest, Dancing on Air, waved her chubby fist in greeting. They walked with the crowds to hear the words of their chiefs.

Kaitlin noticed the same three important members of the new society she'd met last night came forward to join her and the two men. The four others who'd traveled with them: Falling Rock, Dark Horse, Raven's Wing, and Sneaky Weasel also came forward to stand with them.

The gathering in front of the village waited quietly for the drum beat to stop. It would signify that the chiefs and the council were ready to speak. Kaitlin scanned the crowd in nervous dread.

The village of the Crow was smaller than that of the Oglala from what the blonde could tell. She could see the edges of the encampment. The crowd did not stretch for miles although one could not deny that quite a few people were present. The council appeared to be the three leaders she'd met the preceding night, but she was not sure about the woman.

Did women hold positions of power in the village of the Crow? If so, why not in the Sioux communities? This was how it should be: more equality between the sexes.

Yet the women here seemed to downplay their natural beauty. Their clothing was drab and boring. Their hair was cut in unflattering shags and bobs. Most styles only brushed the tops of the shoulder area.

The men, however, wore fine clothes that were adorned with many decorations. Their shining hair hung past their waists. It seemed backward to Kaitlin. These people were certainly very different from any she'd met!

Before Kaitlin had completed mental comparisons, the drum stopped. The golden-skinned woman's heart beat took over the ominous rhythm in her ears. Her throat shrunk, forcing her ability to swallow to depart, and her knees knocked. *Would they execute her before the crowd?* They seemed to be obsessed with her love. All they said in reference to her was the name, '*Woniya Mato*'.

***

"My people," began Chief Midnight Star. "We have great news for you." He paused, "There will be much excitement in the next week or two. We will be warring with the Oglala tribe of Sioux."

The people stared with wide eyes.

"Many of you have met *Sunmanitu Wacitusni*. I want to welcome him into our hearts as one of us." The chief nodded to Sly Coyote. Cued, he stepped forward. "His rightful place is among us, and he joins us now as an honored Crow warrior!"

The crowd clapped uncertainly. They did not yet understand the story about to be unfurled.

"Do you see the yellow eyes that stands with him?" the chief asked his people. Many murmurs of confirmation went up.

Chief Bloody Knife stepped up and stated, "She is the promised one of *Woniya Mato*. They were to join on the next rising of the sun." The multitude went silent as all eyes fell upon the golden-eyed woman.

Chief Midnight Star resumed speaking, "*Sunmanitu Wacitusni* is none other than the first born son of Night Hawk." With this fact revealed, the gathering seemed to hold its breath for the next revelation.

"He was raised by his Sioux mother in the camp of the Yankton. He came to our village several moons ago to reveal a daring and deadly plan. He wanted to reclaim his heritage among our people. He felt that this plot would show where his true loyalties lie."

Bright Sky told the next leg of the story. Her husky voice filled the air of expectation. "He can never return to the camp of the Yankton where his mother lives. They would strike him dead upon his arrival. All will know of

Sunmanitu Wacitusni's courage, cunning, and bravery. His prowess will earn him the highest coup among the Crow!" she bragged.

Bright Sky continued, "He walked right into the camp of our fiercest foe, *Woniya Mato*. During his celebrations before his joining, and he outfoxed the war chief's betrothed into coming with him on her own free will!"

Now all eyes shifted to Sly Coyote. He shifted nervously, but outwardly he appeared calm. He met the eyes of his people with stoic dignity.

"We will finally be able to defeat the mighty bear for we now hold the key to his success: his heart!" she claimed.

The war chief, Bloody Knife, stepped forward. He built anticipation by not speaking for several moments before his part of the revelation. He stood tall and strong as he waited for the rustling to die down. Finally, at the peak of expectation, he spoke.

"There is more to *Sunmanitu Wacitusni's* coup." He paused as the gathering became silent. "Not only did he steal the betrothed right from under the Oglala war chief's nose, but also from under the noses of his other leaders, the entire band, and at least four or five chiefs from other tribes and branches of the Sioux!" He stopped as the community gasped collectively. "We expect swift retaliation. It is *Woniya Mato's* way. In four suns, we will ask women, children, and those too old to fight to go to the nearby cave to wait," Bloody Knife began. "*Woniya Mato's* fury will rule his logic. He will come for his woman, but we will be ready! We have a plan set up to trap his warriors. The mighty bear will not live to ride against us again!" Many shouts went up from the crowd; it was deafening.

Bloody Knife continued, "We have two bands of our brothers from the north coming to help rid us of the Oglala war chief. This plan could not have happened if not for the daring of this man before you!"

Midnight Star spoke, "*Sunmanitu Wacitusni*, son of Night Hawk, a proven Crow warrior, stealer of the heart and soon to be life of *Woniya Mato*, meet your people!"

Sly Coyote stepped forward and met the crowd. He felt more honored than he ever had before in his life. If he'd wondered about his decision to implement his possibly deadly plan, all insecurities were wiped away. He was home, truly *home*!

"To honor our new Crow warrior with the highest coup earned, we have built a small tipi for *Sunmanitu Wacitusni*. He will marry someday and inherit a larger tipi when the time comes."

Bright Sky added, "Arrow Head also wished for Sly Coyote to have his own lodge to keep his slave in. The sight of her triggers many memories in his wife, Wild Flower. If you remember, *Woniya Mato's* first coup was when he took the life of Night Hawk many winters ago. He stole a husband, father, and a brother that night. Wild Flower was left without a provider. She had a small child to care for. This man, Black Bird's brother, is now reunited with his family," she nodded to Sly Coyote, "for he was stolen from Black Bird's side. Because of this reminder of Wild Flower's sad past, she has asked that *Mazaska Zi Ista* stay away from her. In no way does she wish to offend the son of Night Hawk, brother to her son, but she does not want to relive her memories. When she looks upon the golden one, all she can see is the yellow eye's chosen one taking away the life of her lost *hingnaku*."

Many nods of approval and agreement accompanied the voiced affirmations.

"Come, *Sunmanitu Wacitusni*. We show you your lodge."

The three leaders led Sly Coyote to a place of honor. A tipi of medium size stood erected in one of the high-ranking spots for lead warriors. It looked small among the larger tipis standing there.

"With all the women who will want you as a mate, you shall have a larger tipi shortly," revealed Bright Sky with a smile.

"Thank you so much!" Sly Coyote said. He'd never expected such rectitude! "My words flee before such honor you bestow upon me!" He clasped the arms of all leaders and bowed to the people. They cheered in support of him.

CHAPTER THIRTEEN

Clean

Sly Coyote escorted Golden Eyes into his new tipi. She would share the lodge with him. They looked around. A rock-lined hearth was complete with wood stacked neatly to the side and a skin pot was suspended over the place for fire. Two sleeping mats were evident. Furs were placed on top of the mats to ward off the night chill.

There were a set of plates and horn cups with cooking and eating utensils. It was not elaborate, but it was a fine gift for a start! Sly Coyote turned and faced the three leaders.

"I do not know how to show my appreciation for this highest honor," he began. His voice broke with emotion. He was silent for a moment, gathering his wits back about him.

The kindly leaders clasped his arms again.

"There is no obligation to repay. We are still in *your* debt! You have given us a chance to secure the life of *Woniya Mato*!" the head chief exclaimed. "Welcome, *Sunmanitu Wacitusni*."

"Join us when you settle in," Bright Sky invited. "We will be in the ceremonial lodge. We have much to discuss. Our northerly brothers will join us in one sun."

Sly Coyote smiled and nodded in understanding.

***

When they were left alone, Kaitlin went to the mat to sit. She didn't look at her surroundings past her initial interest. Nor did she look at the man who'd betrayed her. The solitary white woman stared dejectedly at her hands clasped in her lap.

Sly Coyote joined her. He put his hand under her chin and gently lifted it up until he could see her face. Her golden eyes were bright with unshed tears.

"*Mazaska Zi Ista*, do not leave this tipi while I am gone," he said.

She didn't respond. He cupped her face and forced her to look into his.

"*Mazaska Zi Ista*. Do you understand? I cannot guarantee your safety unless you stay within this tipi." He repeated, "Do you understand?"

"*Tos*, I understand," she said, her tone flat. As soon as he let go of her chin, golden eyes dropped back to her hands in her lap. Her tears slowly trailed down her face and dripped onto them.

Some of the bliss Sly Coyote experienced dimmed with the sudden guilty twist of the knife in his chest. Whether he wanted to or not, the warrior had begun to care for this beautiful and innocent girl. He didn't know what to say to ease her fear or pain. The reborn Crow man couldn't guarantee what would happen in the next week or two with the expected warfare. He would not lie to her again. Finally, Sly Coyote stood to leave.

"I go to the council lodge. I will be back in a few hours."

She sat listlessly and didn't acknowledge him. He stood for a moment over her, worried, and then stooped down in front of her.

"*Mazaska Zi Ista*, I am sorry you had to be a part of my plan. I truly am. But I could not have achieved my entrance back into Crow society, where I belong, without abducting you."

Again, she didn't react to his words. The blonde continued to sit, staring without seeing at the hands in her lap. Slow tears followed the trails down and joined the other glistening droplets on her hands. Sighing, Sly Coyote stood and turned to leave. With one more concerned look, he left.

***

Several hours later, he returned, once again elated. The Crow man noticed that Golden Eyes had not moved. She no longer cried, but she sat in the same spot and in the same position.

Sly Coyote couldn't take the guilty twisting in this chest. He wanted to snap her out of her depression. He came to stand before her.

"*Uwa Yo, Mazaska Zi Ista.* Bring the water skins," he commanded softly. "I have cleaning supplies. You need to bathe. You will feel better once you do."

The captive still made no move to obey. Sly Coyote was unsure whether she'd heard, so he lifted her to her feet. He placed the water skins in her hands. Then he escorted her to the entrance flap. She mechanically followed him out.

He watched her fill the skins in the spring. Then he led her to the river. He found a secluded place in which she could have privacy. As an added precaution, he brought her during the time most Indians rested. Golden Eyes merely stood where he'd left her and stared out onto the waters.

He placed the soapwort root and absorbent deerskin cloth in her hand. He unlaced her dress. When he began to remove the soiled garment, she came to life.

"*Hiya!*" she screeched, twisting away from his gentle hands.

"*Mazaska Zi Ista*, you must clean yourself. It will help you feel better. We have more visitors expected tomorrow. I want you to look… presentable."

"You leave me be, *Sunmanitu Wacitusni*! I hate you! I hate what you've done to me and my life! I don't care if they kill me! Dying is better than the life I will face in the hands of my *toka*!" she spat and then turned to run, but Sly Coyote was too quick for her.

He snapped her back into his arms before she could take three steps. Her eyes were narrowed in anger. Tears trails were still evident on her dusty face. Her breasts strained against the cloth of her soiled dress as she sucked in angry breaths.

= = =

"You… are so… beautiful, *Mazaska Zi Ista*," Sly Coyote groaned. She made him weak with desire. Her fury was much preferred to him than the empty shell of the woman back at his new tipi. Vehemence could be overcome and turned into passion. Emptiness was to be nothing.

Kaitlin was furious. At that moment, she'd never hated anyone more! How could her hate turn the man on? She recognized his desire just before he began to lower his face to hers.

The blonde twisted at the perfect moment and escaped the lips that intended to plunder hers. Sly Coyote allowed her to twist away although he still held her body in his arms. He looked down and admired it for the millionth time. Her golden skin called for him to stroke it. Slowly and deliberately, he stood her on her feet.

In a deep voice that commanded obedience, he said, "Either you bathe yourself, *Mazaska Zi Ista*, or I will do it for you. You decide. But you *will* be clean before you meet the Crow who will come with the new sun.”

= = =

Golden Eyes was flooded with memories of bathing in another lifetime as another man’s slave. She sighed with longing. Sly Coyote tried to ignore the small sigh of remembrance that escaped her lips; it ignited his desire into a raging intensity.

Kaitlin glared at him in fury for a moment then grabbed the cleaning items from him with shaking hands. She was glad he didn’t use his stronger power and force himself upon her. She needed to escape from his black scrutiny.

“Will you turn your back to me?” she asked softly. She didn’t want her voice to quaver and let him know how much he disturbed her.

“*Tos*,” he granted her this request.

He would love to gaze upon her nude body, but he knew that if he did, all restraint from taking her as a woman would be gone. He mustn't ever let himself see the rare jewels she dangled before him without the barrier of clothes. He reminded himself again how much magic she held over a man. He had to maintain control of himself!

The warrior heard a splash as she dove into the river waters. He quietly let out a breath of air he'd been holding. He focused his mind and let go of the thoughts of desire he held for the golden woman behind him.

When she stated she was ready, he turned to see a dripping woman. She'd washed her dress, but as she had no other garments to wear, she'd had to put it back on. It dripped onto her bare feet. She'd wrapped the soft deerskin towel around her hair. She gazed at him defiantly, daring him to say something.

He did not. He allowed her to follow him back to their tipi. After dropping her off, he went to see Bright Sky.

She was still up during rest time. He, like her, could not think of resting when such a big event was right around the corner.

"Hello, *Sunmanitu Wacitusni*."

"Greetings, Bright Sky."

"Is there something you need?" She smiled when he looked down momentarily.

"Yes. The woman of *Woniya Mato*, *Mazaska Zi Ista*, needs a clean garment. She washed the dress she wears. She is too modest to take it off for it to dry.

"I do have several to spare, but they will be a little big for her. I think I might have one that will do."

Bright Sky went into her tipi and retrieved a fresh dress and female breechcloth for the yellow eyes.

"Give these to our guest."

"Thank you, Bright Sky. Your hospitality is much appreciated."

"You are welcome, *Sunmanitu Wacitusni*.
Come and join my evening fire for dinner this
night. Bring the woman of *Woniya Mato* with
you."

"I would be honored."

He left. The bronzed man gave the items to
Mazaska Zi Ista upon his return.

"I will wait outside for you to change into the
dry items," he informed her. "Then you can dry
your dress on the rock outside."

She merely looked at him. He walked outside
the tipi to wait. When the appropriate time had
passed, he reentered. She'd changed. She left
the tipi to drape her clean dress over the drying
rock.

"Do you have a brush?" she asked upon
reentering the tipi.

"Yes," he said as he handed her the one Bright
Sky had also given him. He placed the beaded
leather tongs along with the brush on her
sleeping mat.

Kaitlin hated to admit that Sly Coyote had been right; she *did* feel better after washing the traveling dust off her body. Her head felt fresh and clean. She was cooled with her damp hair. If only the depressed woman could revive her spirit as she had her body…

Golden Eyes brushed her honeyed tresses until they hung in soft curls. Then she braided them. They stayed out of her face and helped her remain cooler during the heat of the day in this style. She knew that *Sunmanitu Wacitusni* watched her.

Kaitlin had such anger against this man! Why had he brought her here? Yes, it was to gain entrance into the Crow society; he had told her that much, but why did she make the difference? *Woniya Mato* was a renowned war chief, but surely, he could see the folly of following them onto Crow lands! Was the coup simply that Sly Coyote had stolen her away?

She was so stupid! Why couldn't she have seen through his ploy? A war chief's woman should have guessed right away that *Sunmanitu Wacitusni* was lying! Otherwise, *Wawakankan* would have been present!

In despair, Kaitlin lay back on her mat to feign rest. She had no energy to perform any chore without force. The golden girl wanted to openly defy the Crow to force them to kill her, but she was too big of a coward. The only other escape was to trek inwardly.

Sly Coyote also tried to rest. When they awoke, they would go to the hearth of Bright Sky. Maybe they could help prepare the meal for the evening.

CHAPTER FOURTEEN

Bright Sky

Bright Sky saw them approaching and smiled in pleasure. She was glad that the son of Night Hawk had rejoined his Crow brothers. His heart was Crow through and through.

It did not matter if *Woniya Mato* came for his bride. The daring of the coup performed by Sly Coyote was amazing! If only Night Hawk could see his son now!

The yellow eyes following *Sunmanitu Wacitusni* was a beautiful girl. Even the dress that hung loosely on her could not hide her generous curves. Bright Sky had no doubt someone would provide for her should Sly Coyote decide he did not want to offer his protection to her as a slave. However, the leader suspected that he would keep the girl. The oldest son of Night Hawk could not quite hide his interest from her knowing eyes. The Crow man's eyes followed the girl's every move.

Bright Sky would study this light-skinned girl. She had never been near one before and hadn't made a decision toward her yet.

Could it really be true that the sun-kissed woman held such power over a proven warrior? Would that same man, a chief of renowned power and authority, be so foolish as to charge into an enemy camp just to rescue a mere woman? Bright Sky would be very surprised and disappointed in *Woniya Mato* if his instincts didn't serve him better than that!

The others believed the yellow eyes had this very power over the fiercest warrior ever known. Otherwise, they wouldn't have called two other bands of Crow to assist them in the possible war and demise of the mighty bear. Bright Sky was glad she'd thought to invite *Sunmanitu Wacitusni* to her fire this night. She could further study the strong white girl.

The female leader had cooked a stew of quail and vegetables. A tenderloin of mountain sheep slowly roasted over a low fire to accompany the

soup. She'd make pones of fresh bread as well
to top off the meal, fresh berries were offered
for sweetness and nourishment.

The Crow leader even had blackberry juice that
she fermented with a special recipe that had
been in her family for generations. Many Crow
came from all over the territories to trade
numerous things for her brew. She was very
careful with it, however. She'd seen what it
could do under daily consumption. Many men
could easily fall prey to its potent effect.

Once in a while, however, for celebrations such
as this, Bright Sky broke out her treasured drink.
She let the other leaders and head warriors in
her village know her drink was available as well
as announce it to the warriors from another band
that had just arrived. They'd join them early in
the evening and stay until all the drink was
consumed. It was good to connect like this
before expected warfare. It only strengthened
bonds of trust among them.

"Come, sit before the fire. I have many
comfortable mats for you to sit on," Bright Sky
greeted her visitors.

"Can we assist you in any way?" Sly Coyote asked.

"No, it is done except the bread that I am going to cook now. You sit beside the yellow eyes."

Kaitlin watched as the other woman worked. She didn't feel obligated in the least to help these people although none really had been mean to her. Just knowing that they were the enemy of the Sioux was enough for her.

The listless blonde was extremely resentful of *Sunmanitu Wacitusni*. Yet, he held complete power over her. She knew he might be her only protection against a community of enemies. At least he didn't treat her badly… and so far, he had not forced himself upon her. Kaitlin did her best to hide her resentment.

Soup and meat were served. The bread and drink accompanied the meal. After a taste of the berry brew, Sly Coyote looked in amazement at Bright Sky.

"This is a very good, interesting flavor," he said, smacking his lips to savor the taste.

"You like?"

"Yes, it is very, very delightful. What a refreshing change!"

"After a couple of cups, you will note its effects as well. It has a factor that makes one feel free. I will warn you ahead of time… if you drink too much, you will not feel like rising in the morning, and we have many guests coming," she warned.

His eyes twinkled with the challenge.

"I will heed your warning," he teased.

He turned to Golden Eyes and spoke in Lakota, "What do you think of the meal, *Mazaska Zi Ista*?"

Golden eyes looked at him. At first, he didn't think she would comment.

"It is very good," the woman of the Oglala war chief finally admitted. "This drink is… unique."

He nodded. Turning back to Bright Sky, Sly
Coyote asked, "Would you like *Mazaska Zi Ista*
to clean up after you?"

"I think it might be good to give her something
to do," Bright Sky answered in Crow. "I am
sure she has much on her mind with nothing to
occupy her hands."

"Is it… safe for her to go alone?"

"If you trust her. None will dishonor you by
harming her."

Returning to Lakota, Sly Coyote commanded,
"*Mazaska Zi Ista*, Bright Sky has cooked for us.
Honor her by cleaning." He knew that she
wouldn't have understood their conversation in
Crow.

***

Kaitlin stood. She felt like disobeying, but
she'd actually enjoy the time out of the sight of
the disturbing Crow warrior for once. She'd

had time in the tipi alone, but it wasn't the same. The white woman gathered up the dishes and headed to the spring. For the first time since her capture, the blonde had a light spring in her step.

When *Mazaska Zi Ista* reached the water's edge, she put down the dishes and entertained thoughts of escaping by floating down in the river's current. It seemed to flow in a southeast direction… the direction of family. Home was *Woniya Mato* and the Oglala!

Kaitlin sighed and stooped down. She began cleaning the bone plates and fire-hardened bowls and utensils. First the dishes were scoured with gravel. Then she pounded the yucca root to form suds. The slave placed the frothy result on a soft deer hide rag and washed the dishes.

As she was rinsing the plates, *Mazaska Zi Ista* heard the crunch of gravel. When she turned, the white woman saw three Indian females standing behind her. They didn't look very friendly. Kaitlin stood her ground and watched them. They smiled maliciously and approached her.

The solitary slave didn't move. One Crow girl said something in her language which made the others laugh. The blonde heard *Woniya Mato's* name and also *Sunmanitu Wacitusni*'s. They made lewd motions that left no doubt as to the names they were calling her.

"I am NOT sleeping with *Sunmanitu Wacitusni*!" Kaitlin yelled at them. She may be a captive in their village, but she was not a whore!

One girl came forward and pulled Kaitlin's hair. Kaitlin could not contain all of the fury at her situation that had been pent up for days; retaliating, she grabbed a fistful of the girls' black hair and yanked on it with the same intensity as the other showed her.

Seeing this, the other girls came forward to assist their friend. Kaitlin was scratched and slapped until she let go of the first woman. Then, the three pulled her hair and knocked her down. When she stood back up, they kicked her and pushed her backwards into the river. The three laughed so hard that they bent over, clutching their abdomens.

Kaitlin was boiling with anger that led to shaking with defeat. She stayed in the river until her teeth chattered and the women left. It was only a few minutes more until Sly Coyote came looking for her. When he saw what she looked like, he dashed to the riverside.

"*Mazaska Zi Ista*, what happened?"

"I fell in the river."

"Come, I will help you out."

All of her clean dishes had dirt thrown all over them. She nearly cried in her frustration and hopelessness.

"Please take me home, *Sunmanitu Wacitusni*. I can't stand this life! I do not deserve this! I have done nothing to you!"

Sly Coyote ignored her outcry as he helped her from the cold waters. She stooped to look over her hard work. She angrily began to clean the dishes a second time.

"*Mazaska Zi Ista*, I will help you."

"*Hiya!* I do not want nor do I need help from you!" Her vexation was obvious.

 Kaitlin refused his offer to take her back to the tipi to change. She rewashed the dishes and then carried them back to the tipi of the woman leader. The white outcast cared not that she dripped with icy water, had a few minor scratches, and her hair was disheveled.

"What happened?" asked Bright Sky in heavily accented Lakota.

"I fell in the river."

"With help. Who did this to you?"

"I fell with no help."

"Come, now, woman of *Woniya Mato*. I know better. It does not take long to wash dishes and fall into the river."

Kaitlin was silent under the other woman's scrutiny. The blonde had enough enemies in this village and didn't want more by tattling.

The stare was long and intense. Kaitlin could see how this woman had come into a position of power. Still, she was used to the scrutiny of Spirit Bear. No warrior or leader could compare to his stare when he wished to know something. The blonde shifted her weight uneasily, but she would not give. Finally, the woman let her off the hook.

"Come. I have another dress you can change into. I will take this soiled garment in exchange."

Kaitlin's golden eyes lifted to meet the black ones of Bright Sky. This leader also had compassion. The almond-shaped eyes softened.

"Thank you," she offered hesitantly.

The women went into the leader's tipi and secured the flap. Bright Sky handed Kaitlin dry new clothes. She handed her a towel, porcupine brush, and turned her back to give the other privacy to change.

Bright Sky was no fool. She'd noticed the scratches and bright red spots that would more than likely bruise upon the sun-kissed skin of the white girl. The leader gritted her teeth in anger at those who would dishonor the highly esteemed Crow warrior! Even if his slave happened to be the betrothed of their greatest enemy, no one had the right!

This yellow eyes was not at all what she'd expected. How could she expect less of the great man? Bright Sky scoffed at herself. *Woniya Mato* had the choice of many women, and he chose the golden girl in front of her. She must be exceptional, even among her own people. The woman leader had to admit, this yellow eyes was nothing like the stories she'd heard about the white's cowardice and greed. Perhaps she was an anomaly.

When the Crow woman turned back, the slave had fixed her appearance. She was once more the glamorous woman who radiated grace and beauty without effort.

"What would you like me to do with the dirty dress?" she asked. "I will wash it for you."

"*Hiya*, I must apologize for your… *fall* into the river. I never thought my people would dishonor *Sunmanitu Wacitusni* by attacking you."

Kaitlin looked down in modesty. She knew the other woman realized she was not being honest, but she didn't expect Crow woman to confront her.

"I understand why you do not want to tell," Bright Sky revealed. "But I will watch to make sure it does not happen again."

"Thank you," Kaitlin said hesitantly. "What do I call you?"

Bright Sky told her her name in Crow. Kaitlin had some difficulty with the correct pronunciation, but she tried.

"And you are *Mazaska Zi Ista*, correct?"

"*Tos*."

"Let us rejoin the others."

CHAPTER FIFTEEN

Berry Wine

When Bright Sky led Kaitlin back out of her tipi, the slave noticed that a few other imposing looking figures had joined the area around the leader's fire pit. Some she recognized, and some she didn't. All eyes watched them approach but then, out of politeness, the men resumed their conversations. *Sunmanitu Wacitusni* continued to watch the golden one although his eyes were veiled. Black Bird, however, made no pretense; he engulfed her form with his hungry stare. The captor's brother relished making this desirable woman feel his heat.

Feeling compassion for this gentle spirit, Bright Sky filled up her cup with the blackberry wine and looked pointedly at Black Bird until he resumed talking.

"This is really quite good. Do you share this recipe?" Kaitlin queried.

"No. It is actually quite dangerous to indulge in too frequently. This is why I guard the ingredients and processes with my life."

Kaitlin nodded in acknowledgment, but she didn't understand what was so dangerous about the drink. It made her feel quite pleasant. She didn't comprehend the guttural warning issued in Crow about the effects of the drink on the senses the next morning if one consumed more than a cupful or two.

After Kaitlin finished her drink, Bright Sky formally introduced Sly Coyote to the newly arrived band leaders gathered around her fire.

"This man has earned one of the greatest coups! I'm sure you've already heard about it!" Bright Sky announced.

Wide grins and head nods greeted *Sunmanitu Wacitusni* from around the fire.

"How you ever accomplished this, I will never know," one man complimented. *"Woniya Mato* has senses about him that anyone can fathom. He knows what we are up to before we even think it!"

Sly Coyote helped Kaitlin rise and then said, "His Golden Eyes is the reason I was able. She is very beautiful, as you can see. Spirit Bear is consumed by this woman, and her power over him has stolen all of his perceptions. For this, he will fall."

All eyes assessed Kaitlin as a man for a woman and as an object that can wield great power. Kaitlin's eyes flashed, but she was able to stand the valuation with the false bravado the drink was supplying her.

Chief Sidewinder smiled and said, "When you trade her, I will happily take her off your hands."

"I will, too!" agreed Chief Black Bear.

"She is not for trade," Sly Coyote stated. "Golden Eyes has much power, more than you can know. I will not trade her to a leader so that he can fall as well."

Then men laughed in good nature, and congratulations continued long into the night. Kaitlin was happy to no longer be the object of interest, and drank some more of the wine. It helped her feelings of trepidation and anxieties disappear. She was rather enjoying Bright Sky's company.

When Kaitlin became a little giggly, Bright Sky wouldn't allow her to indulge in more. The leader knew the girl would, most likely, wake up with a headache. It was late when Sly Coyote took her back to their tipi. Black Bird wistfully watched them leave.

"She is not for you, Black Bird," Bloody Knife warned.

"Who do you think she is for?" he asked the war chief.

"She has great power. Can you not feel it? *Sunmanitu Wacitusni* is wise. Do not entangle yourself with wanting her."

"How can a man help but want her?" he asked.

"I, too, feel this power she holds over men, but my will is greater. I would not dishonor myself."

Black Bird didn't respond. He left a short while later but wandered off into the dark woods.

***

Sly Coyote started a small fire when they entered the tipi. He mostly lit it so they could see. Kaitlin seemed more relaxed than she ever had been while in his presence. The Crow man hated to see it end. He poured them each a horn cup full of water, for the blackberry drink made them thirsty.

"Thank you," Golden Eyes said.

"You are welcome," Sly Coyote responded tenderly.

The pleasant warmth from the wine made him feel especially kind to the girl before him. The warrior sat down beside her and feasted his eyes upon her. The fair-complected woman turned her head to avoid his gaze. She focused her vision upon the flames.

"You did well tonight," he praised her.

"You mean except for the river incident?"

"No, including that. Most females would want to get the other party in trouble. You did not want to cause more issues. Leaders look favorably upon those who do not look for misfortune. It earns you more respect although we would have liked to have known."

Kaitlin did not say more. She didn't like having to get acclimated to a new tribe. The new drink, however, made her more uninhibited.

"*Sunmanitu Wacitusni*, why did you take me?"

He was silent but continued to study her comely profile. Kaitlin turned her almond-shaped orbs upon him to plead a response.

"I told you it was a way to return with honor to my people of the Crow." Sly Coyote paused, but the drink had loosened the resolve to never admit his feelings for her, even to himself. He added, "However, now I am glad for more reasons than that."

Kaitlin's eyes widened, but she'd suspected as much. The blonde didn't comment on his last revelation. "I thought you were Yankton."

"My mother is. She was captured by a Crow warrior, my father. She escaped when the Sioux raided our camp. She married Hunter of the Skies and had Eagle Talon by him. I did not join her until I was eight winters."

"Why?"

"I was with my father when she was taken. Years later, I went hunting with him. Night Hawk was a great warrior in this village, but our party wandered into territory claimed by the Sioux. A group of them attacked us.

"*Woniya Mato* killed my father. It was his first kill as a warrior; he was only twelve winters. Very few are ever as young as *Woniya Mato* when they are accepted into warrior society. At eight, they still saw me as a child not yet inducted into the ceremonial rites of manhood.

They took me to live with my mother with the Yankton Sioux.

"Why did you want to become a Crow if you could choose between two tribes?"

"I know you do not understand the way it is in a tribe because you were raised white. A native man earns status in two ways: he is born into it by the rank of his father, or in Crow society, the rank of a parent, but he must also prove himself worthy. Surely you can understand my status within the ranks of the Sioux. I have a Crow father, the enemy. I have proven myself with many coups on the war field, but many do not want to trust me because of who I am." He laughed. "With good reason.

"I have always felt my heart belonged here with my father's people," Sly Coyote continued. "I knew if I helped to defeat our worst enemy, your betrothed, I would earn one of the highest coups. Even if he does not come to rescue you from me, I have dared to insult the enemy."

Kaitlin sucked in a sharp breath. "You do not expect him to come for me!" Her voice was incredulous.

"Ah, but we do."

"So *that* is why you chose to take me! I refuse
to be used in this way! I cannot lure the man of
my heart to his death!"

"*Mazaska Zi Ista*, you already have. Through
no fault of your own," *Sunmanitu Wacitusni*
hastily added. "But he will come. Spirit Bear
loves you too much not to. I heard first hand
from Opossum Eyes of the power you hold over
him. She is how I came to arrive at my daring
plan. If not for the mate of Eagle Talon, I
would never have known that any could lure the
great bear into making a decision that will be his
end."

"Not only do you do this for the coup you earn,
but you do this for revenge!" Kaitlin's eyes
blazed golden flames. The blonde jumped to
her feet and began to pace. The light-hearted
mood of earlier evaporated with these disturbing
admissions.

"I cannot deny that I will find pleasure in my
revenge upon the greatest enemy the Crow have
ever known. He has claimed many Crow lives,

including my father's!" Sly Coyote said passionately.

"You make a mistake! He will not die by your hands!" she exclaimed confidently, looking down at him in his seated position.

"You have great faith in this man of yours, don't you?" Sly Coyote asked softly, also rising silently to his feet.

"Yes, I do!" she said defiantly, raising her voice.

"He cannot win!" the Crow man said with a slow smile, looming before her. "We have two other bands that have joined us. You met their leaders this night. Even *Woniya Mato* cannot overcome three bands of united Crow. Then, when the man of your heart is gone, you will belong to me."

Kaitlin screamed, "*Hiya!* I will *never* be yours!"

"I wonder how we compare in other ways?" Sly Coyote challenged, capturing her to him.

Kaitlin squirmed in fear and hatred. How she wished she could strike down this man with a

vengeful heart! This time there was no avoiding
the lips bent on ravishing hers.

Sunmanitu Wacitusni's mouth closed over hers.
The white woman felt no passion, only panic.
He tenderly worked his lips on hers. When she
did not invite him to taste the treasures within,
he lowered his kiss to her neck.

Sly Coyote's breathing rate increased and his
hands raked her feminine form. He moaned low
in his throat as he tasted the sweetness of her
slender collar. His hot tongue traced downward
to the skin bordering the fabric of her dress and
the cleavage just beneath it. He groaned deeply
with desire as one hand began to gently knead
her bottom. Slowly, he moved both hands down
to grab the bottom hem. When he began to raise
the dress up, Kaitlin came alive.

"*Hiya*!" she screamed. She wrenched free of his
hands and pushed him back with all the force
she could muster. The blonde ran for the door.

"Do not dare to leave this tipi, or I swear I will
make you mine in all ways this night!"
Sunmanitu Wacitusni's masculine command
stopped her in her tracks. His voice was husky

with need, but he'd managed to regain control of his body. Although Sly Coyote's manhood didn't agree on who was in control, his mind had cleared enough with her surprising push that he could think once more. Her power was greater than even he'd guessed! He wanted her now with boundless intensity. Sly Coyote must control his desires!

Kaitlin stood as if undecided on whether to risk running into the night, but with his threat, she didn't push it. His words just then were the only thing that could have stopped her flight.

"*Uwa yo, Mazaska Zi Ista.* Lie down. I will not bother you further. You are tired, as am I. The berry drink made me desire what is not mine to take. Someday in the future, maybe it will be so, but you are safe for now."

Kaitlin slowly returned to her sleeping mat. She watched him warily with her golden eyes. He lay down upon his mat to show he didn't intend to approach her again.

Finally, she lay down as well. The fire whispered to both as it crackled and popped in

low frustration. It was a long time before either
of them slept.

CHAPTER SIXTEEN

More Crow Warriors

With dawn, a beating awoke her. Were they banging on drums this early? Or was that the rhythm that pounded in her temples on their own accord? When Kaitlin tried to sit, she realized it was coming from within her. The blonde looked over at Sly Coyote. She was relieved to see that he was already gone.

The white woman moaned and lay back down. Kaitlin didn't move until the need to use the area of privacy became too great. She hoisted her body that had grown heavy overnight to head in that direction.

As Kaitlin made her way back into the village, the young white woman saw the three females who'd attacked her the night before. They snickered and then laughed loudly behind their hands. *Mazaska Zi Ista* smiled sweetly at them.

If that didn't make them seethe! Her smile turned genuine at that thought.

Upon return to the tipi, Kaitlin placed the freshly filled water skins where they would not spill or leak but would be easily accessible when needed. Sly Coyote came back in the tipi minutes later.

"*Mazaska Zi Ista*, be ready to meet some Crow warriors in about an hour."

"Please, *Sunmanitu Wacitusni*, I do not feel like company this day."

Not only did her head ache and her stomach feel queasy, but she was tired. She was depressed, too, for this would have been her joining day to *Woniya Mato*, her only love. How easy it was to sink into the murky depths of despair.

"You must. Do you need some willow bark tea? It will help alleviate your pain."

"*Tos*, please."

He left and returned moments later. He handed her the water skin full of willow bark tea.

"Drink some of this, and you will feel better shortly. Wear your own dress to this meeting."

So he wanted her to look her finest. Why should she? How could her presentation make any difference? Kaitlin *would* have looked her best on this day… her wedding day!

Sly Coyote had already revealed it was *Woniya Mato* they were after. They planned on using her as bait to end his life! Kaitlin could not allow this to happen! She had to do something, but what?

The lonely woman drank the tea and sighed. There was nothing she could do right now except to obey. The golden one didn't want to give Sly Coyote any reason to touch her. She knew he was very attracted to her. The eye-catching girl knew to watch her step, or she would fall prey to her captor's superior strength.

After sipping on the medicated brew for ten minutes, Kaitlin lay back. Slowly, she felt the drink begin to work its magic. The beating in her head didn't go away, but the drumming began to recede. She looked up at Sly Coyote who hovered in nervous anticipation.

"Could you give me a few minutes of privacy to change, please, *Sunmanitu Wacitusni*?" she requested politely.

"Yes, this I will do for you. Come out when you are ready. I will wait close by the entrance."

She dressed and combed her hair then braided it neatly. Kaitlin placed her moccasins on her feet. She wiggled her toes in the soft comfort and was sadly reminded of *Wawat'ecaka*. The alienated woman felt her morale tick a little lower. Silently, the white girl vowed to not let the Crow win.

The golden one didn't want to go, but she let her unwilling feet lead the way to Sly Coyote's side. He looked at her and nodded in approval. A strange light burned in his black eyes as he perused her body. Kaitlin felt like she needed to put additional clothing on to escape his desire.

The honey-haired beauty looked down in embarrassed discomfort. She didn't want to encourage the man in the slightest. It would kill her to have this *toka* touch her in the way that was reserved only for *Woniya Mato's* loving hands.

"Come," he commanded tersely. "We meet the others."

"But haven't I met them already?" Kaitlin asked quietly.

"Another band has arrived. We meet them all."

He led the way toward the ceremonial lodge. Kaitlin had only been in one once, and that memory had scared her to death.

+ + +

Kaitlin'd had to face the tribal council in the Oglala village for them to determine her punishment for her attempted escape. At the time, she'd thought they would prescribe death. She'd nearly fainted when the only difference in her treatment was that she'd had to be escorted by a man everywhere she went. The blonde vividly recalled the masterful arms that carried her back to the chief's tipi… *Woniya Mato…*

Tears welled up in her eyes when recalled bronzed arms securing her body against his powerful, smooth chest. Rapidly, the golden-skinned beauty blinked away the memory. It would not do to present such a weak feminine picture in front of these Crow men. The war chief's betrothed wanted to honor the Oglala leader as much as she was able.

+ + +

On shaky legs, Kaitlin followed in Sly Coyote's wake. The gathering of leaders and head warriors was too big for the ceremonial lodge, so they assembled in the clearing beside it. Only leaders and head warriors were present. Among the crowd were the three privileged of the village: Midnight Star, Bright Sky, and Bloody Knife. Also present were Black Bird, Raven's Wing, and five other warriors from Sly Coyote's band. Twenty-three other imposing figures had fixed their eyes upon her womanly form.

Of the Thirty-three figures present, only five were women including Bright Sky. Sly Coyote signaled Kaitlin to come into the center of the gathering. There, the three leaders of the home village met him.

"My Crow brothers," Midnight Star began. "The son of Night Hawk has given us a wonderful opportunity, one we would never have had if it weren't for his cunning and daring nature. *Sunmanitu Wacitusni* went to the pre-joining celebration of *Woniya Mato* and stole his promised from under his very nose!"

The crowd was greatly impressed with this coup, and all stared in open curiosity at the yellow eyes present among them.

"He chose a yellow eyes over a woman of his own breed?" one rude voice asked.

"I will allow each of you to come close and see for yourself why he has chosen this woman over a Sioux maiden. I've only been in her company for two suns, and already I have felt desire for her," Midnight Star revealed. "According to the tale told to *Sunmanitu Wacitusni*, she'd even been inducted into Sioux society so that she could join with *Woniya Mato*."

Midnight Star was an expert at weaving a magical tale. He knew how long each dramatic pause should be. The chief looked around at the influential faces. He began speaking at the peak of the theatrical moment.

"The Oglala believe it is the will of *Wakantanka* that this mating occurs. They believe that *Mazaska Zi Ista* has been personally blessed by the black bear. Behold the betrothal *wanapin*! When you walk forward to see this girl for yourselves, look at her necklace. It was made by the hand of *Woniya Mato* himself!"

The prominent people began to shuffle forward. Kaitlin shrank against Sly Coyote. He smiled at her encouragingly but gently pushed her forward. Remembering her determination to honor Spirit Bear, she held up her chin and dared to look at the men and four women in the face. She clasped her hands together in front of her to mask their shaking.

Many hands reached for her necklace. None tried to remove it from her neck, but some did lift it to study it closely. Kaitlin felt like a horse on an auction block. Some of the men walked around her, and several even dared to smell her!

When the important men and women returned to their places, Midnight Star spoke once more. "This day is very special to *Woniya Mato* and his woman, *Mazaska Zi Ista*. This day," he paused for dramatic effect, "was his joining day… *Sunmanitu Wacitusni* earns another coup!"

"Are you sure he will come for her?" a voice called out.

The chief nodded to Sly Coyote, indicating that he should answer the question.

"I have witnessed the great love shared between this woman and the Oglala war chief," Sly Coyote admitted. "*Woniya Mato* would challenge the Bird of Death himself for her!"

"That is who he will challenge if he comes for her here!" a male yelled.

More voices joined in the determined hope of defeating their foe.

"What is to be done with the yellow eyes?" another voice asked.

"We will use her as bait. The war chief will come after her here. We have left evidence that she is unharmed along our trial. If we need to lure him into the village by dangling his tempting morsel in front of him, we will," Sly Coyote stated hopefully.

"But what of her after *Woniya Mato's* defeat? What plans do you have for her then?"

"She is my slave. I will make that decision upon the death of the mighty Spirit Bear!"

Another voice questioned, "If *Woniya Mato* thought so highly of his woman, why were you able to steal her away?"

Sly Coyote responded, "That is a very good question. The Oglala had been watching for signs of Crow on their lands. Raven's Wing and Black Bird staged a party to lure the war chief away. During his absence, I told his betrothed that he was injured. I happened to have a horse to whisk her away to see her beloved before he walked the path with *Wakantanka*." He laughed. "It worked as if the Great Spirit willed it!"

The Crow murmured amongst themselves. They were enthralled with the plan that the two sons of Night Hawk along with Raven's Wing had come up with. Now they would be able to confront the Oglala warrior on their grounds. He would fight them on their terms! The tension and excitement built as the men conversed.

"You may return the yellow eyes to your tipi. Then we will discuss war plans upon your return."

Sly Coyote nodded to the group. He looked at Kaitlin who radiated feminine beauty.

"Come, *Mazaska Zi Ista*. I return you to the tipi. Stay there until I return."

She meekly followed him from the ceremonial lodge area. The subdued blonde was relieved to leave the heavy stares of the domineering people. Moments later, she was alone in the hut.

Sly Coyote told her to stay, but he would be busy for several hours or more. That was a long time for the dejected woman to dwell on her wedding day that was not to be. Did she dare risk escape? There were many eyes, but all the warriors were in the ceremonial area… all the important ones, anyway.

Kaitlin knew more warriors rode with the newcomers. She didn't know where they were staying for the moment. Although she didn't want to wait to make good on her escape, the captive might have a better opportunity later. The expansive waters of the river might just sweep her away at the opportune time! First, though, the blonde needed to study the location of the others.

CHAPTER SEVENTEEN

Losing Hope

Kaitlin threw herself down upon her sleeping mat. She visualized her wedding. This day was supposed to be the happiest day in her life, the day she united with her love! It would have begun a whole world of happy days. Now, her husband could very well die, thanks to her.

Because of her own stupidity and the plan of *Sunmanitu Wacitusni*, Kaitlin would never know the happiness found in *Woniya Mato's* arms as his wife. Due to the actions of that man, the golden one was surrounded by many hostile Crow! The white girl sank further into despair; she could hold back no longer: sobs racked her body.

Kaitlin cried herself to sleep. Her misery did not help her comfort level. With her emotional outpouring, her headache returned with fury.

***

Sly Coyote brought back more stew from the night before for their lunch. He stood over her sleeping form and looked guiltily upon her tear-swollen eyes. He could even see the pulse in her temples. The Crow man stooped low to push back hair dried to her face from the river of tears that had flowed.

Sly Coyote would see to it that she drank more willow bark tea upon her waking. The village would celebrate and feast this night. Tomorrow, the men would escort the elderly, women, and children to the cave for their safety. Kaitlin would remain with him during the war fare. The acclaimed warrior needed her beside him in case they should need to show the great man proof of her well-being.

The worried man could not imagine the effects of this battle upon the slender girl. Her beauty should never be marred. *Sunmanitu Wacitusni* knew this delicate creature would hate him forever when her love was killed before her very eyes. Maybe the Crow man could spare her that part.

If it took hitting rock bottom of emotional despondency for her to accept a new man into her heart, he would do it, but Sly Coyote felt that he should proceed with caution; it should be done without Golden Eyes seeing the death of her betrothed. Just the knowledge that her love was gone would be more than she could bear for a while.

Sly Coyote wanted *Mazaska Zi Ista* in his life circle desperately. The extreme precautions he'd taken to resist her powerful magic were for naught. The warrior was helplessly caught in the great web she'd unknowingly woven. Sly Coyote would do anything to fully possess the golden goddess… except destroy her.

The Crow man would protect her with his life before he would strike down his foe. All of this planning was to avenge his father's death and to regain his lost place in Crow warrior society. Now, only a week later, he would sacrifice it all for this magnetic woman before him.
Sunmanitu Wacitusni prayed he would never have to make that choice.

The plan was set into motion. The Crow men were preparing to fall into place. The only thing left was to secure the feeble. They would begin their move on the rise of the new sun.

Kaitlin groaned in her sleep and draped an arm over her pounding eyes. She murmured the very man's name he dreaded to hear: *Woniya Mato*. This intriguing female could dream of the Oglala war chief all she wanted, but she'd never enjoy his embraces again! *Mazaska Zi Ista* would have to find relief with him. At that thought, a smile tugged at his sensuous lips. Sly Coyote was a patient man. He'd wait as long as it took!

= = =

Kaitlin had begun to tremble and cry once more in her sleep. Sly Coyote went to her side and smoothed her hair away from her face. She grabbed onto him in strong intensity.

"*Hiya, Woniya Mato*! Do not come for me!
They will kill you! It does not matter that today
is our joining day! Do not risk yourself for
me!"

Then those glorious golden orbs opened. They
burned brightly through her tears. The blonde
groaned and crashed back the short distance to
her mat. Holding her head, she rocked slightly
back and forth in great pain.

Sly Coyote propped her up and held the willow
bark tea skin to her lips. "Drink, *Mazaska Zi
Ista*. It will soothe your pain."

The beauty drank the liquid he held to her.
Then she focused her eyes upon his ebony ones.

"Why do you care, *Sunmanitu Wacitusni*? You
should feel great pleasure from my discomfort."

"I am sorry you think that about me, *Mazaska Zi
Ista*. Believe it or not, I want you as a man
wants a woman, but a joining between us can
never be."

Sly Coyote almost became angry when he noted
her relieved expression. To make sure she

didn't misunderstand him, he added, "I did not say a mating between us could never be. I desire that very much. However, I will not take you while *Woniya Mato* still lives."

"Then I will never have to lie with you," Kaitlin whispered through gritted teeth. She struggled in his arms so that he would put her down.

Sly Coyote didn't push her because of her feelings of illness. Still, he was hurt that she didn't act as if she were interested in him at all. Gently, he placed her back onto her mat.

It is because I have stolen her wedding day from her. She will learn to care for me and desire me as she did him, he promised himself. *I just need to give her time, especially once Woniya Mato is slain!*

Sly Coyote realized that it would be a long time for her to get over the hate she'd experience toward him at the death of her betrothed. He'd give her time to grieve, for she would need this. However, he wouldn't wait forever. Sly Coyote was only a man and wouldn't torture himself overly so.

The warrior felt one cycle of the moon would be sufficient for the delectable girl to get over the worst. Then he would make her his in all ways. The white slave would learn her place and come to him willingly. With that promise to himself, *Sunmanitu Wacitusni* took out his weapons and began to work on them.

Kaitlin lay still for a long time, babying the pounding in her head. When she tried to sit, she felt queasy. She didn't understand these feelings. The blonde was reminded of the conversation with Bright Sky about the drink being dangerous. She vowed never to drink the berry juice drink again!

The sensations it gave were very pleasant when one consumed the beverage, but the next day was twice as bad as the good it had initially provided! The queasy woman lay back once more.

"*Mazaska Zi Ista*, I have some of the quail stew for you. It will help you to feel better."

Kaitlin glared at Sly Coyote. She wanted nothing from him. He dipped her some into a bowl and brought it to her.

"I cannot eat," she icily informed him.

"I must insist," he calmly said. "I believe you will feel better."

She said in disbelief, "You will not force me to eat!"

A smile teased the edges of his mouth. He leaned forward. "Are you sure?" he asked quietly, his words chalked full of the power he held over her.

"I will become ill if you force me to eat!" she cried.

"Eat a few mouthfuls, and I will be satisfied for now."

"One," she said spitefully as she spooned the liquid into her mouth. "Two," she said between gritted teeth. "I am full. You have won."

Rather than push the issue, *Sunmanitu Wacitusni* allowed the blonde to sit in sullen silence. He took the bowl and placed it back by the pot. Ignoring her, he resumed working on his weapons.

Kaitlin rocked herself as she held her fingers to her temples. She stilled her motion when the world seemed to heave before her. When would her head stop hurting? The girl nearly moaned as a new wave of pain racked her.

Slowly, the golden-skinned woman sunk back to her mat. Before long, she slept more. Sly Coyote was becoming concerned. Surely this illness from the berry drink did not last this long!

Indians were resuming their chores when Kaitlin finally opened her eyes again. She slowly sat upright. She stretched her body and slowly rolled her neck.

"How are you feeling, *Mazaska Zi Ista*?" Sly Coyote's voice greeted her.

"Better, I think."

 "Would you like me to bring you more stew? Perhaps you will feel more like eating?"

"*Hiya*. Right now, I just want to sit."

Sly Coyote resumed attaching the spear point to the long shaft. He had many new weapons ready to slice through the Sioux. He was excited to further prove himself to his Crow brothers.

Thirty minutes passed. Kaitlin stood slowly. She appeared to be testing her strength.

"I will go to the women's area of privacy. Do you need me to fill the *mniapahta*?" She used the Lakota word for the water skin bag.

"If you feel well enough, yes. If not, I can do it later."

"The air will do me good." The blonde grabbed the stretchy skin bags and left.

The brightness of the sky nearly brought back her headache, but Kaitlin stood rooted to her spot until her eyes accustomed to the light. Tentatively, she began her journey to the spring and the privacy area. The golden eyed beauty had just finished with her privacy needs and headed to the spring. As she stooped to fill the *mniapahta,* a noise startled her.

"They trust you off by yourself so soon?" a venomous voice hissed from off to the side of her. Kaitlin knew it was not a friend who stood just behind her at the drinking spring.

"Where can I go in the midst of a Crow camp?" she asked the man with the heavy accent. She turned to face Sneaky Weasel.

His eyes devoured her slender frame, and he took a menacing step nearer. He sneered, "Can you guess what your fate will be once we slay your lover?"

"I can guess the less-than-honorable intentions of the Crow," she slurred at him.

He grabbed her in anger and said, "Slaves have no honor in our camp. They do not earn it, nor is it granted. You will lie beneath many men, whore!"

Kaitlin's face paled despite her resolve to not wilt under his threats. "I do not think *Sunmanitu Wacitusni* has the same plans as you," she nearly spit at him.

His grip tightened on her arm and then she saw stars as he slapped her delicate cheeks with his other. Her head reeled and she fell to the ground under the force of his hit.

"*Sunmanitu Wacitusni* may not want one such as you!" he growled.

"But you do?" she softly questioned as she tenderly touched her face where he'd struck her.

"Only for one need, my delectable whore," he said, fondling himself. His glacial eyes frosted over as he thought of his plans for her.

Steps were approaching the spring. He turned and left her where she lay without a backward glance.

CHAPTER EIGHTEEN

Preparation

A burst of drumming began once more in the
temples of Kaitlin's mind. She shakily rose to
her feet and slowly walked back to the tipi. The
blonde did feel a little weak from the lack of
food. Perhaps she would drink a bit of the stew
broth.

Sly Coyote leapt silently to his feet as soon as
he saw her. "What happened?" he cried.

Kaitlin dragged herself back to her mat.
Ignoring his question, she placed the *mniapahta*
in front of her.

"May I have more of the willow bark tea?" she
asked quietly.

The Crow man immediately grabbed the skin
and placed it into her hands. He gently removed
the water bags and put them up. Then Sly
Coyote squatted down in front of the white

captive. He let her drink the medicine before he grabbed her hands in his. The concerned warrior waited patiently until she lifted her chin and looked into his eyes.

"What happened, *Mazaska Zi Ista*?" he asked softly.

"What do you think happened, *Sunmanitu Wacitusni*? I live with my *toka*. Do you expect them to welcome me with open arms?"

"I do not expect them to attack you, *Mazaska Zi Ista*," he said sadly. "Tell me who did this ghastly deed!"

"*Hiya*, for he would only hate me more."

"He? A man attacked you? Did he only hit you… or did he… hurt you more?"

"He only hit me. He threatened more," Kaitlin admitted as a shudder overtook her body.

"Was it Black Bird?" he asked adamantly through his clenched jaw.

"No, it was not." To change the subject, she said, "Will you bring me some of the broth now? I could try to eat a little."

"*Tos*, I will do that for you, Golden One."

Sly Coyote tried not to slam her dish around as he warmed up the soup, but he was enraged. He took it as a personal insult when a person dared to lay hands upon her fragile beauty, especially a man!

He placed the bowl into her hands. He saw the slight tremor as she spooned the liquid into her mouth. Slowly, the nourishing broth stilled the queasiness that had plagued her all day.

Sly Coyote promised himself to secretly follow her on her chores. She'd several bruises on her arms and two good ones on her legs from her 'fall' into the river. Already the mark on her face showed that it would likely bruise as well. He hoped that none would suspect him of a heavy hand. He preferred to stroke women to passion, not beat them!

Mountain sheep were bought back into the camp for cooking and making into stews to feed the many warriors. Kaitlin was not expected to help, but she couldn't stand to be idle because her mind always returned to *Woniya Mato*. The white captive couldn't bear to think of the Crow's plans for him, nor could she stand to think of her nonexistent marriage day.

The blonde asked Bright Sky if she could assist her. The powerful leader granted the yellow eyes permission. The Crow woman assigned her the task of preparing the meat skews.

Kaitlin had never seen the strange animals with curled horns before. She let the men skin the animals. Then she was allowed a sharp knife to slice the carcass up into manageable pieces. She skewered the loins and ham. The rest was sliced up into stew-sized portions.

The meat slowly cooked over the open flames, sending delicious mouth-watering aroma into the air. Kaitlin busied herself by watching many pieces. She did this to keep busy and avoid meeting the curious stares from the people in the community.

While she was busy overseeing the cooking, Bright Sky approached Sly Coyote.

"Did women attack the woman of *Woniya Mato* again?" she asked.

"She was attacked again. Golden Eyes has not felt well this day. I let her fill the water skins and use the privacy area. When she returned, she had the bright mark across her face." Sly Coyotes anger was displayed by the darkening of his brows.

"Do you think the same person committed this deed?"

"I do not think so, Bright Sky. I assumed a woman, or several, attacked her last night. Men do not typically scratch each other," *Sunmanitu Wacitusni* revealed these clues to her. "She said a man did this but did not reveal who to me," he paused, then added, "Except she said it was not Black Bird."

Sly Coyote noticed the tightening of the leader's lips.

"We will keep a closer eye upon *Mazaska Zi Ista.*"

"Yes."

Many new faces grouped around the fires. There was much laughing and visiting among the village Crow and guest warriors. They all seemed optimistic and in high spirits. Kaitlin did not share in the revelry. She ate very little and stared into the fire most of the evening.

"Come, we wash the dishes," Bright Sky said.

They cleaned the dishes and then washed up afterwards. The water always seemed to lighten Kaitlin's spirits.

"Will you tell me who dared to bruise your face?" the kind woman asked Kaitlin.

"I cannot tell you, Bright Sky. He would make sure I paid the ultimate price the next time he saw me."

"I can see to it that he never bothers you again… and still retain his life."

"It would do no good to reveal his identity. He would only have others strike out at me. It is best I keep this to myself."

"It is a shame that a man would dishonor himself so by attacking a helpless woman."

"*Tos*, I agree with you."

They returned to the village. The pre-war jitters had many sharing coup stories and recounting past victories long into the night. Kaitlin was tired. She'd never fully recovered from the trip with all the fear and anxiety over her own destiny and that of her love's. The white girl asked Sly Coyote if she could return to the tipi. He nodded his permission and watched her until she darkened the tipi's entrance.

"You are worried over the woman of *Woniya Mato's*, are you not?" asked Night Sky.

"Yes. I have never seen her so lethargic and withdrawn."

"Do you expect her to be any other way on her wedding day?" asked Bright Sky.

"No. You are right. I should give her time to grieve… Especially when we take the life of her betrothed."

Many heads nodded.

"She is a good woman, *Sunmanitu Wacitusni*,"
Bright Sky praised her. "What are your plans
for her?"

"I am not sure. I will keep her for a while, I
think." He knew he would, but he didn't know
how the Crow would react to his declaration.

 The three leaders of the village nodded as if in
confirmation. Sly Coyote took it for approval.
He smiled and joined in with the loquacious
talks. His heart had suddenly lightened
inexplicably.

When Sly Coyote entered his tipi, he stood over
Kaitlin as he had many times before. She slept,
but her eyes were darkened and shadowed as if
she had not rested. Her beauty was marred by
the greenish tinge splashed across her left cheek.
His hands clenched in fury. Sly Coyote truly
wished to know who had dared to strike her!
The Crow warrior paced out much energy
before he was able to succumb to rest.

They were aroused early in the morning with the
flurry of movement within the village. Kaitlin
looked out the entrance flap to see what was
going on. She saw many women and children

carrying numerous filled bags of food, possessions, and sleeping rolls.

"What is going on?" she inquired of the man who stood beside her.

"They are going somewhere safe."

"Safe?"

"There is a battle to fight, *Mazaska Zi Ista*. The young, old, and child-bearing women need to be protected."

Kaitlin turned her golden eyes upon him. Sly Coyote met her gaze and then looked away. He didn't know what else to say.   The white woman was silent for a time.

"If you do not care, I would like some tea after I return from the privacy area. I still do not quite feel myself."

"Of course. I will obtain some tea leaves from Bright Sky. Is there a certain kind you prefer?"

"Mint, but any will be fine." Kaitlin stood, signifying she was ready to leave. She took the water skins with her.

Sly Coyote obtained the tea from the leader and returned it to the tipi. Then he stealthily followed Kaitlin.   He allowed her to use the privacy area without looking, but he watched from nearby as she refilled the water. He beat her back to the tipi.

If you will acquire grains, or allow me to, I will make some *aguyapi* for our breakfast."

"Of course. I will be back."

This time he went to the house of his brother. Black Bird was not there; he was helping his family move. He went back to Bright Sky's tipi.

She opened her flap for him.

"Do you have extra wheat or grains that *Mazaska Zi Ista* can make into *aguyapi*?"

"Yes, I have plenty! I will give you a bag of already-crushed grain. Here are some dried buffalo berries, also to flavor it. We will not have time to gather fresh for a while," the heavy implication didn't go unheeded.

"Again, my thanks."

"You do not have to thank me. *Mazaska Zi Ista* can help me gather fresh grain and berries upon our success."

Bright Sky was rewarded with a charming smile full of warmth. She smiled in return. She already felt like *Sunmanitu Wacitusni* was a long-lost brother. The woman leader sent up a thank you to the Great Spirit for his return to her people.

Kaitlin still looked peaked even after she'd drunk her tea. She half-heartedly mixed the flour and added the berries. She cooked the pones on the flat rocks. She gave most of the prepared bread to Sly Coyote. She only nibbled on one piece for herself.

"*Mazaska Zi Ista*, you are barely eating enough to keep a mouse alive. Are you okay?"

"I do not feel well," was all she would say.

He noticed she would eat a little nibble and then her throat would work on swallowing the piece. It was almost as if the blonde were willing herself not to purge herself of the nourishment.

"Do I need to call the medicine chief?"

"No, it is just a little bug. That is all."

Sly Coyote watched over her as he worked more on his weapons. The golden one did nothing but lie around and drink water. She drank a little broth at noon from a stew.

That evening, the village seemed deserted. The warriors still assembled to eat together. It was quite different from how it had been since their arrival.

Kaitlin did eat just a little more at night. She had a small slice of smoked meat, a tiny piece of bread, and a handful of berries. She drank water and sat listlessly and listened to the men speak in their strange tongue.

The men watched Golden Eyes throughout the meal. No one mentioned her apathy or her bruise. Sneaky Weasel even smiled at her when their eyes touched.

CHAPTER NINETEEN

Under the Weather

Black Bird and seven others were to keep guard over the camp throughout the night. The gathering didn't know when *Woniya Mato* would come, only that he would. Everyone's nerves were taunt yet excited. They would be known throughout Indian history for being the one to end the powerful reign of the mighty Spirit Bear!

Although the Crow didn't expect any attacks to come for a few days yet, they were not going to leave it to chance. If they didn't remain on their toes, the bear could take the lives of those in the inner circle. To take the war chief by surprise, the second outer circle of Crow would not attack until the war cry and drum sounded from within the village.

Kaitlin turned in early again. Sly Coyote watched with a worried expression.

"Is something wrong, *Sunmanitu Wacitusni*?" asked Bright Sky.

"It is *Mazaska Zi Ista*. She had not felt well since she drank the berry wine. I do not think that it could still be plaguing her."

"No, the effects would be gone by now," she agreed.

"Perhaps her heart ache causes her pain," Bloody Knife offered. "That is how we plan to defeat *Woniya Mato*, by stealing his heart. It could do the same to her."

"I did not think of that," Sly Coyote admitted.

"She thinks of how we lure him to his death. Her guilt, although it does not belong to her, takes away her will to fight," Bloody Knife offered again.

"Yes, I have noticed a gradual acceptance that she cannot escape since her arrival," Midnight Star added.

"What can I do to help her?" Sly Coyote asked, trying to elicit the advice of the others.

"There is nothing you can do," Bright Sky said. "*Mazaska Zi Ista* must work him out of her heart on her own. It could take her a very long time," she warned.

Sly Coyote looked down momentarily. "It is a shame that an innocent woman must feel that she has to take blame in his death. *Woniya Mato* must die!" he cried. "My father must be avenged!"

Sunmanitu Wacitusni also knew it was the only way he could have Golden Eyes for himself. One day, he vowed, her eyes would shine with love for him, but first, the man who claimed that emotion in her life must be eliminated!

One by one, the men returned to tipis around the village. Each had his weapons readied for the call that would send them running to defend and attack. The seven men would take first watch. When the moon rose high in the sky, seven more men would replace them.

"I am sorry, *Mazaska Zi Ista*, for what I have put you through," Sly Coyote whispered to her sleeping form. "If I could take back your pain, I would, but I cannot. I did not know any other

way to lure *Woniya Mato* to his death. I cannot
say that I regret including you in my life circle!”

He went to his mats but sleep would not come.
The warrior decided to take the next watch.
Sunmanitu Wacitusni yearned for the Spirit Bear
to come. He hoped he could strike the arrows
home!

In the morning, Sly Coyote returned to the tipi
to find it empty. He was panic-stricken at first.
When the acclaimed Crow man noticed the
water skins were missing, he went to the spring.
The filled skins were sitting on the edge of the
bank, but he didn’t see Kaitlin. He searched
further and walked down the bank of the river.
He found her scrubbing her clothes. The blonde
had freshly bathed. Her pallor was fragile, and
she seemed so delicate.

“*Mazaska Zi Ista,* washing clothes so early?”

“Yes, I… I just needed to,” she swallowed,
“Change.”

“You are sure you are not sick?”

“I am fine.”

He stood over her, watching her worriedly. The coyote shadowed her every move. The white woman was too listless to pay him much attention. Kaitlin grabbed the water skins on the way back to the tipi. Then she mixed more grain and berries for the Indian bread. They supplemented the pones with cooked meat.

Although Kaitlin did her best to not draw attention to the food she ate, Sly Coyote noticed she didn't eat much. Within a half hour, she rushed outside. He hurried to the entrance flap to see her making a mad dash toward the river. He followed her hurried flight.

He found her retching her meager breakfast in the woods. She dragged herself to the river and rinsed her face. She looked up into his dark eyes only to look down once more sheepishly.

"Come, *Mazaska Zi Ista*. You must rest. You are ill."

"I am fine. Just… let me sit a minute. I feel better if I can splash the cool water upon my skin"

"How long have you felt this way?" he asked, his deep voice riddled with concern.

"Just since I guess I overindulged in the berry juice. Perhaps it didn't agree with my system, or it masked the beginnings of an illness." She looked up at him again. "At least it doesn't look contagious."

Sly Coyote waited until her nausea had passed. He assisted her back to the tipi. The captor wouldn't allow the white woman off the mat to do anything. Kaitlin rested her weary body and mind. The blonde didn't feel as if she had enough energy to even think. For that, the white girl was appreciative.

That evening, Black Bird's deep voice came from the flap. "Brother, I have returned from moving my family," he said once he'd gained permission for entry.

"Does everyone seem settled in?" Sly Coyote asked.

"Yes, I think they will be fine. They have provisions for a week. As long as it is safe, we will visit daily. A sentry watches over them.

Bloody Knife assigned about ten warriors to guard and protect them."

Black Bird's gaze wandered to Golden Eyes.

"Have you changed your mind about the power she holds over a man?" he teased. "Is this why she has no energy to greet one of her escorts?"

"No, brother, her power is strong. I have not taken her to my mats though I strongly desire to. Until *Woniya Mato* walks no more, I will resist her magic."

"Will you share with your long-lost brother?"

 Sly Coyote laughed deeply. "You do not easily give up!" he teased.

"You do not answer," returned Black Bird with a smile.

"No, my brother. I will not share. I do not think she would like that, either."

"I get first dibs on her if you trade her off," Black Bird warned. "What is wrong with her, then? She usually is so full of fiery eyes."

"The traveling was hard on her. She is ill."

"Ill? How ill?"

"She is sleeping much. She eats little, she is pale and fights to keep food down," Sly Coyote relayed her symptoms.

"When did she begin to act this way?"

"The morning after the special wine juice of Bright Sky."

"Have you consulted with Bright Sky?" Black Bird had never heard of any becoming sick for a time after consumption of the drink, but he was not sure.

"Yes. She said the effects do not last more than the day after if one is ill from it."

"What of the medicine chief?

"I have not called him yet. *Mazaska Zi Ista* does not feel well, but she will live. I will talk to him if she does not get better; it is just he has a lot to prepare for right now."

Black Bird was silent for a time. He said, "We will watch her, *Sunmanitu Wacitusni.* If her symptoms worsen, I will seek the medicine of Magic Waters."

"Yes, brother, I will seek his counsel. Thank you."

"You will share the meal fires tonight, won't you?"

Sly Coyote said, "Yes, I plan to come."

"I will see you then," the deep timbre of Black Bird's voice then bid them farewell.

Sly Coyote was glad that he finally felt prepared to meet the battle successfully. He didn't think he would be able to concentrate on his weapon completion if the task was not already done. His mind continually strayed to Golden Eyes.

He walked over to her. The golden beauty had been sleeping, but she blinked open her eyes as if sensing he was standing over her.

"How are you feeling?" he asked.

"Better, I think." She sat up slowly.

He stooped down beside her and touched her forehead.

"You do not fight the heat demons."

"No, I do not believe I run a fever," she said, "It seems to come and go."

"Can I get you anything?" he solicitously inquired. "Does willow bark tea help?"

The thought of the bitter liquid almost made the nausea return.

"No, I do not think that will help. I think just resting seems to be doing the trick. I think that maybe I pressed my body too hard."

Sly Coyote wished he would stop feeling the surges of guilt that her words brought to him. He didn't think she'd said these things to make him feel badly; the golden one was just being honest. The warrior inquired about her health, and she'd answered him. It was as simple as that.

After rest time, the meal preparation began. Kaitlin was feeling quite a bit better by then. She was glad to get up and out of the hot tipi.

She helped cook a stew in the shade of a large oak.

"It comes to my attention that you haven't been feeling well lately," Bright Sky stated as she approached the white girl who'd earned her respect.

"I do not know why anyone is concerned for me," Kaitlin saucily retorted. She didn't intend to be rude; the captive just didn't understand.

"My dear, you are a guest here in our camp. Even if you do not desire to be one, you are. You are a fine individual – one who did not ask to be put in the position she finds herself in. You have a high honor: to be the chosen one of a great chief who is, to be honest, a walking legend," Bright Sky said honestly. "If we had met under different circumstances, I would be honored to call you a friend. Our situation, however, makes it impossible. While *Woniya Mato* lives, we cannot yet be friends. Not that," she searched for the right words, "I don't enjoy you and your company! For I do! And this is the reason I care."

 Bright Sky's eyes rested upon Sly Coyote. "*Sunmanitu Wacitusni* also hates to put you in the middle of this battle. He has come to care for you in the time you have spent together."

Kaitlin's brow furrowed. She couldn't honestly say she hated Sly Coyote. He'd treated her with kindness and respect, but she didn't trust him. He'd hurt her deeply and betrayed her. When the white girl heard he cared for her, a well of resentment bubbled under her carefully concealed face. It was no secret to her that he desired to take her onto his sleeping mat.

Noting her expression, but not quite understanding it completely, Bright Sky said, "Do not worry about your future should your chosen one join the Great Spirit. *Sunmanitu Wacitusni* will see to your needs."

Kaitlin stood abruptly and said, "I need to use the privacy area. I will return."

Thinking she might be feeling ill again, Bright Sky nodded. She saw that Sly Coyote would escort her without her knowledge. No more attacks would occur against the golden girl.

Kaitlin needed to escape any more talk about her future without *Woniya Mato*. She refused to think of what her life would be like without him, especially if it involved *Sunmanitu Wacitusni*! No man could compare to the mighty war chief!

Woniya Mato was so tall, so bronze, and so muscular. He could stop her heart with a searing look from his ebony eyes. His full lips always had a ready smile for her. Kaitlin pictured his sensuous mouth. It so easily drove her wild! It left her longing for his touch.

The blonde leaned heavily against the tree. She arched her head back until the tough bark supported her. The forlorn woman looked up into the sky.

Please, Woniya Mato! Do not come for me. She silently prayed. *I can bear this existence if I know you live. I cannot be the reason you die! I could never live knowing I caused your death!*

CHAPTER TWENTY

Boredom

Hating to go back but knowing she must, Kaitlin began to slowly trek back. If she had the strength, she'd plunge into the river this very moment. The lack of food and the energy depletion she'd suffered from, though, made escape an impossible feat. Perhaps she would feel better in a day or two… if the battle wasn't on-going by then.

If I have the opportunity to touch Sly Coyote's weapons, I will. I don't believe that my touch could rob them of power, but just in case… I will. I also promise to bump all warrior's arrows that are aimed toward you, the love of my life! I swear it!

Sly Coyote's silhouette darkened the path at the top of the hill. Couldn't she just go to the restroom by herself? *No,* she scuffed inwardly. *You are a prize of war. They cannot afford for*

*you to make an escape attempt. They need you
to lure in the mighty bear!*

"Are you feeling alright?" he asked.

"*Tos*. I just needed to use the privacy area," she
stated, trying to hide her resentment.

"*Come, Mazaska Zi Ista*. It is time to eat."

She followed him back to the shade of the oak.
The Sioux woman prided herself on being able
to eat a bowl full of the tempting stew. It was
not a large bowl, but it was more than she'd
been able to eat lately. Kaitlin hoped her
strength would be back in full-force on the next
day. Then she'd allow herself to be 'swept'
down the river.

The golden one retired early, once more, for she
did not relish listening to others speak the
foreign tongue. Even if they spoke Lakota
normally, she'd not have wanted to listen to
their coup and battle stories. Every night that
they prayed for success, she prayed for the
Crow's fall.

Mercifully, Kaitlin fell asleep quickly even though it seemed like she'd spent the whole day sleeping. Her body just seemed so heavy. Wearily, her eyes closed on their own accord. The stressed woman didn't know any more until morning.

When the new day smiled on her, Kaitlin gently awoke. She tentatively tested her body. It seemed to respond. She stood and went to relieve herself. Then the blonde filled the water skins. Upon her return, she cooked wild grains and was given honey to flavor it. The young woman, thankfully, felt a little better.

Golden Eyes ate a small breakfast. It kind of made her feel queasy with the first few bites, but it passed. Kaitlin did not push it and over indulge, but she ate enough to help bring her strength back. The captive wanted to 'fall' into the river as soon as she felt she had the strength to battle the current.

"You seem as if you are feeling better this day," Sly Coyote said, relieved. He didn't want to think about her falling ill because of him. The proclaimed Crow man had enough guilt where she was concerned!

"*Tos*, I am glad. Being sick is not fun!" she said in a teasing manner.

"*Hiya*, it is not," he agreed.

Kaitlin saw the few remaining villagers carry the last of their items toward the concealing cave. She couldn't see the cave, but she knew it lay to the northeast of the village. She longed to conceal her identity and pretend to leave for the cave, too.

Kaitlin had never been in a village before with nothing to do. Her boredom was obvious. With most of the inhabitants gone, there weren't even people to watch.

The men only touched and rearranged their weapons. They watched her and would pace from time to time. Kaitlin found it difficult to believe that men got excited over the prospect of dying or killing!

Bright Sky and one other woman beyond herself were the only females left. She sat at Bright Sky's outside fire pit under the oak whenever she could. The more time that went by, the more anger she felt in her heart at Sly Coyote's treachery.

"Bright Sky," Kaitlin asked curiously, "will you fight when the time comes?"

"Yes, but I will not fight as the men fight. I will stay here and defend what is ours."

"Have you fought before?"

Bright Sky looked at Kaitlin and nodded seriously. "I have defended my camp against our foes many times. This is how I earned enough coups to become leader."

"I do not mean to offend you, but why do the Sioux not allow women the same privileges as the Crow?"

"I am not sure. I would guess that they believe women are sacred. Females can plant a man's seed within her body and bring forth a child from a mating. I believe they see this ability as a revered one from the Great Spirit. For this reason, they believe women are like children and need constant protection. If the women are killed, how will the tribe be replaced? Men are not as important, for one man can have many wives and plan many seeds. Do you understand?"

"Do the Crow not believe this as well?"

"Yes, we do, but we also believe that the Great Spirit can call forth female warriors and leaders as well. We live our lives as He sees fit. We do not argue with the Great Spirit."

"That makes sense," Kaitlin murmured to herself.

The golden skinned girl didn't want to fight in wars. She didn't think she could ever kill a person, but Kaitlin did think women could make good leaders and come up with valid decisions and points on the council. It always infuriated her that men always put themselves so high on the pedestal!

"Is there anything I can do?" Kaitlin asked, desperate to fill in her time.

Understanding flooded Bright Sky. She didn't have anything to do at the moment, but she thought she could give something to Golden Eyes to take her mind off imposing matters.

"I do not have much, but if you want to keep busy, I always make the berry wine. With our next celebration, we will want some. Do you want to strain the pulp from a batch?"

Kaitlin nodded. She smiled sheepishly and said, "As long as I do not have to drink any!" She didn't want to offend the leader, so she quickly added, "It was very good; it just made me so ill!"

"I am not offended. Some choose not to indulge in the drink because of the after effects."

Kaitlin couldn't keep the look of relief from her face. She followed Bright Sky into a separate tipi. It was very large and plain. It was made from old hides that needed replacing.

"This is my work tipi. I cannot leave my berry process elsewhere because of those who would swipe it. I use weathered hides to keep it from the sun."

The leader ducked into the dwelling. Kaitlin followed. There were many containers of the drink in various stages of completion. Bright Sky led her to three huge containers made from hardened earth.

Kaitlin stared at wonder at the texture of the containers. It was like glass but was not! Bright Sky gave her fresh containers and braided horsehair net. The net was very closely woven until it was a cloth-like texture.

"I will show you what I need done. It is much work, but it will fill your time." Bright Sky placed the net over a fresh container and secured it with rocks. She allowed the center to droop inwards slightly. Then she took a fire-hardened wooden scoop and began to fill the smashed, fermenting berry liquid into it. She dumped the mixture onto the top of the net.

"No offense, but that stinks!"

Bright Sky smiled at her. "Yes, rotten berries never smell that great."

Bright Sky scooped several bowls of liquid onto the top of the net. It bubbled and popped softly in protest. Then she smashed the accumulated pulp on the top to squeeze the excess juice through.

"That is all I want you to do," Bright Sky said. "When the top becomes too full of pulp, remove it and place it in this container. We will carry it off from camp later."

"This does not seem like much work," Kaitlin said.

"Tell me that after you smelled and felt this most of the day."

Kaitlin thought about curing leather with *Wawat'ecaka*. Straining fermented berries from the juice would be like a walk in the woods compared to smearing days-old brains into the skin of the animal it came from. Kaitlin smiled wistfully. Oh, what she wouldn't give to be smearing brains in to hide this moment by the motherly woman's side!

Kaitlin began the time-consuming chore of filling the new container and removing the pulp. Her mind still wandered to her love. Her hands were busy, but their movement didn't require her mind to concentrate.

The golden one felt much better, but the yeast smell and the way the berries smeared all over her hands made her feel like she could become ill at any moment. What was wrong with her? When had she developed such a weak stomach? Yes, Kaitlin had retched the first few times she worked in the curing cave with *Wawat'ecaka*, but who wouldn't? The strong ammonia and feces smell that the master curer used on her leather was enough to make anyone revisit their breakfast contents!

When one urn was filled, Kaitlin removed the net. She wanted to wash it off at the river before filling a fresh container. When the material became too saturated with the pulp, some sneaked through. She went to Bright Sky to tell her this. The female leader followed the white captive back to check her progress.

"You are doing a magnificent job!" Bright Sky informed Golden Eyes. "You are probably straining the berries better than I do myself! Do not worry if some fall through, as long as most do not. I will strain this once or twice more before it is complete."

"I will wash off this net before I begin a fresh pot."

Bright Sky nodded her agreement. She accompanied her to the river. Together, the net was easier to clean and wring out.

Kaitlin had finished the second container before the heat of the day. The golden-haired beauty walked back to the edge of the river to clean the net again. Then she dumped the pulp she'd removed from the top of the brew.

The white girl washed up and returned to the tipi. Sly Coyote watched her enter. He sat next to the fire pit.

"Bright Sky said you are a wonderful help to her," his rich voice filled the tipi. "She brought some food."

Kaitlin walked toward the pit and sat. She accepted her bowl and ate slowly. The first few bites always made her feel ill, especially when she saw the degenerating berries every time she blinked.   Slowly, the blonde felt better.

Sly Coyote watched her closely. Kaitlin felt like screaming at him to stop staring but didn't dare. They'd worked out a truce between them. The Crow man hadn't tried to touch her again since the night they consumed the berry juice, so the white girl didn't want to do anything to tempt him. Her capture could retaliate by touching her. Kaitlin did her best to continue to act as though she didn't notice his weighty stares.

The prisoner froze as Sly Coyote leaned forward and wiped back a wayward strand of gold that kept trying to enter her food bowl. The blonde didn't want to encourage or offend him, so she waited silently. Then she resumed eating.

The effects of his touch didn't go unnoticed by Sly Coyote. He was trying hard not to become more entangled in her powerful spell, but she always was so beautiful and kind. The white girl worked because she wanted to. His respect for her knew no bounds. Even after working with rotting berries, her smell was clean and fresh. The warrior wanted her as he had no other woman.

Kaitlin could feel Sly Coyote's aura surround her. His attraction for her was as thick as a knife. She could feel it pulsating. Suddenly fearful he'd force himself upon her; she pushed back her bowl and went to her mat. Hopefully her sudden distance and her will to rest would cool his ardor.

The golden one sighed and rolled away from his onyx looks. The beauty yawned and made a show of being tired. She discovered it was no act. A short while later, blissfully, she slept.

= = =

"Soon, my Golden One, it will be me who fills your mind… and your body. It is so difficult to make myself wait!" Sly Coyote softly promised her sleeping form.

The warrior stood and paced the tipi. He was frustrated in more ways than one. The Crow man longed to take *Mazaska Zi Ista* into his arms and make her whisper his name in passion. He longed to take the life of the man she loved. Only then would he be free to truly pursue her.

"Why won't you come?" Sly Coyote asked himself aloud. They hadn't really expected him to arrive before this day. The Crow may have to wait days more, or the strike from the masterful war chief could come this very moment!

= = =

When Kaitlin woke, she returned to complete the final berry siphoning. She still didn't feel back to her normal self. It seemed that either upon waking or eating, she felt like she would be sick. At least it wasn't an illness that put her down for the count. Still, she didn't like the weakness that overtook her at times.

The blonde had to escape no matter how she felt, or *Woniya Mato* would be dead, and she would wish to be. She planned on attempting it either tonight or in the morning. She cleaned the berry net and empty pots and carried them back into the tipi one at a time. Then the captive helped Bright Sky clean some freshly killed rabbits to roast. They ate *Tinpsila* and the pones of bread with the freshly cooked meat.

Everyone was on edge. It seemed that the littlest noise had the men whirling, weapons ready in-hand. It pinched Kaitlin's nerves as well.

The blonde returned to her tipi and wondered how to prepare for escape. The captive wished she could prepare some food to take. The trip would be very taxing on her still-not-well body, but if she planned to use the river to escape, she wouldn't be able to carry anything unless she tied it to her head.

That evening, *Sunmanitu Wacitusni* and Black Bird spoke together by the fire pit. Kaitlin sneaked towards the privacy area. She hoped she could have a nice swim afterwards, but her plans to escape were foiled when she saw two Crow warriors on the opposite side of the river down steam. They were smiling and joking as if they didn't have a care in the world. They stopped to watch her leave the covered canopy of foliage that served to protect women from straggling eyes.

Kaitlin gnashed her teeth in frustration. Why did it always seem that someone prevented her escape? She nearly stomped in rage. The golden one paused by the river and took a few deep breaths. She had to calm her frayed nerves before she faced Sly Coyote once more.

Finally, the white woman returned and dragged herself to her sleeping mat once more. She was aware that Sly Coyote's curious eyes were upon her. She didn't care. The blonde lay down and forced her breath rate to calm.

"Did something happen to upset you?" Sly Coyote's voice came from behind her. "Did someone bother you?"

"*Hiya*. I just want to go home, *Sunmanitu Wacitusni*. I am tired of this. Can't you understand how I feel?"

"*Tos, Mazaska Zi Ista*," his voice gentled with comprehension. "I do understand. I, like you, was taken from the home I knew and raised as a Sioux."

"Yes, but you were with your very own mother!"

"I was with my mother, *tos*, but it is almost worse on a man who is the blood of the enemy. I do not expect you to understand."

She raised up to face him. Her resentment at her situation was evident. "YOU, of all people, do *not* understand, *Sunmanitu Wacitusni*! You do not understand how it is to be a woman with no rights. You do not know what it is like to be at the mercy of every man, woman, and child. Men think they can do as they wish with me. They are stronger, and therefore, can force me to do whatever they please!" Her golden eyes flashed fire.

"*Mazaska Zi Ista*, did a man make you do something you did not wish?"

"Yes. YOU!" Kaitlin turned to sob into her sleeping mat.

=   =   =

How *Sunmanitu Wacitusni* longed to hold and comfort her, but he dared not. If he touched her glorious body, he would prove her words true. He might force her to give more than she was willing. The Crow man could easily overpower her and take, but he didn't want their first joining to be so forceful. He wanted to please her as much as she would him.

Sly Coyote sighed and slowly walked back to his spot. Black Bird was taking first watch over the village. He would take over later in the night. Midnight Star would watch over his tipi during his visage to make sure no harm came to *Mazaska Zi Ista.* Now he was glad.

Each night, her powerful aura reached out to him. He smelled her womanly scent, and it played havoc on his rest. *Mazaska Zi Ista* was slowly robbing him of his sanity. He now understood the power that *Woniya Mato* had succumbed to. He stood and walked out into the cooling air. Her sobs wrenched at his heart, but he could do nothing.

The Golden One was right. She had the lowest rank in the village. A slave was held above none. A newborn had more status than a slave. And *Mazaska Zi Ista* was right about men. He would take from her if she didn't give when he could no longer resist her charms. *Sunmanitu Wacitusni* was no longer sure if he could give her a full moon to grieve the loss of *Woniya Mato*. The self-proclaimed Crow man cared for her, but he wouldn't sacrifice himself; he was too intertwined with desire for her heart. If Sly Coyote lived, Golden Eyes would be his. A soft smile warmed his lips as he dreamed of the day.

CHAPTER TWENTY-ONE

Opportunity

When Kaitlin awoke, Sly Coyote was gone. She breathed a sigh of relief. The white slave made her way to the privacy area and filled the water skins. It was eerily quiet. It dawned on her that she was alone! Was it true? Was she *really* alone? The men were off, preening themselves for a war. The womenfolk were hidden and safe. That left her… *all alone*!

Quietly, the captive waded into the river. She smiled in pleasure as the cool waters swirled up around her. She back floated into the current and allowed it to carry her downstream. She was mostly submerged for about thirty minutes.

An overwhelming sense told her to hide. Immediately listening to her immerging Native instincts, Kaitlin went to the side of a bank.

Fronds were drooping over a section of the water, and the blonde secured herself from sight. A short time later, she heard *Sunmanitu Wacitusni's* voice speaking to another brave. She couldn't understand them as they spoke in Crow, but she knew it wouldn't be long before he returned to the village and discovered her absence.

Loud heart beats thundered in her throat. The escapee was almost certain her captor would hear its echo on the rippling waters in which she hid. Kaitlin willed her breathing to slow as to not quiver the fronds that secured her from his sight. It seemed forever before they quietly walked from the river edge.

Patiently waiting on anxious toes, ten more minutes edged by before *Mazaska Zi Ista* resumed her trip down the waterway. Her heart beat madly, and she feared discovery. The white captive vividly recalled Sly Coyote's threats to make her his in all ways the night she nearly ran from him. It had been the only thing that had stopped her flight. The golden-eyed girl hated to think of his punishments for her when he discovered her absence. Oh, if only

she could make it to *Woniya Mato's* side before
it was too late!

Kaitlin went another thirty minutes before she
became so cold she had to leave the waters. She
didn't leave the river's edge, however. She
knew many powerful trackers lived in the
village. The men would be on her like hounds
after a fox when they discovered her gone.
Nevertheless, she had to get the bulk of her
body out of the cold depths to warm up for a
while.

The beauty walked on the slippery stones near
the water's edge. She hoped the wetness of the
river would quickly erase her passage before
those stealthy eyes discovered the bottom
disturbance.

Kaitlin looked down, mostly to avoid falling and
slipping. The splashing noise would alert any
Native to an anomaly in the river. The escapee
could not allow for discovery!

The white girl raised her eyes to look around
periodically but mostly focused on her feet.
Kaitlin came close to screaming when she
nearly walked on a wet moccasin-clad foot.

She stood, mesmerized. Slowly, her eyes traced the moccasin up the masculine leg attired in soft buckskin leggings.

Bit by bit, her eyes continued their ascent until they met the leering grin of Black Bird's. His predatory gleam left her no doubt of his intentions, and it wasn't to take her straight back to his brother. Then, to make matters worse, Sneaky Weasel materialized beside him.

"Going somewhere?" Black Bird's deep voice drawled in heavily accented Lakota.

Kaitlin could do nothing but watch him as his hand drew her wet one to him.

"Come. We need to get you out of the cold water," he said.

His tone was falsely calm; Kaitlin knew he didn't care for her welfare at all. She had no choice but to walk to the bank with him. Sneaky Weasel followed closely beside her.

"Please," she whispered, her teeth chattering half in fear and half in cold.

"The first thing we need to do is get you out of these wet clothes. What do you think, Sneaky Weasel?"

"Definitely the first thing we need to do," he echoed.

"Sit, *Mazaska Zi Ista*. I will start a fire to warm you," Black Bird commanded.

She knew his words were sympathetic, but his kindness was a façade. The malicious aura that encompassed him belied his thoughtful actions. The reclaimed woman could do nothing but note the derisive smiles that passed between the two men as her body continued its shaking reaction.

They began a fire and then spoke rapidly in Crow. She didn't know what they said, but she knew they argued over her. Sneaky Weasel removed a sleeping mat and placed it close to the fire.

"Take off your clothes, *Mazaska Zi Ista*," Black Bird ordered.

"*Hi – hiya…*"

"Come now. Surely you realize we need to get you dried off! You will catch a cold if we do not warm you up!" he chuckled in amusement.

"D – do you… have something I could cover myself with?" she stammered.

"Oh, yes," Black Bird smiled wickedly. He rose agilely from his crouched position by the fire and came to stand over her. "Can you guess what I intend to cover you with?" he asked coldly. His tone changed to reflect his raw hunger and power over her.

When she didn't answer, he turned to Sneaky Weasel. Still speaking in accented Lakota to prolong her terror, he asked, "What about you, my friend? Do you have any suggestions on how we can cover *Mazaska Zi Ista* to warm her up?" His evil laugh flooded over any forthcoming response from Sneaky Weasel.

He began to unlace the drenched ties on her dress. The blonde's eyes were as wide as a doe's. She began to shake more uncontrollably and move her head back and forth slowly in denial.

"*Tos*, my yellow-eyed friend, I think you do know what I intend to cover you with!" Black Bird again laughed nastily.

Sneaky Weasel couldn't help but to send their barbs home quicker and deeper. "I told you, whore; you would lie beneath many men! First it will be us! Then *Isnala Sungmanitu* won't want a soiled woman!   Because," he stepped closer to her, "that is what we are going to do to you!" He sneered maliciously at her.

Kaitlin's face went ashen as Black Bird slowly finished untying the laces on her dress. He wanted her to watch his every move. The son of Night Hawk hated *Woniya Mato* with a passion. The unforgiving Crow man would work his revenge out on the man in a much more fulfilling way!

The victimized white didn't try to fight. What was the use? Her strength was no match against two men.

"We do not want to destroy this very becoming dress," Black Bird informed her. "And," he added, "We won't tell Sly Coyote about our... fun... if you don't."

Black Bird really didn't know how his brother
would react to the discovery of what was about
to happen, but he was too into his lust to truly
care. Still, he attempted to persuade her to keep
her silence.

"Then, *maybe*, he will keep you because he
won't know that you really are just a whore," he
paused. "We won't tell him about *this*," he said
as he pulled the dripping garment down from
her shoulder.

"Or this," Sneaky Weasel was at her other
shoulder, pulling down on the dress. Both men
gawked in wonder at her delicately exposed
chest. Both nipples peaked at them through the
clinging wet deer leather.

"Oh, I can't wait!" said Sneaky Weasel in Crow.
His breathing was heavy with desire.

"Get back," Black Bird said through gritted
teeth. "You can help me hold her down if she
fights." He switched back to accented Lakota to
inflict fear, "She must want this as much as we
do!"

Black Bird finished removing her dress from her body and pushed her back onto the mat.

"Please… Black Bird!" she gasped. "Don't do this!"

His only response was his narrowed glittering eyes as he removed his leggings. He seemed to relish how his slow reactions appeared to immobilize her with fear. Only the attractive girl's panicked orbs flashed her feelings.

Sneaky Weasel still had on his clothes, but a hard bulge was evident between his legs as he anticipated watching the first union with the yellow-eyed girl.

Black Bird's long member sprang free when he untied the breechcloth.   He allowed her to see. Then he squatted to lie beside her. He leaned forward and kissed her mouth in a brutal assault. His hardness burned against her still adorning breechcloth.

Slowly, he began to untie her female covering. He stared at the perfection of the body gleaming beside him.

Black Bird wanted her eyes to look into his as he claimed victory. He wanted her to feel his dominating power over her before he plundered her body and robbed it of all will. The golden one would totally submit to him before he would take her back to the village. He didn't care if it took all day!

"*Mazaska Zi Ista*, Look at me," he commanded.

The blonde would not obey. He reached down and touched the tip of her beast. She cried out and screwed her eyes shut.

Kaitlin might not be able to prevent what they intended, but she didn't have to fully cooperate. She would not give them the satisfaction of begging again. She vowed that at the first opportunity, she would kill both men!

Instantly, her cheeks were held in an iron grip. Black Bird turned her face to his. He said tersely, "Look at me! I want you to look into my eyes as I take what *Woniya Mato* has taken before me."

All of a sudden, she roared, "*Hiya*! You will never possess what *Woniya Mato* has!" and pushed with all of her might.

CHAPTER TWENTY-TWO

Invasion

Kaitiln succeeded in making him fall backward, yet he managed to catch himself with his hands. She crawled away frantically, but he caught her foot and dragged her back. Sneaky Weasel grabbed her arms and held them down once they flipped her back onto the mat.

"Care to tell me that again, *Mazaska Zi Ista*? Black Bird taunted her as he looked down at her body. Lust dilated his pupils. "I will have that very treasure within minutes. And when I am finished, Sneaky Weasel will have a turn. We may take many more turns before we tire of your wonderful cha – ahhh…"

Kaitlin screamed as he suddenly slumped forward onto her. Tremors began anew. However, she noticed he'd loosened his grip on her body. Why had he stopped? Then she noticed that Sneaky Weasel's grip was absent from her wrists as well.

Perhaps he believed Black Bird could handle his evil deed without further help. The terrified woman lay quivering in shock, trapped beneath the manly form of Black Bird. She couldn't see the double arrows with red and black feathers driven deeply into his soulless heart. His partner-in-crime lay nearby with an arrow protruding from his eye socket.

Suddenly, a shadow loomed above her. The weight was lifted from her body, and she saw the heavenly sight of *Woniya Mato*. His war-painted face was furious, yet strangely happy as well. His body was taut with unleashed savagery.

"*Woniya Mato*!" she screeched over and over. Uncontrollable sobs wracked her fragile form. He swooped her naked and helpless body into his arms. He covered her with the mat upon which she lay.

She clutched at him, nearly in hysterics. "Is it really you, *Woniya Mato*? Or am I dead and in heaven?"

"Oh, *Mazaska Zi Ista*! Are you alright? Did they hurt you?" he whispered, smoothing her hair with his gentle hand. He could not bear to hear if they had. Already they deserved to die many times at his powerful hands.

"*Hiya, Woniya Mato.* But they almost… They almost…" and she couldn't finish. She burst into fresh sobs. Now that she was safely in her love's arms, it seemed she couldn't stop her emotional outpour.

"It is okay, *Mazaska Zi Ista*," he soothed, "I have you now. No one will harm you any further. Shh, *mita wastelaka*," he tried to console her.

Spirit Bear knew his warriors would be on the lookout for more Crow while he reunited with the woman of his heart. He cradled her to his strong chest until her cries subsided.

"Oh, *Woniya Mato*! I never thought I would see you again! I am so happy to see you! I love you! I love you!" she cried.

"And I love you, Golden One, you are my heart. You are my life!" he looked down into her blissfully happy face. His worried concern was smoothed by her complete joy as his lethal body wrapped protectively around hers.

"Tell me how they treated you, *Mazaska Zi Ista*. I must know exactly who to extract slow revenge upon," his jaw muscles bulged as he clenched in rage. "One name I do not need to be told. He will die by my hand this day!" he swore.

He looked down again, searching her beautiful face for answers. His eyes narrowed when he noticed the blue-green color displayed on her left cheek.

"Who dared to strike you, *Mazaska Zi Ista*?" he snarled.

"He already lies dead at our feet, *mita wastelaka*," she informed him. "It was Sneaky Weasel who struck me."

His tone gentled. "Who has dared to harm you, *mita wastelaka*? I must know."

"No one hurt me. These two were going to," she tried to hold back a fresh sob and turned her head into his neck to hide their evil bodies from her sight.

"Are you telling me that *Sunmanitu Wacitusni* did not… he did not…" He couldn't bear to utter the words.

"Hiya, Woniya Mato. If you seek to know who has taken me on the sleeping mats, none but you, my wonderful warrior!"

Kaitlin smiled up into his stalwart frame. The valiant war chief knew no fear in the face of death, but he trembled when he thought of her shame and pain. Her heart went out to him and was a willing captive in his intrepid embrace.

"But they would have," she added, trembling at the thought.

He captured her attention with his commanding stare, demanding to know more.

"*Sunmanitu Wacitusni* planned on killing you first…" she broke off. She took a few deep breaths to calm herself. "He planned on me being his slave in all ways after you walked the spirit path."

"After I see to you, *Mazaska Zi Ista*, I must go to seek revenge."

At his words, she tightened her grip on his vibrant body. "I can't bear to let you go! I want to come with you, *Woniya Mato*. Do not leave me!" she beseeched him.

"I must, *Mazaska Zi Ista*! I am here to rescue you and to see that they do not strike against me again. They asked for the revenge of *Woniya Mato*, and this is what they will receive!" His eyes flashed with blazing black fire.

"At least take me with you! Please, *Woniya Mato*! Please!"

"*Hiya, Mazaska Zi Ista*. I go to make war, not love," his impassive face softened as he looked down into her beauty. "But I will have time for that later," he paused meaningfully. Then he continued, "War is no place for a woman. You have already witnessed that. This time, it will be worse, for my foes wish to crush me. They are different from the white dogs; they, like Lakota, are warriors of the land… worthy opponents. However, they have unleashed my rage!”

“*Woniya Mato*! I must warn you! They have met up with other bands of Crow. I do not know their locations, for I do not understand their language. I know that several suns ago, many men came into camp. They do not stay in the village, so I think they wait for you!” Again, her grasp tightened protectively on his powerful bronze frame.

He stood with her cradled in his strong arms. Yellow Feather, *Watila Hehaka*, and *Wawakankan* materialized beside him. The men greeted her with their eyes and a relieved smile.

“*Wawakankan*? You came?” she whispered in surprise.

“Yes, I brought him,” the war chief acknowledged. “We left Lone Wolf back in camp to protect. I needed most men with me, especially *Wawakankan*. It is not logical to go into war and plan on escaping without injury. Who better to treat our wounds than our very powerful medicine man? Spirit Bear's eyes twinkled in humor at the awed surprise on Golden Eye's face. "He is also an excellent warrior!"

Kaitlin rewarded the shaman with a bright smile then turned to the third man. "Brave Elk, I sure wish you'd have been following me on that day!" she laughed. Her friend affirmed with a nod.

Golden Eyes turned to her betrothed. "*Woniya Mato*, I do have one request," she said softly, returning her attention to his obsidian eyes.

"*Tos*, my Golden Bird?" he paused suspiciously. "I have already said that you cannot come with me to war."

"I know," she responded, looking down. "There is a woman. Her name is Bright Sky. She leads among the Crow. She has been very kind and has protected me. Please have mercy on her, even if it means a quick death. She is an honorable woman. Do this for me," she implored.

"If she protected the *winyan* of *Woniya Mato*, Oglala chief of war, against my *toka*, the Crow, she will be honored!" he cried.

While their powerful leader reunited with his love, Yellow Feather and Wonder Worker dragged the bodies of the two fallen Crow into the river. They moved on quiet feet to help the gentle one of their chief cope with the ghastly scene. Both men loved the *winyan* and were very angry that the Crow could count coup on them through her. Their bodies longed for revenge! Noiselessly, they returned to Spirit Bear's side.

The fierce war chief turned to his friends. "Alert the others to what *Mazaska Zi Ista* has revealed about the Crow," he tersely ordered. "Guard each other's backs and return to me before dark with band leaders. I will decide what needs to be done with *Mazaska Zi Ista* to protect her while we slay our *toka*. We attack this night!"

The men whistled for their mounts and soundlessly disappeared into the foliage. Kaitlin barely heard their fleeting steps. When

Woniya Mato turned to face her, she held his total attention.

His handsome face perused hers. Spirit Bear's eyes engulfed hers with an intense blaze that had nothing to do with the heat of the day. "My body burns with a fever for you, *Mazaska Zi Ista*. I have been so worried about you! I feared for your life!" he admitted. "I worried for your tender heart if they abused you! I could not bear to live without you!" Spirit Bear's voice was hoarse with emotion. He would not let the other warriors see this tender side of him that he erroneously saw as weakness.

"*Mita wastelaka*, this was their plan!" she exclaimed. "They planned to use me to cause your downfall from power. Me!" she cried. "I cannot be the cause of your death!"

"You will not be," he promised.

His striking features softened with desire for his golden love. "It has been many suns since I have held your naked form in my arms," he teasingly spoke. "I do not think I can just hold you."

"I would be crushed if you could," she sparred back.

His sensuous mouth captured hers, much as an eagle would swoop down on a rabbit. It was precise and masterful, stealing the very breath from her lungs. Kaitlin's heat fluttered madly against the cage of her ribs.

His searing midnight eyes blazed with unspoken magic into her very soul. A handsome smile captured his artful lips when he broke contact.

"Never will *toka* take you from me again," he softly promised. His voice held unending power.

"*Woniya Mato*, love me," she requested softly into his bronze skin covering his masculine neck.

He groaned as he lay her down in the grass. He unwrapped the mat protecting her body from wandering eyes. His onyx stare feasted upon her luscious curves before his lips rejoined hers for an enticing dance with her tongue. Moments later, he wore only his breechcloth and a look of appeal.

His hands worked enchantments upon her heated skin. The golden allure of this *winyan* could not be resisted. Her enticements were too great for any man to withstand.

His wife-to-be purred from deep in her throat. Her gentle fingers danced upon his taunt chest. The blonde explored with carnal lust. His arms, shoulders, neck, and chest submitted to her circular motions. Her hand wandered over his flat, muscular belly. It responded by drawing tighter with her soft caress.

Kaitlin reached up and licked his trapezius muscles, nipping them as her breathing rate bespoke of her great excitement. Her arms worked around his superb body to fondle the hard power of his back. Spirit Bear groaned. He could barely take this teasing assault on his senses!

His mouth meshed hungrily on hers, and he whispered her name into her ears. His hot breath tickled her and made her squeal. Kaitlin's breath became ragged, and she continually whispered his name.

***

The war chief knew that danger could still lurk. It was possible that their passionate cries could have alerted an enemy to their location. As he held her closely after their ultimate joining, he listened for stealthy foot falls that only his ears could detect.

After the raging passion of their lovemaking, Kaitlin still found she could not keep her hands off his body. She touched his perfect face many times. Her fingers traced his full lips. Kaitlin's lips kissed his eyelids. The freed woman continued this welcomed torture until his even, white teeth laughed under her ardor.

Spirit Bear returned her caresses with vigor. He, too, had missed her with a passionate longing he didn't believe he was capable of. The great war chief loved his *winyan* more than anything in this world. His enemy had sought to destroy him through her, and they very nearly had.

Many, many times, Spirit Bear had imagined her death at their hands. In his worst nightmares, they'd held her up before his war party and sliced her delicate throat in front of him. Then they'd laugh when he'd collapse to the ground, handing them his very life.

Other times, the living legend worked himself up into a livid tantrum over them using her gorgeous body to appease their needs as they worked the most horrible revenge against him. He thanked *Wakantanka* every moment since he'd seen the evil devils about to rape his Golden Bird because The Great Spirit allowed him to prevent it. Spirit Bear thanked Him again now, for He had completely spared his *winyan* from all treachery!

The reunited couple made slow, passionate love. It was a mindless and blissful sharing that removed them from the warring world they would soon partake in. Both needed the physical and mental relief from the anguished they'd suffered when each believed the other had been lost to them forever.

Finally sated and loved thoroughly, the war chief looked down into the relaxed and happy face of his promised.

"Will you marry me when we return to our village?" he asked, knowing the answer before she spoke it.

"I will marry you here, now, if you wish," she replied.

The chief teased her back, "I was not sure when you disappeared before our joining. I thought you stood me up!"

"The most eligible bachelor in Indian history?" she squealed quietly. "I think not! I love you, *Woniya Mato*. More than life itself."

"And I, you, Golden One."

Spirit Bear looked down on her flushed body and said, "I better redress you before my body yearns for yours again. It would not be good to be caught in a compromising situation when my warriors return!"

Kaitlin quizzically cocked a brow at him and said, "Are you sure?" she murmured seductively. She captured his dark hair in her hands, fisted it, and brought his sensuous lips onto hers, crushing her mouth with force. She smiled in triumph when his lips responded to her teasing caresses.

"Perhaps they won't return for another hour," he huskily groaned.

CHAPTER TWENTY-THREE

Worry

By the time Kaitlin rinsed off and redressed, the garment had been dry for quite some time. Gone were her pale cheeks. They'd been flushed many times, and some of the pinkish color still tinged her face.

Woniya Mato prepared himself to ride. He rinsed off and donned his clothes. Then he reapplied the red and black markings to his face that bespoke and alerted his *toka* that it was he, Spirit Bear, who stood before them. He wanted no doubt as to who dealt the Bird of Death onto the Crow camp.

"I know you have used up much of your energy this day escaping with your daring swim, so I know that you will need to replenish your strength," he teased. Both knew how she'd depleted her liveliness.

Kaitlin smiled and took the pemmican he handed her. The warrior shared the meal time with her, eating together as they had time and again within the privacy of their own tipi.

"I know I keep saying it, *Woniya Mato*, but I just can't get over how much I missed you. I thought you were lost to me forever!" she did not cry, but tears glimmered in her golden orbs like jewels in the sun.

"Hush, *Mazaska Zi Ista*. Now is the time for happiness, not tears. We will not be ripped apart again. I am going to have *Wawakankan* watch over you while we wreak havoc on the lives that have done so to us."

"Come back to me, *Woniya Mato*! I cannot bear to live without you!" she whispered vehemently.

"Do not worry, *mita wastelaka*. The mighty bear has power once more!"

A short time later, Spirit Bear was in the midst of many band leaders. Sky Warrior, Yellow

Feather, Wonder Worker, Brave Elk, Gray Fox, Shooting Star, Beam of Light, and about twenty more men from the Bear Claw Clan were present. Many faces Kaitlin didn't know were also in attendance. They gathered around and shadowed the war chief as he laid out his plans for them to share with the other warriors under their leadership.

One pair of eyes searched for Kaitlin after the warriors sat to eat before the night raid.

"Chief Hawk Eyes! You are here!" she exclaimed.

"*Tos, Mazaska Zi Ista.* You do not think that I could allow our mutual *toka* claim such a prize beneath all of our noses without retaliation, do you?" he smiled warmly at the girl who'd pulled the heart strings within his chest.

"Chief Wise Owl also joins us," *Woniya Mato* announced. "You did not get to meet him. He is the chief of the Yankton Sioux."

The realization of who this proud man before her was came to her abruptly. Kaitlin looked into the kind eyes of the imposing man.

"Thank you for coming," she whispered, for his presence had stolen her breath.

"You are welcome, *Mazaska Zi Ista*. I am honored to meet the *winyan* who holds the heart of the mighty bear! I am deeply sorry that one I protected caused us all such harm."

Another man stepped forward. She'd only met this man once before, yet he was oddly familiar.

"I, too, am deeply shamed that my brother has caused such chaos within our camps."

She had a suspicion of who he was but had to ask anyway, "You must be… Eagle Talon?"

Kaitlin could see the resemblance more distinctively now. He was a little taller and more sleekly built than Sly Coyote, but they both were muscular and handsome. Eagle Talon had the same nose and lips as his brother. Sorrow etched miniscule lines around his eyes and mouth.

"*Tos*. I never suspected that my half-brother would cause such shame among our people. We accepted him into our hearts as Sioux."

"Eagle Talon, I must tell you that your brother never harmed me. Although what he did was horrible, he never treated me without honor or respect."

"Thank you for your kind words. It is a relief to know you were not wounded in any way." His eyes brushed against the bruise on her cheek.

"The ones who tried to hurt me are now dead," she stated as if in answer to her visible injury.

"You are truly worthy of *Woniya Mato*!" Eagle Talon's voice was choked with gratitude. The golden beauty honored him when she let him know she had not been defiled by one of his blood. Although he had come to seek revenge, Eagle Talon loved his brother. Still, he could not allow him to commit this disloyalty and debauchery upon his integrity without payment for it.

"I know you all would not harm the women and children of the camp," Kaitlin began, "so I disclose to you that they are not within the boundary of the village. They are safely tucked away in a cave to the northeast."

"There is a woman inside the village who deserves honor above all others," rang the authoritative voice of the war chief. He stood tall and proud as all eyes settled on him. Spirit Bear was a man of distinction in an area full of superior beings.

"She is a leader who answers to Bright Sky. She protected *Mazaska Zi Ista* against harm and sheltered her. She is to be treated with honor and respect!" he cried. He repeated the last sentence succinctly, noticeably stressing it so that all would know his wishes.

"Also," he paused," before we ride, I want the man, *Sunmanitu Wacitusni* to be left for me. I do not want any to kill him unless it is to save a life. Capture him. *Woniya Mato* has spoken!" his masculine form eluded power and dominance as he spoke with a noble air.

Voices echoed agreement within the gathering. Many were eager to get their hands upon the sly coyote, but he would be dealt with by *Woniya Mato* alone

Spirit Bear approached Wonder Worker. He did so discreetly, for he wished to give tribute to his closest friend.

"*Wawakankan*, will you honor me by protecting *Mazaska Zi Ista*? I cannot allow my heart to wander freely in the domain of our *toka*."

Wonder Worker had expected his friend to ask him for such high praise. "*Tos,* I am pleased you asked me."

"If you will mount up, take *Mazaska Zi Ista* to the spot where we last camped. We warriors will return upon the mark of the new day"

"*Tos*, my chief. You will know where to find us."

"Watch yourself," Spirit Bear needlessly advised. "She is now in your capable hands."

Wawakankan mounted his mahogany-colored mare marked with splashes of white and black on her rump. Before *Woniya Mato* handed Golden Eyes up to him, the chief savored the feel of her weight pressed against his vibrant body. He looked into her shining eyes and whispered words of love for her ears alone. Their lips met in a lingering embrace.

None would tease the living legend for his show of affection to his chosen one. He'd handled the loss of power through the coup well. Not many could handle the abduction of their loved one just before their joining day and maintain a cool head in a game of war!

Kaitlin looked back and saw the proud Sioux man leap astride his large tri-colored stallion. His noble silhouette marked him as he sat with warrior's grace upon the great steed. His eyes never left hers until they rode out of sight.

The betrothed woman knew to be quiet for the three-hour ride back to the camp where the men had stayed the night before. She rode behind the stolid frame of *Wawakankan*. Kaitlin tried to hang onto the horse without touching him, but with her strength still not up to par, she was not able. She lightly held on to his waist. By the end of the ride, she had slouched against his warming support.

Wonder Worker dismounted and helped her from the back of his animal. She unrolled their sleeping mats and lay upon hers. She was so tired, but how could she sleep when the man she loved could be fighting for his life?

Wawakankan watched as *Mazaska Zi Ista* rolled and sighed many times into the night. She did not seem like idle conversation was on her mind. Perhaps he should give it a try to distract her. A *winyan's* mind was not like a man's when it came to war.

Wonder Worker hadn't spoken because he'd wanted to maintain the silent air of safety until the warriors were engaged in battle. Now, however, the shaman felt the danger had passed. He'd keep his ears open for the slightest vibration on the ground.

"Do not worry over your chief, *Mazaska Zi Ista*. He is the greatest man to walk on earth."

"I know, *Wawakankan*. It is just that we were only just reunited, and he is taken from my side so soon," she nearly wailed.

"It is necessary, *Mazaska Zi Ista*. To strike against *Woniya Mato* is a deadly mistake. His reputation is well-known. He is a fair and honest man, but he is lethal if you are *toka*. The Crow have earned his wrath."

"I know what you say is true, *Wawakankan*, but I do not have to like it," the golden one replied in misery.

"Your friends are worried over your safety," Wonder Worker said to change the subject. "You should have seen how they wounded *Woniya Mato's* pride!" he chuckled softly. "I believe he was glad to escape their harping voices."

Kaitlin's eyes immediately brightened with a happier light. "Oh, I cannot wait to see them! How is *Skeca Ecaca*? Your mother, *Wawat'ecaka*? I will be so happy to hug them all! *Unjinjintka Can Koica*! *Haspa Nableca*!" she sat up in excitement.

"I think it is they who will be happy to see you!" the medicine man said with a smile on his full lips. "They will break you into two pieces with all of their hugs!" he claimed.

"I shall welcome all the hugs I can get! Oh, *Wawakankan*, it was awful," she admitted.

"Being a slave is never fun, but to be one and know they are planning to set up a trap to lure your love to his death is the greatest misery of all!"

"They will not lure our war chief to his death."

"I know, *Wawakankan*, but at first, I feared this trick of theirs. I could not live if I was the cause of *Woniya Mato's* death!" she vowed.

"*Sunmanitu Wacitusni* is to blame for everything," he consoled her. "You have no share in what happened."

"I wish I could say that was true," she moaned. "He tricked me into leaving with him."

"How?" Wonder Worker's deep voice asked.

"When my love rode after the Crow, *Sunmanitu Wacitusni* came to me and told me that *Woniya Mato* was dying from a possibly fatal injury and that he was sent to fetch me. I just blindly followed him when something whispered to me not to trust him. But I didn't listen!" new tears of guilt leaked from her eyes.

"Anyone could have fallen for his ruse, *Mazaska Zi Ista*. Do not blame yourself so harshly."

"*Tos*, but when I stopped panicking, I realized he would have had *you* with him," she whispered.

"Answer me this," *Wawakankan's* voice consoled. "Do you think if you hadn't come with him, he would have allowed you to walk away? Do you think *Sunmanitu Wacitusni* would have watched all his deceitful plans go awry? You would not have been able to leave his evil grasp, Golden Eyes. *Wakantanka* protected you from his harm and treacherous acts that night. He may have harmed you if you hadn't been tricked."

Seeing the truth of his words, Kaitlin felt a tiny grip of guilt lift from her heart. It had plagued her daily since her enlightenment to Sly Coyote's plans. "Thank you, my *kola*," she said and smiled softly at him.

Now that the shaman had the interest of Playful Otter, Wonder Worker was better able to resist Kaitlin's charms, but her smiles designed just for him could still make his heart flip in his chest.

"Rest now, *Mazaska Zi Ista*. I will watch over you."

After another restless hour or two, the fatigue in Kaitlin's body usurped her power to remain awake. She slept more restfully than she had in some time. In her dreams, Kaitlin was nestled in the fearsome arms of the Oglala war chief.

CHAPTER TWENTY-FOUR

To Meet Again

The groups of warriors riding against the Crow were glad that *Mazaska Zi Ista* had managed to dupe the *toka* while they were preparing for their arrival. If it hadn't been for the betrothed of the war chief, they could have ridden into a trap.

Conquest was impossible. *Woniya Mato* would never admit defeat while he lived and breathed. Nevertheless, it would have set them back. The injuries suffered and death toll would have been more heavily on the Sioux side if it hadn't been for the Golden One's timely warning.

Woniya Mato's group rode directly between the two bands of Crow warriors waiting in ambush. His other war parties were circling around. On their way to the center of the Crow village, they would silently take out any Crow parties encountered.

Spirit Bear wanted to be one of the first on the scene. He couldn't wait to meet Sly Coyote once more, face to face. His anger knew no bounds when he'd faced the prospect of living life without the pride and joy the other had stolen from him. Although *Sunmanitu Wacitusni* would pay as he faced death, *Woniya Mato* didn't intend to fully torture him. His only mercy would be that he did not force Kaitlin to succumb to his passions. Still, the wild dog's desire for his betrothed angered the chief. A man could sense when another sniffed with interest around his *winyan*.

The only reason *Mazaska Zi Ista* was not forced to lie with *Sunmanitu Wacitusni* upon his mats was because of the protection of *Wakantanka*. The Great Spirit protected her in many ways until Spirit Bear could come to possess her once more. Slowly and silently, the Oglala weaved their way into the heart of Crow country.

A Crow sentry suddenly gave warning. The approach of the Sioux was no longer unknown to their *toka*. A drum began to sound.

Woniya Mato's eyes gleamed in welcome. His body yearned to unleash his superior power onto these men who'd stolen happiness from his heart for a time. They would pay! He readied his weapons as an opponent jumped out at him.

Woniya Mato jumped from his stallion's back and slashed a vicious blow to his adversary. His war knife barely had time for the enemy's blood to splash on its blade before he whirled to slice another man's neck as he hurdled out from the brush. Three arrows from his fellow warriors pierced another Crow's body, and he fell from the tree above. Then the Oglala fanned out. To stay too closely grouped was to welcome death. *Woniya Mato* became one with the trees. His superior hearing detected the silent feet of his foes.

With covertness, the war chief crept five hundred feet to where a small group of *toka* waited. When he leapt, he noted the surprise on the warriors' faces. He stabbed the first man while simultaneously sinking his tomahawk into the head of another. Holding the body of the man he just stabbed in front of him like a shield, he swiftly whirled as four arrows vibrated into the dead man's back. Spirit Bear threw down the body and issued a war cry that made those who heard tremble in fear. The bear had been roused!

He fired four arrows in quick succession. Three of four warriors fell. One man had wisely ducked behind a stump. Spirit Bear listened for his hasty retreat. He stalked forward, slaying his opponents as he met them. No matter how many attempted to slay him, all met with death. He was the spirit he was reputed to be, for none could touch him.

Suddenly, the woods came alive with Crow. *Woniya Mato*'s predatory sense heard his enemies' feet attempt to enclose him.

The Crow attempts to surround me, he thought, nearly amused. *They try to outwit the bear? I think not!*

Spirit Bear crawled through the tight underbrush and leaped onto a fallen tree. It gave him a better vantage point. His arrows became missiles of death. Before the others realized it, five men were left of a party of eighteen.

= = =

The Crow warriors could not seem to get in range to shoot their shafts before *Woniya Mato*'s already filled their bodies. What power was this? How did he get such distance from his arrows? Was he really blessed by *Wakantanka*?

When the five Crow finally reached the place where the spirit of the bear had just been, no trace of the man was evidenced. Even the bark on the tree where he'd stood barely showed his weight. Only the arrows that bore the mark of the Oglala war chief verified that he truly was a man.

Maybe he actually was a vengeful spirit! The Crow men felt a wave of terror before their bodies crumpled to the ground…

***

Sunmanitu Wacitusni found himself surrounded by a party of Sioux men of war. Two other Crow were alive other than himself in the village. Bloody Knife and Bright Sky stood beside him in the middle of smiling enemy warriors. Bloody Knife was still armed, but the war party held them at bay.

Midnight Star had been slain as he unnecessarily protected Bright Sky from capture. He didn't know that the Oglala war chief had ordered her unharmed. Sky Warrior had claimed his life with daunting grace.

When Sly Coyote or Bloody Knife tried to encourage a fight for his life so that he could die with honor, the men would only grin wider and prick him with the sharp tips of the crimson-stained lances until they were forced back into the center of the circle. They were waiting; *Sunmanitu Wacitusni* knew what fate awaited him.

"He comes for you," Bloody Knife said needlessly.

"Woniya Mato?"

"Who else?"

Sly Coyote turned to face his leader. "I think he comes for both of us," he said.

An ominous voice thundered, "You both are correct!   I have ordered you both spared from easy death. You have earned my personal vengeance."

The circle of Oglala surrounding the Crow parted as *Woniya Mato* walked into the core with arrogant dominance. He stood before them. His lethal body shone like copper in the light cast from the moon. He eerily resembled a spirit come to strike doom upon those who stood in his path.

"We meet at last, Bloody Knife," Spirit Bear acknowledged his foe in accented Crow. Then he turned to the man he truly wished to see. "and we meet again, *Sunmanitu Wacitusni*. I do not think these are the conditions you envisioned seeing me under, but you have called for me, and I have answered."

The two Crow only met the war chief's stare as the domineering man addressed them. Both felt the power of his aura, and they inwardly admitted his victory. They knew they would not die easily.

Two other Sioux stepped forward to address Sly Coyote as well.

"Brother! How could you betray us like this?" Eagle Talon's voice barely masked his deep wound over his sibling's treachery.

"I have many reasons. None have to do with you, Eagle Talon."

"Tell us your reasons," *Woniya Mato* commanded. "I, too, am curious to know of these 'many reasons'."

"First and foremost, you have stolen my rank and honor from me," he revealed passionately to Spirit Bear, his eyes flashing with the remembered past.

"I do not recall this event," stated the war chief.

"Do you remember your very first war coup?" Sly Coyote asked, his voice deep with pain.

"The one where you were just a boy and were taken to rejoin your mother?"

"Yes."

"How did this remove your honor and status?"

"You killed my father! Night Hawk had much honor in my tribe. I never told anyone that your mighty deed, this coup celebrated and retold for years, was the death of my own father!" he revealed as his voice filled with anguish.

Understanding lit in the blackness of Spirit Bear's eyes.

"Our mother never stated the warrior's name who planted his seed within her," Eagle Talon stated. "You yourself never offered this knowledge."

"Mother hated being a captive. It is a great dishonor for a woman to be at the mercy of an enemy. Father cared for her, but she never returned his feelings. She would not name him for it renewed shame in her heart."

"But she always treated you with honor!" Eagle Talon defended.

"Yes. But I was not her favored son."

Chief Wise Owl said, "We respected you within our tribe, *Sunmanitu Wacitusni*. You earned your right as a great warrior and provider! Why did you do this thing when we loved you as our own?" His voice also reflected his betrayal.

"You, my chief, did honor me," Sly Coyote admitted. "But many others did not. They spied upon me at every turn. They spoke behind my back. They played cruel games upon me. They did not back me in raids; Many did not trust my Crow blood," he paused. "This planted the seed for growth. If I could not earn my honor in the place I lived, I would seek it elsewhere.

"My brother, Black Bird, welcomed me into the ranks of the Crow. The leaders also honored me as the son of Night Hawk. I knew respect as it has never been given to me before."

The chief's face revealed that although he did not agree, he understood. However, it didn't lessen the pain of treachery in his heart.

Sunmanitu Wacitusni continued, "With this high honor, I also wanted to seek an extraordinary coup as well as revenge of the man who'd taken my life from me." He was silent for a moment. "That is why I took your promised from your side. I had hoped to slay you for the pain you have caused me," he stated, holding the weighty stare of the powerful chief.

"And what was your plan for *Mazaska Zi Ista*?" The fearsome man's voice deepened only just perceptibly. Spirit Bear suspected he knew Sly Coyote's reason and struggled to keep the possessive anger from his tone.

"Once you were out of the way, I planned to replace you in her heart and on my mat," he answered honestly.

A silent curtain fell upon the gathering. *Woniya Mato*'s muscles were clenched in rigid rage, but he said with control, "Instead, you will die."

CHAPTER TWENTY-FIVE

War Chiefs

The Oglala leader turned to face the other war chief. "But first, I challenge you, Bloody Knife. You will personally be an example of what happens to war chiefs that plot to destroy me!"

The crowd surged forward. They pinned Sly Coyote and forced him to the side. He found himself standing beside Bright Sky. She'd remained silent through the recent admissions.

The two powerful war chiefs stripped until they were only dressed from their waists down. A wide circle encompassed the two men, but there was plenty of room for both surviving Crow to watch the events unfurl.

"You honor me with a fight to the death?" Bloody Knife asked in surprise. He thought he would find death through hours of torture.

"*Tos.* It will be the last honor you face on this earth. I want no questions as to how or why you met your defeat. I want the Crow Nation to realize who dealt it to you, as well."

The long blade gleamed wickedly from *Woniya Mato's* hand. The moon shone equally as brightly on the blade tossed to the Crow war chief. He picked it up and tested its weight in his hands.

The two honed warriors circled each other warily. Their eyes missed nothing as each studied the panther-like grace of the other. *Woniya Mato* allowed the enemy to initiate the battle.

Closer and closer padded the Crow. The mighty bear was not afraid. The enemy surged forward and sliced with his blade. He missed the man but nicked his buckskin. *Woniya Mato* met the challenge. He swooped down and cut a shallow slice from the side of Bloody Knife's arm.

The Crow's surprise was evident. He didn't expect Spirit Bear to draw first blood. He charged to sink in his knife; it had earned him his namesake. Before he died, Bloody Knife planned to plaster his knife with the life force of the great man before him.

The surge was parried and both men regrouped to circle the other once again.

"You are a worthy opponent," said the Crow war chief begrudgingly.

Woniya Mato only nodded his acceptance of the praise. At this gesture, the other once again struck forward with his blade. At the same time, he swiped his foot to trip his foe. Spirit Bear jumped and drove his dagger across in front of him, marking his enemy once again. This time the horizontal mark dripped crimson from his chest.

"You are quick!" the Crow praised. "But you will feel my blade."

"Not as deeply as you will feel mine," Spirit Bear responded.

This time, the Oglala man lunged. Bloody Knife jumped back, but *Woniya Mato* expected this move and leaped forward again at the same moment. His blade sunk into the top part of Bloody Knife's chest near his shoulder. It was not a death stab, but one that would slow him. The man's only auditory acknowledgement of the deed was a sharp intake of breath.

Spirit Bear backed off to let the other recuperate. He wanted to savor this victory. He would work out his anger towards those who dared to strike at his heart. The defeat of his *toka* would purify his soul.

***

Bloody Knife's dominant hand had not been injured. He would still be able to strike back at his foe. However, a different tactic would be required. So far, the Oglala man had parried and blocked his every attempt. He must touch the bear and make it bleed to prove it could die.

Perhaps if the pride of the Sioux war chief was great enough, he would brazenly invite Sly Coyote to a challenge after him. If Bloody Knife could tire the other man and possibly give him injury, the Crow could still prevail by wiping away the predominant reign of the current master leader through his death. *Sunmanitu Wacitusni* would, no doubt, join *Woniya Mato* with his walk with *Wakantanka*, but it would be a Crow victory, nonetheless.

The other man was obviously giving him time to recover from his injury. Perhaps if he feigned his recovery just a little longer…

***

Woniya Mato could tell his strikes had surprised his foe, but he was ready for his charge at any point. He'd battled enough *toka* to guess many of their tactics. He was also man enough to realize it was a very real fight to the death: anything goes. Spirit Bear had seen many men nearly be victorious in a one-on-one challenge and fall at the last moment.

He walked on the balls of his feet, ready to either pounce or jump defensively. His reactions were agile and quick. Spirit Bear was a supreme athlete and warrior. His defeat would be nearly impossible, but there was always that chance.

With a distracting cry, Bloody Knife thrust his knife forward. He contrived a downward blade motion, then dove. His body slammed on the earth, and he slid on the ground while he sliced up. *Woniya Mato* jumped back and missed the deadly blow, but the blade caught and cut his left calf muscle. He purposefully fell on his opponent's knife hand, knocking the blade free. Quickly, he stabbed this opponent in the back with his own edge.

= = =

The Crow chief grunted and rolled away. His
knife gleamed on the ground near Spirit Bear's
feet. *Woniya Mato* smiled at his foe and tossed
his weapon back to him. Bloody Knife nearly
did not catch the blade. He was moving slower,
but he still had much stamina and power. He
would once again trick the other into believing
he was tiring more quickly than was true.

They circled again, much more slowly and
warily than at the onslaught. *Woniya Mato*
didn't limp from his cut, but Bloody Knife knew
which leg was injured. He would again target
his weak side for a blow. Yet, the Oglala man
had his own bag of tricks.

***

Bloody Knife faked a dive right but went left,
kicking at Spirit Bear's leg. He made contact.
When they broke apart, Spirit Bear reached
down to feel his injured leg. His eyes only left
the other's for a second. When *Woniya Mato*

looked down, at that instant, the Crow man charged.

Expecting this reaction from his ploy, *Woniya Mato* laughed as he easily jumped aside with lithe precision. He punched the other's side with his pass. His foe made an "oof" noise, but whirled quickly and left a narrow cut on Spirit Bear's forearm.

The next charge came almost immediately! Bloody Knife lunged, and it appeared that he'd knocked Spirit Bear off balance, for he fell backward. The enemy was on top of him in an instant. The Sioux men collectively drew in shocked breaths until *Woniya Mato* threw the dead man's body from off the top of him.

"Did you doubt me, my *kolas*?" his voice was filled with amusement.

War cries went up in the air, and they surrounded their idol. They chanted his name over and over. Then they reformed the circle.

"Next?" taunted Spirit Bear.

CHAPTER TWENTY-SIX

The Final Encounter

"I don't plan to be," Sly Coyote's deep voice steadily retorted.

"No one plans to die, but I promise, you will. You sealed your fate when you took what was mine!"

"But what of what was mine?" cried the younger man.

"When I took from you, my intentions were honorable. Yours were not. For that, you pay with your life. You are very fortunate that you did not harm her in any way. This is the reason you are honored enough to die a man. "

The proclaimed Crow didn't feel honored, but he realized that he could've had many tortures inflicted upon him. Sly Coyote nodded once toward the chief to acknowledge his mercy. Still, he couldn't miss a chance to provoke him.

"Kiss *Mazaska Zi Ista* for me," the warrior said in derision, "when you find her," he paused then added, "Her lips *are* like honey!"

Woniya Mato's lips tightened just a minuscule amount with the thought that his foe had the audacity to press his lips to his woman's… though the chief didn't want his foe to know his remark was upsetting.

"I already have. I greeted her as only I can," returned the Oglala warrior, refusing to be needled. "She was *very* happy to see me!"

It was Sly Coyote who became angered. He wanted Golden Eyes, and now she was lost to him forever. Somehow, the Crow man would make the man before him pay! "So you have already met up with her?" he said in incredulous surprise.

"*Tos*, many times," said the powerful man with a smug smile. His onyx eyes glittered malevolently.

The snickering behind them made *Sunmanitu Wacitusni* lose his temper. He charged in anger. It was his first mistake.

Woniya Mato did not make child's play with the dog before him. He brutally stabbed the other in the thigh. It wouldn't kill him, but he would feel agony with every step.

Sly Coyote hissed in pain but did not voice an oath.

"That is for stealing *Mazaska Zi Ista* from me," Spirit Bear stated. He stood there, hands down in relaxed confidence.

"You are too arrogant, *Woniya Mato*."

"Perhaps you'd like to take me down a notch?" the chief countered a taunt.

"Perhaps I will!" he parried.

Woniya Mato smiled in invitation. His eyes sparkled with the challenge. The leader held up his hand, palm facing his chest and motioned for him to come.

Sly Coyote knew he couldn't face a master warrior with a hot head. He had to be quick but also use his head. He cautiously circled the leader. As he did, the Crow man tested his injury so he could judge how he could respond accordingly.

Suddenly, the war chief leaped forward and sliced the hamstring in the injured leg. *Sunmanitu Wacitusni* hissed an oath. His leg definitely wasn't going to respond like normal.

"That is for kissing my *winyan!*" Spirit Bear informed.

Sly Coyote charged. He drove his knife forward, but Spirit Bear caught his hand before he could make contact. The chief slashed at his opponent, but luckily, *Sunmanitu Wacitusni* jumped back and avoided the damage. Wrenching his hand free, he backed up to recoup. He really just wanted to wipe the taunting smile from the Oglala's face!

The two men met in the center of the circle. Each grasped the other's free hand. Blades cut at the opponent, but neither would release the other. In this deadly game, all deep wounds

were parried. Still, the crowd held its breath.
Blood dripped and skin sliced. It was difficult
for the observers to know where the next nick
would come from.

Finally, Sly Coyote shoved Spirit Bear back, his
chest heaving with the effort. Both men had
been touched by the blade of the other, but no
real harm had been done. Spirit Bear did not let
his adversary rest. He leaped forward to injure,
but *Sunmanitu Wacitusni* jumped to the side
while slashing outwardly. Spirit Bear countered
with a quick swipe toward him that met with his
ribs. The cut gleamed deeply.

"Let us finish this, *Woniya Mato*!" the Crow
man cried.

Spirit Bear threw down his knife. His
supporters behind him seemed to hold their
breath. They wondered about this new tactic!
They had tremendous faith in their war chief,
but to throw down a weapon in the face of a
worthy adversary? Only the very confident
would risk this!

With a victorious smile, *Sunmanitu Wacitusni*
pranced forward, all injuries momentarily

forgotten. "You shouldn't have done that, *Woniya Mato*," he growled.

The war chief's sardonic smile only deepened. Sly Coyote lunged and cut toward the face and neck of his foe. Spirit Bear, surprisingly, caught his knife hand and delivered a brutal uppercut to his stomach. Then he let the man with his knife fall back. His smile broadened to show his white teeth.

The chief's grin made Sly Coyote feel as if he were merely playing a game. It infuriated him!

"You want me, boy, come and get me!" Spirit Bear continued to challenge and harass his enemy with his words.

A frustrated scream of rage tore from *Sunmanitu Wacitusni* as he raced toward the man he'd hated for years. Once more, his knife met with empty air, and he found himself pounded several more times by the other's fists. The final kick to his stomach had him doubled over for a moment.

Woniya Mato stood proudly, waiting on his enemy to recover. His stance continued to be relaxed yet ready. His feet were shoulder-width apart and his muscles rippled with power.

"Are we finished yet?" he asked softly.

"NO!" the other bellowed hoarsely.

Sly Coyote did not charge madly again. He knew the war chief was needling him until he surged forward, blind with rage. He could never defeat the Oglala man unless he used his brain. The honed battle skills and hand combat techniques of the war chief were far superior to his own, but when Spirit Bear threw down his knife, he'd evened the odds.

This time, when *Sunmanitu Wacitusni* approached his opponent, he stalked forward as a hunter. He eased his mind and his muscles and let them control his actions rather than his anger.

Woniya Mato noticed a change in his foe, but still didn't believe he'd made such a drastic transformation. Yet, the other seemed much more in control. As he advanced this time, it was a steady hunt, not a blind attack.

When *Sunmanitu Wacitusni* assailed him, Spirit Bear's eyes widened in astonishment when he found the knife held by the smaller, less experienced man had pierced his flesh. He'd managed to catch the knife hand as the blade was being driven about an inch and a half into his dermis. *Woniya Mato* watched as he removed the offending blade from high on his upper pec by guiding the other's hand and forcing it back. It wasn't a serious injury, but it would draw his attention when he moved for a week or two. It was also one he hadn't been as prepared for. The war chief chided himself.

"That was for my father, Night Hawk!" His words echoed the leader's earlier words.

Sunmanitu Wacitusni reluctantly retreated. It was his turn to smile into the temporarily surprised face of the Oglala warrior. He began to prowl forward again, his earlier success bringing new confidence into his step. *Woniya Mato's* stoic mask once more erased his facial expressions of emotion.

"Do you want your knife back now, chief?" Sly Coyote sneered. He found he could parley as easily as his enemy.

"*Hiya*. I do not need it to kill my *toka*. You had your one chance. You should have dealt the death strike. Your blow did not go deep enough to halt my wrath. I will not play with you further. You will die very soon, *Sunmanitu Wacitusni*."

The way the powerful man spoke sent chills of fear racing down his spine. Still, Sly Coyote *had* managed to sink his knife into the other's flesh. It was more than he'd anticipated! The blade hadn't sunk in as deeply as he'd liked, for the bigger man had halted its downward descent, but perhaps he'd taken some of the daunting confidence from the indomitable *Woniya Mato*!

Again, he approached Spirit Bear to strike. He was wary, for he knew the other had changed from game-minded to serious-minded. If he took one wrong step, it could prove to be fatal, even from the unarmed man!

Sly Coyote noted how *Woniya Mato* stood. His stance was easy as he waited on the Crow man to make his move. His hands twitched slightly as they anticipated his actions. It was very intimidating to attack this powerful adversary even though he possessed no weapon except his cunning and experience! The man of war's eyes were narrowed as they assessed him. They mocked him as the moon shone in their black depths and glittered danger!

Sly Coyote moved as close as possible to the Oglala man. Then, with all the power he possessed, he attacked. He held the blade with both hands, aiming for the chief's heart. He intended to rip it out and eat it to prove his prowess!

Without quite knowing how it happened, *Woniya Mato* was at his back, his arm wrapped tightly around his throat. His windpipe was slowly being crushed under the pressure. *Sunmanitu Wacitusni* wildly stabbed back in the direction of his foe, but somehow his blade missed each time.

A disdainful voice taunted in his ear, "Know that you have lost all while I have won, *Sunmanitu Wacitusni*. You will never sleep with *mita wastelaka, Mazaska Zi Ista*! You could have been my *kola*, but you chose *toka*. Know, also, you could have defeated me had you taken *Mazaska Zi Ista's* life from me."

Sly Coyote gasped, for his effort to talk was severely impaired, but he managed to croak, "No matter what, *Woniya Mato*, I could never defeat you by killing your *wastelaka*. To kill *Mazaska Zi Ista* would be to kill myself. I know it is difficult to believe, but I love her." With that thought, his lights dimmed, and he knew no more.

Although the fighting was over, and the Oglala was victorious, *Woniya Mato* felt winning was bittersweet. He'd known it would come down to a battle between the leading men and himself, for he had a reputation and tribe to protect, but he never took life lightly. Both men slain in hand combat had begrudgingly earned his respect.

Woniya Mato slowly approached the remaining Crow, the *winyan* leader. She trembled in fear but met his eyes with strength that surprised him.

"Is it my turn next, *Woniya Mato*?" she huskily tried to jest.

To her bewilderment, the mightiest warrior of all time knelt down on one knee before her. He held out his hand to her, so she placed hers in his grasp.

"You are Bright Sky, are you not?" he asked, bestowing an honor she couldn't imagine upon her.

"Yes," she answered his accented Crow.

"I owe you much."

Her eyes were wide with wonder at his words.

He continued, "You honor me by taking *Mazaska Zi Ista* under your wing. You protected her and gave her friendship in a village of enemies. I am in your debt."

Bright Sky didn't know quite how to react. She stood quietly in front of him.

The chief was not quite finished. "*Mazaska Zi Ista* is my heart; she is my life. Because you protected her, I grant you your life back. Your people will need you to guide them in this time of great loss. We spared no one that stood against us. You have lost many warriors and hunters on this night. I am sorry for your loss, but I have my own people to think of."

"I am greatly honored, *Woniya Mato*," she said, accepting his terms. "You are truly a wise leader. You are a great man to show mercy and respect. I know now why you have reigned so long and yet you are still so young. You are, indeed, an impressive man!" Bright Sky took a shaky breath and persisted, "I can see why you also own *Mazaska Zi Ista's* heart. I thank you for your great spirit and understanding."

Woniya Mato stood once more, towering over the female Crow leader.

"I ask a few things from you before I allow you to return to your people, Bright Sky," Spirit Bear's masculine voice added.

She angled her head up to look into his understanding features. "Yes?"

"I want your people to know who killed Bloody Knife and *Sunmanitu Wacitusni* and why. I want it announced that those who plan to count coup on me will have his coup chanted with his death rites. Those who plan treachery against me and the Sioux will have to answer to me personally!" He took a breath.

"I also wish my mercy to you to be known. You
are a leader who did not partake in this sordid
affair, so you were spared. I am not a monster,
nor do I take another's life shallowly without
reason. I mourn those who fall by my hand, for
I know they were loved as father, brother, and
son by my foes."

He turned to gather his men and leave her to
grieve and give her people strength. With a
final thought, he turned back to her.

"I normally would not do this, but you have
proven to *Mazaska Zi Ista* that you are *kola*, so I
will also empower you with my trust. In about a
week, I plan to marry her. If you would like to
come to the ceremony, I grant you passage.
None will harm you. Several of my active
warriors are present here tonight and have seen
who you are. They will alert others to your
identity.

"I understand that this is not a time for you and
your people to celebrate. We, too, have suffered
casualties of war, but my offer stands should
you wish to honor us with your presence. I will
not allow for any to accompany you with
deception on their minds. I will slay them on

the spot should I suspect them of foul play. I prefer only you, but I know it is unwise for even a woman warrior to travel alone."

Bright Sky nearly staggered under the weight of his trust that he extended to her. He was here on war purposes! She'd just watched him slay two superior warriors, and now he invited her to his wedding? It was too much!

Chapter Twenty-Seven

Medicine Man

"I will think on this invitation, *Woniya Mato*," she said softly. "I can promise nothing. I am greatly honored. If it is possible, I may come, but my people will go through much at your hands. I do not think it would be a welcomed decision for me to attend your wedding."

"I understand. I did not expect you to take me up on the invitation, but I wished you to know the depth of my gratitude to you and your protection of my heart. You are wise. I accept your decision to either stay or come. Good luck to you. May *Wakantanka* bless you and the lives of those you touch."

"Farewell, *Woniya Mato*. I am glad to have met you although I cannot say I favor the circumstances."

"Goodbye, Bright Sky."

The men whistled for their obedient steeds, mounted, and disappeared into the night. There was much rejoicing over the victory of the battle, the rescue without injury to *Mazaska Zi Ista*, and the minimal casualties. Approximately eighteen men had received moderate to severe injuries, but only a handful were slain.

Sky Warrior and a group of about twenty men were overseeing the travois-building to bring back the bodies. The Oglala had three casualties. The other three braves killed were Yankton. No Cheyenne walked the spirit trail.

The men's victory cries reverberated through the night as they rode for their former camp site. The men raved over the two-individual hand-combats performed by the Oglala war chief. Spirit Bear had given his men heart and stamina to prevail over any tragedy. He'd also given them the will and endurance to concur any threat.

About thirty minutes before they reached camp, *Woniya Mato* stopped. He turned to his men.

"We have many numbers among us tonight. We have been victorious!"

The men cheered in support of his words.

"I have my promised to bring home. She cannot travel as we men can. We are warriors with hardened bodies. She is a woman with a soft body."

The men began snickering among themselves at the way this fearsome warrior's deadly eyes softened and weakened at the mere thought of his love. They were glad that their mighty war chief could possess both kind heart and lethal accuracy. They teased him out of love.

"Do I hear men mocking me?" Spirit Bear raised his brow in challenge. "I am not so tired nor weak that I cannot prove my prowess among my own!"

The result was louder, raucous laughter. The men brazenly taunted the man they respected above all others.

"We see how your eyes light up at the mere mention of your *winyan*!" they teased. "We know the real reason you want us to ride ahead!"

Spirit Bear leaned back with the force of his laughter. "So you know what I was going to suggest," he said heartily. "With so many of us," he said looking at the numerous men that stretched for many horses beyond him, "I thought it would be less overwhelming if we did not all ride as one group." He smiled as they still ribbed him.

"Aw, come on, chief. Just tell us you want to start the honeymoon early!"

"Men, my *winyan's* modesty is renowned. She is a wild cat when she thinks other could learn of our… deeds," his smile widened. "But my point is that many of you will want to return quickly to your families. I plan to have a joining ceremony the same time we celebrate our great victory. I want all of you there. Ride on to prepare yourselves and your travels. I know there are men from the Cheyenne tribe, the Yankton tribe, and a few Arapaho warriors among us. They may need a little more time for preparation. I say ride on and take the time you need. I have waited too long as it is to take my *winyan* as my mate.

"I will gradually make my trip homeward. I will wait to accompany the fallen men as is my role as war chief. Do not feel you have to wait for me. Go home, men! You have made me very proud. I am honored to have such a loyal and worthy following! We celebrate our success upon my return!"

The men yelled and shouted praise for quite a while before thundering toward their homelands. *Woniya Mato* watched them leave. He thanked *Wakantanka* and rode for his love.

Before he crushed his Golden One to him, he felt he should clean himself. He stopped to bathe at a cold-water stream. He did have quite a bit of blood covering him from his chest injury and from several lacerations he'd received from Bloody Knife and Sly Coyote. He also washed the last traces of the war paint from his body. Then lastly, he applied a medicinal salve to his deeper wounds.

Spirit Bear arrived at the camp just as *wi* sent glorious beams of light onto the earth. *Mazaska*

Zi Ista still slept wearily upon her mat. Placing his fingers to his lips so that his closest friend, *Wawakankan,* would not alert his *winyan* to his presence, Spirit Bear lay down beside her. He covered her face lightly with butterfly kisses. She sighed and smiled happily. When the Golden One realized he was no dream image, she squealed and hugged him tightly.

Immediately, Kaitlin shrieked in horror as she noticed the many cuts upon his body. Nothing could tarnish his masculine beauty, but just the knowledge of the danger he'd faced sent icy tremors shooting throughout her now-fragile system.

"Oh, *Woniya Mato*! I am so glad to see you are all right! I love you so much! I worried horribly over you! Are you okay?"

"*Tos,* Golden One. I have never been better. I am with you now."

Kaitlin would not take no for an answer. She made the domineering, unconquerable man go before *Wawakankan.* Spirit Bear felt like he was answering to his mother once more.

Sheepishly standing before the medicine man, he asked in a bemused voice, "*Wawakankan,* before we leave this day, will you treat my… injuries?"

As if he were a well-rehearsed actor, *Wawakankan* replied calmly, "*Tos,* my chief. I would be honored to. Give me a few minutes to fix the supplies. Then, at your convenience."

Snickering under his breath, Wonder Worker began preparing an antiseptic wash and poultice for the forcible treatment. He was sure there'd be others to treat, for the severely injured would be coming in directly with the arrival of the slain.

Kaitlin sat with her arms wrapped around her knees. She looked up into her love's eyes when he reclined by her on the sleeping mats. She had many questions swirling in her head; questions she was afraid to ask.

"You wonder what happened, Golden One?" his masculine voice inquired.

"*Tos, Woniya Mato,* but I fear to hear all the details."

"Then I will modify them for you. Any danger
to you no longer exists. The woman you asked
to spare has been granted her life. Bright Sky
has a great job before her. Many will be
grieving, for the war was not pleasant. The
Crow's fatalities were great. Some of the other
band's members escaped in the night and
returned to their home lands. Bright Sky has a
big responsibility placed upon her shoulders.
She will gather her people and help them recoup
their losses."

"Oh, *Woniya Mato*, thank you! You are, indeed,
a merciful man!

"Not all I encountered would agree with you,"
he said, his gorgeous mouth curving into a smile
that had an immediate and delightful effect on
her senses.

"*Tos*, but I am so glad you spared Bright Sky!"

"I wanted to honor her for her treatment of you.
I also wanted her to relay two things to her
people. She agreed to communicate to the Crow
that all *toka* who'd plotted against me were slain.
The message that any further schemers will
meet with the same fate will be spread. Not

only did I want her to portray me as an undefeatable adversary, but I want the Crow to know I am merciful. I am not a man filled with hate and vengeance on all of one race. I only seek revenge against those who have provoked me.”

“You are the best man I know,” Kaitlin soothed lovingly.

“I am not perfect, but I try to do the bidding of *Wakantanka*.”

“Oh, but you *are* perfect,” she whispered.

He smiled down at her, devastating her with his charm, “As long as you think so, *mita wastelaka*.”

“I am ready to treat your injuries, my chief,” came the teasing voice of *Wawakankan*.

“I am coming.”

Kaitlin watched as the medicine man wrapped the two deeper wounds on *Woniya Mato's* lithe body: his calf and his upper chest. He dressed the other lacerations with the cleansing wash under the instruction and watchful eye of *Mazaska Zi Ista*.

When they finished, the three ate a breakfast of pemmican while they waited for Sky Warrior and the others before heading homeward.

A short time after eating, Kaitlin experienced a wave of nausea. She stood then walked to the stream. After rinsing her face in the cold water, she felt a little better. She sat there for a little while, periodically cooling her face.

"Are you alright, *Mazaska Zi Ista*?" Spirit Bear asked, materializing beside her. He caused her to jump at his silent approach.

"I am fine. I just feel… refreshed if I rinse my face. It helps when I do not feel the greatest."

"You do not feel well?" he asked with concern lacing his voice.

"I am fine," she repeated. "It is just a sensitivity I've had since I drank the fermented berry juice of Bright Sky's. Remind me to never indulge in that again!"

"I have had that drink before," he reminisced.

"You have?" she asked in bewilderment.

Her confusion was greeted by laughter. "Not Bright Sky's concoction, to be sure. There is another who brews this in the Yankton tribe. It is a quite popular drink, but we have no one who is skilled with making the brew in our village."

"I would offer to make it; it seems simple enough, but I would need the recipe. I just will not drink it if it causes one to be ill for so long!"

"How long have you felt ill, *Mazaska Zi Ista*? From my experiences, the unpleasant effects should not last over a day or two."

"This is what Bright Sky said as well, but I have felt this way for a little over a week."

"Has your ailment passed, Golden One?"

"*Tos*, I think so."

"*Uwa yo*. Now I insist that *you* seek *Wawakankan's* consultation. A week is far too long for your feelings to be caused from the berry wine."

He led Kaitlin to her sleeping mat and then
called Wonder Worker to her side. He
explained what she'd divulged to him.

CHAPTER TWENTY-EIGHT

Raspberry Leaves

"So, for about a week, you've felt this strange illness, *Mazaska Zi Ista*?" the shaman asked.

"*Tos*, that seems to be about the right amount of time."

"How else have you been feeling that is different from normal?" he pressed, probing for more symptoms.

"I do not know what I can contribute to my sickness or what I can attribute to my stress at worrying over whether the Crow would succeed in killing *Woniya Mato*," she began.

"Tell us all, *Mazaska Zi Ista*. I will decide whether you have a strange sickness or if it is stress related," *Wawakankan* advised.

"I get tired a lot," she revealed. "It seems like I need to rest a lot more and I sleep a lot harder, but I'd traveled hard for suns," she said to justify her lethargy. "And I have been so depressed!"

"Go on," the medicine man encouraged.

"I have been moody, but I did not want *Sunmanitu Wacitusni* to pressure me. The villagers were not especially kind to me which was also stressful." A look from Wonder Worker had her adding, "I also do not feel well when I first rise from sleeping or when I try to eat. The feeling usually passes, especially if I have cold water to splash upon my skin."

"Anything else?" he inquired solicitously.

"This is strange, but I feel heavy. It's like I am filled with led. My arms and legs require great energy, at times, when I want to move."

"Hummm. Anything else?" he asked, a smile curving his full lips.

"What is so funny?" she asked, playfully punching him. "I do not feel well, and you smile?" she looked at *Woniya Mato* for support. Kaitlin saw he also closely watched this curious reaction from his friend.

"This next question may embarrass you, but I also think it will enlighten you to your… condition," he paused meaningfully. "*Mazaska Zi Ista,* when was your last visit to the tipis apart?"

The dawning of the implication stunned both she and Spirit Bear. Kaitlin looked at both men in shock. Each man's eyes drilled into hers, each waiting with baited breath for her answer.

"I – I have only been in our home village," she stammered.

Woniya Mato was instantly on his feet. He arched his head back and screamed in pure happiness and amazement. His arms were lifted to the sky.

"*Wakantanka* truly has blessed me this day!" he cried. "I am going to be a father!"

Kaitlin sat in shocked silence. She was pregnant? She was going to be a mother? She was going to have a baby with *Woniya Mato*? It seemed unlikely… but how else could she explain her symptoms and lack of monthly flow? She was going to be a mother!

After taking a few moments to accept facts, she stood on shaky legs. Spirit Bear looked down at her happily, swooped her up in his powerful embrace, and swung her around, laughing deeply.

"Oh, *Woniya Mato*! Don't swing me! Put me down! Put me down! *Now*!"

Worry etched in his face as he instantly obeyed. She ran quickly to the edge of the woods and became ill.

Instantly, he was at her side. "Oh, *Wastelaka*! I am so sorry! Can I get you anything?"

"Just *mni*, please," she panted as another wave of nausea passed over her.

He retrieved a *mniapahta* with fresh, icy water. Kaitlin splashed it on her face. Her pallor peaked, so Spirit Bear gently carried her back to her mat to rest.

He hovered like an excited hummingbird over her. The blonde lay back on the mat and closed her eyes. Shortly, her breathing deepened.

"These suns have been much for her, my *kola*," *Wawakankan* stated. "We will have to make our trip home even slower to make sure she is fine."

"My brother! I am going to be a father!" he enthusiastically whispered. "I cannot believe it! I do not care how long it takes me to get home! I will have a pregnant woman to wed as soon as I get there!" His wide smile seemed glued to his face. *Wakantanka* had a way of rewarding those who followed his path!

"*Tos*, my friend! It is a great honor to gain a *thawicu* and child of your blood at the same time!" he paused then smiled slyly. "Talk about prowess!"

Woniya Mato laughed heartily, although he tried to keep his robust volume down for Kaitlin's sake. Off in the distance, a procession became noticeable.

"There is *Wawakte Towanjila*! I will go and help them!" Whistling to *Runs with the Wind*, Spirit Bear took a flying leap onto the stallion's back and cantered toward his other close friend. They arrived at camp a short time later.

Sky Warrior dismounted and glanced curiously at Kaitlin's reclined form. She was beginning to stir with the noise made by the men's arrival.

"Have you worn out your *winyan* already, my *kola*?" he asked, a brow rose in question. A ready smile teased his lips as he jabbed at his friend.

Spirit Bear chuckled heartily to his friend's teasing. "It is not what you think, my brother! She sleeps because of her condition."

"Her condition?" he questioned. "What ails her?" he asked suddenly concerned.

A beaming smile split the war chief's face. He lowered his voice, "We have already honored the dead by starting a new life!" Then he whispered conspiratorially, "Do not share this with all yet. I first want to tell close friends. We will announce this at our joining ceremony."

The two men clasped forearms in agreement.

"I am pleased for you, my *kola*. The Great Spirit honors your might in many ways!"

The chief nodded in agreement. Then both leaders turned to help *Wawakankan* treat the more seriously injured braves. Three additional men had moderate injuries, and a few others had a few deep but not serious wounds and several mild abrasions.

Kaitlin roused and wandered toward a group of trees. Spirit Bear's eyes watched her proudly. He had the greatest coup of all! He'd planted himself within another. All men desired many sons to follow in their footsteps. When she returned, Golden Eyes approached the group of men.

"What can I do to help?" she asked

Wawakankan said, "Can you find me four short straight and sturdy sticks? I need to set this man's broken arm, and I need them to keep it in place."

"*Tos*, I can do this. *Woniya Mato*, may I borrow your tomahawk?"

"Of course, *Mazaska Zi Ista*," he said, handing her the dangerous weapon.

The tomahawk had two purposes; for this reason, he had two separate tools. He had a war tomahawk which he kept in a sacred location, but the wood tomahawk was for any to touch. This is the weapon he handed to her.

He called after her, "Do not strain yourself, *mita wastelaka*! If you need to chop a lot, come for me!"

Kaitlin turned back, "I will listen to my body, *Woniya Mato*. I will be fine."

Wawakankan smiled at his friend and said, "I thought she'd rather look at sticks than at bones protruding through flesh," as he worked on restructuring the man's arm.

He thoroughly cleaned the arm, flesh, and bone. He set the man's arm, sewed it with sterilized sinew, and then he set the arm again with precision. By the time Kaitlin returned with the splint, he was ready to apply the wrap to secure the bones in place.

"I think your arm will heal with minimal damage. The break was clean. As long as you do not push it, you should regain full use, Night Stealth. Here," *Wawakankan* said, handing the injured man the *mniapahta* with a specially prepared strong pain killer.

The shaman had performed the necessary rituals to prepare the leaves of the American White Hellebore before the men had left the village. Because of the intense ritual and preparation of this medicine, it was reserved for the most painful wounds. For less severe injuries, yarrow, slippery elm, and willow bark was used to alleviate discomfort.

While *Wawakankan* prepared to treat the next severe injury, he turned to *Woniya Mato*. "We will be here most of the day. If we travel at all, it will be near evening. For this reason, I will have time to formulate a drink that will help your *winyan*. You can take her to collect raspberry leaves to be used in a tea I will prepare. This will help her feelings of nausea.

It is a good herb to drink all during her experience." He winked at Spirit Bear.

"You do not need me to help?" he asked in surprise. It was a well-known fact that the war chief was nearly as proficient at healing as the medicine man!

"I have *Wawakte Towanjila* to help me if I need strength. I have everything else essential to clean, wrap injuries, and treat pain. You go get *Mazaska Zi Ista* her herbs."

Kaitlin watched the masculine grace of her man as he left the circle of injured warriors. His eyes were only for her as she stacked firewood for the evening meal.

"*Uwa yo, mita wastelaka.* I will bring my bow and kill rabbits for a meal. You can gather plants as we look for raspberry bushes."

"Are you hungry for raspberries, my love?" she teased. "Perhaps you want raspberry *aguyapi*?"

"I look for the plant's leaves for you, *Mazaska Zi Ista*," he said with a smile.

"I do not eat the leaves, my chief," she retorted in astonishment.

The chief rewarded her with a deep chuckle of amusement. "*Wawakankan* will make a tea from the leaves for you to drink each day. This will help you with your sickness."

"Oh!" she said with sparkling eyes. "I love you! I love him!"

"Just remember it is me you are marrying," he responded.

"How could I ever forget?" she breathed. "You are my life!"

Kaitlin gathered tubers, wild onion and garlic, burdock, chicory, cucumber root, chickweed, and groundnuts to accompany the many rabbits Spirit Bear killed. She didn't have a basket, so she used a leather bag to stuff her wild greens into. They also found several raspberry bushes and filled another bag with the leaves.

Before returning to camp, *Woniya Mato* led her into an area with long, sweet, wild grass and several trees that secluded the area from sight.

He smiled down at her tenderly, noting the look upon her face.

"You know why I brought you here, do you not, *mita wastelaka*?"

"You wish to look for more raspberry leaves?" she asked breathlessly.

"*Tos*," he admitted.

Spirit Bear untied her dress and gently pulled it down. He laid her back in the soft bedding that the grasses made. The gentle man placed a raspberry leaf on her left breast.

"I found one right here," he whispered as he bent over to kiss the leaf aside. It fell into her cleavage.

"And here," the leader said as he trailed a wet path of molten lava down her womanly curves to tease the valley in between mounds with his tongue.

After lavishing attention to both, Spirit Bear took the tip of the raspberry leaf and traced a path down her flat stomach, followed by his exploring lips. He dipped the leaf into her navel.

His tongue swirled the hole before dipping in.
The bronzed perfection nipped and bit at her
ticklish abdomen.

"There are many raspberry leaves in this
location," he teased her.

The handsome chief tortured his captive wife-
to-be until she begged for mercy.

"Your wish, *mita wastelaka*, is my command,"
he said as he surged forward to meet her request.
"This union will have to last us for a while,
Mazaska Zi Ista, for we will be on the road
home with company."

"Perhaps we will need to look for more
raspberry leaves along the way, my love,"
Kaitlin said huskily as she arched against him.

His body possessed hers with much skill. They
moved on one another until they became one.
The happy couple lay passionately embraced,
welded together after the pleasurable spasms
had faded.

"We need to return to camp, *Wastelaka*," he said
as he regretfully lifted from her form.

"I know," the Golden One said with love shining in her eyes.

CHAPTER TWENTY-NINE

Torn Between Worlds

The soon-to-be married pair returned to camp together. Kaitin walked side by side with Spirit Bear until just before entering the camp. Then she walked the respectful distance behind the warrior that was appropriate for a woman following a man.

The golden girl walked to the pit and began a fire. *Woniya Mato* skinned the rabbits and skewered them over the fire for his *winyan* to watch so they would not burn.   Then the chief went to check on the progress of the doctoring of men.

"We are nearly finished treating the injured," Sky Warrior told Spirit Bear. "We will eat and then leave this night. We can travel for three or

four hours until the men need to rest. It will be
a long, slow trip for the more severely injured."

"*Tos*. This is good for we need to travel slowly
anyway for *Mazaska Zi Ista*," Spirit Bear
assented.

Kaitlin roasted the meat to perfection. The
greens were served either roasted or fresh. The
men smiled in appreciation of her efforts, for
they had eaten pemmican for many days.

After the meal was consumed, bed rolls were
packed and medicines were placed carefully in
special bags. The men mounted up. The horses
that carried the travois-laden bodies followed
the procession.

Kaitlin was happy to be nestled once again in
front of the hard frame of her soon-to-be
husband. He made a wonderful backrest! She
looked up frequently into his handsome features
as the war leader led the men on their homeward
journey.

= = =

Woniya Mato watched his delicate beauty more frequently than she watched him although she was unaware of this. He'd nearly lost his manhood when she'd been taken from him. It'd taken every ounce of training and control he possessed to remain the calm, masterful leader he was well-known for.

The chief sighed silently in relief as her womanly curves molded to his masculine hardness. His hand momentarily tightened possessively on her frame. Yet again, he thanked *Wakantanka* for her safe return.

Spirit Bear was still in awe that he was going to be a father! He couldn't believe his blessings! They were numerous and vast! A baby!

"I think we should name our first son Warrior Bear," he whispered to her.

"I like that name," Kaitlin said thoughtfully. "But what if it's a girl?"

"Hummm. I shall have to think of a name for a female *wakanheja*."

= = =

They were silent as they continued to trek on, each lost in dreams consisting of the other. The war party traveled past the settling of *wi* on the horizon and into the dark. The moon was high before they stopped and unrolled their sleeping mats. All the men's injuries, if severe, were rewashed and redressed with fresh poultices. Each was given a good dose of analgesic if he required it as well as the antibiotic before they rested.

Kaitlin dropped wearily to their shared mat. She looked at the other men lying in circles around them. There were many men but she knew that the majority of the others had ridden on. The blonde snuggled up close to the warm protection of the head chief who'd led the victorious party.

The honey-haired woman was still in reverence at the fierceness of her man; yet he possessed such a gentle, caring side as well. Spirit Bear was esteemed amidst friends but inspired fear among his enemies. The war chief was always so tender and generous with her. Kaitlin still couldn't believe that he wanted *her* out of the many women he could have chosen from.

Still, the blonde had to admit concerns. The baby had opened up a whole new realm of issues in her mind, especially with the resentments of the man who had recently held her as hostage. Sly Coyote's troubles derived because he was born between two worlds.

"What troubles your mind Golden One?" Spirit Bear asked her. "You are tired yet you toss and turn."

"I am sorry. Am I keeping you awake?" she asked, avoiding his question.

"*Tos*, but only because I can never rest while you are awake. It is partly my training, but I would not be able to rest much anyway. When we are on the warpath, or coming from one, I cannot sleep, especially when we still lay on *toka* territory."

Kaitlin had realized that she'd never fallen asleep after he had nor arisen in the morning before him, yet she'd never really understood what it meant. How strange that she'd never really thought about it before.

"So?" his warm tenor voice asked, startling her.

"*Tos?*"

"What is on your mind, *Mazaska Zi Ista?*"

"It is just – I… I am thinking about our baby."

The concerned warrior propped up on his arm and looked down into her face. His midnight mane tickled her check as it waved in the gentle breeze.

"What bothers you, *mita wastelaka*? Are you ill? I know you are excited for this sharing of our love. Tell me, Golden One, what eats on your mind?"

"*Woniya Mato*, it is *Sunmanitu Wacitusni.*"

She took in a breath as she noticed the slight narrowing of the war chief's eyes and the miniscule flare of his nostrils.

"What does *Sunmanitu Wacitusni* have to do
with our baby?"

"Nothing, yet everything. *Sunmanitu Wacitusni*
was born between two worlds; worlds at war
with one another."

Spirit Bear's face instantly relaxed. "*Mazaska
Zi Ista*, our child will be different. He will have
much honor and opportunities amongst our
people simply because he will be the chief's son.
It is the will of *Wakantanka*."

"*Tos*, but *Woniya Mato*, what if our child learns
to hate? What if others do not accept him... or
her? What if – "

"*Mazaska Zi Ista*," he said, taking her face in his
hands and kissing her eyes, "Do not worry. Our
child will be loved as much by our people as he
will be by us. Do not fear. Our situation is not
at all like *Sunmanitu Wacitusni's*."

"I was a slave that became pregnant by her
captor."

"Do you love your captor?" he asked with a hint of a smile. "Do you wish to share your life with me until you walk the spirit path?"

"*Tos*, with my whole soul."

"See? *Sunmanitu Wacitusni's* mother never grew to love his father. She never treated her son as a Yankton child. Her actions caused others to follow in her steps. His mother never realized what she did to him. Our situation could not be further than that of *Sunmanitu Wacitusni*'s," the wise chief justified his beliefs.

Kaitlin smiled up into his hypnotic gaze and smiled. Tears glimmered behind her golden spheres. Thank you, *Woniya Mato*. You always manage to dispel all of my fears."

"That is my duty, Golden One. *Istinma wanna*."

The influential man encircled her body with his bronze arm and secured her to him. He smiled in the dark as he listened to her settling down, preparing for sleep. He'd significantly eased her mind.

Spirit Bear didn't realize the depth of Sly Coyote's influence on his *winyan*. At least he'd quelled her fears before they grew large. He couldn't suppress his renewed anger at what the younger man had unnecessarily put Golden Eyes through. At least *Woniya Mato* had won another war against the ghost of *Sunmanitu Wacitusni*.

The high leader forced his mind away from the Crow-Sioux man. He'd spent too much energy on the one man in the past two weeks. He was finished consuming his mind and time with him!

The men only rested five and a half hours. They'd spend equal times resting and riding. Frequent breaks and redressing of wounds were necessary for recovery. Before the war chief woke *Mazaska Zi Ista*, he brewed the tea of raspberry leaves for her.

As soon as she sat, Spirit Bear handed her a steaming cup of it. The blonde rewarded him with a brilliant smile.

"Thank you, my love! I do not know what I did to deserve such honor or to be held in such high esteem as the ultimate man!" Her eyes sparkled with love mixed with mischief.

Kaitlin sat for at least twenty minutes, giving the tea time to work on her system. It was wonderful! She only had one little bout of nausea for an instant; then it was gone. Normally, it plagued her for at least the duration of the morning!

"*Wawakankan*, I love you!" the recovered blonde smiled happily in his direction and blew him a kiss.

"I will protect my honor!" *Woniya Mato* exclaimed, masking his amusement with a fierce look. "Do I need to remove this threat from my *winyan*?" He stood as if ready to do battle.

"*Hiya*!" Kaitlin yelled and ran to him. "I may love him, but you have stolen my heart!" she giggled.

Wonder Worker jokingly retorted, "I may adore her, but I would never risk my life battling you for her, my *kola*! Especially after the stories I have heard!

After making sure she was fine to travel and treating the men's wounds, the warriors loaded up supplies and continued to travel toward their homeland. When Kaitlin grew too tired to keep her head up, she leaned into the powerful arms of her man. He supported her frame as the steady pace continued.

The journey continued like this for most of the first days. They would stop to eat, rest, and treat wounds in equal slices of time. Slowly, the men's strength began to respond to the continual treatment of the expert shaman. Gradually, the time weighed more heavily toward transportation.

Both *Woniya Mato* and *Wawakankan* kept a careful watch on Kaitlin. Then knew the new demands on her body would be taxing, especially with the endless traveling, but the golden-eyed girl was young and strong. She no longer experienced the stress of separation from her true love. Gone was the worry about the threat to his life that had been placed on her shoulders. The blonde also now had a wonderful new tea that dealt with her pregnancy-induced nausea.

Spirit Bear was frequently caught smiling by his men. Most who didn't know the true reason behind it thought he was on Cloud Nine because of his victory over the Crow and his reunion with his love. Shortly after they returned to the village, the happy couple would unite as husband and wife. The unsuspecting warriors didn't deduce that he was not only joyful for the reasons they believed, but also for the child that grew within *Mazaska Zi Ista's* body.

Spirit Bear's men loved the two personalities that resided in the unsurpassed strength of the young chief. He treated *Mazaska Zi Ista* with tender care and compassion that most men couldn't hope to achieve with a *winyan*. It was such an elite privilege to watch the special love the two shared, knowing the flip side was the rage of a wild bear that knew no mercy on its attackers!

The followers of the war chief were glad that he reigned over their lives. If he were the leader of another tribe, they would join ranks with him rather than oppose him in war. The Crow were foolish for the deed they pulled. They'd be licking their wounds for a long time to come.

The legend of the Spirit Bear would grow to unsurpassed limits. None could hold a candle to his fame. The warriors realized the blessing and challenges that would come to pass when they rode alongside such a mighty leader.

The great thing about being under the wings of such a famous chief was that many would avoid confrontation because of his reputation alone. They'd opt for peace when presented with war. It made for less death.

But the flip side was wearing. No warrior could count a higher coup than to target the most legendary man of all. Many young men would risk foolish deeds just to say that they witnessed the wrath of the impressive bear! Warrior status could be obtained immediately if one lived to tell of a risk against the famed *Woniya Mato*!

About half way through the trip, the Yankton men broke off from the Oglala to make their way home. Kaitlin loved what they did for her and *Woniya Mato*: they risked everything!

"Goodbye, Chief Wise Owl! Bye, Eagle Talon! Thank you so much! I cannot show you how much what you've done means to me!"

"*Mazaska Zi Ista*, you do not need to thank us. We are honored to fight!" Chief Wise Owl told her.

The chief turned to his equal and said, "*Woniya Mato*, do not join with your lovely *winyan* until we arrive. We will go home, perform the death ritual to honor our fallen men; then we will return if you will have us."

"I would be honored. But do not delay too long. I know my *winyan* will attack me if I do not join with her before long!"

Kaitlin punched him and squealed, "I will attack him for making me look like a wolf! It is he who is impatient!" she smiled then softly added, "Well, we both are."

The honeyed-blonde waved bye to all of them. Kaitlin was so blessed to have such kind and caring people to call her friends!

CHAPTER THIRTY

Emotional Tears

Finally, the group was within an hour of their home village. Kaitlin was so relieved, she almost wept with joy! At last, no more traveling!

Woniya Mato taped his golden-eyed beauty's arm and pointed to a blue bird. They were lovely fowl that made her heart sing with joy. It was a foreshadowing of the joyous greeting to come.

It was nearing the evening meal time when they pulled into the village. People were swarming everywhere. Then men dismounted. Kaitlin walked into the village beside her chief; he would have it no other way.

The crowd surged forward. Many voices cried out to them. Everyone touched, hugged, and spoke to them simultaneously. Kaitlin couldn't hold back her tears.

The greeting from the community was more tiring than the trip had been, but it was welcomed. The white girl hadn't ever cried so many happy tears. This was truly her home!

After the salutation died down, *Woniya Mato* and *Wawakankan* took Kaitlin to *Wawat'ecaka*'s food fire.

"*Mazaska Zi Ista*, we leaders must go prepare the fallen warriors. We have traveled far. The deceased's spirits will want to rest. We will build the scaffolds, and then we will eat. Before *wi* sleeps, we will sing the death chant."

"I understand, *Woniya Mato*."

Kaitlin watched his manly form disappear back to the area where the horses roamed free. *Wawat'ecaka* came immediately to the young woman and wrapped her motherly arms around her.

"My daughter, I am so glad to see you returned to us unharmed! You were dearly missed!"

"I missed you, too! Oh, *Wawat'ecaka*! What I would have done to be able to smear brains into hides with you!" Both women laughed.

Within minutes, the three best friends approached the leather maker's hearth.

"*Mazaska Zi Ista*, we were so worried about you! We never have been so scared before!"

"I was scared, too, Desert Rose!"

"We all were!" Apple Blossom revealed.

"Yes, and when all of our fiercest warriors went riding off to your rescue, we knew they'd bring you back, but we never were more concerned!" Playful Otter exclaimed. "They were riding into the heart of Crow territory!"

No one mentioned the thought they all shared. No one had known if any of them would return. Yes, *Woniya Mato* and the *Cante Tinza* were legendary in their war techniques and prowess, but a victory was never a guarantee, especially on the enemies' turf! To verbalize doubt in the men's success was to doubt the warrior's ability. A combatant could receive no greater insult.

"I have some news to share," Kaitlin lowered her voice mysteriously.

"What is it?"

"*Woniya Mato* wants it to remain among friends until our joining," she said, capturing the unwavering attention of all of her closest friends.

Golden Eyes revealed, "We are going to be parents!"

Great squeals came forth from the four women. They swarmed around her, hugging her at once. None hugged her tighter than *Wawat'ecaka*.

"You have made this woman very happy!" she exclaimed. Tears of joy leaked out of the corners of her eyes. "I never thought I'd see this day!"

Pretty soon the congratulation pats shifted from Kaitlin to Gentle Rabbit. The women were all smiles as they shared bliss at the news and consoled the deliriously happy woman.

"When did you find out?" asked a curious Apple Blossom. "Were you in the Crow camp?"

"*Hiya.* I drank some blackberry brew one
evening during my… visit. I felt ill ever since.
I thought I had some reaction to it. It wasn't
until our trip home that *Woniya Mato* made me
talk to *Wawakankan*. He is the one who figured
it out!"

"Oh, my son! It will be his turn soon!"
Wawat'ecaka glanced toward Playful Otter with
a smile. The shy woman looked bashfully away.

Gentle Rabbit was still beaming when she went
to check on the choice cuts of roasting elk. Pots
of stews cooked, and vegetables steamed. There
would be maple pones of bread and the typical
berry *aguyapi*.

"So, how are you feeling now?" asked Desert
Rose. "You said you'd been feeling ill ever
since the wine…"

"Much better. *Wawakankan is* a miracle worker!
He made a tea for me out of raspberry leaves
that mostly makes my nausea disappear! I still
tire very easily – more than I ever have, but I
guess that is the way it goes."

= = =

Apple Blossom was especially quiet. She was very happy for *Mazaska Zi Ista*. She just remembered her brief experience with pregnancy. The unfreed woman eventually wanted a child, but she'd never wanted one with Snake Strike. Still, any child from one's own body was special, and she often felt sad over her lost *ojilaka*.

Someday *Haspa Nableca* would be proud to bear a child for *Wawakte Towanjila*. He was more man than she'd ever expected in her life. He was brave, strong, and very giving, especially upon the sleeping mats. The leader was virile and handsome. He made her heart flutter. If only she weren't considered a slave…

Apple Blossom tried not to hope for the same happiness as *Mazaska Zi Ista*. Golden Eyes had been a slave most of her experience with the Sioux village. She was once more a slave when she was captured by the Crow. Now she was an Oglala *winyan*, preparing to join a chief! And she already carried his child!

Haspa Nableca couldn't help but to compare the both of them. Now she was the slave of a handsome and powerful chief. Could she someday achieve the same? Could the Pawnee woman become adopted into Oglala society and marry Sky Warrior? She hoped so. If she continued to show her value as a *winyan* and *kola*, perhaps her dreams could come true as well.

***

The men returned to camp. Each went to his own fire except for the four leaders. Spirit Bear, Sky Warrior, Wonder Worker, and Lone Wolf sat down at *Wawat'ecaka's* hearth to eat. They were served by the women.

"So he took out the war chief first?" *Isnala Sungmanitu* inquired.

"Only after he killed about half of the Crow's warriors on his own!" Sky Warrior informed with pride. "We wondered what was taking him so long to get there!" and laughed.

Lone Wolf responded back, "I had to stay here and miss all the excitement. Tell me once more about these hand-to-hand combats. You actually thought he lost the first match?" his deep voice reflected disbelief.

"Only but for a second, my *kola*! *Woniya Mato* is a very skilled warrior. It was a trick all along!" retorted the deep timbre of *Wawakte Towanjila*. "He did have us going for a moment!"

Spirit Bear noticed the men had the rapt attention of the women. He cleared his throat.

"I have not yet related the in-depth version for the *winyans*," the war chief stated. He could see the shock written clearly on *Mazaska Zi Ista's* face. He knew that all would be revealed at the celebration, but with her delicate state, the father-to-be didn't want to stress her unduly.

Golden Eyes stood, pale in complexion. *Woniya Mato* rose as well.

"Are you all right, *Mazaska Zi Ista*?" concern laced his voice.

"You… you nearly lost a fight?" she spluttered.

Sky Warrior realized his mistake. He immediately tried to rectify the situation.

"*Mazaska Zi Ista, Woniya Mato* was never in danger for his life. I did not mean to alarm you! A warrior must have many tricks up his sleeve to win in warfare. He tricked his enemy. That is all."

"Wh – what happened to m – make you think he lost?" she whispered.

"*Iyotaka*," *Woniya Mato* interrupted. I will tell you what you wish to know. It is over," he reminded her. "I have won."

"I – I know. I did ask for the m – modified version of the war. It is not your fault that I did not hear all the details. I am sorry," Kaitlin said softly, looking up into his striking face.

"Do not be sorry, *Wastelaka*. What do you wish to know?" he soothed.

"You finish eating. We can talk later."

"You are sure?" Spirit Bear asked, looking down at her.

"*Tos*. I did not mean to overreact. It was just a shock."

To help make amends and switch the subject to a more soothing matter, Sky Warrior said, "*Woniya Mato*, share with *Isnala Sungmanitu* the news for close friends."

Suddenly, all the fire of *Wawat'ecaka*'s were beaming. Lone Wolf looked toward his friend. *Woniya Mato* cleared his throat before he spoke.

"*Wakantanka* has blessed the Oglala. A life he took during the war has already been recouped."

"What!?" Are you saying…" *Isnala Sungmanitu* paused to switch looks from *Woniya Mato* to *Mazaska Zi Ista* and back again. "that you are going to be… parents?" he swallowed.

Wawat'ecaka couldn't help the loud squeal that escaped her mouth the second revelation of the news. She rushed forward to hug Spirit Bear with enthusiastic arms.

Lone Wolf laughed heartily. "I will take that as a yes," he smiled.

"Do not say anything. They will announce their news at the joining," Desert Rose advised.

"*Tos*, your secret is safe with me," he said eyeing the two with a pleased look on his face.

The women began collecting the men's dishes and utensils. While they ate, everyone shared happy smiles with the expecting couple.

After the nightly chores, the women began to prepare for the upcoming farewell ceremony for those who now walked the Spirit Trail. It would be brief, but this respect was vital. Kaitlin was happy to put on her nice dress and shoes.

The community gathered and walked behind the men carrying the bodies on the death scaffolds. They would carry them to the burial place to rest with other cherished family members. After the ceremony and parting gifts were given, men would erect the structures into the air for the bodies to become one with the spirits around them. Their physical essences would be reabsorbed by the elements as was the Indian way.

Chief Spirit Bear stood before the gathering with Wonder Worker. On either side of them were the other two leaders, Sky Warrior and Lone Wolf.

Woniya Mato began the address: "My people, we have gathered here this evening to say goodbye to loved ones. These men were esteemed members of the *Cante Tinza*. They earned this right to fight and will walk as an established warrior by *Wakantanka's* side.

"These fighters and protectors died honorably. They were taken by ambush by Crow warriors. Sky Warrior and Brave Elk killed these foes, but not before it was too late for our brothers."

Sky Warrior continued the ceremony by telling a little about each man and who he was survived by. He also made a statement of comfort to the families. Lone Wolf added that each family would be provided for until other arrangements could be made.

Wawakankan took over. He, as spiritual leader, would perform the death chant and supervise the gift-giving by the people. The shaman took out hollow bones and gourds for the necessary Release-of-Spirit incantations. He also had boughs of evergreen limbs. He placed the branches around the bodies adorned in finery. Then he began a strange and forlorn song.

Upon the lonely melody, *Wawakankan* began the death chant with the accompaniment of implements. The spiritual man appealed to the four sacred directions. He spoke of fire, earth, wind, and water. He relayed thanks and appealed to the Bird of Death and the Great Spirit. Wonder Worker asked for guidance onto the spirit path and spoke of the beauty of the world beyond.

It was strange and beautiful to Kaitlin. She'd never witnessed anything so magical before in her life. Watching Wonder Worker weave the tale of the afterlife was fascinating and magnificent. He was artful and creative in his portrayal. The man who was knowledgeable in the mysteries of beyond made the blonde woman want to weep and laugh with joy simultaneously.

Finally, the families and friends came forward with their departing gifts. Beam of Light was given his weapons, baskets of food, and most of his cherished possessions. They were placed into the scaffold with him to ease the trip onto the spiritual path. This process was repeated for each of the fallen warriors.

When the ceremony was completed, the men wrapped the bodies tightly in each person's blanket and lifted the scaffold up into the air. The elevation, it was believed, began the spirit journey and helped the fallen warrior find his way to *Wakantanka* easier and quicker.

Before the community trekked back to the village, a wailing, keening cry was shared amongst the grieving members. It was a lonely, sad sound that Kaitlin had never experienced before. It caused tears to streak down her cheeks, and she thanked the men for giving their lives for her.

CHAPTER THIRTY-ONE

Passions of the Heart

Upon return to the settlement, Kaitlin was completely drained of energy. She sank onto the mat on the floor. Spirit Bear helped her undress. Neither wanted the fine garment ruined by sleeping in it. After *Woniya Mato* stripped, he placed his finery in a secure spot and lay by Golden Eyes.

She was asleep almost before her head touched the sleeping mat. Spirit Bear smiled down on her. He couldn't be more pleased with the recent turn of events.

Not long after his *winyan* succumbed to the land of slumber, he allowed himself to follow. He, too, needed rest. The war chief had not slept peacefully for over a month.

In the morning, before Golden Eyes began to stir, Spirit Bear once more began a fire and made her raspberry tea leaf drink. When she roused, she thanked him. The chief found his bride-to-be very inviting with her sleep-tossed mane of gold and soft shining lips that smiled up at him.

"*Woniya Mato*, you spoil me."

"It will be our secret," he replied back.

The happy blonde watched his manly form carry out the woman's chore. He rippled with power with every movement. Her heart swelled with love and pride for this magnetic man.

Spirit Bear brought her a steaming cup of tea and stretched his brawny length out beside her on the mat. Kaitlin blew on the hot liquid to help it cool. The warrior was content to watch.

How he made her feel with the weight of his stare was much different than her reaction under *Sunmanitu Wacitusni*'s. *Woniya Mato* made her squirm with desire when those fiery black eyes raked her tender curves. Sly Coyote only made her uncomfortable and angry.

Pushing thoughts of the deceased enemy aside, the young woman began to tentatively sip the prepared liquid. Her eyes met the heated ebony depths of the Oglala leader. Soon, the tea was consumed and quickly forgotten.

Kaitlin stretched out beside Spirit Bear with a becoming smile. She began to show her interest in him by tracing a rigid pectoral. The blonde touched his hard chest with a feathery fingertip, outlining the taunt muscle. Her finger worked back and forth across the bulge and dipped in the flat spot between. Kaitlin tentatively kissed his injury.

The white woman leaned forward and took his nipple into her mouth. She nipped it lightly and circled it with her tongue. Kaitlin looked up as she blew on his chest; the *ska winyan* was scorched with his look of fierce possessiveness.

The golden girl continued to practice her magic upon his senses. She worked her mouth down his supreme example of masculinity. Kaitlin traced every muscle with a burning need. Golden hands touched his superior abdomen; she was not only impressed with its flatness but also the packs of muscles evident beneath her hand and mouth.

Kaitlin's hand rubbed on his lower torso, across his lean hips, and wandered lower. His nostrils flared, and he closed his eyes with the sensations she was inspiring. After a time, he could take no more of the sensations stirred from deep within. He usurped control. Grasping her, he rolled her to her back, his member protesting by waiving at the sudden movement. Her eyes were drawn to him.

The way his woman hungrily watched his manhood was almost more than Spirit Bear could stand. When such a beautiful woman wanted a man, it was difficult to control the joining of the bodies. But *Woniya Mato* wanted her to derive as much pleasure as he.

"My turn," he told her with a wicked smile.

Soon, his lips and hands drove her to the same frequency of passion that consumed him. The chief was magical and mysterious. She never knew where his fingertips or mouth would burn next.

When their union finally happened, both were so highly aroused that the pinnacle of passion was reached within a short time. They lay happily in each other's arms, grinning into the face of the other's.

"That was very sexy," Spirit Bear stated.

"I agree. *You* are very sexy!" she breathed. Kaitlin would never tire of looking at his god like beauty. It truly was a masterpiece!

"How do you feel this morning?"

"Glorious!" she purred.

His deep laughter followed her statement.

"I meant, do you have any nausea?"

"No. I would say *Wawakankan* found the magical solution. The man is a genius!"

Woniya Mato placed his bronzed hand on her pale stomach. She didn't look pregnant except for maybe her breasts were a little fuller. Her abdomen was as flat as ever. It was truly a gift from *Wakantanka* that a woman could go from normal to having a complete child formed in nine months.

Spirit Bear smiled as he leaned over her tummy, "Hello, Warrior Bear. I cannot wait to meet you, son!"

When Kaitlin's look was slightly worried, he added, "Or Sun Flower."

"Sun Flower?"

"It is just an idea. If she is golden like you, then Sun Flower might describe her. I will have to see our child before I determine a name for sure."

She nodded her agreement. Kaitlin began to imagine what a little one of theirs would look like. *Would the baby have midnight hair and eyes like his father, or would the ojilaka have honeyed hair and golden eyes like she? Would the youngster have straight or curly hair? Or would the child be a unique combination of the two of them?*

Both *Woniya Mato* and she were muscular in stature and taller than average. Their offspring were sure to stand above others. If they had a boy who was half as daunting as his father, he would be an imposing figure. Kaitlin smiled tenderly as she imagined.

"What brings such a sweet smile to your lips, *mita wastelaka*?" asked *Woniya Mato*, intruding on her thoughts."

"I dream of what our child will look like," she responded.

"I, too, wonder who a *wakanheja* of ours will resemble. No matter what, our child will be *gopeca,* just like his mother."

"My love, *you* are the true beauty in this tipi!" her eyes raked over his lean physique as she spoke.

"If you look at me like that again, we shall be truly late on rising. All will know why," he said with a mischievous look.

For once, Kaitlin was able to meet the new day relatively embarrassment free. She no longer cared if others knew what kept her in her tipi for long periods of time. The golden beauty had the best man in the world at her fingertips!

However, she also realized that if her friends began to tease her, she would blush.

The couple dressed and ate a breakfast of cold roasted elk and fresh *aguyapi*. Then each of the lovers went their ways to begin the chores of the day. Kaitlin felt a desire to gather food close to the village for the mid-day meal. She did not intend to wander very far because the recent kidnapping was still too fresh in her mind. The golden-skinned *winyan* wandered in the direction of the river, still in clear sight of the village. Once she'd reached the edge of the valley, a cold premonition swept over the recovering blonde's frame, and Kaitlin's breath caught in her throat. A man was standing just beyond the trees!

"Brave Elk! You startled me!"

"I did not mean to scare you, *Mazaska Zi Ista*."

"Are you out just wandering around, or are you following me?" she teased with a relieved smile that made his heart flutter.

"Actually... I just want to make sure you are safe." Brave Elk had developed a crush on the golden woman of *Woniya Mato*. He'd known there was something special about her from the moment he laid eyes upon her, but Spirit Bear was his idol. He'd never do something to offend the mighty warrior.

"Thank you so much for everything you've done for me, *Watila Hehaka*!"

"I am honored to have been a part of your return to our people, *Mazaska Zi Ista*. The people need their princess," he paused then added, "and so does the chief…"

"Thank you for the compliment, mighty sir," she teased. "How many times is it now that you've saved my life?"

"Only two."

"At least this time you did not receive any arrows!" she said, seriously.

"Snake Strike was not a warrior. Had a true man of war hit me with one arrow, I would have walked the spirit path."

"I still do not know how you shadowed me for so many suns while I endured my 'punishment'! I bet it was boring for you!"

"*Woniya Mato* bestowed a great honor upon me. I, who was not yet a warrior, was asked to protect and watch his most precious treasure. Besides, I would not know you as I do if I had not."

+++

The near brush with death had bonded the two. When Kaitlin had been recaptured after her attempt at escape from *Woniya Mato*, Brave Elk had followed her everywhere when Spirit Bear could not as part of her consequences. The youth hadn't yet been inducted into manhood or warrior society at the time.

When Snake Strike attacked her to seek his revenge upon *Woniya Mato*, Brave Elk had thwarted his attack. He'd been shot in the back twice with arrows. Now, the man, member of the *Cante Tinza*, stood proudly before her. He was three years her junior and had already obtained an honor far above those of men much older than he.

Brave Elk smiled down on Kaitlin. Although he was not his full height yet, he was tall and lean. He possessed the build of a warrior. Someday, he'd make a fine leader!

+++

After Kaitlin was satisfied with her gathering of greens, they walked back to the village. Brave Elk disappeared to help the hunters obtain game for the huge feast to occur in several days as Kaitlin turned to stack her wood by the outside fireplace. Then she sat to work on a waterproof basket.

Golden Eye's friends were scarce. She didn't even see *Wawat'ecaka* which was very unusual. She wondered if they were gathering something nearby.

Kaitlin relished the time to sit. Her body was still exhausted from the endless days of traveling and the stressful time in the Crow village. It didn't take a lot of energy to deftly weave the basket. There were some challenging corners, but it was relatively not labor-intensive work.

About midday, the women and men returned, animals of all varieties had been obtained for the feast as well as many greens, vegetables, and fruit. Elk stew was served with *aguyapi* for the noon meal. Preparations for the feast in approximately two days would begin after rest time.

Woniya Mato entered the tipi at noon. He smiled upon his betrothed. She was lying on her mat already.

 "How are you doing, *Mazaska Zi Ista?*"

"Fine. I just thought I'd…"

"*Tos,*" Spirit Bear interrupted. "Do not feel guilty for needing to *istinma*. Your body makes many new demands on you. I wanted to check upon you. I am going to help the men skin the animals now. Do you need anything?"

"*Hiya, Woniya Mato.* Just to sleep. I will feel like work when I rise."

Spirit Bear walked to his *winyan* and placed a kiss on her brow. He touched her cheek tenderly, and then left her to rest. Kaitlin fell asleep almost immediately afterward.

CHAPTER THIRTY-TWO

Gifts from Special People

Upon rising, Golden Eyes found the village a flurry of motion. It seemed like a fire was built in almost every pit and large pieces of meat were being cooked. She walked to *Wawat'ecaka's* fire.

"I am so sorry, *Wawat'ecaka*. I did not realize I slept so long."

"You needed to rest, *Mazaska Zi Ista*. You have been through much. Do not be hard on yourself if you need to sleep."

"What do you want me to do?"

"You can watch the meat cook. I need to gather more greens. I want to make a new dish for the feast."

"Are you sure you would not like me to collect the greens?" Kaitlin asked.

"*Hiya*, you do not know what all I need. It is easier for me to do this myself, but your offer is appreciated," Gentle Rabbit responded.

Kaitlin spent a hot afternoon tending the roasting meat. She caught the drippings to use in the bread and other dishes for flavoring. Even though it was not a difficult job, it did require a lot of bending and walking to turn the main dishes to keep them from burning. It was hot, tiring work.

As evening approached, a sentry announced the approach of visitors. The Cheyenne and Arapaho had returned for the joining ceremony. It was a happy reunion.

After eating, the group sat around the fires to share tales. Chief Hawk Eyes and his wife, Wild Flower, gave Kaitlin happy hugs.

"We are so glad you were returned unharmed. *Wakantanka* truly blesses you," Wild Flower confided.

"I am really fortunate because my many friends came to my rescue!" she replied back with a smile.

"Now we can *finally* watch the joining of the century!" Chief Hawk Eyes stated.

Kaitlin blushed. She was still nervous about getting up in front of many people, but not so much as she had been before her abduction, for she'd bonded to all of these wonderful natives who'd risked their very lives and livelihoods for her!

Woniya Mato and *Wawakankan* smiled because they saw her acceptance of her new friends. Life was good. Wonder Worker looked toward the golden woman and rose.

"I will be right back," he said.

Spirit Bear watched his retreating back. The medicine man soon returned with a bulky item covered up in a colored wrap of woven wool. He walked toward the war chief's *winyan*. Spirit Bear stood and joined them; his curiosity was piqued.

Wawakankan stood before Golden Eyes. When he had her full attention, he knelt down on one knee before the honored one. Her eyes widened in wonder.

"*Tos, Wawakankan*?" she asked. He surely had something important to say or he wouldn't have knelt.

"*Mazaska Zi Ista*, I wish to pay homage to you and my hearth brother, *Woniya Mato*, I have my wedding gift for you completed. If you would honor me, I would like for you to have it now."

At first, Kaitlin didn't know what to say. She merely stared in stunned silence before Desert Rose nudged her from the side.

Kaitlin looked up into the attractive face of her fiancé's closest friend. He smiled at her and handed her the wrapped bundle. Wonder Worker seemed nervous as he waited for her to open the gift.

Slowly, the blonde woman unwrapped the items. Just the wool shawl covering the gift was of the softest texture. The colors were bold and pristine. Touching its dreamy fluff made her sigh in pleasure.

"Oh, *Wawakankan*! I will be the talk of the tribe with this lovely wrap! It is beautiful!"

The shawl had orange, black, red, and white patterns woven into it. Fringe hung from the bottom of the wrap. When she held it up, the tiny amber beads alternated with the red and black feathers that were a symbol of her soon-to-be husband's whispering softly.

Kaitlin was so entranced with the covering for her shoulders that she didn't immediately see the bulky items they covered. A startled sound of awe left her lips when she spied the hand-carved pieces. Squealing, she stood to hug Wonder Worker fiercely.

"Oh, *Wawakankan*! Thank you so much! It is just what I wanted! But how did you find the time?"

The Golden One looked down with pleasure at the finely sculpted wooden plates. The top had been intricately carved into a pattern of sun flowers and bears. It sparkled with some sort of a hardening finish.

Wonder Worker's eyes danced with gratification. He'd hoped for such a reaction. The *winyan* of *Woniya Mato* had come to mean something to him personally as well.

"*Woniya Mato*, look!" she still spoke with great excitement. "Aren't they beautiful?"

Her promised picked up a plate and examined it closely. He ran a finger across the finely sanded hallowed place and then across the top of the flattened decorated rims.

"This is fine work, *Wawakankan*!" he praised his spirit brother. "Would you like a hug from me as well?" he asked with a teasing smile.

"*Hiya*, just one from your *gopeca winyan* is plenty! It is all a man could dream of," he needled his chief.

"Just remember that is all you can have of my betrothed!" he returned in fun.

Not to be outdone, Lone Wolf then went to his home and returned. In his arms he held about ten fine pelts. Most were luxurious fox pelts, but there were two bobcats and a raccoon pelt as well.

"Thank you, *Isnala Sungmanitu*! They are fine furs! I am honored to have them!"

He leaned forward and smiled. He looked conspiringly at *Woniya Mato* and said, "Now you can make warm furs for the *wakanheja* when he arrives!"

Kaitlin blushed and agreed. She hugged his neck as well. She was surprised to note he flushed a little.

Desert Rose also retrieved her wedding gifts. She had two baskets of the finest weave. They were very colorful and highly decorated. Much time and skill had gone into the creation of the artistic pieces.

Kaitlin would never get tired of handing out hugs. She had tears of happiness because of the fine gifts these loving and respected people bestowed on her. Their generosity was unexpected and a glorious experience. The golden eyed girl was nothing but smiles.

The rest of the evening was spent enjoying each friend's companionship and storytelling. Kaitlin was so happy she felt she would burst. She couldn't believe that all of the people and events about to occur revolved around her!

Kaitlin leaned her cheek on *Woniya Mato*'s strong shoulder. She adored him and still couldn't seem to be close enough. The feeling was reciprocated. He also could not get enough of her.

"Do we need to move the ceremony up a day?" asked Chief Hawk Eyes warmly.

Spirit Bear laughed deeply, "We can wait one more day for the feast to cook, my *kola*."

"I only tease you for I know there is nothing like fear to strengthen bonds between you!"

"That is the truth!" Kaitlin agreed. "I never need to have my bonds strengthened like that again!"

"Nor do I," admitted the war chief. "I never thought I was a fearful man, but I learned the definition of the term when you were taken from my side."

"*Tos*, as did I when I learned of the deception they were going to use against you!" Kaitlin added vehemently.

"But we have returned safely," Chief Hawk Eyes reminded them.

"*Tos*," *Woniya Mato* agreed. "It was the will of *Wakantanka*." Many heads nodded agreement.

Before long, even with the festive air, Kaitlin found herself bobbing with fatigue. The new demands on her body made her so tired. She wished she would remain awake and enjoy her friends, but her physical side had other ideas.

Sky Warrior elbowed his friend and snickered when he lifted his golden woman into his arms and carried her to their tipi. *Woniya Mato* smiled back. He rather enjoyed his friends pointing out his prowess on the mats.

Gently, he laid Golden Eyes upon their bedding. He stripped her and then himself. He lay down beside her and watched her as her eyes blinked slowly a few times and then closed. Kaitlin knew no more until the morning.

The little bright bird awoke with a song in her heart! This was the day before the wedding ceremony. The last time she'd experienced this, it was with great remorse. Kaitlin had thought for over a week that she'd never wed the man of her heart. Those long days had seemed like a lifetime to her. Now, in one day, she would be the *thawicu* of a powerful chief.

The first visitor to her tipi was Apple Blossom. She brought a strange item into their dwelling. She sat down beside her friend as she sipped her morning tea of raspberry fruit, leaves and mint.

"I have brought you my gift," *Haspa Nableca* stated shyly.

"What is this?" Kaitlin asked, fingering the object. It was a smooth, sanded board with straps on it.

"It is a cradle board for your infant," she stated. "You will find great use for this after the baby is born."

"Oh, thank you, *Haspa Nableca*! You are such a wonderful friend!"

"I also give you these," Apple Blossom held up tiny moccasin boots for her baby.

Kaitlin hugged her friend fiercely with tears in her eyes.

"You don't know how much this means to me, my friend!" she cried.

Apple Blossom smiled back. Moments later, Sky Warrior's deep voice asked for permission to enter. When it was granted, he entered carrying a strange looking woven item. Not wanting to appear rude, she smiled her thanks when he handed it to her.

"Do you know what this is?" he asked with amusement warming his voice. He suspected she did not, as she was still new to Native culture and ways. The golden-skinned one had learned much but still didn't know all.

"I am sorry, *Wawakte Towanjila*, but I do not."

"Do not feel badly. I will explain my gift to you. This is called a dream catcher. Parents place this over where the *wakanheja* sleeps, and it will keep bad dreams away. It stops them from coming through. It only allows good and peaceful dreams to pleasure the little one's thoughts as he sleeps."

"What happens to the bad dreams captured in the dream catcher?"

"They disappear upon the light of day."

"Thank you, *Wawakte Towanjila*! I will treasure it always!" Kaitlin said sincerely.

"I have one more thing for you, but you shall not have it before your ceremony. I will give it to you in a day or two."

"You do not need to give more," the gracious and humbled woman replied.

"I wish to. Your eyes will light up more with this gift," he said secretively. "I know you will like it."

I will await the day, then, my *kola*," she responded, touched by his desire to please her. "Thank you, both! You are special people," the

blonde informed them. Hugs were given again
before they left.

CHAPTER THIRTY-THREE

Cherry War

The special woman embraced the day. Kaitlin wanted to seek out Gentle Rabbit. She was busy with many other women tending to the cooking of meat and other dishes.

"*Wawat'ecaka*, will you help me? I do not know what to do in preparation for the ceremony tomorrow. Do we have the joining ceremony in the morning, midday, or at night?"

"*Mazaska Zi Ista*, do not worry. You will be prepared by your friends during the day tomorrow. You will join as the sun begins its journey to sleep."

"Thank you, mother. I do not mean to disrupt you."

"You are not, daughter. You are just nervous and excited. It is normal."

Kaitlin asked Moon Eyes, Playful Otter, and Apple Blossom to accompany her to gather berries. She wanted to attempt to make a sweet dish made from the berries to celebrate her love for the war chief.

There were many chokecherries left. Most black berries and raspberries were gone for the season. Kaitlin could make what she wanted with the cherries.

"What do you plan to do with so many cherries, *Mazaska Zi Ista*?" Playful Otter asked.

"I am going to make a special pie for you."

"What is a pie?" Apple Blossom asked.

"You will see. You will like it. I will make as many as I can with these cherries."

After she and her friends had gathered several baskets full, they returned to the tipi area. Kaitlin began by starting a fire in her pit and placing the cast iron skillet over the flames. She added water and boiled some of the pitted chokecherries.

When the mixture began to bubble slowly and thicken, she added honey to sweeten the sauce. She dumped the cherry-honey mixture into a skin pot and repeated the process until she'd used all the cherries they'd collected.

After cleaning the skillet, she placed a gruel of grains into the bottom and sides of the pan. She cooked it slowly until it began to rise and firm. She added some of the cherry mixture and folded the tartlet and did her best to pinch the sauce inside. After the blend thickened and hardened, she glazed it with more honey.

Kaitlin continued to perform the procedure time and time again until she had many pies and had used all the cherry mixture. Her friends watched her with curiosity, for none had seen the strange pastries from white culture.

The blonde wasn't sure how the pies would turn out. In white society, there was good white flour, white sugar, butter, and lard to use in baking. There were also ovens made from fire-hardened earth to cook in. In Indian culture, there was grain flour, honey, and fat. Judging by the looks and smells of the pastries, they would do just fine.

Spirit Bear returned to the tipi just as she finished cooking the last pie. He looked at the moon-shaped item with interest.

"They look delicious," he commented.

"You will have to wait until the feast to try them," she warned.

"Come, now, Golden One! You would not even spare one for your future husband?" he teased her. His black eyes shone with an ornery glimmer.

"Just because you have tasted most of the fruit you'll have access to on your wedding night does not mean you get to taste *all* the fruit before your wedding night, *mita wastelaka*," Kaitlin jested.

"Is this a test, *Mazaska Zi Ista*? If so, I rise to the challenge!" the mighty war chief approached her with long strides and grasped her shoulders firmly, turning her to face him.

"Possibly," she teased with a smile.

"You wish to see how I respond to any challenge?" his eyes sparkled dangerously.

"Oh, no, my powerful chief! I will bend to your will. Release me, and I shall serve your every wish."

Slowly, Spirit Bear released her but eyed her suspiciously. He watched as his *ska winyan* approached the skin pot. She dipped her hands along the lining, filling her fingers with goo.

"*Uwa yo, Woniya Mato*, so your *winyan* can serve you your treat," Kaitlin encouraged her soon-to-be-husband to come to her.

She'd never have heard his approach, but she felt his presence behind her. The blonde whirled and placed her thick, sticky red hands upon his bare chest and then dashed away.

***

The powerful warrior looked down at his messy chest. A smirk painted the edges of his lips. He watched his betrothed disappear through the tipi flap, giggling in glee as she made her escape. The stealthy Sioux would allow her to think she'd escaped, but he'd be the victor!

The unwavering man watched as his *winyan* raced for the woods. Her glorious eyes glanced back to see if he pursued her. Oh, he would, but she'd never see it coming!

***

Kaitlin raced upwards, for *Woniya Mato* would probably guess she'd go down toward the safety of the river. She found her feet approaching the blue pond. It was the place they shared many wonderful memories.

The white woman climbed into the branches of the willow tree. She sat quietly, trying to still her ragged breath. She snickered when she recalled the look on *Woniya Mato*'s face as she'd smeared his body with the sticky cherries.

Kaitlin sat for about fifteen minutes. *Had she really escaped from the legendary war chief?* Somehow, she doubted it. Still, the blonde smiled at her success. Another five minutes ticked by. *Perhaps he wasn't going to come after her?* That was okay, too.

Kaitlin would have another coup to count against him. She'd scored! Then the pastry cook began to think of all her unprotected pies in the tipi. *What if he were eating them?* Then she'd be the one to have a coup counted on!

Hurriedly, she clamored down the tree. Darn him! The war chief had tricked her! He'd pay for duping her.

Suddenly, the white beauty was caught in a vice of masculine strength. She started to scream but her mouth was ravaged in an impassioned embrace. Her wide eyes looked up into the domineering ones of her promised.

She gasped, "*Woniya Mato*!"

"*Tos?*"

"You do not play fairly."

"And you do?"

"You scared me," she pouted prettily.

"Just remember, Golden One, I always win."

His eyes raked her feminine form. Kaitlin pressed a hand against his chest and found he hadn't cleaned off the sticky mess. She smiled as she wiped the mess onto his lean cheeks.

"This means war, *Wastelaka*," he promised.

"Oh, and it would be so fair, too, my love," she responded. "Your brawn against my brain."

"War is not fair, *Mazaska Zi Ista*."

"So just what are you going to do to me, oh mighty captor?"

"Torture you, of course." He smiled as his eyes rippled up and down her firm frame. His eyes managed to burn a flame to life inside her.

"Oh, no! Not that!"

"*Tos, Mazaska Zi Ista.* It is time for you to learn your place." The dominant male lay her down on the bank of the pond. He unlaced her dress and removed his leggings.

"I have a very entertaining way of passing the rest of this day," he promised.

Kaitlin reached up and touched her tongue tentatively to the smeared cherry on his chest. "Um, you are very tasty, my chief," she murmured.

He swiped a finger through the mashed cherry sauce and wiped it upon her chest. Then he lowered his head and licked it off.

"You are right, Golden One. This is very good!" and he captured her firm peak in his hot mouth.

"Oh, *Woniya Mato*! This is so unfair," she moaned. With a spare hand she reached for his member, but he anticipated her move and rolled away from her seeking fingers.

"*Hiya, Mazaska Zi Ista.* I torture you, not the other way around" he said with humor warming his voice. He loved to see the profound effect his lips had upon her senses.

The golden skinned woman pressed his weight away from her with her hands, but he didn't budge. "This is not fair," she wailed again.

Chuckling at her feeble attempts, he captured her hands in his larger, stronger ones. He kissed her palms and nibbled his way down her arms.

Kaitlin never realized her arms had so many tender, ticklish places. She wiggled to no avail. The blonde couldn't escape the enticing lips and tongue of her master.

When Spirit Bear reached the full circles upon her chest, he attacked them with relish. Her answering gasps of pleasure and thrashing were very nearly his undoing.

Spirit Bear was determined to maintain control. He wouldn't enter her entreating body until he'd tortured her to the brink! He moved lower. The chief tantalized her flat abdomen, her rounded hips, her delectable derriere, and her long, lean legs. He lay upon her legs and even tasted her toes and nipped the bottoms of her feet. She squealed in sexual pleasure. Finally, his body relinquished his barely maintained command; they found pleasure in each other.

"I… had no idea… war could be so… pleasurable," she gasped.

"Nor did I, my sweet!"

The loving couple lay in each other's arms, gazing into each other's eyes for a time. They rinsed off in the invigorating waters of the spring pond and returned to the tipi.

"Are you sure I cannot have one of your pies?"

"*Hiya*! You will have to wait."

"I have a turkey for you to prepare for our supper. I even found some of your favorite tubers to cook as well!" The obsidian eyes shone as she inhaled in pleasurable surprise.

"Thank you, my chief! I will begin preparing them now!"

Chapter Thirty-Four

Jitters

Kaitlin didn't lie down as most during the heat of the day. She was too excited and had a lot to do. The meal was prepared to perfection, but the wife-to-be could hardly make herself eat.

After the meal, the women went to the river to clean the plates and utensils. They joked around and also took every opportunity to tease Kaitlin.

"Are you still nervous, *Mazaska Zi Ista*? You shouldn't be. There are only going to be four or five-hundred people staring at you," Desert Rose joked.

"Do not scare her," chided Apple Blossom. "We do not want her running for it again!"

"Do not worry! Nothing will stop me from joining *Woniya Mato*! Not five-hundred people and not Crow warriors!" Kaitlin exclaimed.

The women laughed jovially at her fervent display. They were glad that it seemed as though nothing could prevent the ceremony this time! They collected the cleaned items and returned. All the men's eyes were upon them as they entered the gathering.

Just to be ornery, Kaitlin's friends suddenly fell in line behind her, forcing her to walk first. When the blonde tried to shrink back, they pushed her forward, giggling.

"You need practice for tomorrow," whispered Playful Otter.

Blushing, Kaitlin walked into camp. The men all had grins on their faces as they recognized the mischievous antics of her friends; the bride-to-be's self-conscious walk and timid look endeared the golden-eyed one even more to their hearts.

When the women rejoined the men, many stories and laughs were shared. The men teased all of Kaitlin's friends. It truly was a time for bonding and uniting tribes.

"Are you telling me that in the short months *Mazaska Zi Ista* has been with the Oglala, she has learned to cure leather with *Wawat'ecaka*, mastered the art of pattern and water-proof basket weave, and she is good with drilling holes in jewelry stones?" asked Wild Flower.

"*Tos*, this is true," affirmed Playful Otter with nods from Desert Rose and Gentle Rabbit.

"She also makes perfect *aguyapi* every time," *Wawat'ecaka* added to her prowess.

Little Foot, Hopping Robin, and Soft Touch all looked impressed. Kaitlin could only look down in embarrassment. She was proud of her accomplishments but was modest about them when others' praised her.

Both Chief Hawk Eyes and Chief Wise Owl teased *Woniya Mato* by stating, "If you ever decide you tire of her, please send her our way!"

Even the men's wives didn't look insulted. A woman such as *Mazaska Zi Ista* would bring much honor to their tipi. But everyone knew this would never happen. The war chief had just ridden into the center of enemy territory to reclaim his stolen *winyan*. That deed alone spoke of the great love and loyalty the war chief had for his soon-to-be wife.

At last, the people around the campfire retired for the night. *Woniya Mato* led his woman to their tipi. She still looked wide-awake yet exhausted at the same time.

"*Uwa yo, Mazaska Zi Ista.* You need to *istinma.* I want you to be fully awake and ready for tomorrow."

"Oh, *Woniya Mato*! You are right; I am very tired. But I am also so excited about our joining tomorrow; I fear my mind will never let me sleep!"

"Come. Lie beside me. I will make sure your eyes are closed."

Wrapped in the safe and powerful embrace, the chief did indeed have a way of relaxing her. Kaitlin had never desired to be anywhere but wrapped in his masterful arms. Hadn't he shown her time and time again how safe she was with him?

Before she realized it, the morning light kissed her awake. The blonde sat up and drank her tea in the company of her promised. She kept stealing looks at his handsome profile. Spirit

Bear grinned at her and left the tipi just as her friends entered.

"Good morning, sunshine!" sang New Moon.

"Good morning. What are you all doing here?" Kaitlin asked suspiciously.

"We have come to prepare the bride for her special day!"

"But it is just morning. I won't join him until tonight."

Gentle Rabbit said, "We will use the whole day just for us! We help prepare you for your man!" Her eyes twinkled with unhidden joy.

"Go relieve your needs; then come to my tipi," *Wawat'ecaka* commanded. "We will have our fun with you then!"

Kaitlin used the brisk walk to the river to finish waking up. She looked over the river that sparkled gold in the sun as it blessed the lands it watered. Birds and butterflies darted along the path in front of her.

When she walked back to *Wawat'ecaka's* house, she saw New Moon, Playful Otter, Desert Rose, and Apple Blossom waiting for her. They all accompanied her into the tipi wearing wide smiles.

Kaitlin looked at them doubtfully. "What are you all up to? I feel as though you are up to no good," she confessed.

"Oh, my friend! You are so far from the truth!" Desert Rose exclaimed. "Just wait until you see what *Wawat'ecaka* has for you!" Kaitlin turned her golden eyes upon the motherly figure. She got down a bundle of soft rabbit fur. She brought it over and placed it with reverence upon Kaitlin's lap.

Mazaska Zi Ista felt the incredibly soft pelts and nearly sighed with pleasure. She knew, however, that there was something more within the folds of fur. She felt the supple folds of leather before she saw it.

The blonde nearly screamed in startled surprise when she saw the fine workmanship upon the leather pelt that she'd helped to cure. Kaitlin held up a dress made from the sacred white hide of the elk!

The bride-to-be jumped to her feet and held the dress up to her. It was cut to fit her perfectly. It would mold to her hourglass figure and cling in an attractive manner. All men would be captive prisoners of hers on this night!

The dress had a V-neckline. The slightly scooped collar above the V was lined in crisp, fluffy rabbit fur of the whitest white. The down waved delicately as the breeze moved the air in the tipi. Kaitlin was mesmerized as the breath caressed the softness. Hanging slightly below the white fur were light amber beads sewn in tiny half-inch streamers. They tinkled slightly when she moved the garment. The bottom of the dress was done in the same fashion: fluffy, snowy rabbit fur lined the hem with amber streamers strung to clink freely together below.

The V would dip far into her cleavage area when she wore it, but a white strip of leather crisscrossed, connecting the sides of the front together to keep the dress from gaping open and showing off the bride's wedding goods. The end of the laces hung down over her breasts and contained a cotton ball of white rabbit fur.

The waist of the dress had more of the amber beads sewn onto the garment with no streamers. At the top of the creation, two eagle feathers and two red feathers with black tips were attached to the sleeveless shoulder area. The feathers would hang down onto the top part of her arm.

The dress was a masterpiece. Kaitlin turned to *Wawat'ecaka* and all of her friends with tears in her eyes.

"It is the finest thing I've ever seen! Oh, thank you! How can I ever thank you enough!?" she cried.

"Should we show her more?" asked Apple Blossom.

"I don't know! Do you think she can handle it?" parried Desert Rose.

All women looked toward Gentle Rabbit with questions in their eyes.

Playful Otter brought forward a leather bag. In it were many beads of amber and other gemstones, all drilled for decorating.

"Oh, Playful Otter! Thank you so much! You need not give me all of these! I bet it took you forever!"

"Not as long as it did for me to do the beading on your wedding dress!"

"You did that?"

"*Tos. Wawat'ecaka* did the dress creation with the fur and design, but I added the bead strings under her watchful eye and instruction. She had the design in her mind. I just followed orders."

"Thank you so much for your gifts!" Kaitlin breathed. She gave both women hugs for their hard work. The dress would be cherished forever! Not only would she marry the man she loved in it, but the women who meant so much to her had made it!

"There is more," Apple Blossom said. She brought forth another bag of leather. *Mazaska*

Zi Ista wondered what was in it. She didn't
have to wonder for long!

Kaitlin pulled out two white moccasin boots
with criss crossed leather stripped down the
front. The fluffy white rabbit fur ran down the
seams and encased the top rim where the boot
would touch her upper calves. The amber bead
fringe was present on these creations as well.

Kaitlin did leak a few tears this time as she
hugged her friends. However, they weren't
quite finished with her. New Moon and Desert
Rose approached her with a tiny basket. They
placed it in her lap.

Inside the basket was a white headband beaded
with more amber. The amber beading made
intricate patterns around the center of the
adornment. A fluffy white feather flanked by
two of her husband's would rise above her
forehead when she placed it on. Lining the
outside rims of the band, a tiny strip of the
rabbit fluff was attached. It was finery fit for an
Oglala princess!

"Wow! I am humbled. I just don't know how to thank you! I am at a loss of words to explain the depth of my gratitude."

"First time for everything," Desert Rose mumbled in a teasing manner.

"Now," said Gentle Rabbit, "We bathe you."

"Bathe me?" squeaked Kaitlin.

"*Tos*, on your joining day, we pamper you. It may be the first and last time ever! So enjoy it and don't resist!"

CHAPTER THIRTY-FIVE

The Ceremony

The women escorted Kaitlin back to the river. They made her strip and enter the clear water. The spot they picked was warmer than usual. It was just a little further away from their normal bathing location. The full sun warmed the refreshing current.

They washed her body and scrubbed her head despite the protests that she could at least wash her own self. Strawberry-smelling cream was massaged into her scalp and long tresses to scent it and make it easier to comb.

When all the soap and conditioner were rinsed away, the blonde was brought onto the banks of the shore. The women wrapped her up in a large colorful blanket and sneaked her back into *Wawat'ecaka's* tipi.

New Moon, Apple Blossom, and Playful Otter brought forth oils scented with a hint of lavender. They had Kaitlin lay down on an older piece of soft leather of Gentle Rabbit's and began to work the oil into her skin.

Kaitlin was not comfortable with others washing, rinsing, and rubbing on her nude form, but her friends didn't give her a choice otherwise. They were raised to be at ease with their bodies, not to feel as if they'd sinned by showing skin. The white woman realized the differences in the two cultures, but the fair-skinned beauty didn't think she'd ever get over her shyness.

"Her skin is so golden!" New Moon said. "It is almost the color of her eyes!"

"And it is soft to the touch!" agreed Apple Blossom.

"No wonder *Woniya Mato* wants to join with her so quickly," laughed Desert Rose as she got a squeal from the light-skinned woman.

"Her hair is so silky, too," stated Playful Otter. "It curls around your fingers," she said in awe. She was combing Kaitlin's strands as the others worked oil into her skin.

"Knock it off, guys!" stressed *Mazaska Zi Ista*. "This is hard enough for me to endure without all of you critiquing my body and hair!"

"We have said nothing about your body!" denied Desert Rose. "But now that you bring it up…"

"Oh, don't you dare!" Kaitlin shrilled excitedly.

"Relax, child," *Wawat'ecaka* said to her. Then she directed the next command at the group of her friends.

"Do not over excite our bride," Gentle Rabbit began. "She has much going on today."

"Oh, all right," mumbled Desert Rose. Under her breath, she added, "Didn't have to ruin our fun!"

New Moon placed some sweet-smelling incense on the fire. It added to the relaxing atmosphere of hands massaging Kaitlin. Before long, she found that she'd managed to doze off. All too soon, the blonde snapped awake.

"I'm so sorry! I didn't mean to fall asleep on you!" she cried in shame.

"This is a good thing on your joining day,"
Wawat'ecaka stated. "It means we are
pleasuring you and relaxing you so that you can
doze before your special time. There is no
higher honor than this for the group of friends to
the bride!" revealed Gentle Rabbit.

"Oh. Well, then… carry on!" and she laughed.
Kaitlin's friends giggled at her enjoyment as
well.

At noon, Apple Blossom stole freshly smoked
venison and bread for their meal. Although the
nervous bride tried to deny the food, the group
wouldn't allow her to skip out on the meal.

"Do you want to pass out during your joining
ceremony?" asked Gentle Rabbit.

"*Hiya*!"

"Then you better eat. I have seen many, in the
stress of the moment, weak from not eating,
pass out. Also, it is very important to remember:
do not lock your knees!"

"Really?"

The other women nodded. Just three years ago they'd witnessed the bride do this very thing. It was an embarrassment to the maiden. Still to this day, it was a subject that still brought her shame!

Mazaska Zi Ista managed to eat a small amount of the mouth-watering food. Then all the women rested. Really, they visited and spoke about the ceremony…

"The joining ceremony will happen first," Desert Rose stated. "Then we will feast."

"*Tos*, and then the men will share stories of coups," added Playful Otter.

"Does this mean they will retell the Crow victory?" asked Kaitlin. She nearly dreaded to hear the answer.

"Of course," *Wawat'ecaka* affirmed. "We must celebrate the many blessings bestowed upon us by *Wakantanka*."

"*Tos*, I know, my mother. I just do not like hearing of death."

"I understand, child, but be proud of your man and what he does. It is who he is."

Kaitlin had never thought of it in quite those terms. She'd try to be proud of him, but the innocent white couldn't stand to think of torture. She nearly went into a coma when she witnessed Jed's anguish. Perhaps it was not the same thing in the present situation.

"I am proud of him," *Mazaska Zi Ista* whispered.

Her friends smiled and patted her with understanding. In no time at all, the drum beat began to pound. It spiked Kaitlin's heart rate.

The women in the tipi all appeared a little nervous, for it was infectious. However, Gentle Rabbit accepted the challenge. She'd waited a long time to begin to see her men joined with worthy women!

The women dabbed a delicate scent of wild jasmine onto Kaitlin's neck, chest, and hips. Then they had her step into her enchanting joining dress. She looked beautiful and shined with a golden light brightened by the white.

Playful Otter rubbed glossy oil into Kaitlin's hair and finger combed it once more so that the natural curl didn't frizz as it was prone to do. Then the women carefully placed the headband onto her head, centering the feather. They used her nose as a guide.

Next, Gentle Rabbit had *Mazaska Zi Ista* sit and extend her shapely leg while she fitted her foot into the moccasin boot. She laced up the mid-calf footwear and tied it. The lace with the rabbit fur ball hung, adding more to the decorative look on the fine gift.

Kaitlin looked down at herself and gasped at the beauty of the garments. It was finery fit for a queen! She hugged all of her friends once more.

Wawat'ecaka turned to the other women and shooed them all out except for Kaitlin. She wanted them to find their spots so they could see and welcome the bride to the groom's side when the drum beat changed.

Kaitlin paced nervously within the confines of the tipi. She tried not to, but her body refused to be still. Even with the subtle glances from Gentle Rabbit, she couldn't still her feet.

After a seemingly endless time of pacing, the crowd was finally assembled. The drum beat changed, quickening the blonde's heart.

"Oh, *Wawat'ecaka*!" she whispered intently. "I am so scared! What do I do?"

"Golden One, once you see your man, nothing else will matter. He is a handsome one, fitting for your beauty!"

And it was true. When *Wawat'ecaka* led Kaitlin forth from the tipi, the crowd parted and allowed her a wide berth into their midst. Her eyes found *Woniya Mato* immediately.

Indeed, the chief was a striking figure. His male beauty was etched into her mind for all time. He stood tall and proud before her. His bronze skin gleamed, contrasting against his white wedding garments.

Spirit Bear's new white fringed leggings matched his tunic and breechcloth. Woven into the fabric were red, black, and tawny quill patterns. Kaitlin comprehended that his colors and hers were intertwined, joining them together for all time.

Her man wore a fine cape of white leather sporting more decorative quill patterns. The white down of the rabbit's also adorned the top and bottoms of the cloak. It was made for the king!

The warrior sported his chieftain's headdress, and he held his ceremonial staff as well. He would've been an intimidating figure if not for his happy smile and blazing eyes that compelled her forward. Kaitlin's feet took happy steps to his side while his eyes devoured her in a hungry gulp.

When she was beside the imposing man, the drum beat stopped. It was a strange experience to be in a crowd of over five-hundred people with total silence. *Woniya Mato* took her soft hand in his warm one and squeezed it softly to encourage her.

Mazaska Zi Ista looked into his dazzling smile. She saw white, even teeth that contrasted starkly against his bronzed features. His long, black mane shone with the sun's dying light, sending glimmers of blue down its silky lengths.

Wawakankan stood before the powerful couple and began a happy, yet eerie chant. He used bones and rattles accompanied by a dance of twirling steps around the joining couple. Then he stood still before them once more.

The shaman held open his palm, motioning toward the war chief. *Woniya Mato* placed the ceremonial staff into his hands. *Wawakankan* held it high above his head. Then he began a beat with it by tapping on the ground in front of the couple. The drum beat began once more to mimic it.

The priest of the Oglala turned to the instrumental players and pointed to the woodwind flute. Immediately, a beautiful melody pirouetted in the air. A simulation of a hawk cry was introduced periodically in the flow of music.

Gourd rattles began with a point of the staff. Then came the small kettle drum, a different sound than the main. It was an enchanting song for a time to unite dreams.

Wawakankan continued to tap his rhythm with the staff to the man and woman standing before the masses. He stopped and handed the rod to Lone Wolf. After motioning the musicians to continue, he brought forth the sacred ceremonial pipe. Filling it with *chan-shasha,* a red willow-bark tobacco for all to witness, he lit the carved pipe before walking four slow circles around the joining couple.

The medicine man blew smoke on the man and woman, then held the pipe high in the air. The smoke was to remind the witnesses of fire and of the breath of *Wakantanka* and the life bestowed upon the people by Him. Wonder Worker chanted to the Great Spirit, asking Him to attend and bless the joining.

Next, the shaman held the pipe next to the earth. He spoke of the grasses and how the earth feeds the animals which in turn, fed the people. He spoke of ways the Indians lived off the land. The great circle of life made all related; each was a part of the family of brothers and sisters.

Water was the next thing *Wawakankan* mentioned. The cycle of rain was also circular. It rained and fed the plants on earth. It flowed into rivers. Eventually, the water evaporated back into the sky to rebirth life.

The last of the directions was air. Wonder Worker spoke of winds bringing change. He spoke of opening one's mind to new ideas, enlightenment, and clarity.

"There are seven pipe ceremonies," *Wawakankan* began as he addressed the crowd as well and the joining couple. "It stands for the seven tribes present in the Sioux Nation in these plains. The circles on the base of the pipe represent love, for the pipe was made by both man and woman."

Kaitlin listened with rapt attention. This was a story she'd never heard. It was intriguing.

Wonder Worker continued, "The warrior carved the pipe, but the woman placed the decorative quills upon its bowl. When the pipe was made, both man and woman held the ceremonial pipe together."

Sky Warrior came forward and tied *Woniya Mato*'s and Kaitlin's hands together with a earth-red cloth. Both Sky Warrior and Wonder Worker smoked the sacred ceremonial pipe, drew the chemical-laden air into their lungs, and blew it simultaneously onto the couple's joined hands.

"Now this man and woman have been tied together for always!"

Wawakankan turned the newly joined couple to meet their people for the first time as husband and wife. They walked together, hands still tied, into the throng of congratulating friends and village members.

Kaitlin couldn't say how long they met and were congratulated by the multitude of people, but she bet it was at least an hour. At the end of the period, she and her daunting and handsome *hingnaku* took her back to the ceremonial spot again. He removed his long hunting knife from the sheath at his waist and cut the restraining cloth from their wrists.

Wawakankan addressed the crowd once more, as tradition required.

"You see that *Woniya Mato* has severed the wrist tie. This does *not* sever his recent binding to his *thawicu*. Instead, this action signifies that he is an individual, as is *Mazaska Zi Ista*. Both are joined for life, but each is an individual in this union. Each will assume their roles as man and as woman, but they are united in spirit forever."

Kaitlin turned to her handsome *hingnaku* and melted into his arms. The war chief could not help but to kiss his new *thawicu* in front of the crowd. He loved this *winyan* with all of his heart!

Shouts and hurrahs rushed excitedly through the air. A new drum sound began to pound in the multitude to signify the beginning of the celebration. Their mighty chief had finally joined!

CHAPTER THIRTY-SIX

A Surprise Guest

"Come, *Mazaska Zi Ista*. Let us share our joy with our people. I want to dance with you."

"B – b – but *Woniya Mato*! I don't know how."

"It is easy, *Wastelaka*. Let the music move you. Become one with the rhythm. It is the essence of all. The secret to life is melody."

Swallowing her timidity, she followed her *hingnaku* out where they had a little more space. The beat of the drum slowed and became an alluring seduction. Kaitlin closed her eyes and felt her body sway gently with the beat. *Woniya Mato* also allowed his body to slowly move in time.

When the white woman looked up, she saw the gentle smile playing about her husband's full lips. She grinned bashfully in response.

Their people encouraged the newly wed dancers and began to join in. Kaitlin released her body; she was free to dance unencumbered. Spirit Bear's eyes sparkled with pride and joy as he, too, let the music take control.

After the dance, the chief gathered his *thawicu* into his arms and whispered into her ear.

"Very impressive, *mita wastelaka*. I am honored you are my wife."

"I also am honored, my *hingnaku* and chief," she said softly back.

Just then, Brave Elk thundered into the clearing on his war horse.

"What is it, *Watila Hehaka*?" the chief's voice was laced with concern.

"I think you will be pleased, *Woniya Mato*!" Brave Elk responded. "We have new visitors."

"Indeed?"

"Yes. Bright Sky is approaching with a small party."

The leader's smile brightened his face. "She may be disappointed to have missed our ceremony."

"I think she has a gift for you," Brave Elk grinned, swinging off his horse.

Woniya Mato led *Mazaska Zi Ista* back to the chieftains' spots to watch the procession of the approaching party. The progress was steady and unhurried. The Oglala festivities continued around them; the people were not concerned if their chiefs were at-ease.

Kaitlin could see the group consisted of about ten Crow. The leader was, undeniably, Bright Sky. Several horses were led sporting two large barrels each. Suddenly, the newly acknowledged Indian princess realized what gift the other was bearing!

Finally, the group was close enough that the villagers took notice that Crow were joining an Oglala celebration. Slowly, dancers stilled their feet. Subtle eyes watched the chiefs for any sign of concern.

By the time the small party reached the communal setting, even the music had stopped. Kaitlin could tell that Bright Sky was a little nervous as she approached the band that'd diminished hers by vast numbers, but most would only see a strong, brave woman leader from another tribe. Kaitlin smiled encouragement to her friend.

As the woman dismounted, her warriors did the same. It was a sign of peace and respect to the Sioux; they wanted to show no hostility was intended.

The war chief approached the woman leader with a wide smile of welcome. He grasped her forearms in greeting, and Kaitlin stepped up to the Crow woman as well.

"Good evening, our new friends," *Woniya Mato* stated for all to hear. "Welcome to our humble celebration!"

"I see I am just a little late," Bright Sky said with a trace of disappointment.

"Only by minutes," the chief responded. Laughter rippled around the meeting.

"I am sorry we missed it," Bright Sky added genuinely.

"We can repeat the ceremony," Spirit Bear offered with a wink. Kaitlin vigorously shook her head.

Laughing, Bright Sky said, "I will not put my dear friend through the turmoil again. I am sure *Mazaska Zi Ista* relished the ceremony and being tied to you, *Woniya Mato*, but I also am aware of her dislike at being the center of attention."

Spirit Bear threw back his head and laughed. "That is why I considered repeating the performance for your pleasure."

"*Woniya Mato*!" his wife gently scolded. His laughter only deepened.

"Please, Bright Sky, eat, dance, and be merry! Join us at the ceremonial spot. There is always room for more."

Bright Sky nodded her head in acceptance. She stated, "I have a gift for you and your people, *Woniya Mato*."

"I see you bring offerings," Spirit Bear acknowledged.

"I brought my special drink to bring more merriment to your celebration. I also intend to fully share with *Mazaska Zi Ista* the rest of the secret to making this brew."

Kaitlin hugged Bright Sky. Then she whispered, "I hope you will pardon me if I don't indulge in any this time. I do not wish to offend."

Bright Sky giggled in humor. "I did not expect you to, my dear. It is more a peace offering to your husband. It is thanks to you both for your friendship and honor. Not many would allow mercy in a revenge raid."

"Oh, thank goodness," Kaitlin sighed.

"My gift to you, my young friend, is that I will share the secrets of the recipe. I know you already know a lot, but not all. This will only increase your value. However, I must insist that this recipe only be used for special celebrations. It is not for daily consumption."

"You have my word, Bright Sky."

"I am sure you have not heard the real reason *Mazaska Zi Ista* did not feel well after she drank your potion," *Woniya Mato* grinned.

Bright Sky's brows curved delicately upwards and then a knowing smile donned her face.

Kaitlin nodded at the woman's perception.

"Oh, how *wonderful*! You are to be parents! The Great Spirit truly smiles on you and blesses you!" she breathed.

"*Tos*, Bright Sky. It is true, and we are very thankful."

Brave Elk stood forward and said, "Thank you for watching over and protecting our leader's lovely *thawicu*. We are forever indebted to you. I will select a few men to find you lodging for your stay."

"Thank you, *Watila Hehaka*. I will need only two tipis. Five of my warriors will be returning tonight as our village is still recuperating. I will stay for a short period of time to celebrate with you before I must return. I do want to share my gift with *Mazaska Zi Ista* to show how much I care for her.”

Brave Elk acknowledged her with a nod and turned to find her a temporary place to call home.

“Come, Bright Sky! I want to introduce you to my family and friends,” Kaitlin invited. The blonde put her hand on the Crow leader’s arm and gently guided her to the ceremonial spot occupied by the other chieftains and their interests.

“I want to say how *gopeca* you look in that exquisite wedding dress, *Mazaska Zi Ista*. It suits you well.” Kaitlin offered a shy smile of thanks.

Kaitlin led her over to an elderly woman with kind eyes. “*Wawat’ecaka*, this is Bright Sky. My friend, Gentle Rabbit is my mother figure. She is the creator of my dress. Her skill is unsurpassed with leather creation.”

"Unsurpassed until you came to learn from me, my dear," Gentle Rabbit announced. "It would be difficult for you to differentiate my leather form *Mazaska Zi Ista's*," she complimented.

Bright Sky clasped arms with Gentle Rabbit in admiration.

"She is also our shaman's mother, and she, likewise, claims two of our leaders as her sons," added the blonde.

Bright Sky's eyes widened. "You *are* an accomplished woman!"

Although true, Gentle Rabbit wasn't comfortable with a lot of compliments at one time; she subtly blushed. Kaitlin smiled but then turned to introduce her other family-like members.

Spirit Bear had joined his chieftain brothers and were smiling at the women as they turned.

"Bright Sky, this is *Wawakankan*."

"Yes. I have heard of you. A skilled healer. I see your mother's strength in you, young man."

"And this is Lone Wolf, our leader of large hunts, and Sky Warrior, chief of village affairs, peacekeeper, and warrior."

Kaitlin let her husband introduce Bright Sky to the other band leaders that were visiting for the wedding.

The men smiled and greeted her in the respectful Indian way.

"These are my best friends: Apple Blossom, Playful Otter, and Desert Rose."

"I am honored to meet you," Bright Sky greeted with a charming smile.

The men that accompanied Bright Sky began to unload the great barrels of drink from the horses. They set it up near the chieftains' area. Three men dragged two barrels off in the wake of Brave Elk toward the dwelling he'd secured for them.

"Are the men staying here going to be… comfortable… during our celebration?" Kaitlin asked hesitantly of Bright Sky.

"My men will not enjoy all aspects of your formal celebration. I am sure you will not only rejoice your joining, but all will also revel in the victory over your recovery... and our defeat. This, of course, will be the details of the fight reconstructed. My men will not enjoy this, but they were aware of what you'd be celebrating when they volunteered to come with me." Bright Sky paused and added softly, "Thank you for feeling empathy over our comfort level, *Mazaska Zi Ista*."

"*Tos*, if you are sure."

"If we feel too uncomfortable, we can go to our temporary tipi. We are aware of all that you rejoice."

Kaitlin offered a shy smile. "Why did your men agree to come?"

"Believe it or not, they actually respect *Woniya Mato* for his honorable treatment of the people who survived… and also for those who did not. In addition, they were determined to see me safely here."

Kaitlin smiled but the tiny worry line was still present on her forehead.

CHAPTER THIRTY-SEVEN

New Friends

The two women stood thoughtfully, each lost in her own thoughts as they watched the Oglala people look curiously to where the barrels were set up off to the side of the feast. The chieftains were gathered together, speaking with gestures to one another, as still others milled around, finishing the elaborate feast set up with all the furnishings.

After nearly an hour had passed, Kaitlin's closest friends had a better grip of the personality of the Crow leader. Finally, a drum beat signaled the beginning of the celebration in honor of the newly married leader and his wife, as well as the war victory. The chief approached his spouse with a smile.

"Come, *Mazaska Zi Ista*. We need to begin our people's celebration with a very important announcement… or two." His white teeth flashed brilliantly against the contrast of his dark complexion.

Although Kaitlin thought she was over her nervous state, the new member to high status learned that indeed, her anxiety still had a life of its own. The blonde beauty allowed her smaller hand to be consumed by her *hingnaku's* larger one. Spirit Bear drew her into his warm side and let her absorb some of his strength.

"Ready, Golden One?" his warm voice asked.

"*Tos*, I am ready."

The tempo of the drum picked up, and when they reached the clearing, *Wawakankan* joined them. In the sudden silence, the shaman stepped forward followed by the newly wedded couple.

"My people," Wonder Worker began. "We are here with our leader and his *thawicu* to celebrate their new joining, but also to rejoice in our victory over the Crow."

A few nervous looks shuffled through the crowd.

"I see you have noted our guests," *Wawakankan* noted. "They are our honored friends who have acted upon our welcomed invitation to join us on this day." He paused for effect. "They are our friends and wish to be with us tonight although they know all we celebrate. I will let *Woniya Mato* elaborate. However, I have a very important announcement to make before I let him tell his tale."

Wonder Worker began to work his magic. He waited until he captured every eye before knowing the exact moment to speak. "Your chief and leader, *Woniya Mato*, is very skilled at taking out the enemy."

The crowd nodded in eagerness.

"And… he is very skilled at… bringing in new life."

A collective gasp shattered every lip. The crowd pressed forward with exclamations and congratulations, surging around the happy couple.

For Kaitlin, it seemed hours later before the drum once more captured the attention of the village, proclaiming it was time to begin a new kind of celebration.

Spirit Bear faced his people with his wife by his side. "Thank you so much, everyone, for making this the most special day in my life. I have the best woman in the world! One could not have been more suited for me, and *Wankantanka* knew this. He created many avenues and events to make me realize she was truly Oglala at heart and that she is one of us."

His people sustained his confessions by raining them with cheering support; in addition, they respected them by dropping a curtain of silence just as quickly. The community waited with baited breath for *Woniya Mato* to continue. Many were extremely curious about the Crow's presence within the village, especially at a time they'd be soon sharing a victory over their destruction.

"As you know, my *thawicu* – then my fiancé – was abducted by *Sunmanitu Wacitusni* as a means to earn a great coup and become an honored member of the Crow band."

Some angry voices echoed his words.

"Peace, my people," he commanded in a lowered voice before continuing, "We will tell more of that story in a little while." The war chief's black eyes glittered against the night. "Bright Sky, a woman leader in the Crow village, was *Mazaska Zi Ista's* protector and companion for many suns. She communicated with her in Lakota to make her feel at home. She translated Crow for her, and provided clothing, food, and other necessities. Bright Sky did this not because she was asked to and not because she was required to; she did this because of the graciousness of her heart. She is a true leader. Bright Sky is a friend of Oglala!"

Lone Wolf and Sky Warrior escorted Bright Sky into the clearing to stand to the side of the war chief. She stood proudly erect, her stoic features were hardened as she was greeted with many curious stares.

Spirit Bear turned back to *Wawakankan* to retrieve a package wrapped in the softest rabbit hide. Then he turned to Bright Sky, facing her, and knelt, extending the gift offering before him. All eyes widened and watched.

"Bright Sky, friend of Bear Claw Clan of the Oglala, please accept this gift."

Once the smile shattered the nervous hardness of her face, the Crow leader respectfully reached for the plush softness of the hide. Spirit Bear stood. Wonder Worker came forward to stand to the side of Kaitlin so that both women faced each other and were sandwiched between two leaders of the community.

Bright Sky delicately unwrapped the fine flute and pipe within the soft folds. Her mouth made an easy O as she breathed in pleasure of the gift. She looked closely at the fine sculpting and engraving on the sides of both items. Someone had etched a tiny black Crow intermingled with black bears. One was dominant on the land, and one in the skies. It stood for peace and harmony between two opposing forces.

"I am honored, *Woniya Mato!*" she exclaimed huskily. Fat tears brimmed in her eyes. Bright Sky held up the items to the crowd for them to see. "This is of the highest honor!"

"All of our leaders had a part in the construction," the war chief revealed. "It is a creation we all composed for you."

The response was deafening!

Bright Sky looked up into each leader's face, the distinctive white girl, and then faced the Sioux people and stated, "I, too, have brought a wedding gift – a gift for your community as you share in the joy of the joining of your leader to his wonderful bride. It is berry wine. Many of you may have indulged in this before, but for those who have not, let me forewarn you: it is a powerful drink. It will make you feel nice and warm. It will make you feel happy or like you could do anything. This makes one want to drink more. To drink more is to become ill with the effects of too much. You will wake up with a headache and dry mouth, or worse: you can become ill. The effects are short lived. I also will give this gift – the power to make this drink – to *Mazaska Zi Ista* to use sparingly in your village. It is an influential gift that cannot be abused."

The crowd again surged forward, wanting to thank the very brave and giving Crow woman. -

Sky Warrior stated, "Let us rejoice in our newly found alliance by allowing our guests to eat first!"

Again, the community supported their leaders. The Crow were served first, followed by the newlyweds, then the rest of the Oglala leaders and their women. Finally, all could fill their plates as their society permitted.

"What a wonderful celebration!" Playful Otter exclaimed once they were all sitting again.

"It will be a tale to be told for many generations to come," agreed Gentle Rabbit.

"I am so honored to be such an esteemed guest," Bright Sky said in astonishment. "I really was quite nervous about coming."

Kaitlin laughed gently. "Oh, believe me, I can relate!" The others laughed with her. She added, "We are really glad you did, though!"

"Although my community is going through a lot of reconstruction and grieving, we felt it was important for me to make an appearance here. I really wanted to be present, but I didn't know if I should leave my people in a time of need."

"Don't get me wrong, I am so *happy* you did, but what made you decide?"

"You may know how the outcome of the war raid turned out, but I don't think you all realize the extent of the devastation of my village. I am not saying this to cause guilt to surface; it is simply a fact. However, my people realize that had it been any other than *Woniya Mato*, none of us would have survived. Every single one of my people would have been annihilated! It is his generosity and the support of his people that allowed us the graciousness of life." Bright Sky paused as a tear of gratitude filled her eyes. Taking a breath, she continued, "We just felt that making an appearance and bringing a gift took precedence. Initiating and maintaining a good relationship with such a man and supportive community is in our highest interest now."

Kaitlin didn't say a word but got up and quietly wrapped her arms around Bright Sky. The resilient woman didn't cry, but she hugged her back, demonstrating a need for friendship, understanding, and support. There was much responsibility hanging on the woman's shoulders.

After much celebrating and eating, the drum once again signaled ceremonial change. Children were put to bed. Kaitlin noticed the Crow men looked nervous. She slid up to her husband's side.

"*Woniya Mato*, it is safe for our new friends, right? No one would get angry and want justice as you tell the tale tonight?"

"*Hiya, Mazaska Zi Ista*. They will know as I begin that all the threats are destroyed. Only our new allies are left of that particular group of Crow. They are our honored guests. Of course, they do not have to watch this ceremony. I am sure it will raise some hard-to-deal-with feelings."

"Can I suggest to Bright Sky that the men go away from the camp for a few hours?

Bright Sky could go to her temporary tipi… or I'd even be willing to sit with her in ours?"

"Of course, *mita wastelaka.* I would not put them through emotional turmoil if it is not necessary. I will wait for your response."

Kaitlin made a beeline for Bright Sky and relayed her ideas. Bright Sky did seem interested for the sake of her men; she knew they were intimidated in the middle of a very powerful Sioux tribe. The Crow and Sioux had been long-time enemies. A friendship alliance was still very new and raw, especially on the tips of broken wings.

"For me, however, I will watch the ceremony by your side. I already know of all the events. Yes, I will feel many emotions, but I would be honored to be allowed to see such a ceremony by a different tribe."

"*Tos*, my friend. I will tell *Woniya Mato.*"

CHAPTER THIRTY-EIGHT

Victory Celebration

Upon Kaitlin's return to sit by her friends, the chieftains left to prepare for the war ceremony celebration. Kaitlin was proud of her man, but she still couldn't repress a shiver of fear when her *hingnaku* assumed his fierce paint. He no longer was the man she knew but assumed the identity of a warrior capable of anything.

It didn't seem long before the drum quieted once more. Instead, gourd rattles and a flute became the major instruments; it was the lull before the action. When the performance was ready to begin, a menacing kettle drum began the heartbeat of life. Suddenly, the celebration clearing was simulated into a Crow battlefield. Sioux men began creeping into the ambush set up by the Crow. The crowd held its breath, fearing for their men although they already knew the outcome of the reenactment.

Instantly, the Oglala men looked directly at the men pretending to be Crow warriors, indicating that their strategic plans for attack were known to the *Cante Tinza*. After a group of Crow men were "taken out", they faded away until only *Woniya Mato*, his extraordinary bow of unbelievable range, and "Crow" warriors remained. The war chief demonstrated how he found his way into the heart of the enemy village. He was a ghost warrior that none could touch! His weapon blessed by *Wankantanka* allowed his path to be cleared as he pirouetted out of range without a trace.

Sky Warrior was dressed and painted like Bloody Knife who was held in the clearing by Oglala men. Yellow Feather and Brave Elk held the man decorated as "Sly Coyote" who was really Lone Wolf. A "female" figure was also there to resemble Bright Sky.

The deadly dance began between the two war chiefs. Gasps and startled noises erupted from the crowd when Spirit Bear struck Bloody

Knife. Kaitlin could barely watch. She leaned into Bright Sky and the two women supported each other.

Air whistled between Kaitlin's teeth when "Bloody Knife's" blade caught *Woniya Mato*'s left calf. She held her breath then the enemy sliced her husband's forearm, but she literally screamed and jumped to her feet when Bloody Knife attacked Spirit Bear and fell on him appearing to make the death strike.

Bright Sky and the many friends surrounding the blonde used gentle hands to pull her back to her seat.

"Shhh, *Mazaska Zi Ista*. Your man is fine. Watch his mastery of the dance with death!" Bright Sky soothed with awe.

"Do not doubt his prowess," *Wawat'ecaka* commanded. "He would never leave your side!" The motherly figure smiled tenderly at her adopted daughter.

"Here, hug me," Desert Rose commanded. "Do not watch."

With tears of fear in her eyes, Kaitlin said, "I am fine now. I will not shame him again. It just scared me, and my emotions are a little crazy right now."

Currently, her *hingnaku* and "Sly Coyote" were seizing each other up. The pregnant woman vowed she would not scream again. She gritted her teeth and watched. Many hands of comfort stayed on her to lend support.

Bright Sky watched silently but her eyes were bright with unshed tears as she watched the confrontation between the Yankton men and *Sunmanitu Wacitusni*, demanding the reasons for his betrayal. Kaitlin wanted to comfort her, but she couldn't tear her eyes from her husband's prowess and strength. The blonde knew what he did in battle, but it left her weak in the knees when she had to witness how close the blades came to taking him away… and with a terrible war cry, the battle began.

Kaitlin nearly bit her tongue. She didn't think a one-to-one battle could be more terrifying than the fight against the Crow war chief, but she was mistaken. When both Sly Coyote and Spirit Bear held each other's forearm and slashed at the other with their lethal daggers, she whimpered softly. However, the blonde could not watch the finale when her *hingnaku* threw down his knife and needled the other to anger. Bright Sky patted her along with friends crowding in to block her sight.

Finally, the combat was over. Kaitlin calmed herself and put an arm around Bright Sky. *Woniya Mato* approached the simulated female Crow leader. He honored her by dropping to his knees in front of her. The Oglala crowd became very still in awe. Spirit Bear thanked the Crow woman for protecting his chosen one and for treating her nobly as Bright Sky simply stared in wonder at him.

The mighty warrior continued, "You honor me by taking *Mazaska Zi Ista* under your wing. You protected her and gave her friendship in a village of enemies. I am in your debt."

The opposing leader could not speak; all she could do was politely watch him. The war chief resumed standing before her and announced that he granted the rest of the surviving Crow their lives back, and he wished Bright Sky to help them heal.

Nevertheless, Spirit Bear was not finished. He turned to his people so that they could clearly hear the rest of what he relayed to the Crow leader.

"I ask a few things from you before I allow you to return to your people, Bright Sky," he said, his tone lowered. "I want your people to know who killed Bloody Knife and *Sunmanitu Wacitusni* and why. I want it announced that those who plan to count coup on me will have *his* coup chanted with his death rites. Those who plan treachery against me and the Sioux will have to answer to me personally!" The Crowd applauded their chieftain's words. Spirit Bear waited for the gathering to quiet once more.

Still speaking to the posing Bright Sky, he added, "I also wish my mercy to you to be known. You were not involved in the planning, execution, or completion of taking my woman, so you were spared. I am not a monster, nor do I take another's life shallowly without reason. I mourn those who fall by my hand, for I know they were loved as father, brother, and son by my foes."

Finally, the infamous man stated, "I normally would not do this, but you have proven to *Mazaska Zi Ista* that you are *kola*, so I will also empower you with my trust. In about a week, I plan to marry her. If you would like to come to the ceremony, I grant you passage. None will harm you. Several of my active warriors are present here tonight and have seen who you are. They will alert others to your identity."

All war chiefs turned to look at the real Bright Sky. *Woniya Mato* took a step toward the real Crow leader. "Bright Sky, do you wish to honor us by joining us in the clearing?"

Standing precariously on her feet, she walked forward. A shaky smile warmed her features, and she hurriedly wiped an escaped tear from her eye.

When she stood before the leaders again, all four men took a knee to her. Bright Sky allowed her hand to be held by the council.

Then they stood, reiterating their support of the surviving Crow band.

The crowd went wild with cheering. Drums took presence and the throng surged forward to rejoice. They swept Kaitlin with them in elation.

"I – I just don't know what to say!" stammered Bright Sky. "The ceremony was so… profound… and so *real*. It was a true account of what happened."

"Are your ceremonies different?" Kaitlin asked.

"Many are embellished for better storytelling," the leader revealed, "but then again, I don't imagine *Woniya Mato* needs to enhance!" She chuckled.

"This is true," agreed *Wawat'ecaka* heartily. "None could make up a fight more thrilling!"

Exhilarating rhythms again took over, and members of the community began to dance. Sky Warrior initiated the wine rations. Soon, many more people were moving to the cadence of the music.

Momentarily, the Crow men returned from the outskirts of the community and headed to their assigned tepees.

"Please excuse me a moment," Bright Sky said. A short time later, she led her men into the clearing to join them. The Crow woman retrieved each cup of wine.

"This will help them relax," she revealed. "Most of my men only speak limited Lakota. I've explained that the ceremony was a very good depiction of true events. They have nothing to fear. The community supports their leaders' philosophies; they are safe."

"I can understand their discomfort and fear," *Mazaska Zi Ista* stated. She smiled at the brave men.

CHAPTER THIRTY-NINE

Generosity

Kaitlin caught the eye of two of the men who smiled back at her. The Indian princess motioned for them to come closer.

"Please tell them that they are honored guests. We want them to sit in the place of honor; in the chieftain circle… if they won't be too uncomfortable."

Bright Sky beckoned them in Crow. The men appeared dubious, but then came with a smile. They sat close to Bright Sky where they were most relaxed. They would also need her to interpret.

"I think another cup of wine would help after they finish eating," *Wawakankan* suggested after he resumed his seat by Playful Otter. "It does great for relaxing nerves."

"This is true!" agreed Kaitlin, remembering, so she advocated to her friends to help her get them more.

"We shall get it, my friend," stated Desert Rose. "You are now *thawicu* to a chieftain. It is no longer your place to wait on others unless it is in your personal tipi… and even then, one may be appointed to serve guests."

Kaitlin was silent, absorbing still another Sioux custom.

As the wine loosened nerves and brought about a relaxed aura, the Crow men smiled and talked amongst themselves and Bright Sky. They began some small talk with the leadership group. Kaitlin could tell they were somewhat subdued around Spirit Bear. He was a legend of war, but it was an honor to be able to talk with him.

After an hour of visiting, one man directed his speech to the war leader, "If I may ask," he hesitated and swallowed, "how you… come cross… such bow?"

"I made it with the breath of *Wankantanka,*" Spirit Bear replied. A smile crinkled his eyes.

The man nodded with a slight grunt and said, he muttered 'priceless' in Crow but settled for "It good gift."

Kaitlin could tell he wanted to ask more questions about it, but all knew that *Woniya Mato* would never reveal trade secrets with another band. It would cause the warrior society, *Cante Tinza,* to lose power.

"Speaking of your bow," began Lone Wolf, "we need to practice targeting bison before long."

"*Tos*, my friend. We will hunt in the next few weeks."

"We, too, need to hunt," revealed a sad Bright Sky.

Spirit Bear nodded in consideration. "If you would like, your people are welcome to hunt with our band. I know you do not have many men left. We have plenty of hunters to take down enough for us and for you. You would need to process your own meat, however.”

Bright Sky was incredulous, “You would do this for us?”

“I would not see hunger take more people from your lives,” he responded with a nod.

The woman turned to the men and spoke rapidly in Crow. Their eyes widened and their mouths dropped open. They all began conversing in excited bursts.

“We accept with gratitude. A few of our people will join in the hunt, and if you don’t mind… there will be a woman or two. We will bring our community to process what we need.”

“That sounds great!” Lone Wolf assented with a nod.

"I will need at least three weeks to teach *Mazaska Zi Ista* the basics of wine making. Then we hunt?" Bright Sky asked.

"*Tos*, that is fine. Or we can hunt in two weeks, and you stay with my *thawicu*? Finish teaching her the arts correctly. There will be plenty of time for you to join. As you know, preparing for winter with bison takes weeks as well."

"Yes, thank you, *Woniya Mato*. I will send Speckled Owl back to speak with the rest of our band. He is a good man. I think he has leadership ability."

Speckled Owl piped up, "My Lakota improving. I understand. I go and will come again." He smiled brightly.

"Yes, in the morning," Bright Sky added.

All had a lighter heart and celebrated more enthusiastically.

"That was very nice," Kaitlin murmured against Spirit Bear's shoulder. "There are so many reasons why I love you so much!"

"Loving you makes me a better man, *mita wastelaka*." He placed a tender kiss on her lips.

The celebration lasted long into the night. Many great memories were made with friends on this wondrous occasion. Kaitlin's head began to bob and nod with fatigue. The renowned warrior gently scooped her up and cradled her in his arms.

"Good night, all," he said with a smile.

"Ahhh, so you have *sleep* on your mind?" *Wawakankan* jested.

Sky Warrior added, "I think not! It *is* his wedding night!"

Male laughter echoed behind Spirit Bear.

His grin only got bigger at his friends' ribbing. The warrior walked purposefully toward their dwelling.

Kaitlin nestled her head against her husband's sculpted chest; the gentle rocking motion nearly tipping the scales into sleep. Her *hingnaku* gently laid her on the soft bedding. A dreamy sigh of his name escaped her pink lips.

Spirit Bear stripped and lay beside his beautiful rare flower. With practiced hands, he unlaced her dress and slipped her clothes. Kaitlin barely stirred. She murmured something unintelligible against his warm flesh.

"Shhh, *Mazaska Zi Ista. Istinma.* We have the rest of our lives to love one another. I would rather you rest your body now and save some energy up for the morning." He softly chuckled as his words fell on deaf ears. The baby growing inside his wife stole her away from him at night. Kaitlin succumbed to sleep much more easily since her body began going through changes.   He smiled. He didn't mind and couldn't wait to meet his child!

The stalwart warrior watched the peaceful confines take his mate deeper into its chamber. He enjoyed just looking at her exquisite beauty relaxed with sleep. He felt he could never get enough of drinking in her magnificence. Finally, he drew her into his embrace and slept.

The next morning, pink fingers of light subtly fluttered around the newly married couple. Kaitlin opened her eyes to find her husband watching her with hungry, onyx eyes. He was propped on one elbow as he watched awareness liven her face.

"*Woniya Mato*! I fell asleep on you last night!" she breathed in.

"*Tos*. It is true, *mita wastelaka*," Spirit Bear smiled tenderly into her mortified face.

"I am so sorry!"

"For what, *Mazaska Zi Ista*?"

"It was our wedding night… and I fell… *asleep*… on you!"

Spirit Bear chuckled. "Do not worry, Golden One. There is plenty of time for love."

His smile never left his expression as he lowered his face to hers. A gentle kiss claimed her lips, and passion kindled immediately. Spirit Bear's hands began exploring her chilled morning flesh. Kaitlin moaned softly as his fingers found and kneaded her breasts.

The golden-skinned woman's hands traced the hard lines of the muscular warrior's body, massaging here and there. Spirit Bear's breath began coming in quick, staccato bursts. Her hands dipped lower to find him hard and wanting. He growled deep in his throat as he rolled her to her side.

"You lay still, my *gopeca* wife. Let me explore!"

"*Hiya, mita hingnaku*! Love is a two-way endeavor!"

"Then," he whispered with an air of command, "You will have to learn the hard way." He grinned as he captured Kaitlin's hands in his. Guiding her arms above her head, he captured one of her hardened peaks in his mouth. Swirling the tip with his tongue, he sucked and flicked the bud.

"You don't play fair," the white woman moaned. The chief allowed her to work a hand free, and she fisted a handful of his hair and gave a playful tug.

"Oh, you want to play that game?" Spirit Bear asked mischievously. "Two can play at that!"

Purposefully, the war chief slid his arms underneath his wife's body and grabbed light fistfuls of golden hair. Softly, he tugged her hair until Kaitlin's head was arched back, revealing a long, slender throat.

The bronzed man licked to taste, then breathed on her moistened skin. He nibbled, and kissed his wife's silky skin until her breathing had quickened into soft mewing. Her throaty sounds of desire nearly broke his restraint.

Kaitlin broke free and pushed him to his back. Taking charge, she straddled him and attacked his body with frenzy. The assertive white girl kissed and tasted every inch of his frame. Finally, neither could take any more, and they satisfied their carnivorous cravings.

"Wow, *Mazaska Zi Ista*! That was worth waiting for!"

Kaitlin's cheeks pinked subtly, but she grinned. "I'm glad you approve, my chief!"

"I more than approve, *mita wastelaka*! We may have to have a repeat performance!"

When the married couple emerged several hours later, no one said a word. Kaitlin saw all the satisfied looks of happiness others expressed toward them. Her friends wore little smirks, but the Indian princess didn't mind. She was sure she wore a contented look herself.

In the days before the bison hunt, the tribe relaxed before they'd begin weeks of arduous work. It was a time full of fun and games. Each night friends gathered around camps and told stories. Finally, Crow members began arriving to help prepare for the hunt.

CHAPTER FORTY

Wine Making

During the weeks of "rest", Kaitlin and Bright Sky made daily trips to the tepees where the wine making took place. The Crow leader had brought many late summer wild grapes with her as part of her gift. The two women smashed the fruit in a bowl with large, pulverizing stones. With each bowl readied, Bright Sky showed Kaitlin how to begin the fruit processing. The older woman would chew about a quarter of each small bowl and spit each mouthful into the vat to help the break-down process. Then she'd stir to distribute the enzymes as evenly as possible.

When a large container was filled (a several day process), the women let it sit for a few more days. The temperature was important to keep constant. Ventilation flaps were opened during the day to increase the air flow when the temperatures rose, and a low fire was kept burning throughout the night as temperatures dropped.

After about five days, slight bubbling became evident in the fermenting mixture. Bright Sky waited a few more days and added a honey mixture to the concoction. She explained to Kaitlin how important all the processes were and knowing when to add ingredients at the right time was crucial for the brew to turn out.

The first container would need to sit for several weeks before it was ready for straining and syphoning. After it sat for four to six weeks, Bright Sky explained that Kaitlin would need to skim off the floating fruit debris, strain it, and pour most of the liquid into a second container to sit as many weeks again. After another month or two of sitting, another round of straining would take place. As much of the fermenting fruit as possible would need to be separated from the bulk of the liquid.

One large container was in the "third round" of the fermenting process. Bright Sky clarified that she'd brought the container along so that she could continue teaching the wine process to the newly married woman. The next few days, the women strained the third stage of the grape juice for the final time, separating even more pulp from the liquid. It was a job that didn't sit well with Kaitlin's stomach. The future wine left a sour taste in her mouth, tortured her sense of smell, and left her feeling slightly queasy. However, the job was finally completed.

"Now we wait," Bright Sky informed with a smile as she plugged the jar as tightly as she could.

"No, now we rest so we can begin to process meat soon!" Kaitlin stated.

The women were actually able to do all the preparation of the wine in a little over a week and a half, so they'd be able to help with the processing of the bison fully.

The chief's wife glanced around the camp teeming with many Crow. It was a powerful site to see two strongly opposed people getting along peacefully in one community. It was a humbling experience. Kaitlin thanked the Great Spirit and her *hingnaku* for this phenomenon.

Spirit Bear announced that the hunting and processing groups would head out in the morning. The blonde noted that many travois that were being readied to leave with the processors.

"*Wawat'ecaka*, why are there so many travois?" she asked.

"We cannot possibly carry all the meat and animal parts back to camp with us," she answered with an understanding smile. "The bison are very large and powerful animals. They are heavy. We must chop up the meat to even put it on the travois."

"Will we bring it back to camp to process?"

"We will process much of it on the spot. It won't weigh as much for the horses as we bring it back to camp. Plan on being at the kill site for at least a week."

"What all will I need to pack?"

"Bring your skinning tools, sharp knives, and scraping knives. You will need many knives and sharpening tools. We will have a lot of meat to dry before coming back to camp."

"Thank you, *Wawat'ecaka*. I will pack now."

Kaitlin left. Really all she needed to pack was a few garments, soaps for cleaning, oils for possibly tanning hides, and a lot of sharp knives and skins to pack the meat in. Still, it made for a bulky pack.

At the hot point of the day when the village rested, Kaitlin settled against the warm skin of her husband's chest.

"*Woniya Mato*, how do you all decide who gets what on the killed animal? Don't some people have to stay at the camp to take care of the children and such?"

"Technically, whoever kills the bison owns it, but we are one with the people. We all share."

"But who gets the hides? Who gets the prime choices of meat?"

"The hunter who takes down the animal always has a choice of what he does with the animal parts. Most of us will take what we need. If we need the hide for blankets, bed roles, clothing, or shoes, we take it. We kill more animals than what we need so that we provide for all in the village. Those whose needs are greatest for certain items get the claim to what it is they seek."

"What about *Wawakte Towanjila*? He usually stays to protect the village. How does he get a rightful share?"

"Ah, you are worried about my friend, Sky Warrior?" an amused glimmer sparkled in her husband's eyes.

"I am just trying to figure out how all this works still," Kaitlin said with a laugh. "My eyes are only for you, my handsome chief!"

"Sky Warrior will have first choice in the prime things we bring back. We chieftains decide who gets what and allocate accordingly. *Wawakte Towanjila* is aware of village matters and is primarily responsible for distribution decisions."

"Will it go the same way with the Crow people?"

"Basically. We will kill as many animals as needed for both tribes. It will look like we take too much at first, but *Wakantanka* knows we do not waste. He will provide all of what we need. Bison blanket the prairie. Our needs will be very small in relation."

A soft sigh of relief escaped the beautiful blonde's lips as she drifted off to sleep. Spirit Bear enclosed her resting form in his protective embrace. "*Istinma, Mazaska Zi Ista.* Dream of me." He smiled into her hair and forced his mind to relax. The afternoon would be a flurry of activity to prepare for the morning's departure.

CHAPTER FORTY-ONE

Bison Hunt

It was early, still dark, when most of the village was packed and mounted or walking behind horses pulling travois. Most travois supported the packs that would be on voyagers' backs on the return trip. Many women and older children walked, but some rode with their husbands. Progress was slow, but the travelers didn't mind; it saved energy for the hard work ahead.

By night fall, the throng had reached its chosen spot to camp. It was near the site where vast herds of *tatonka* were milling. The great animals' noises could be heard for miles.

The women began preparing makeshift bedding and fire pits where huge amounts of meat would be prepared and dried. Children gathered wood for fires. The men checked over their weapons and horses after the day's long journey. It wasn't long before the community had settled in for the night.

Kaitlin wiggled into the traveling mats next to her new husband. Spirit Bear placed a protective arm around his wife and drew her into his body. He breathed into her hair how much he loved her.

"*Woniya Mato*, is hunting the *tatonka* dangerous?"

"*Tos, Mazaska Zi Ista*, but we do not take unnecessary risks."

The blonde turned to fix her golden eyes into his ebony ones. "How many risks are there?"

"It is a great honor to hunt *tatonka*. It is the highest blessing *Wankantanka* can give us. We demonstrate our appreciation by showing our prowess, cunning, and daring. We try to spare the animals' pain and terror, but we must confuse them as we herd them into frenzy. With such hunting methods, there is always risk."

Kaitlyn's eyes were haunted.

"Relax," her husband reassured, pulling her once again into his comforting embrace, "we have hunted *tatonka* many times. You know how *Wankantanka* protects and provides for us. Do not worry."

"*Woniya Mato,* it must be my job to worry!" Kaitlin nervously laughed. "I mean no insult to you. Not only do I fear losing you after all we've been through, but we now have a child on the way."

"I will never leave you, *mita wastelaka. Nimitawa ktelo*: you are mine, forever." He lowered his face and tenderly caressed his lips over hers. Pulling back slowly, he whispered, "*Istinma* now. You will need your strength for tomorrow."

"*Tos, mita hingnaku.* Just please, *please* be careful!" Soon, both drifted off into a light sleep.

***

Woniya Mato sat astride his powerful stallion, waiting for the right moment to signal his hunters. Bands of light began to explode in the east, slicing the blackness of night. Surrounding the chief, well over two-hundred men, painted to aid their prowess, suppressed their eagerness to begin the mighty hunt.

The predators were hidden in the trees that flanked both sides of the prairie on the southern end. Opposite *Woniya Mato, Isnala Sungmanitu* readied his equal number of warriors in preparation for the securing of life for two tribes.

The large hoofed animals were beginning to stir when the sound of many Indian warriors and hunters undulating from the foliage set off alarm within the herd. The brightly colored men on many shaded steeds poured from both sides of the prairie boundaries to greet the masses. Madness lit the men's eyes and their warrior cries shattered the stillness of the morning.

A defense mechanism for the bovine was to run as one unit, stampeding to safety. When pack animals charge, it makes it difficult for predators to single out one individual. Another technique employed by the mighty bison was to surround the young within a protective, inner circle and face their enemy.

The humped beasts began making sounds of distress. Because one side was being driven toward the other, the herding mammals could not organize and blundered about in fright. The panicked animals began bawling loudly, slinging saliva high into the air. In the jumbled milling, the young began falling under the sharp hooves of the adults. Bison bulls billowed anger, horning anything close. The warriors rapidly closed the distance to keep the animals from consolidating.

About the time the first arrows began to fly, a dominant bull broke free from the massed bunch and charged. Because Yellow Feather was close, he turned his horse to herd the mammoth back, knowing he'd take the beast down if he could. Just when he sent a brightly colored arrow at his target, five additional large bulls swung toward the man as well, following the lead of the head bull.

The brightly colored arrow punctured the on-coming male high on his shoulder. Although it ripped part of the muscle, it didn't seem to slow him. Several arrows were necessary to weaken the massive creature before one could get close enough to finish the job with a lance. Yellow Feather's eyes brightened considerably in surprise. While he was prepared to take on a single bull, he simply could not fight off six.

Many men were focused on targeting individual animals and did not notice the swift challenge for life. Brave Elk gave a piercing whistle that cut through the terror and excitement of man and beast alike, alerting many to the now grave situation.

Twenty-five men of the hundreds were close enough to make a difference. Immediately, they sent their horses barreling across the prairie to try to stop the disastrous event. Unfortunately, their altered course seemed to add speed to the furies on hoof rushing toward the single man.

= = =

Yellow feather stopped his mount; there was no need to turn and run. Horses were typically faster than *tatonka*, yet being the target of six charging bulls did not lend to confidence. The *Cante Tinza* member chose to immobilize and face death proudly.

Taking a deep, steadying breath, Yellow Feather aimed and shot arrow after arrow. Mark after mark, the arrows sunk deeply, but the man could not hit the beast fatally when they were facing him in a stampede.

Many hunters' arrows began flying and striking the rampaging bulls. The four lagging bulls began to slow as men flying on horses swooped closer. Still, the front two bulls didn't seem to be shifting their course.

The ground thundered with approaching death. Yet, Yellow Feather calmly continued to shoot feathered missiles. The bison were so close now that he could see the red membrane inside their widened nostrils as the bulls huffed daybreak air with their exertion. Steam rose off their backs as their heat met the cool morning temperature. The beasts' small eyes were focused on him, and they were reddened pools of black fire.

Right before the master bull reached Yellow Feather's horse, a black-tipped red-feathered arrow pierced the animal's eye. It screamed and dropped, sliding into his mount. Yellow Feather's horse jumped in the air, but it could not move entirely out of the monster's path. When the horse came down, it fell on the creature, unable to gather secure footing. The second bull, also downed with a twin weapon protruding from its eye socket, slid into the man and beasts. Yellow Feather blacked out as the tons of animals pushed him down into a dark, furry grave.

Hours later, it seemed, Yellow Feather was finally able to crack his eyes open. They were hot and swollen, but he smiled when he realized he was still alive.

Wawakankan stood over him with a rich broth. "Drink this, my friend," he stated. The medicine man leaned down to support his head as the bison-flavored brew soothed his parched mouth. Then the shaman gave him a strong, bitter medicine that seemed to rob his orifice of any moisture.

"More broth," he croaked.

"Only a little to wash the medicine down. You will need your strength, and I do not want to challenge your stomach. You have been through much on this day."

"My horse…"

"Did not make it. He broke his neck when the second bull collided into him. You were more fortunate. Your horse took the brunt of the force as well as your arm. It will heal, and I believe you will make a full recovery."

With a nod, Yellow Feather sank back into oblivion.

***

The leaders of the successful hunting party were gathered around *Wawakankan* and his patient after the excitement from the hunt was over. Provisions of food, hides, and fat would see two tribes of Indians through the winter; it was an enormous success. There were some minor injuries, but the main one was the warrior lying before them. His injuries were not life-threatening; *Wankantanka* had blessed them once again.

There were many drying meat fires around the site. Most of two villages were busy cutting, slicing, cooking, and drying various parts of the bison. Fat was stored in intestinal tubes. Tendons would be secured for making sinew thread for shoes and clothes. Bones were piled to make into tools and utensils. Hooves were amassed to make into glue or other needed material. Much of the drying would be completed on site, but a lot of the work would be taken back to each band's community.

Kaitlin and *Wawat'ecaka* had just finished rolling up the head bull's hide and that of a prime pelt of a cow. Also secured was the mammoth head of the dominant male. These were placed in sight of Yellow Feather so that he could see them once he was awake again. It was an honor to be chosen by such a powerful totem and live to tell of it. The spirit of *tatonka* was with the warrior forever now: he had been marked.

Woniya Mato was proud as he watched his wife work without complaint. All the women would fall into exhausted slumbers only to wake again a few short hours later to check on the meat. Children assisted the women with chores. They also gathered water and wood for fires. Men would be guarding the killed animals from hungry vermin throughout the night. It took everyone who was able to work to secure the future of the tribes.

CHAPTER FORTY-TWO

Celebrating the Hunt

Finally, everyone settled back home. There was still much to do. Pemmican would need to be made, sinew would have to be stretched and dried, bones would need to be boiled and cleaned of debris, and many other items would need to be finished into usable products. Then the curing of hides would have to take place.

Kaitlin wouldn't have it any other way. She felt exhausted but satisfied each night as she fell into a deep sleep. Once all the work was completed, the *winyan* could begin sewing new winter clothes and baby items. It was an exciting prospect!

When things had begun to settle back into normalcy, the tribe began to talk about a celebration ceremony. The community had had too much work and meat to secure to even think of spending energy on rejoicing, but once everyone was rested, they needed time to relax and thank the Great Spirit. Nothing would serve their purpose better than a gathering of recognitions!

The communal agreement was that they would take a day of rest, and then take a day to prepare for a large feast. Everyone always looked forward to this type of a gathering!

***

Kaitlin had just settled into the chieftain's circle. A merry fire was blazing in the clearing, and the delicious aromas of the abundance of prepared food tantalized her senses. Her stomach growled in anticipation.

Friends were gathered closely, all smiling at one another. *Wawat'ecaka*, as usual, was a butterfly with her ceaseless fluttering over platters of food. A large drum began to signal the attention of the community.

Spirit Bear along with Wonder Worker, Lone Wolf, and Sky Warrior were gathered in the ceremonial clearing that would serve as the stage. They were smiling happily, well pleased with their bounty of meat before the weather turned for the worst.

It was not long before the village was greeted by *Woniya Mato*'s manly voice.

"My people! It is time to thank *Wankantanka* for blessing us with plenty for the upcoming seasons. As we all know, winter is a very trying time that robs us of young and old alike, especially if our *tatonka* hunting has not been successful. Although we are not finished with all of winter's minor preparation, we have secured enough meat and hides to weather us through."

The throng all called aloud in agreement that *Wankantanka* had, indeed, been full of blessings for their people.

"Tonight, we rejoice in the many gifts of *Wankantanka*. We will eat, dance, and be merry! Then, a group of warriors will reenact Yellow Feather's daring stand against the spirit animal that marked him forever!"

The crowd went wild with cheering!

Kaitlin beamed at her man just to be elbowed by a grinning Desert Rose.

"Hey!" she said with a smile.

"I had to get your attention some way!" Desert Rose teased. "You can't rip your eyes away from your *hingnaku*! I've missed you!"

"You see me nearly every day!" Kaitlin laughed.

"*Tos, Mazaska Zi Ista*, this is true, but when do we have time to have fun?"

"I agree. We have been very busy lately!"

Both friends hugged one another.

"I have missed you, too, *Unjinjintka Can Koica*!"

Another arm snaked around Kaitlin from the opposite side. "And have you missed me as well?" asked Apple Blossom.

"I have missed you all!" The blonde woman replied. She was suddenly surrounded by all of her friends: Apple Blossom, Desert Rose, Playful Otter, and even Fresh Water, New Moon, and Singing Cicada.

Singing Cicada giggled and fluttered flower petals in the air over Kaitlin as she did a childlike dance that was somehow womanly around the gathering of friends.

"What are you doing, you little busy beaver?" laughed the adopted Indian princess.

"I am soo happy NOT TO BE WORKING!" the child-woman replied. "I'm celebrating already!"

"Look, Singing Cicada! Silver Fox watches you! He must be enjoying your dance," teased New Moon.

Indeed, a young Sioux brave was hungrily following the graceful yet playful antics of the young woman in her circle of friends.

"She is too young to be looked at so!" gasped Kaitlin. Her friends just chuckled. "You should know men will look at any with curves!" Playful Otter teased.

Fresh Water, ever protective, threw the young man a motherly glare. Immediately, he looked away.

She chastised, "Singing Cicada, please sit. I know you are having fun, but act more properly."

"Yes, Fresh Water."

The signal was given to begin the meal celebration, so women began serving their men. Kaitlin happily retrieved one of her wedding plates and filled it with tender *tatonka*. She drizzled wild onion and meat dripping dressing over watercress tossed with poke and raisins, freshly made berry pones of bread, and a slice of tuber drenched in meat sauce. She also filled his cup with flavored water.

"My love?" she said, gently placing the aromatic meal in his lap.

"Oh, *mita wastelaka,* this is splendid! Look, *Wawakankan*! She uses your plate gift!"

"It is nearly too beautiful to use," Kaitlin admitted, "but what good do they do if we never use them?"

Wonder Worker flashed the Indian princess a white smile. "They are to use however you see fit."

"Thank you," she grinned back.

"Go fill a plate for yourself, *Mazaska Zi Ista*, then return to my side."

All the women filled plates and sat in the chieftains' circle.

"How is the berry drink coming along?" Desert Rose inquired.

"It is going very nicely," she answered. "I do find, however, that great skill comes with great smell." Her friends all laughed at her response.

"But I like the smell of berries," Singing Cicada said with a pretty pout.

"You wouldn't like the smell of these," Kaitlin teased. "They are similar to berries that have sat in rain water for a few weeks. They do NOT smell nice."

The young woman wrinkled her nose prettily.

"We need to have a ceremony soon to induct new women," *Woniya Mato* suggested.

Wonder Worker, Sky Warrior, and Lone Wolf all agreed. Every single person turned their eyes upon the blossoming young lady. Singing Cicada blushed furiously. It was the only time Kaitlyn had ever seen her speechless.

Talking was postponed as the women consumed their meal. When they finished, dishes were collected and washed. It was time for the reenactment of the hunt!

A deep base began a solitary beat. The leaders excused themselves from the chieftains' circle to prepare for the "hunt". Before long, the audience was enthralled in a man-portrayed version of the hunt. When the Natives performed events for the congregation, all felt as if they were there. It sealed the feeling of togetherness. At the performance's end, two men carried the massive head to Yellow Feather.

Yellow Feather stood proudly and watched as they brought the skull brightly decorated with scenes of the hunt across the forehead. Feathers were adorned and attached with leather streamers. It was a fine piece of art.

"The spirit of this *tatonka* chose Yellow Feather to guide on the day of the hunt," *Wawakankan* began. "The great beast warrior marked his human equal forever with his protection."

The crowd cheered madly. The gathering looked at the man standing with his arm in a sling.

"Yellow Feather will make a full recovery because both the spirit of the *tatonka* and *Wankantanka* will it."

Lone Wolf stood and added, "He will be even more stealthy and protected on hunts. Other spirit animals will have to get around the *tatonka* guide to harm him." Lone Wolf laughed. "Not many would risk that!"

Again, the Sioux people went crazy with support.

Spirit Bear added, "Yellow Feather is already *Cante Tinza*, but he has been marked for more prowess in war raids and those to protect our community!" *Woniya Mato* held the bison skull high in the air for the crowd and shook it with meaning. The multitude surged forward to the men on stage and surrounded them.

When the excitement died down, another drum signaled the upcoming revelries. The dancing and actions of celebrations began. Yellow Feather joined the chieftains' circle upon the men's return.

"How does your arm feel?" Lone Wolf asked.

"It feels fine. The swelling is down. Now it just needs to heal."

"Our blessings are many," Spirit Bear agreed, smiling at his wife.

Quiet Deer and Yellow Feather's two children also joined their group. The friends talked long into the night. They danced, sang, ate and drank more, and teased each other. Finally, everyone headed to their personal dwellings to rest.

CHAPTER FORTY - THREE

Disagreement

The next few weeks were a flurry of motion. Final preparation for winter was procured. At last, the tribe had some time to restore energy levels. The hard work was worth every person it saved, but now was a time for less intense exertion. Life was an act of achieving balance.

Kaitlin was excited to begin construction on garments for her child. At an evening fire outside of her tipi one night, she sat down with cutting tools. She didn't really know where to begin. How large or small should she make the attire? There was no child to measure it against. If the expectant mother waited until the child came, he (or she) would be naked and cold until she could make the item.

Wawat'ecaka noticed Golden Eyes staring at the cutting tools and leather in her lap.

"*Mazaska Zi Ista*," she called, "Would you like some help?" The elderly woman approached with quiet feet. "Do you not know where to begin? I assume you want to begin sewing for your new one?"

"*Tos*, I do, and *Hiya,* I do not know where to start. How do you measure clothing if the child is not here to compare?"

Gentle Rabbit chuckled softly. "*Mazaska Zi Ista*, do not worry. Our new child garments are constructed so that they fit most children when they get here. It is a type of frock, similar to what I constructed for you upon your arrival here except it is not open at the sides."

"Even for male children? They wear a gown?"

"*Tos*. Even males wear a robe. They do not yet have an ego to support."

"But their fathers might."

Gentle Rabbit chuckled. "It is our way.
None will question. Let me help you with your
first construction."

Kaitlin watched as *Wawat'ecaka*
cut out the garment for her. It was a very simple
design that was genius. The blonde began to
sew with the softest rawhide bindings available.
In no time, she had her first gown completed.
She held it up to admire. The leather was like
silk and was a lighter yellow color.

"Do you decorate newborn's clothing?"
Kaitlin asked as *Wawat'ecaka* nodded her head
with approval.

"You can, but most do not. New
children like to spit up a lot. It is easier to clean
the clothing when there are no adornments."

"I see."

"But you will want many frocks as they
tend to get dirty quickly."

"How many?"

"Three or four per day."

"So I should make two suns' supply?"

"If you have the time, supplies, and energy, it would be wise."

This time *Mazaska Zi Ista* cut the fabric under *Wawat'ecaka*'s watchful eyes. Before long, Kaitlin had several usable gowns for a new child. She'd work on making more that evening. For now, she'd check the berry wine and rub oil on some pelts.

At noon, she returned to her tipi. Her husband smiled brightly at her.

"I see you've made some new clothes," he said.

Kaitlin grinned back. "*Tos*, I will make more, too. *Wawat'ecaka* says I will need three or four outfits each day."

"You may want to make some undergarments as well."

"Ohhh, yes! I can't forget to do that!"

Kaitlin began to construct a soft diaper that could be tied on the sides. While she did, she became pensive. Spirit Bear noted a difference that overcame her.

"What holds your thoughts, *Mazaska Zi Ista?*"

"It is my family."

"We are your family now, *mita wastelaka.*"

"*Tos*, always and forever, my love, but still. My heart wonders how my father and brother fare. I wish to show them our new child someday."

"I do not think this is possible… Or wise."

"Why not?"

"*Mita wastelaka*, you gave up your *wasicu* ways when you became Oglala. You can never return to that life."

"*Woniya Mato*, I do not wish to return to that existence. Ever. But I do wish to see my family. I know they did not treat me well, but it does not mean I do not care for them. At least they would know I live."

"They will not welcome me with open arms, and I will not allow you to travel alone."

"At least you could converse with them now that you know the rudimentary elements of our language."

"Did you not hear me, love? I am War Chief. They see me as an enemy."

"My father and brother did not live in the town. They had the house outside of the walls. We could see them, just you and me."

"We have winter coming and the band to think of, *Mazaska Zi Ista*. I am a leader and now is not the time to do this."

"Then when? In the spring? Before the baby comes, or after? I think I am due in May."

"Someday, we will see. I am not going to promise anything. I do not think travel is wise while you are heavy with child. Travel with new children is also not always best."

"*Woniya Mato*, why do you not want me to see my father and brother?"

The war chief was silent for a few minutes. Finally, he said, "*Mazaska Zi Ista*, your father chose the man Jed to be your *hingnaku*. I am the one who took his life. I also took his brother's life. Then *Zuzeca Pazan* masqueraded as me and killed more *wasicu*. How could they know I mean them no harm? I know the ways of man. They will have blood lust running in their veins, fueled by fear. It is not wise to go." Spirit Bear did not add anything about his anger toward her father over Jed.

Kaitlin looked down and studied the diaper in her lap. Idly, she fidgeted with the strings to tie the garment. She did not hear her husband approach but felt his presence.

"*Mita wastelaka*, I do not deny you based on your will to reunite with your family. I deny you because my warrior's sense says no. This is how I have survived as long as I have. I do not want to lose you or our child you carry. The *wasicu* are not honorable men. Words to explain past events will fall on deaf ears. I do not trust them, even those who carry your blood."

He squatted down and wiped the lonely tear slowly trickling down her cheek.

"I am emotional, and I can't help but want to see them, my *hingnaku*. I know you speak wisely, but my heart is still sad. Promise me that someday you will change your mind. Maybe you can take me and melt into the woods while I visit my family?" Her hopeful tone pulled at the leader's heart strings.

"I will not say *tos*, *Mazaska Zi Ista*. But I promise to think on this."

"Thank you, my love."

***

Fall was in full swing. The band continued to collect seasonal things in preparation for the cold months. Even mushrooms were gathered and dried to help flavor soups and stews.

When the weather turned brisk and windy, Kaitlin noticed that the herds of animals began to migrate. The community, also, seemed to be a flurry of movement. She noticed Fresh Water bustling around.

"What is everyone doing, my *kola*?"

"We are preparing to move."

"We are moving? Why?"

"When the animals have eaten the grasslands down, they leave the area. With winter approaching, we usually follow the animals' lead and travel to lower ground. This spot is optimum for hunting and gathering, so we will return in the spring."

"Where do we go now?"

"It is hard to describe but it is about nine suns from here if we ride normally, more with the slow pace we will have to take."

Kaitlin began to roll up the newly cured hides and store them. Really, she felt at a loss. The blonde looked at the plethora of gifts they'd received and all the stored food and hides. How would they ever move it all?

At rest time, *Wawat'ecaka* stopped by to eat with Kaitlin. Wonder Worker joined the couple and his mother at their hearth. *Mazaska Zi Ista* had prepared a venison, carrot, mushroom, and *Tinpsila* stew. She served sweet *aguyapi* with the meal.

"Fresh Water tells me the village is moving soon," Kaitlin almost couldn't contain herself.

"*Tos*," Gentle Rabbit confirmed. "We shall move in a few suns."

Kaitlin's face must have held a level of panic, for the tender old woman soothed, "When have I failed to help you when you have need?"

"Never!"

"Do not doubt me now!"

Kaitlin turned to her husband, "But, *Woniya Mato*, how will we ever move all that is in our tipi?"

"*Mazaska Zi Ista*, do not worry!" he chuckled with amusement. "We are one big family. We help one another."

"But everyone else will have their own belongings to pack. It is so much!"

"I am chief. I have many horses. There are enough animals to pack all of our belongings and that of many in the village. *Wankantanka* blesses us."

Finally, Kaitlin was able to take a sigh in relief.

Wawat'ecaka said, "Women friends gather together to help each other disassemble our dwellings. Before this, though, most have things ready to place on travois for the move."

Wawakankan added, "I will bless us with a prayer tonight so that all goes smoothly." He flashed a grin at the worried woman.

"When will we need to have the majority of things packed?"

The chief said, "We will most likely move in seven suns."

"That will just barely be enough time to get everything gathered. And the wine…!"

"*Mita wastelaka*, all will be taken care of. Take a deep breath and calm yourself. It is much to do, but many hands help."

After lunch, each went to their dwelling to rest. It was difficult for the blonde to relax, so Spirit Bear knew he needed to take her mind off all she needed to do: it was time for romance.

"*Mazaska Zi Ista, uwa yo.*"

"*Tos, mita hingnaku?*" Kaitlin stopped her pacing to approach him on the mats.

He patted the bedding with a smile.

"I have so much to do!"

"*Tos*, I know." His smile widened. His vivid white teeth flashed against the bronze of his skin.

Kaitlin's heart fluttered. She knew he was determined to get her mind off of her present anxieties. When she settled beside him, he kissed her gently. Slowly, his hands guided themselves to her clothing and smoothly removed them. Then he shed his own buckskins.

Kaitlyn's eyes mesmerized him as he saw her hungrily drink in his lean body. Her eyes caressed the outline of his prominent muscles. The blonde grinned very deliberately.

Spirit Bear cocked a brow. His member responded. The stalwart warrior approached his wife and became malleable in her soft embraces. Both took what they needed from the other. The chief received unconditional love and support which he returned in full. Kaitlin's nerves were rejuvenated as well. Soon they rested, nestled in each other's arms.

CHAPTER FORTY-FOUR

New Ground

The next few days were a flurry of motion for the village. Women were busy loading up travois and binding possessions in wraps such as blankets, furs, and baskets. Food items were bundled but kept in the tepees until the last possible moment.

On the morning of the move, women gathered together to disassemble the many dwellings. It was a collective effort. The men caught horses and attached the many travois to prepare for travel. Children began to find spots on the wayfaring devices to load up with packed food.

The wind was gusty, but not overly so. Kaitlin decided to braid her hair to keep the puffs from making it sting her face.

Wawat'ecaka brought forth some feminine leggings for Kaitlin to wear and also some matching lace-up boots. Both were a chestnut color with wool lining the inside. To top it off, she gave her a riding cloak to match. Not only would Kaitlin travel in style, she would be plenty warm!

"Oh, *Wawat'ecaka*, how can I ever thank you? You have done so much for me, and you always do too much!"

"It is nothing, daughter! I am honored to make you happy!"

Before the elder woman knew it, the blonde had thrown her arms around her neck and gave her a bear hug. The startled female ended up hugging her back.

"Look, *Woniya Mato*! See what your mother made for me?" Kaitlin did a twirl to make the cloak flow prettily.

"It is perfect for you, *mita wastelaka*! It is made for a queen!" He paused an appropriate amount of time after the compliment before adding, "Is everything loaded up on the travois?"

"Yes, my chief."

"Then *uwa yo*. We must be on our way."

Spirit Bear leaped onto the back of his stallion and swung her up in front. Gentle Rabbit was on the line-backed dun, and Wonder Worker was on his mare. The many horses held either people or pulled loaded travois.

Because the tribal council members were the ones to lead the procession, Kaitlin could see the vastness of the community behind them. Between two and three hundred families flanked them. Warriors were strategically placed throughout the crowd to quickly be able to handle any threats.

"My *hingnaku*, where will we go to find such a home as this that will house our entire band?"

"There is land on the other side of the *wasicu* that we always reside during the time when the winds war with the land. It will be dangerous as we trek through that area."

Kaitlin's eyes rounded with hope.

"*Mita wastelaka*, have I not told you that it is not the time to go seek your family?"

"I know, my chief. But maybe one day once we're settled…?"

"Do not get your hopes up."

"How far away from the settlement will we be?"

"Three days."

"*Woniya Mato!* Will it be safe?" her inhaled breath gave away her surprise.

"It is not ideal. It is our land, and we will defend it. I just hope it does not come down to that."

Kaitlin was silent. This idea definitely was NOT ideal. She could not stand any casualties of war. The men in the settlement had flintlocks. At least her Lakota family knew what they were now and the power they wielded.

The journey was long and wearisome, especially for Kaitlin. Many days blended into nights. The Lakota princess lost track of the time. Finally, the camp that would be their winter home lay on the horizon. Kaitlin was wearily ecstatic.

The first night was spent sleeping as they had on the trial. Makeshift bedding was placed around campfires. Tepee erection would commence with the morning, for the travelers were too exhausted.

Kaitlin nestled against her husband's warmth. His strength seeped into her bones. Spirit Bear's closeness blanketed her in safety and before she knew it, the *winyan* was deep in slumber. Her *hingnaku* lay quietly by her side for a time, then gently arose.

Woniya Mato, chief of war, took first guard. The white settlement was near, but not so near as to be on high alert. Still, it was the first night in the old site, and a sentry was needed. Any of the *Cante Tinza* would be happy to stand on guard; however, the leader wanted his warriors to rest after the days of travel.

With morning came a flurry of communal efforts. By midday, the Lakota village was completely resurrected in bulk. Minor preparations continued on into the late evening. Meals of pemmican and dried items were shared one final time before fresh meat would be procured.

Kaitlin gathered enough firewood to last through the night. Just as the fire died back, her husband entered. He did a few things then retired to their furs.

"*Mita wastelaka, uwa yo*. I need to hold you in my arms."

He had stripped and was only wearing his breech clout and a smile. She grinned at his open invitation.

"Shall I undress?"

"*Hiya*. Let me have the honor!"

The golden skinned beauty's silhouette was bathed in the warm light of the fire. She truly looked like the *wi* goddess coming to pleasure him. His grin deepened with eagerness.

Slowly, seductively, Kaitlin approached her bronzed god. She purposefully swayed her hips. Just as she was about to reach the bedding, she turned away and giggled.

"*Mazaska Zi Ista*!" His voice was deep and hoarse.

His wife turned and batted her eyes innocently. "*Tos*?"

"*Uwa yo!*"

"I am just an arm's length from you, my chief!" her laughter tinkled around them like tiny silver butterflies.

The Oglala leader's eyes narrowed dangerously. Kaitlin took a nervous swallow. Still, she continued to torment her husband. She fluttered about with teasing wings.

Swiftly and silently, the war chief struck. Kaitlin squealed in a high-pitched voice when he'd whisked her in the air then cradled her next to his hard chest.

"You dare to defy me, Golden One?"

"N – no, my chief! I do not know what you mean!"

"Oh, but I think you do! You shall pay dearly for that little trick!"

"B – but what are you going to do to me?

Spirit Bear's laughter rumbled deep in his throat, nearly sounding as much a bear as his name indicated.

"Do you tremble with fear? …Or anticipation?" her intrepid warrior asked softly.

"I tremble with desire for you, my *hingnaku*!" Kaitlin responded.

Swiftly, the couple returned to the sleeping mats, and the chief gently nestled his wife in the furs. He then dropped down beside her. Kaitlin's eyes were wide saucers.

The bear prowled his domain, lurking here or there, but never devouring his prey. *Woniya Mato* would hover above the mounds on her chest, but did not touch. Kaitlin's breathing rate increased.

"What is it you desire, *mita wastelaka?*" he asked huskily.

"I want you… to love me!" she panted.

"*Tos?*" he lowered his head until his lips were just above her straining chest. He breathed on them as he watched her. The blonde instinctively arched her back. Spirit bear touched the fabric stretched over her pronounced nipples slightly with his tongue. He was rewarded with a delicate moan.

Spirit Bear began to undo the bindings of her dress, deliberately taking his time, to torture her like she had him. His fingers would slightly touch her skin as he unlaced the material. Kaitlin raised up and began to nibble on his throat. Her arms slid around him, bringing him to her. Suddenly, the slow lovemaking turned into a frenzy.

Clothes were whipped away and strewn about their dwelling, and slow touches became fiery embraces. Tongues twirled, teeth nipped, and hands explored. It was not long before the two lay back, sated, in the soft comfort of the bedding furs.

"*Mazaska Zi Ista*, before we sleep, will you practice *wasicu* tongue with me?"

"*Tos*, my chief. You wish to learn more of our language?"

"I am interested in the ways of your old people, but it may not be for all reasons you will like," he granted.

"For what reasons, *Woniya Mato*?"

"*Mita wastelaka*, know you hold my heart. Without you, I could not live or breathe. The *wasicu* are not honorable men. I would like to understand their language so I can understand them."

"How will it help you understand them?"

"I study them and their ways. I hear them speak but do not know what they say."

"You spy on them?" his wife held her breath.

"If you must think of it that way, then *tos*. I never underestimate the *toka*. When I do, I will lead no more."

"Do not say that! You will lead for a long time, my chief! I will do anything to help you!"

"Shhhh, *mita wastelaka*. You help our people when you help me. Do not worry."

Kaitlin allowed herself to snuggle deeper into his embrace before they began practicing the language of the *wasicu*.

***

The next morning came bright and early. There was a scratch at the flap just as the sun awoke.

"*Tos*?" Spirit Bear answered.

"It is I, *Wawat'ecaka*. I have brought breakfast."

"*Hau*, come in and join us!"

The elderly woman softly padded in with a plate of quail and fresh pones of bread.

"You have been busy, mother."

"Actually, *Wawakankan* has been."

The chief arched a brow in response.

"*Wawakankan* felt like maybe I worked too hard at my age with the move, and the same for your *thawicu*, with this first experience traveling so far, with the many preparations, in her new condition."

Spirit Bear laughed heartily. "You must tell my brother how deeply appreciated he is! Why did he not come to share the meal?"

"*Wawakankan* wanted to see if his stores of herbs were full for winter one last time. He will make a search of this new location to replenish anything lacking."

"Well, I invite you both to share a dinner fire tonight. I will tell the others in the tribal council to bring their love interests as well."

Kaitlin's eyes lit up. She scrambled forward to share food with *Wawat'ecaka.*

"Thank you, mother."

"You must thank *Wawakankan!*" she answered with a smile.

"I must also thank you for preparing it!" she beamed right back. "Would you care to join me for some morning tea as well?" Kaitlin was already pouring water into a new *tatonka* pot over the pit as she asked.

"*Tos*, I would enjoy that."

While the tea brewed, Spirit Bear finished his breakfast and began gathering hunting supplies. The women were nibbling on the pones when he bent down to kiss his wife on the forehead.

"I will see you at midday with fresh meat to roast for the evening meal, *Wastelaka.*"

"*Pilaka*, my *hingnaku*. I am thankful for nothing is better!"

The blonde's eyes never left the manly form until he was gone.

CHAPTER FORTY-FIVE

Settling In

When the tea was ready, the two women sat, side by side, and thoughtfully sipped the beverage.

"What should we do today?" Kaitlin asked. "I know there is much, but I do not know where to begin."

"It shall be busy for a bit, but our lives will slow down a little now that we have basically prepared for winter. There are still things to gather and organize, but our storages areas are nearly brimming. We will focus on nuts, mushrooms, and items like this. We will try to gather wood into a closer location so that we won't have to travel as far when the snow blankets come. Winters can be very harsh. We often lose the very young and very old if the winds are especially cruel."

+++

Kaitlin became pensive. How well she remembered the cruelty of the winter. The former season was spent miserably. Her *wasicu* clothing had been thin and ragged, and her shoes had been in an equal deplorable state as well as highly uncomfortable, and she'd had to struggle to find enough material to heat their dwelling. On especially harsh days, her men folk would help, but it was a rare occasion. The lonely blonde very nearly became ill from lack of adequate warmth. On cold nights, she'd huddle under threadbare blankets while her meager kindling vanished under hungry flames.

+++

Kaitlin shook her head. She couldn't imagine being in a worse predicament than last winter. With all these wonderful people who worked to help one another, she could get through anything! If someone needed food, it would be donated generously. The same was for clothing, furs, and such. Most in the community did their fair share and did not require a large amount of contributions.

"Today, let us organize your storage tent so that we can see if anything is still amiss. We will string up sinew so that we can thread mushrooms for drying. Does this sound acceptable?"

"*Tos*, of course."

The band made the *thawicu* of their chief her very own storage tent. *Mazaska Zi Ista* had many skills, and she needed additional space for her wine making. The structure was large enough for additional storage. Not only was there room for her large fruit processing equipment, but also for her many tanned hides, her basket making items, and jewelry tools.

Kaitlin nearly blushed when she saw all that the community gave her. Never had she had so much abundance! The fair-skinned beauty was humbled and nearly embarrassed when she looked at her acquired lavishness.

Wawat'ecaka smiled gently at the golden one. "You make our community proud, *Mazaska Zi Ista*. We think the world of *Woniya Mato* and of those tied closely to him. The tribal council rules with a fair hand and protects and cares for all. It is how we show our appreciation."

Kaitlin nodded slightly in acknowledgement. It was just so strange going from the lowly status of a slave to the highest rank of wife of a chief with more possessions than she knew what to do with. Somehow, it didn't seem right.

After they strung up the sinew, they threaded the mushrooms and prickly pears they'd gathered along the way. When they finished, they took baskets and gathered many kinds of nuts along with cactus. The flavorful hard-shelled delicacy added an important part in winter diets with the nutritious protein and fat.

"*Wawat'ecaka,* do we eat a lot of cacti?" Kaitlin asked as she sucked on her finger newly pricked by the spines of a large pad.

"They have many uses," the motherly woman responded.

"But we eat them?"

"They are good as a fiber source to add to soups or even to eat raw. One must be careful, however, because the cacti also has a medicinal use. If you need fiber, eat a lot of this, and you will not need fiber for some time!"

The women laughed.

"What else do we do with these?" Kaitlin had never eaten the cacti that she was aware.

"We use the spines for needles and to clean our teeth," Gentle Rabbit informed. "When dried, you can use the skin for many things. The sap from the pads can be used to treat minor wounds, and I've noticed that mosquitoes do not really like the smell."

Kaitlin nodded in acknowledgement. The plant may be tough to gather, but it was worth the benefits. Along the way, the Indian princess found some late blooming elderberries, mostly gone or in a varied state of drying but gathered them. She thought she could make a sort of small pie. Both women returned to their respective dwellings to complete minor chores before the mid-day meal.

Kaitlin began to boil some water in a skin pot and added the elderberries. When the fruit had hydrated, she moved them into the iron skillet with some of the water and added honey. The *winyan* reduced the concoction while adding more honey and a little gruel. When the creation jellied, Kaitlin began to fill small, crepe-like dough with the blend. After fat sizzled and popped in the pan, she cooked the pastries until they were a golden brown. Smiling with satisfaction, the Indian Princess gave a slight nod of accomplishment. When her friends came over to dine, they would have a wonderful treat waiting for them!

It was nearly time to eat lunch by the time Kaitlin had cleaned up the area used to cook. Her husband brought five freshly killed rabbits and a gobbler home. Golden Eyes was clearly surprised.

"*Waniya Mato*! I'm sure this is for our evening meal! What do you want me to prepare for midday?"

"*Mita wastelaka*, begin with the turkey. There is no way we will eat even a fraction of it, but at least we won't eat the same thing for both meals," he replied with a smile. "I will skin the rabbits while you pluck the bird."

"*Tos*. Can you also skewer them for me?"

"Of course."

Kaitlin took notice of how his eyes were glued on her pastries. She smiled warmly. "*Hiya*, my chief. Those are for our evening when we have guests."

"Oh, really? Do you remember the last time you made pastries of this type for me, *Mazaska Zi Ista*?"

"How can I forget, my chief?" she snickered. "If I had the time, I'd challenge you to a repeat dual."

"After we eat and retire for the heat of the day, I accept your challenge," he parlayed.

"Deal."

Kaitlin cleaned the bird then removed two of the drumsticks. She skewered the rest of the fowl. Slowly, she roasted the legs. The rest of the meat would be put over the dying embers after rest time.

She made pones of bread with elderberries, and prepared some poke she'd previously dried. The rehydrated vegetable reminded her quite a bit of spinach. Ever ready to sprinkle over the meal was her favorite salt brush solution.

"Um, *Mazaska Zi Ista*, that smells wonderful!"

"Thank you, my chief. I hope you like it."

They took their plates into their hut. The heat of the day was no longer hot, so the small fire simmering in the pit had the temperatures just right.

The husband and wife team settled down to their meal. Hot juice from the turkey leg burst forward with nearly every bite. The skin was slightly crisp and seasoned flawlessly.

"*Mita wastelaka*, I knew you were perfect, but now I have even more proof!"

"It is you who is perfect!" she countered.

"I do not think so." He reached over and followed the juice running across her hand with his tongue. Slowly he trailed down her arm. When he reached the tender inside of her elbow, he scraped his teeth lightly, causing a small squeal.

"The meal must not be as pleasing as you say, my chief!"

"Oh, the meal is delicious, but how can I think about food with such an enchanting woman before me?" Slowly, the warrior took both of the plates and set them down close enough to the fire to keep the food somewhat warm but not as to dry it out.

Kaitlin stood, waiting for him to return. She slowly unlaced her bindings and lowered her dress. Keeping her eyes on her predator, she very deliberately slid the breechclout down her silky thighs.

She stood again, almost defiantly, and motioned her finger indicating him to come. There was no hesitation. He growled deeply in his throat before scooping her up and nestling her to him.

Spirit Bear's chest radiated heat and Kaitlin began to lightly trace her nails over his firm pectorals. She licked his collarbone and nuzzled her way up to his neck where she continued lightly clawing him and teasing him with her lips and tongue.

Woniya Mato groaned and gently lowered her to the sleeping mats. Nestling her into the furs, he stood and removed every article of clothing. The warrior proudly allowed her gaze to admire his manly outline before he answered her unspoken command to pleasure her.

"You are so beautiful," the war chief whispered in understandable English.

"And you, *mita hingnaku*, are very *gopeca*, too," she whispered back. His male magnificence was like no other. Beauty was the only word she could think to describe it.

With a kiss, their tongues danced leisurely. Spirit Bear grabbed handfuls of her hair and pulled her closer. The blonde made a noise that could have been mistaken for a purr. With his free hand, he slowly followed her curves down and back up, massaging here and there. Kaitlin arched against him, her hands exploring as well.

After a wonderfully slow session of love making, they lay quietly in the serenity that followed. Before she knew it, Kaitlin was breathing deeply. *Woniya Mato* looked down at his wife, happiness beating with every pump of his heart. He noted that her tummy was filling in a little and smiled.

When Kaitlin awoke, Spirit Bear handed her a plate of freshly warmed food. It steamed and tantalized her taste buds. The smile he gave her had a drum pounding in her ears.

"Do not smile at me so, or I will never get to eat!" the golden skinned girl exclaimed.

Spirit Bear lowered his head to her navel and spoke gently, "Do not worry, *wakanheja*, I will see to it that your mother feeds you!"

Kaitlin's eyes sprang tears. "Oh, *Woniya Mato*, you speak to our baby!"

"Warrior Bear or Sunflower must know of our love early," he responded. "Now, *wota*."

Golden Eyes began to eat while admiring the man of her heart. Although Spirit Bear longed to make love to his *thawicu* once more, he turned to do a few things before guests would begin arriving.

CHAPTER FORTY-SIX

Friends

Kaitlin cleaned the dishes and used the area of privacy after she finished eating. Then the gentle white got to work preparing the meat. She made soup with the roasted turkey meat. The fowl was accented by tubers, carrots, and onion in a smooth, creamy broth.

Each rabbit was stuffed with a mash made of tubers, wild onion, and garlic that would firm up into cakes as it cooked and flavor the meat at the same time. They would prepare nicely in the embers.

Desert Rose was bringing some vegetable varieties; Playful Otter offered to supply the group with a cactus dish for Kaitlin to try, and Apple Blossom was to provide more treats. It would be too much food, but it would save until the next day.

Kaitlin was getting excited to see her friends. It seemed forever since they had all just had time to visit. The move and setting up the village had been very taxing on all of them. However, now they had less to do. In the next few weeks, they would gather firewood and heap it in several communal spots so that when the weather was dangerous, they wouldn't have to go far.

Kaitlin loved the temperature best in the sixties through the eighties. She dreaded the winter. The season in South Dakota was not pleasant. In early November, the highs were already in the fifties. Kaitlin put on her colorful shawl, a wedding present from her husband's hearth brother, Wonder Worker.

Golden Eyes sighed as the soft heat billowed around her. It was a little warm, but she welcomed the comfort. Besides, she wanted to be seen in style and show her appreciation for the gift.

In an hour, all the food was prepared. Kaitlin began setting up her wedding dishes as a serving vessel for her friends. She saw Sky Warrior carrying two bladders of prepared drink followed by Apple Blossom.

Delighted, Kaitlin got up and quickly approached the couple.

"*Haspa Nableca*! I am so happy to see you!"

Sky Warrior arched his brow.

"Oh, *Wawakte Towanjila*, I do not forget you! I missed you, as well!"

The chief flashed her a dazzling grin, and Apple Blossom hugged her as she balanced the dish in her other hand.

"I have missed you so much, too!" Apple Blossom stated. "It seems as though it has been many moons."

"*Tos*. Speaking while you work is enjoyable, but it is not as satisfying as giving one your full attention."

Golden Eyes put her friend's food among hers then they sat on a small log close to the fire.

"How are you feeling, *Mazaska Zi Ista*?"

"I feel wonderful! I still get tired a little easier, but I do not feel ill anymore."

"Have you felt the *wakanheja* move?"

"Move? I do not think so."

"Yes, I am told it feels similar to gas bubbles moving but it stays in the same spot. It may resemble a muscle twitching as well."

Kaitlin shook her head. "Not yet."

"Before long, then." Sky Warrior piped in.

Spirit Bear, with the rest of their friends, approached the fire. Kaitlin jumped up and happily squeezed all of them.

"Reunion!" she cried.

"*Mazaska Zi Ista*, it has been way too long!" Desert Rose exclaimed, pulling her close to hug her yet again.

"*Tos, tos*! It has!"

Playful Otter lifted up a corner of the pretty wrap. "I do love your shawl!"

The group all turned to look at Wonder Worker.
He smiled in amusement and winked.

"I think *Skeca Ecaca* desires one for herself,"
Kaitlin said out of orneriness. She knew her
friend was bashful and would turn vivid shades
of red.

Right on cue, Playful Otter looked down in a
deep crimson hue. Kaitlin snickered.

"I would like one the color that you are
right now," Desert Rose declared.

"Aww, leave her be," Lone Wolf jumped to her
rescue. "She has a tender heart."

"We know. I think she realizes we tease her out
of love."

"Yes, but she still is deeply shy," Apple
Blossom stated kindly.

"We are sorry," Kaitlin said as she dropped her
arm around Playful Otter.

The young woman was smiling and said,
"It is okay. I wish I didn't turn red like this!"

"Well, we will take your mind off of it!"

"Come! I will show you the garments I am making for the baby."

Playful Otter perked up and was happy to make an escape from the ever-watchful eyes of the shaman.

"These are very nicely done, especially for your first time!" breathed Apple Blossom.

"Everything she does is extraordinary!" Desert Rose professed.

"*Wawat'ecaka* showed me how. She is the reason I am good at everything!" Kaitlin said, passing the buck. "She and you all!"

"Oh, sure. Include us as an afterthought," provoked Desert Rose.

"I could do nothing before I came to your village!" Kaitlin proclaimed.

"I find that hard to believe!" Playful Otter disagreed.

"She was just unschooled but a natural," agreed Apple Blossom.

It was Kaitlin's turn to blush.

"Now look who is a pretty shade!" Desert Rose pointed out.

Laughing, Playful Otter said, "I will not prolong it like *others* I know!"

Still a pinkish hue, Kaitlin batted her eyes, giggled, and said, "I do not know what you speak of!"

Playful Otter crossed her arms over her chest and said, "Oh, really?"

"Do you have garments you can wear with the growth of the *wakanheja*?" Apple Blossom cut in.

Kaitlin's slightly surprised face said it all.

"You do not want to be in winter without garments to wear," Apple Blossom mildly scolded.

Kaitlin said, "I made apparels for my baby but not for myself! I did not think of this!"

"You have plenty of time. No worries," Playful Otter reassured.

"We can help, too!" Desert Rose offered.

Kaitlin was choked with gratitude. "I have the best anyone could hope for!"

They all smiled. Then they went back to the yard to begin serving their men.

The warriors were all conversing and laughing, but they all became quiet as each had eyes for no other than the woman of their heart.

The women settled down with plates after serving. "You have to try my cactus dish!" Playful Otter said, "I made it especially for you!"

"I would love to try some," Golden Eyes responded, holding out her plate. The recipe dished onto her plate looked tender as it had been sautéed with onion, bison fat, and broth. It also smelled divine.

Kaitlin took a little rabbit and a bit of the patty cooked within. She spooned a tad bit of jellied prickly pear as well as splitting one of her pastries with her hubby. She made sure every plate had a half of her small pie.

When she sat down to eat, she noticed *Skeca Ecaca* closely watching.   She tentatively took a bite of the cacti dish.

"Ummm, this is very good!" exclaimed Kaitlin. "It reminds me of my old home, surprisingly."

"Why is that?" *Woniya Mato* questioned.

"We had a vegetable called green beans there. It reminds me of green beans with a slightly nutty taste. I like! Thank you!"

"You are welcome," Playful Otter responded happily. "I am so glad you enjoyed it!"

Wonder Worker said, "*Mazaska Zi Ista*, I shall become overweight if you make many of these pies!"

Spirit Bear added, "And these prickly pears, *Haspa Nableca!*"

"And I really love your special vegetable dish as well, *Unjinjintka Can Koica,*" Lone Wolf added.

"Yes, it is really quite good," Sky Warrior added. "It almost has a sweet taste."

Desert Rose had made yams with honey. They were a star dish.

The women cleaned up while the men smoked a pipe for a brief time. Then they settled around the fire to tell tales and tease one another.

"When will we have another ceremony?" Kaitlin asked.

"Why?" her husband asked grinning. "Do you wish to address the community?" He knew very well she did not wish to be in front of the eyes of all.

"I was just wondering. Our people honor life in all forms. Do we honor winter as well?"

Wonder Worker responded, "We do honor all because that is what makes life complete. We will have a ceremony to honor the fall season. Our winter honoring will not come until spring."

Kaitlin nodded in understanding.

Sky Warrior stated, "We do need to meet as a counsel and discuss this."

"Yes. We will hold a ceremony soon."

The friends visited and teased one another until long in the night. Finally, the women were noticeably beginning to nod off, resting heads on one another. The men chuckled and said their goodnights, escorting their women folk home.

CHAPTER FORTY-SEVEN

Breakfast

The next morning, Kaitlin arose early. She prepared a raspberry leaf tea with honey and warmed up leftovers. She made enough for both Wonder Worker and his mother, Gentle Rabbit.

"*Woniya Mato*, let us go to your hearth mother's tipi and serve them breakfast."

"As you wish, *mita wastelaka*. Do you grow lonely for company so soon?"

"*Hiya*, but I feel guilty because *Wawat'ecaka* did not join us last night. She had to know we had a get-together."

"Do you not think it pleases her to see that her 'sons' have interests and are close with each other?"

"Of course, my *hingnaku*. It is just… I feel like we left her out."

Spirit Bear walked quietly to his wife and wrapped his arms around her. "Do not feel guilty, *Mazaska Zi Ista*. My mother is your mother, and she understands that sometimes youth needs to have time together."

Kaitlin understood what he was explaining, but she couldn't help but feel the little twang of guilt upon her heart. The blonde rested her head on her husband's vibrant chest and gave a soft sigh.

Golden Eyes enveloped her shoulders with the colorful garment and carried the meat platter out the entrance flap. Her husband grabbed the pies and hot drink. Together, they stopped by Wonder Worker's hut.

"*Wawakankan*, come and join us."

The timber of his voice came from within, "Is all okay?"

"*Tos*. We cannot get enough of your attention," Spirit Bear laughed.

"In that case," Wonder Worker popped his head out of his entrance flap, "I am here!"

"Let us go eat with your mother."

"Wonderful. I see you brought hot food!"

"*Tos*. It is a peace offering."

"For...?"

"*Mazaska Zi Ista* feels sad that we did not have your mother over last night."

"I am sure she was happy to rest!"

"Oh, I did not think about that!" Kaitlin responded. The older woman was always bustling with so much energy, the young woman never thought she rested!

When the trio approached Gentle Rabbit's tipi, they noted a welcoming smoke coming from her ventilation flap.

"*Hau, Wawat'ecaka*!" It was the custom to greet before entering another's dwelling.

"*Hau,* my family! Come in!"

"We brought breakfast!" Kaitlin exclaimed.

"I have made a drink for you to try," she responded.

"I also brought tea."

"Good. There is not a lot of what I made, but I want to see what you think."

As the group settled near the fire spit, each was served a small horn cup of a dark, steaming liquid.

"Coffee!" Kaitlin exclaimed.

"What?" Gentle Rabbit asked.

"It tastes like coffee!"

Spirit Bear said, "What is 'couffe'?"

"Cof-fee," Kaitlin slowed the pronunciation for easier replication. "It is a *wasicu* drink. This is very good. It reminds me of it."

"It is dandelion root with honey," Gentle Rabbit answered.

"It is very good," repeated Golden Eyes. "However, I still prefer tea."

"As do I or you would have drunk this every day," teased the motherly figure.

Kaitlin and Gentle Rabbit served the men then sat down to eat.

"I thank you for this nice surprise. It is not every day a mother is greeted by two of her sons and is fed breakfast."

"*Mazaska Zi Ista* thought it would be nice," Spirit Bear began. He hastily added, "As did we!"

"It made this old woman happy!" Gentle Rabbit agreed. She turned toward Kaitlin and asked, "*Mazaska Zi Ista*, what do you have on your agenda for today?"

"This morning, I want to finish up all I can on my berry wine. It will not continue to do well now that the cold is coming in. I have to keep the fire going all the time to keep it fermenting at a constant temperature. I feed the flames, but they can't rage!'

"Would you like help?"

"I think I can manage. I know you always have a lot of things to do."

"I do have a project I'm working on," the mother figure responded with a soft smile.

"What of you men?" Kaitlin asked.

"We will probably go to meet at the Council Lodge."

"I have a request. I don't know the process."

"*Tos*?" Spirit Bear answered.

"It is about *Haspa Nableca*. Is she to forever be a slave?"

"Ah, you are concerned for your friend."

"*Tos*. I feel she has proven worthy, trustworthy, and she is happy here. But who can be truly happy with the status of slave, even if she is with a chief?"

"Why do I get the feeling there is more emotion tied to those words than it sounds?" her husband asked with a grin.

"I must advocate for her."

"We will discuss the possibilities."

Kaitlin hugged her husband tightly, then hugged Wonder Worker.

"I am glad to see you like the wrap I gave you," Wonder Worker stated after being released.

"I absolutely ADORE it! It is so warm, soft, and *gopeca*!" She did an admiration twirl.

Gentle Rabbit laughed gleefully.

"Did you make this shaw, *Wawat'ecaka*?"

"No, I did not."

"Where did you get this, *Wawakankan*?"

"I do not divulge my secrets!"

"Oh, it's a secret, is it?"

"*Tos*. I have many women to please with such gifts, evidentially, from last night's revelations."

Both Spirit Bear and Kaitlin laughed together.

Gentle Rabbit inquired, "What did I miss?"

Spirit Bear responded, "They like to embarrass *Skeca Ecaca*. They wish to have shawls the same color as her cheeks."

Gentle Rabbit smiled happily and looked at her son. She was ever hopeful for a wedding announcement. Things were going very well as far as *Wawat'ecaka* was concerned. The budding romance between Wonder Worker and Playful Otter was off to an ideal start!

"My son tells me you tried a cacti dish?"

"*Tos*. It seems that I've been reminded of my roots as of late. With the cacti tasting like green beans and your drink reminding me of coffee, I don't think there's much you all can't do!"

Gentle Rabbit's eyes brightened. She knew Kaitlin meant it as a high honor. "I do like the tuber patty you made in the rabbit, too. I will use that idea."

Wonder Worker smiled, for he benefited from his mother's cooking.

Spirit Bear gave his wife a tender kiss then nodded to Wonder Worker. The men ducked out, and Kaitlin followed shortly after helping Gentle Rabbit clean up. The Indian Princess enjoyed making wine, but she would be glad to complete the last batch. By mid-November or sooner, it would be complete. She would start fresh with the ripening of a new berry crop.

At noon, she ate a light lunch of leftover soup and lay down because she knew that council meetings usually lasted a while. As always, she slept soundly. She was warm, the low fire crackled, and she couldn't be happier!

CHAPTER FORTY-EIGHT

Good News

It was later in the afternoon before *Woniya Mato* showed up. Kaitlin served more of the turkey soup and fresh *aguyapi* to her husband upon his arrival.

"Sit with me, *Mazaska Zi Ista*."

After settling by him, she looked up expectantly. He ate a little more and took a long drink.

"Do you really wish for *Haspa Nableca* to be one of us?" he chuckled.

"*Tos*! I do!" she exclaimed, leaning forward in her excitement.

"It has been voted on by the counsel." Spirit Bear's authority rang. Then her *hingnaku* chose that moment to eat and drink more.

Moments passed before Kaitlin could contain herself no more, "*Woniya Mato*! Do not leave me hanging like this!"

Grinning, the war chief deliberately took another bite. He chewed slowly to add to her vexation. Finally, after taking an extra drink, he looked into his wife's exasperated eyes.

"How am I leaving you hanging? I am before you with the answer, am I not?"

"You know very well how you're torturing me!" she said. Although she was aggravated, she could not resist his handsome smile.

"It is as you wish. We have voted and the council agrees. She is worthy of adopting into Sioux status."

Although somewhat prepared for his wife's reaction, he was not quite ready for her to fling all of her weight upon him.

"I am so happy! Thank you, *Woniya Mato*! I love you!"

"And I, you, *mita wastelaka.*"

"Would you like to finish your lunch, now?" Kaitlin asked sheepishly.

Spirit Bear lay, with her on top where she'd landed. His hands started to caress her derriere and belly. "Not really," was his husky response.

Kaitlin straddled him and took his lips passionately with hers. Their tongues danced, and teeth lightly scraped each other. Both sets of hands were roaming and exploring the other's bodies.

"Let us go to a more comfortable location, *Mazaska Zi Ista.*" He sat up and in one fluid motion, scooped her up as he stood. The golden eyes flew open wide. Kaitlin never ceased to be amazed by her man.

Nestling her down, he lazily unlaced her dress while kissing every inch of exposed skin. Kaitlin's focused eyes viewed his every move. Casually, she stroked his back as he continued his very all-embracing exploration of visible skin. Ebony eyes were watchfully anticipating her responses.

When her increased breathing rate amplified and he noted her dilated pupils, the man of war stood and shed his garments like lightning. He turned to throw a few more sticks on the fire, then lay back down.

Kaitlin propped up on her elbow and saw his eyes lower to her chest. By intention, she suddenly pushed him down and straddled him. The blonde goddess began a ravishing exploration of his manly outline.

"Oh, *mita wastelaka*, how much do you think a man can take?"

"Let me show you, my chief! It may not always be you who are in control."

"Are you sure?"

She found that part of his anatomy that made him a man, and he melted in her hands. "*Tos, mita hingnaku. I am sure.*"

After a bit of aerobic exercise, Kaitlin found she was able to take another short rest snuggled deeply in her husband's arms. When she awoke, she donned a work dress and noticed it was a tad bit snugger than she'd noticed before.

"What is it, *mita wastelaka*?" her husband asked when he noted her etched brows.

"It is nothing that cannot be fixed, *Woniya Mato*. All I need is a few of my soft hides to work with."

Understanding dawned, and a grin split his face. "I cannot wait to see our baby grow! You are precious, and it makes me very proud to see my *winyan* grow heavy as she carries my child."

Kaitlin nodded a bit bashfully, and her cheeks grew slightly pink. Spirit Bear lifted her chin and looked into her eyes. He lowered his head and kissed her.

"I am proud of all you are," he stated seriously.

"I love you, *Woniya Mato*!"

"Not as much as I do you!"

"That is not true."

"Who convinced whom that they were in love?"

"That does not matter."

"Oh, yes it does!"

"No, it does not!"

"Um hum. We shall see."

"Agreed!" Kaitlin giggled.

Their friendly argument was interrupted by a noise at the entrance flap.

"*Hau*," called Gentle Rabbit's voice.

"Come in, mother," Spirit Bear answered.

Once inside, the warrior grinned deeply. There was a mischievous light in his eyes.

"Mother, who loves whom more?"

"Why, I love you more! A mother always loves her son more."

Chuckling, Spirit Bear said, "I was not asking between you and me, mother. I know there is no love like that of a mother for her *ojilaka*, but between *Mazaska Zi Ista* and myself."

"You plan to pit me against one of you? I see this as a situation where I am the loser, no matter what."

"You have always been wise, *Wawat'ecaka*. We will not be angry or hurt. Who do you see as the strongest giver of love?"

"I would say it is equal, now, my son. At first, however, you could not hide your infatuation with *Mazaska Zi Ista* although you tried."

Kaitlin coughed into her hand to hide her amusement. The look on the chief's face was priceless. Onyx eyes pierced her façade. The blonde did her best to sober up.

"It looks like it is a draw, *Woniya Mato*," she declared.

"I do not feel this is fair."

"But you won, right?" Kailin asked, still smiling.

Gentle Rabbit also laughed softly. "I do not mean to injure your pride, my son."

Spirit Bear smiled. "I gave up pride long ago, mother. At least when it comes to *mita wastelaka*."

"This is a good thing, my son." Turning to Kaitlin, Gentle Rabbit asked, "Would you like to go for a walk? I plan to begin gathering wood for the winter."

"*Tos*. I would love to walk."

"You must be careful, my family. You are my heart, and we are too close to the *wasicu* for my comfort."

"You speak wisely, my chief," Gentle Rabbit responded. "We will keep out an eye."

The women gathered large baskets to begin the arduous task. They saw a few piles other women had already started around camp.

"We will add to these piles. All will increase the growth."

"*Tos*. I love how the community shares work."

A few hours later, Kaitlin wiped some wayward strands off her sweaty brow and said, "*Wawat'ecaka*, I have an idea."

"*Tos, Mazaska Zi Ista*?"

"If we were to hook a travois up to a horse, we could go further to gather and bring back more wood."

"That is a wonderful idea!" Gentle Rabbit praised. "Perhaps tomorrow? I think we have done enough for this day. Come. I want to show you something."

CHAPTER FORTY-NINE

More Reminders

Kaitlin followed Gentle Rabbit back to her home.

"Sit, *Mazaska Zi Ista*. Close your eyes."

The blonde gratefully sunk into the furs. Soon, something soft was placed in her lap.

"Now open them."

In Kaitlin's lap were two new garments of the softest leather. One was a dark bison leather dress, the other a lighter shade of chestnut from a mule deer. When Kaitlin looked up, her eyes were saucers.

"*Wawat'ecaka*, are these what I think?"

"*Tos*, my daughter. I made them of special construction. There are leggings to go with them. They are made to tie in the back and let out as the *hoksicala* grows."

"Oh, *Wawat'ecaka*, thank you! You do too much!"

"Let an old woman be happy. The love you and my hearth son share is one-of-a-kind. I could not be more honored with my daughter-in-law!"

After giving her mother-figure a hug, Kaitlin held her new dresses against her frame. The material whispered of luxury, they were sensual to the touch: the leather was typical of Gentle Rabbit. However, the new garments were of a thicker, more durable material. The hides were taken from animals preparing for winter. The apparels were plain in nature and of a simple design. They were perfect.

The leggings were constructed of the same material. They also let out in the back. They were soft and warm. Kaitlin couldn't be more pleased!

"Now you do not need to worry about new clothes. Focus on the *hoksicala*."

"*Tos*, thank you!"

"You have a few weeks, maybe a month left you can wear your own dresses. You can make the switch now or wait until then. The choice is yours."

"I will wear mine for another week or so. When the weather bites more, these are what you will see me in!"

Gentle Rabbit laughed. "I am glad you are happy."

"How could I not be?" The elder woman received one more hug before Kaitlin parted ways to go do the evening cooking.

After the meal, both Spirit Bear and Kaitlin sat in the yard by the fire. It was a nice flame and put off adequate heat.

"Do you get bored in winter time?" Kaitlin asked.

"*Hiya*. One would think that one would, but as a leader, there are usually more than a fair share of disputes to settle."

"Why?"

"When people are forced to share a small space, especially families, a lot of squabbles break out. Sometimes we have to step in. Usually, the council designates Sky Warrior to handle most local issues, but there are times he needs assistance."

"It is hard for me to see our community not get along."

"People are people wherever you go. We do have an excellent community, but the dregs of winter and the spirit of unrest affects us all."

"I understand." Kaitlin doubted she'd see the discontent she'd seen last winter. Who could be more quarrelsome than two men without money who still managed to get drunk every night?

Kaitlin was quiet for a time. All the flashbacks to her old society had her wondering about her men folk again. They were only three day's ride from the settlement. Yet, she knew that her husband would not agree to take her. The blonde needed more time to work on obtaining his permission.

How was her family doing? What were their lives like? Did they still live in the lonely cabin? Were they still drunks? Were they even still alive? The questions echoed again and again in her mind and continued to plague her long into the night.

When the couple entered the tipi, Spirit Bear noticed his wife's apathy.

"*Mita wastelaka, uwa yo.* Lie beside me."

When she melted into his side, he wrapped his arms of love around her. They snuggled together under a newly polished bison cape.

"What weighs on your mind?" he gently asked.

"It is my family. I wonder how they are. There have been a few reminders of *wasicu* life lately that has triggered my mind to think of them."

The chief did not say anything but continued to soothe her nerves by softly massaging her neck, arms, and back. After a time, Kaitlin spoke again.

"Did you know of the surprise from *Wawat'ecaka*?"

"*Hiya*. What is it?"

"She made me two dresses that will grow with the *hoksicala*."

Spirit Bear propped up. "Really?"

"*Tos*. They are simple and of excellent construction. They have matching buckskins. And they look warm."

"I will need to thank her in person as well."

"I am so grateful to have her. She is the best mother anyone could ask for."

"I agree." Spirit Bear lay back down and scooted in closer to her. "*Istinma wanna.*"

"Good-night, *mita hingnaku.*"

"Good-night, *mita thawicu.*"

The next morning was the first noticeably colder day. There was a chill nearly warded off by the freshly kindled fire, but Kaitlin knew she'd be trying out her new dresses quite a bit earlier than she'd intended. The wind had picked up and was snarling around the closed entrance flap.

"Thank you for the fire, my love."

"I do not want you to catch a cold! I am honored to warm my family!"

"I am honored also!"

When she arose from the bedding to dress, she noticed Spirit Bear's eyes were drawn to her chest. Suddenly bashful, she quickly slipped on her new dress and leggings.

"*Wastelaka*, I do believe your body is changing before my eyes."

"What?"

"You are growing in nice places," Spirit Bear chuckled.

"My breasts are sore, thank you very much."

Her husband's only response was a deeper laugh.

Kaitlin donned a thick bison robe made for working in winter.

"Where are you going?"

"I need to rekindle the fire in my wine hut. If it went out, perhaps I can still save all my hard work."

"*Mazaska Zi Ista*, I will go. You start your morning drink. Stay warm during the coldest part of the day."

"I love you, my darling! Thank you!"

Kaitlin began warming up stones to drop into the skin pot to heat the water. After it was

going, she began making breakfast. In no time,
her husband returned.

"All is well with your wine."

"Thank goodness! Thank you!"

His answering kiss was his response.

They sat by the fire as Kaitlin passed a bowl of
berry and honey hot grains for breakfast and
berry *aguyapi*. She also gave him a cup of her
tea.

"Do you think we should try to gather as much
wood as we can in the next few suns?"

"You will have enough time in the next few
weeks. Although it is cold today, the weather
will not stabilize at these temperatures at this
time."

"Good!"

"Because of the cold on this day, I wish for us to
stay inside and work on things during the
morning. By this afternoon, it may be better for
you to gather."

"*Tos*, my chief. As you wish."

"And as you wish, too?"

Kaitlin giggled her happy response. She came over to her husband. The golden one knew of the best way in the world to stay busy inside on a cold morning.

CHAPTER FIFTY

Gathering Wood

After midday rest time, Kaitlin put her new dress back on.

"I meant to tell you I like your new dress. It looks warm." Spirit Bear commented.

"*Wawat'ecaka* made it for the growth of the *wakanheja*. She put ties in the back that I can loosen it as he grows as well as the buckskins."

"He?"

Kaitlin smiled. "I am happy with a she, as well."

"As am I. My happiness knows no bounds."

Golden Eyes then asked her husband about her travois-horse idea. Spirit Bear nodded his head.

"*Tos*. The dun mare will be gentle enough for you to use."

"Thank you! It will save our backs," Kaitlin said with a smile as she stooped to wrap her arms around her husband.

He was sitting, and she peeked around his shoulder. The sideway glance he sent her from under the fringe of his dark lashes set her heart aflutter. She smiled and rested her head on his, happy this striking man was all hers.

"When do you wish to leave, *mita wastelaka*?"

"As soon as you're ready to prepare the horse. The heat of the day has arrived and lasts for a few more hours. I do not wish to be out longer than that on a day like today."

Right on cue, a gust of wind rattled the entrance flap.

"I do not want you to go alone."

"I will ask Gentle Rabbit and Desert Rose."

Spirit Bear nodded. "If you see *anything* that tells you something is not right, you return immediately."

"*Tos*. I will listen to my instincts, not my heart.
In no way do I want a repeat of the past!"

"Thank you. Nor do I!"

While her husband went to get the horse, Kaitlin
gathered her friends. Everyone was bundled up
and warm, ready to get to work.

Spirit Bear led the gentle mare to his wife and
handed her the rope tied around her neck.

"Remember this horse?" he asked. "It belonged
to the *wasicu*. She is well-trained and behaved.
She will not act crazy or hurt you."

"*Tos*, how could I forget her?" Kaitlin answered.
"Thank you, *Woniya Mato*. I will ask for her
often as we gather wood."

"She is yours, now. You can use her any time.
This mare is also easy to ride."

"I love you, *mita hingnaku*."

Her response was a sweet kiss before they
turned to go.

About fifteen minutes into their walk, Desert Rose stated, "It is going to be a long winter."

"How do you know?" asked Kaitlin in a worried voice.

"Because today was the first day I didn't have much to do, and I was bored."

Wawat'ecaka leaned her head back and laughed. "I would look forward to the time to rejuvenate my body if it weren't for the cold."

"I wasn't bored." Kaitlin said then turned pink.

"Why, what were you doing?" Desert Rose stopped and looked suspiciously at her friend.

"Um, sleeping!"

"*Toooosssss*, right."

Kaitlin's cheeks deepened their rosy hue.

Gentle Rabbit didn't say a word, but the knowing look she gave had Kaitlin flushing profusely.

"Sleeping, huh?" Desert Rose said.

"Look! There is wood we can gather!" Kaitlin said pointing, effectively getting them to change the subject.

"Let us gather that on the way back," Gentle Rabbit suggested. "That way your mare won't get as tired."

"That is a good idea," Kaitlin agreed.

They walked further. The terrain was new to Kaitlin as she had never lived at this site before, but the two women she was with appeared to remember how to navigate.

"Let us go in a southerly direction," Gentle Rabbit suggested. "There is a grove of trees by a river where we will find quite a bit of firewood if my memory serves correctly."

"*Tos*. We will bring back a lot with our horse friend," Desert Rose added.

The wind was gusty, and the women bent their heads to avoid the cold air from surging down their garments.

"*Mazaska Zi Ista,* I just noticed your dress! It is amazing! When did you do this?"

"It was *Wawat'ecaka*. She surprised me with two dresses and two leggings that will fit me as the *hoksicala* grows. I will show you it better once we return to warmth."

Desert Rose teased, "But I want to see now!"

"Not going to happen."

The women had walked over forty-five minutes to reach the river. Then they trekked downstream a bit to get to the grove of trees.

"It is beautiful here!" Golden Eyes declared.

"*Tos*. It is very beautiful," Gentle Rabbit agreed.

"I still like our other location better."

Both women nodded. Desert Rose said, "The camp we left is one of the most beautiful places. It has everything we need and is a little up in the mountain. Nothing can compare."

The statement was met with wholehearted agreement.

"Here we are! Look at all the wood!"
Wawat'ecaka stated. It will take us more than a
few suns to collect it all!"

"Good! We won't have to travel as far
looking," Desert Rose said.

The women began to gather, all spanning out
from the other to create different piles.
Eventually, they would bring the mare to each
compilation to load onto the travois.

"I think I will wander a little farther into the
wood there," Kaitlin said, indicating a direction.
"I also need to use the bathroom."

"And so it starts," Desert Rose informed.

"What starts?"

"Needing to use the privacy area more
frequently. The bigger the *hoksicala* grows, the
more often you will need to go."

Wawat'ecaka nodded again.

Acknowledged with a soft smile, Kaitlin turned
to the trees. She knew they were trying to help
prepare her. Crunching through the underbrush,

she looked for the perfect spot. Finally, the young woman found \an adequate location.

After retying her clothing, the chieftain's wife froze. Suddenly, goosebumps prickled her flesh, and it wasn't from the cold.

I will listen to my heart, Kaitlin reminded herself. *Something is not right; I feel it. Is it an animal? I will tell the ladies we need to go.*

The blonde looked around but did not discern danger. However, the feeling of eyes upon her was strong. Kaitlin shuddered, briefly thinking of Sly Coyote. Although the foliage in the grove was somewhat thick with the remnants of weathered members desperately clutching onto branches for life, the floor was fairly dense with the skeletal remains of leaves. Gusts of wind would hurl them into the air and force their rickety bones to do a violent dance before throwing them apart. It was impossible to hear friend or foe. Kaitlin swallowed.

Tentatively taking a step, she began to walk lightly. If there were bears or wolves around, she did not want to startle one… or be started.

The young white woman crept up to a large oak
and hugged the base. She peeked around the
side. Suddenly, a hand clamped over her mouth,
and manly arms pulled her back and imprisoned
her against a wall of chest.

CHAPTER FIFTY-ONE

Surprised

Kaitlin felt herself being dragged backwards into thicker undergrowth. She struggled and tried to bite her capture's hand. As she twisted and fought, the grip tightened. The control on her ribs was tight enough to bruise.

"Kaitlin!" a familiar voice whispered in her ear. "Be quiet! I ain't gonna hurt yuh but I can't let yah go if yur gonna scream or sumthin'!"

As soon as his grip slackened, Kaitlin turned, surprise deeply etched in her features. Her eyes were gold silver-dollars, and it was quickly followed with elation.

"Bobby?" Kaitlin was incredulous. "B – B - Bobby?" she stammered, "How… how did you find me?"

Her long-lost brother let her go, and the fair-haired woman flung her arms around his neck.

"I was out tryin' to hunt, and I saw a Injun girl with blonde hair. I just knew that had ter be yah."

Kaitlin looked up from carefully dusting off her clothes and said, "You… hunt?"

"Things changed when yuh got taken."

"You hunt?" She echoed. Rapidly a smile erupted on her face. Kaitlin paused and asked falteringly, "How's… papa?"

"He's hangin' on. He's a not doin' too well, but he's a hangin' on."

"Wh – what do you mean?"

"Pa's a bad drunk. His belly is a stickin' out and his skin's a turnin' yellah. He gets sick to his gut quite a bit."

"Oh, no."

"Yup."

"Bobby, what about… you?" his sister was still totally shocked to even see him, but to witness her brother trying to provide for himself and not

be stumbling around drunk? It was
unbelievable news: wonderful, but stunning.

"I gave up drinkin' a month ago. It really
changed muh when yuh left. Guilt got a hole of
muh! At firs', I drank more. Then Jed
disappeared say'n yuh got taken by them
Redskins. It made muh think o' mama and her
thoughts a how she'd a wanna'd us ta tern out."

Kaitlin was deliriously happy to hear his words.
"But how did you stop?"

"I dunno. I just decided to do it. Papa sold yah
to Jed and I knowed he'd a killed ya, Kait. Papa
done it to pay off some o' that debt. It was
wrong. He regrets doin' it, but I din't wanna be
like that. It took muh awhile, but I jus' up and
quit."

Kaitlin's eyes watered up and she hugged him
one more time.

"If I could, I'd like to see papa again."

"I'll take yah. But yu'll hafta stay outside the
town until I can fine yah sumthin' ter wear.

Yah can't be goin' in ter town dressed like a Injun."

"I can't go right now. I'd have a lot of people I care about mad at me."

It was Bobby's turn to be startled. "What yuh mean?"

"I mean, I have a whole community of people who love and care for me. I have more acceptance now than I've ever known… except for mama."

"Yah talkin' about them Injuns?"

"Yes, Bobby. They are good people."

"I thot I was a savin' yuh."

"And I love you for that!"

"Yah can't be a goin' in ter town talkin' o' luvin' Redskins."

"I realize that."

"An' I gotta fine yuh some clothes."

"Yes."

"Yuv gained a little weight. It's good. Yah always were too skinny."

"It's hard when you're the sole provider."

Kaitlin didn't say it to be mean; it was simply fact. Bobby had the decency to look down.

To help his mind move on, she asked, "Are you here alone?"

"I got a couple o' friends wif muh somewheres."

"They won't hurt my companions, will they?"

"Them women? Nah."

"Good. I never want fighting and warring between the two groups of people I love."

"I haf no desire to fight them warriors."

She smiled, "Keep it that way." After a brief hesitation, Kailin asked, "Bobby, do you have any money?"

He looked away guiltily.

"Can you sell things?"

"Yep. Or trade."

"I'll be back in this area – IF it's safe for us – to collect more wood. I don't want any other white people around. I want just you because I don't want any chance for something ugly to happen. I can give you some furs and leather I've cured to help you buy a dress for me so I can come and see Papa."

Her brother's eyes widened. "Yuh can make leather?"

Bobby, this community is wonderful. They take care of each other. We do our best to make sure no one is hungry or cold. I wish our world cared enough for that. The Native people have taught me many skills that I've grown to be quite good at, and I've only been with them a short while."

"Is yer leather as good as what yer wearin'?"

"Just about. The maker of this leather taught me."

A strange little light went on in the back of her brother's eyes. "Yah, bring muh sum of that leather. It will get ma a little sompthin' to eat and get yah a dress."

"Deal. I'll try to come back in a day or two, weather providing."

"Okay."

"*Mazaska Zi Ista?* Where are you?" Gentle Rabbit's Lakota echoed through the tree grove.

Kaitlin answered back in Lakota, "I will come shortly. Give me a moment."

Her mother's footsteps turned back. Kaitlin pushed her brother against the tree. "I've got to go now, Bobby. I love you. Please be safe and please don't bring anyone with you when you come back. I have to insist."

"Okay. I luv yah too, sis."

Kailin gave him one more little hug, grabbed an armload of wood, and walked away.

CHAPTER FIFTY-TWO

One Request

"Are you alright?" Desert Rose asked. "You were gone a little too long for our liking."

"*Tos*. Just a little cold." Her shiver wasn't embellished.

The wind pulled at Kaitlin's bison cape and the thick skirt above her leggings as if it were an insistent child. It snapped her hair back and forth under the warm bison fur-lined hat like an angry cougar's tail. Winter was coming and whistled a cheerful tune through the branches of nearby trees.

"Let us go home," Gentle Rabbit suggested. "I also could warm in front of the fire."

The women loaded as much wood as was humane for their horse and led the way back to the village. They didn't talk much due to the wind. The temperatures weren't unseasonably cold, but the gusts dropped the chill to at least twenty degrees below average. Kaitlin couldn't wait to stoke the fire and lay down under some piles of fur. The horse saved her back from much, but it was still complaining against the strain.

Upon reaching the village, the women made quick work of unloading, taking care of the horse and travois, then of bee lining it to their homes. Kaitlin made a fresh batch of tea to help her body warm quicker. Settling back with a steamy cup, she allowed her mind to roam.

Bobby was doing fine! He was hunting and seemed to be taking care of himself. He'd been genuinely happy to see her! Kaitlin's heart banged on a loud drum in appreciation. However, the news disclosed about her father was very disheartening. The blonde hoped it wasn't serious. If her father was drinking more than he had been in the past and was now sick, the combination could drive him to the grave very quickly. Winter was not the time to play with one's health! Kaitlin would see if she could talk some sense into the man when she saw him.

Kaitlin was having difficulty visualizing a pleasant way she might tell her *hingnaku* about her reunion. *Woniya Mato* would not be pleased, but she hadn't planned to meet up with her long-lost brother; it had just happened. Still, the blonde knew the leader would not be happy about it.

Would Spirit Bear let her go to see her ill father? Kaitlin knew she should tell him, but how and when? It was tempting to just omit meeting up with Bobby and head to the settlement on a wood-gathering day. However, the *wasicu* village was a three day's ride away. Kaitlin decided her husband would definitely notice her absence. She gnashed her teeth slightly and sighed with frustration.

Even with all that Kaitlin had on her mind, her cognizance drifted into a world of dreams. The fire crooned a sweet lullaby and the furs were deliciously warm. Seconds later, it seemed, her *hingnaku* was gently touching her arm to wake her.

"*Mazaska Zi Ista*, it is time to rise. I have prepared a meal for you."

"You cooked for me?" Kaitlin asked sleepily.
"Thank you, *Woniya Mato*!"

Her husband's smile lit the tipi with brilliance.

"*Tos*, for you."

Golden Eyes sat up, and he handed her a plate
of freshly cooked grouse and a mash made of
crumbled flat bread, sage, and broth from the
bird. It was delicious.

"You are so good to me," Kaitlin groaned. "I
love you so much!"

The blonde was rewarded with another smile.
"and I, you, *mita wastlaka*. Eat then we will
work on small things this afternoon. I also
stoked the fire in your wine tent."

Gratitude flooded her. How in the world did she
ever land the leader of the tribe, the most
handsome man she could ever imagine, and one
who actually cared about her and what she
thought? He was a war chief, and the man was
waiting on her!

"What brings a smile to your lips, *Mazaska Zi
Ista*?" he asked.

"You, my chief! I am the luckiest woman alive!"

Spirit Bear laughed heartily. He knew what an honor he was bestowing on her, and he was also glad she recognized it.

"I do… have something I need to tell you about," Kaitlin began.

"*Tos*?"

"Well… you are not going to like this."

"What, Golden One? You can talk to me."

"I know. It's just… we've already talked about this, and you have already told me the answer."

"Is this about visiting the *wasicu*?"

"*Tos*." She looked sheepish. "I did not mean to go against your wishes, but my brother came to me today."

"What?" Spirit Bear spoke softly, but a lot of power was behind the word.

"He has changed, *Woniya Mato*! Bobby no longer drinks, and he told me my father is ill."

"How did he come to you?" Spirit Bear's face was devoid of emotion, but he still spoke quietly. Kaitlin was intimidated although she knew her husband would never harm her.

"H – he was at the place we gathered wood. I went into a grove of trees for privacy, and on my way out, he was there. Bobby thought I was taken against my will by our warriors, and I told him I love my people. He was going to rescue me. My brother!" Kaitlin nearly whispered it and her eyes were bright with unshed tears. "*Woniya Mato*, he is a good man now. He told me father is ill, so my brother said he would get me a dress so I could visit him."

Spirit Bear stood and paced by the fire. "You know my feelings on this matter."

Kaitlin looked down.

"I have told you my fears. It does not matter that your brother is a good man now." The war chief paused to consider, "How do you know this for certain?"

"I saw Bobby with my own eyes. He *has* changed, *mita hingnaku*." She repeated, "He no longer drinks. My brother was providing food for himself. He was cleaned up and had serviceable clothes. He was genuinely happy to see me!"

"I do not trust this situation."

"*Woniya Mato*, he could have taken me if he so chose."

Her husband was silent once more. He circled, prowling the fire pit. After many noiseless minutes, he stopped in front of his wife.

"*Mazaski Zi Ista*, my instincts scream that this is a silly notion. I cannot give you permission to walk into the *wasicu* environment. What if you needed help? I could not just walk in and assist you."

"Would you at least meet my brother before you say no?"

More soundless moments dragged by on turtle legs. "I will go with you to meet your *wicowe*.

I promise nothing. I want you to be translator.
Speaking the *wasicu* language is my secret.”

“*Tos*, *Woniya Mato*. It is as you wish. Thank
you!” Kaitin wrapped her arms tightly around
his waist. “Thank you!”

The rest of the evening was a quiet one. Kaitlin
knew her husband was upset. She didn’t know
how to assuage his suspicion. In reality, she
didn’t blame him. The whites and the Sioux
weren’t exactly friends. In the past, her brother
never once tried to protect her from the actions
of her father.

Still, losing her father was a thought Kaitlin
wasn’t willing to accept. Papa wasn’t a bad
man; he simply didn’t handle her mother’s death
well. The blonde didn’t like it, hated his
choices, but it didn’t mean she never wanted to
see him again. Her father was consumed by a
disease. Evidentially, it was killing him, and
Kaitlin wanted to say her good-byes.

All the tragedy in Bobby’s life had finally
transformed him. If he would have continued to
follow Papa’s footsteps blindly, he would also
be very sick, and Kaitlin would never have seen

either one again. The golden girl sent up
another prayer of thanks. She also sent up a
plea for her husband's permission to see her
father. It meant more to her than he would ever
know.

The fair-skinned woman got out her jewelry
equipment. It took quite a bit of concentration
to drill holes. It wasn't really a thought-
provoking endeavor, but it would keep her fairly
focused.

Spirit Bear did a similar exercise but for men.
He made more arrow heads. This work also
took a lot of skill and dedication.

CHAPTER FIFTY-THREE

Making Amends

The next morning when Kaitlin awoke, Spirit Bear was gone. He hadn't really spoken much the rest of the prior evening. Currently, however, it was rare for the chief to be gone before she awoke without at least telling her where he'd be.

Kaitlin got up and around. She prepared tea and breakfast. Still, her husband did not return, so the blonde donned a robe and went to Gentle Rabbit's. After entering and having a seat before the fire, the fair-complexioned woman could not remain patient.

"*Wawat'ecaka*, have you seen *Woniya Mato*?"

Gentle Rabbit looked quizzically at Golden Eyes. "I believe he is with *Wawakankan*."

"Do they hunt?"

"*Hiya.* I believe something of importance needed to be discussed. Have you no idea?"

Kaitlin had the decency to look guilty.

"What is it, my daughter?"

"*Wawat'ecaka*, please do not be mad. It happened yesterday. In the tree grove, I met my brother. It was not by design. Bobby thought I'd been kidnapped, and when he saw me, he was going to rescue me. I told him of my love for our people, and he told me our father is ill. Bobby said he could get me a dress so I could return to the *wasicu* to see my papa."

"And you said nothing yesterday?"

"I am sorry. It was too much for me to process. It was also very cold."

Gentle Rabbit scurried around her home for a short time before letting her off the hook.

"*Tos*, child. I do understand. If I were in your shoes, I would need time to think as well."

"Thank you, *Wawat'ecaka*."

"My hearth son does not understand as deeply. He is a wise man, so he looks not only at your desires but at the whole picture which involves much danger for one such as you."

"I know. I would be with my brother."

"Is your brother a man of war?"

"*Hiya.*"

"Then how could he protect you?"

Kaitlin didn't know quite how to respond. "He knows the *wasicu* ways…" she trailed off.

"Do you now see the dilemma your *hingnaku* faces? Your chief loves you more than his own life. If something happened to you or your child, he would never forgive himself. *Woniya Mato* would lose all will to live."

Kaitlin nodded sheepishly with understanding.

"You cannot go against your husband's command."

"I will not, *Wawat'ecaka.*"

"Good. Now, what do we do today?"

"Um, I don't guess we should gather wood?"
Kaitlin smiled wistfully.

"Probably not the best idea under the current
circumstances."

"Let us work on sewing. Then, when the day
warms, is there anything we need to gather?"

"Sewing is good. I can show you how to
construct winter shoes. I know you have some,
but I don't think you've made any yourself?"

"*Tos*, this is true."

The women gathered the needed materials and
began cutting the soles.

"Since I have a nice pair, I wish to make some
for my *hingnaku*. I just don't want to make
mistakes."

"I am here to help. I won't let your work go to
waste."

Kaitlin smiled gratefully at her mother figure.
"*Wawat'ecaka – .*"

"*Tos*?"

"Thank you. You are always here for me. I am sorry I did not tell you immediately."

"You are forgiven, Golden One. Do not worry."

A tear leaked out of Kaitlin's eyes. She attributed it to her haywire emotions. The subdued woman dropped her head so that Gentle Rabbit wouldn't see.

A few hours later, Kaitlin returned to her tipi to begin lunch. She prepared a thick creamy soup of bison and vegetables. Sage and elderberry *aguyapi* complimented the meal as well as horn cups of berry drink. Finally, her husband returned.

"*Hai*, my love," she greeted delicately.

"*Hai, Mazaska Zi Ista*. The food smells delicious."

"Thank you." Kaitlin sat by him to eat.

They ate quietly for a bit. Finally, Kaitlin spoke up.

"Woniya Mato?"

"Tos?"

"I am sorry if you are angry with me."

"*Mita wastelaka,* I am not angry; I am concerned. You have put me in a difficult situation, one I am not sure how to handle. The consequences either way weigh heavily on my mind."

"What did *Wawakankan* have to say?"

"He agrees with me for the most part, but he did advocate for your side as well. He suggested I hear what your *wicowe* has to say before I make a final decision."

Kaitlin nodded, her eyes again shiny. She picked up the Indian bread to avoid detection.

"*Mazaska Zi Ista,* I know this means much to you. This is why it is such a heavy decision for me," Spirit Bear said gently.

"*Tos,* my chief. I know."

"When did you say you would meet up with him?"

"In a day or so when the weather was not excessively angry."

"It will just be the two of us when we go to meet."

"*Tos*. I also wanted to give him some furs and leather to help pay for my dress. He is just getting back on his feet again."

"We have much to spare."

"Thank you so much, my *hingnaku*! You are such a generous man!"

"I love you, *mita wastelaka*."

"I know. I am so grateful you do!"

Spirit Bear drew her to him in a tender embrace. Unhurriedly, their passions kindled, and the leader showed her, again, how much he really cared. His **thawicu** was his passion in life, and he burned deeply with his adoration for her.

Not to be outdone, Kaitlin received and returned his hunger full-force. He was not to be exceeded, and soon it was a game neither could seem to stop. Before long, it no longer mattered who was winning; they could not think of a better way to spend their afternoon.

CHAPTER FIFTY-FOUR

Surprise!

Two days later, Kaitlin was riding in front of her husband on his painted stallion. She'd selected four deer hides, a bison pelt, and a bundle of rabbit fur to bring for her brother. It should be plenty for a modern dress, food, and needed items for her *wasicu* family if so needed. Although Bobby was trying, the blonde was not confident in his skills to provide. One month of being sober and provider did not leave much time for skill development.

Spirit Bear was silent and strong behind her. He was not suspicious of the situation but neither did he trust it. If any *wasicun* could change, it would be his wife's *wicowe*. The challenge for this man would be determined by his power of will to stay away from the drink he so loved. Once one tasted it regularly, that individual became unpredictable. It would kill his *thawicu* to find deception in the man she called 'Bobby';

for now, she had hope. Spirit Bear did not suspect trickery, but when the wealth was placed in the *wicowe* hands, what the *wasicun* did with the money would be totally at his disposal.

They arrived at the grove of trees much quicker on horseback than the women had by walking. Spirit Bear stopped while still in the covering foliage.

"Will your *wicowe* come forward if he sees me?" Spirit Bear asked quietly.

"I suspect he will not, *Woniya Mato*. He would not know if you're here as friend or foe."

"*Tos*. I will wait here while you explain the matter to him. You call for me when you are ready. I will be near."

Kaitlin nodded her head as he placed her gently into the leafy carpet covering the ground. When the blonde glanced back as she walked deeper into the groove, the warrior was already one with nature.

"Baaaahhhh-bbeeee?" she called. "Bob-beeee?"

Kaitlin walked deeper and continued to call.

"I'm a here, sis," came the voice she knew so well.

"Where are you?"

"By the old oak to yer right."

Kaitlin looked over and saw her beloved brother. He'd just managed to get a young deer, but he was experiencing great difficulty with skinning it.

Kaitlin nearly got sick as she looked at the poor remains. Bobby really didn't know what he was doing. The deer was mangled and its leg hung in an odd angle. Blood was smeared in quite a few locations.

"What in the world?" Kaitlin managed, covering her mouth from the stench of gore. Reflexively, she gagged.

"Gee, Kait. I ain't meanin' to make yah sick!"

"H - how did you kill that poor deer, Bobby?"

Her brother sported pink cheeks. "I - I'm ashamed ter tell yuh how."

The gentle woman touched his arm. "Bobby, you're doing the best you can. I am *proud* of you, no matter how you got it. You got a deer!"

"Weeelll, the poor babe' stepped in mah trap. I didn' want ter hurt it, but meat is meat." He peeked at her from under his too-long hair.

"Bobby, I am proud of you," she repeated. "But if it won't hurt your feelings, I will sit over here until you finish."

Bobby tried and tried to get the skin off the young doe, but he kept taking hunks of meat with the hide.

Suddenly, a bronze hand took Bobby's knife from him and made short work of skinning the animal.

"What the hell?" Bobby nearly screamed.

Spirit Bear was his alias and had materialized from air. The ultimate warrior was not there, then he was. Kaitlin nearly stifled a shriek herself.

Bobby scrambled back from the carcass as fast as he could on his hands and knees.

"Kait! Git… behind meh!" he croaked. Bobby was trembling from head to toe like a weathered leaf cracking in the wind as he stood shakily to his feet.

"Bobby…" Kaitlin gently touched him. Her brother jumped and whimpered. He protectively held an arm in front of her. He was too frightened to notice that the Indian hadn't done anything more than skin the deer and turn to face him.

"Look, ah, mister Redskin. Yah kin have that there deer. I don' need em tha' bad." Bobby's knees were knocking.

"Bobby," Kaitlin tried again. "Bobby?"

"Kait, hush! Make no sudden moves!"

"BOBBY!" she yelled.

Both men regarded her.

"Are yeh outta yer mind?" Bobby whispered.
He quickly returned his attention to the bronzed
warrior in front of him.

"Bobby, meet my husband."

"Yer…. WHAT?" Bobby's remaining color
rapidly drained.

"I'm sorry he scared you. I didn't know he was
going to appear like that," Kaitlin said
meaningfully with a pointed look. "He scared
me to death, too."

No movement came from Spirit Bear. He
continued to stand stoically and watch the two.

"Yer… married… to an Injun?"

"Yes, I am."

"That guy?" Bobby swallowed noisily. "He
looks meaner than a box o' rattlers that ain't eat
in a year. An' I thot Jed was bad!"

"Bobby, he's saved my life time and time again.
He is a good man and a good leader. And I love
him."

"S'cuse meh, but got ter sit down." Bobby dropped to his knees and fell the rest of the way into a seated position. His skin was crisply white, and sweat had popped out all over his head. "Nearly mussed muhself," he grumbled.

Kaitlin smoothed his hair back from his face. "He means you no harm, Bobby. My husband is here because he wants assurance that it is safe for me to go into town. He fears I will be in danger."

"Tell meh. Does that man ever move? I mean a'side from when he wuz a usin' a knife."

Kaitlin couldn't help the smile that broke out on her face. She thought she saw her husband's eyes crinkle in a flash of amusement.

"Yes, Bobby," Kaitlin said between her smiling lips, "he does move."

"Yah better not be a smilin'."

"*Woniya Mato* gave you a gift of skinning your deer for you. He wanted you to have some meat left." Kaitlin gave a short burst of laughter.

"Tha' ain't nice, Kait!" Bobby grumped. But his sister knew just what to do to get him back to being Bobby.

When Bobby dared to look at the Sioux warrior, he saw white teeth smiling at him, too.

"My husband is very perceptive," Kaitlin informed.

"Yer tellin' me that I'm a gett'n made fun by o' Injun?

"It appears so."

"Kin he understan' meh?"

"No, but he reads body language well."

"Will yeh tell 'im… thank ya for skinnin' muh deer?"

"Yes, I will." Kaitlin relayed the information in nearly fluent Lakota.

"Goodness, Kait! When didja lern to speak Injun?"

"I lived with them for a span of time now, Bobby. You find the will to learn fast when you can't talk to anyone."

Bobby's eyes widened. "I'm sorry, Kait. I couldn' save yeh from pa. I coudn' save yeh from Jed." He sniffed and wiped his eye.

"Does it look like I blame you? I have a better life now, Bobby."

"Yeh don' know how glad I am ter hear that." Bobby was silent a moment before asking, "Yer sure you wanna see pa?"

"Yes. I've forgiven him. I still love him, Bobby. I don't want to see him suffering. I want to help if I can."

"Is yer hubby gonna let yeh?"

"That's up to you."

CHAPTER FIFTY-FIVE

Consideration

"What do yah mean?" Bobby squawked. He started to act nervous again.

"*Wonoiya Mato* wants to be sure it is safe for me to travel down there. He wants to make sure Pa isn't going to try to sell me again and that there aren't any Jed Coldwater supporters down there to extract revenge on me."

"Naw, Pa ain't strong no more. Yeh could git away from 'em if'n yeh needed to. A'sides, I'm a here ta help. I won' let nothin' happen to yeh. I cain't take no more guilt. As far as Jed Coldwater goes, his clan's dried up and blowed away. Thur's a new man with power in town. I don't rightly know him good, but he seems honest enuff."

"A new man?"

"Jus' got here bout a month ago… 'bout the time I dried out."

"Who is it?"

"Nobody ya'd know. His name is William somethin'. Goes by Will. He's a one of thos' rich fellers."

"Rich?"

"Ya, he brought up a bunch of supplies for the town and now we got a'nother store. He has a teen daughter that is running a place. I mean, he's tha backbone, but he's behin' the scene unless she a needs 'm. Yeh can eat a home cooked meal, buy supplies, and there's a few rooms ter rent above tha'. They just a opened up."

"Really? Wow."

"Yep. I managed to get Pa a room cuz he's a need'n to stay in town. He just ain't up to making that trip no more."

"How much rent does he charge?"

"Well, I made 'm a deal. I clean up the rooms every weekend to pay fer pa's room. I sleep on the floor when I'm a there.

"Do they include the food?"

"Naw. I've a been a tryin' to provide the meat. It's been hard though. As yeh kin see, I ain't no hunter."

"Bobby, there's nothing to be ashamed of. You're doing great! No one has been around to teach you. Papa has been wrapped up in himself since mama left us, and you have, too. You fell into some bad decisions but papa is to blame for leading you that way. Now here you are, doing your best. Who could complain against that?'

"Pa."

"He has no right."

Spirit Bear said something in Lakota.

"What did yer man say?"

"He said if you prove to be honorable, he'd be happy to teach you to hunt."

Bobby turned toward the leader with an incredulous expression. "Yeh'd be a willin' to teach some ole white man ter hunt?"

Spirit Bear's response was one nod.

"He can tell by your expression, Bobby," when he turned his surprised face back to her.

"I cain't believe it!"

"Maybe he will even teach you how to skin one, too," Kaitlin said chortling.

Spirit Bear said something that made Kaitin burst forth with a trail of laughter.

"What did he say?"

"The name he gives you is 'Deer Slayer'."

Bobby didn't know what to say, but he did sport a grin even though he was deeply embarrassed.

"He can't even call meh by muh name?"

"He doesn't feel the need to learn white man language, *and* he's very hard-headed. Let him call you what he wants."

In the corner of her eye, she saw her husband raise a brow toward her.

Ignoring him, she continued, "Believe me, you couldn't learn under someone more skilled."

"That is mighty kind o' him. I don' know quite what ter say. He don't know what he's a getting' in ter."

"I think he may realize it," Kaitlin giggled.

Spirit Bear spoke again.

Kaitlin interpreted, "*Woniya Mato* needs to know if you feel there is any danger to me in town. Many know I was 'kidnapped' by Indians, and he wants assurance that if someone remembers, they wouldn't hold it against me or hold me captive to get him."

"Heck, Kait. I cain't think o' no one. I mean Bradley always liked yeh but he'd never do anythin' to hurt yeh."

"Okay." She relayed the information to her husband in Lakota. He could understand most of what Bobby was saying, but she filled in the blanks. They conversed for moments before Kaitlin turned back to her brother.

"He says we will discuss this. I have some furs and hides for you to use to purchase what you need."

Bobby got a tear in his eye. "I shore don' deserve ya, Kait. I'm actually surprised yeh don' hate me."

"Bobby, I saw what was happening. I saw how you couldn't go against Papa. I also saw how his own decisions were hurting him; all of us. I love you, and forgive you. I just couldn't blindly give myself to Jed, so I ran away. Now, I'm here, and you've changed. I know you have a way to go, but you're on the right path."

Bobby wiped at his eye and turned away from them. He sniffed before turning back around.

"How are you getting to town and back?" his sister asked.

"With mah feet."

"I guess you don't have a horse."

"Naw. Cain't afford one yet."

In Lakota, Kaitlin asked Spirit Bear, "Do you think we could stay a day with him? I could show him how to dry the deer and preserve it so that most of the meat isn't wasted. Then, could we give him a ride near the town?"

"I will need to return for another horse, then, but it would not take long for me on *Runs with the Wind.* Are your brother's friends around? I would not mind you staying until I can return, but I will not leave if they are here."

"Oh, *Woniya Mato*! Thank you!"

"You are welcome. Ask," he said with a nod toward her brother.

Kaitlin asked Bobby his question.

"Naw, they left me yesterday. I wanted to git more meat firs'."

"Would you want me to stay with you to show you how to preserve this deer?

"Wud yeh?"

"Yes. My husband said since your friends left, I could stay to help you. He's going to return here in a few hours so we can give you a ride to town."

Bobby's eyes again teared up. "I don' deserve yeh, Kait."

"Just say 'thank you'."

"Thank yeh."

"You're welcome."

Kaitlin turned to her *hingnaku* and kissed him deeply. Bobby cleared his throat uncomfortably. Then Spirit Bear whistled for *Runs with the Wind*, leaped onto his back, and was gone in a flash.

"How does a man move like tha'?" muttered Bobby. "He's like a ghost. He's a here one minute, gone the next, and is a very scary guy."

Kaitlin arched her head back and laughed. "He is known as 'Spirit Bear'. Come on, Bobby. Let's get started on that deer."

CHAPTER FIFTY-SIX

Generosity

"Yeh shore did lern a lot from them Redskins," Bobby said in appreciation as he bit into the freshly grilled tenderloin. It was seasoned to perfection.

Bobby's campsite was basically a few weathered blankets thrown over a stick structure and held down with rocks by a fire pit. There was deer meat strung up everywhere, but most was close to the fire to discourage vermin and facilitate drying.

"I really have. They have so much more on every level than our kinsmen, Bobby. They have a skilled shaman who is the spiritual leader, but he also is very schooled on making medicines. Their people, for the most part, are like one huge family. No one goes hungry, and everyone is cared for."

"Man, I'da like ter live with yeh."

"Who knows, Bobby? Maybe you can, but you'll have to earn trust. One step at a time."

"I know."

They were quiet while they ate. Just as Kaitlin began cleaning up, her husband returned. He'd brought back a young black mare with a star and four socks. He also had Kaitlin's mare.

Spirit Bear said to his wife, "Tell your brother that he may have this horse. It is his to own, but he may not sell it. He will need to return it to us if he should no longer be able to care for it. She is not to be sold or traded for drink, to pay debt as I have understood from your world, or anything else. The only string attached is that she is not broke to ride, but she is gentle."

"*Woniya Mato*! Really? I am so happy, and I cannot believe it! Why, *mita hingnaku*? I am not questioning your judgement, but I am just so happy because that is much more than I ever expected you to give. You are truly generous."

"*Mita wastelaka*, I give to your brother, *Tahca KatA,* because he is an extension of you, and he has no one else. If I can help him walk the path to becoming a whole man, then that is what I want.”

Kaitlin happily hugged her leader. She was so ecstatic that her eyes leaked with joy.

“What is goin’ on here?” her brother asked.

“Oh, Bobby! My husband is truly generous! He brought back that beautiful black mare as a gift to you!”

Bobby’s jaw dropped, and he stood there, dumbfounded. “Kait, I’m a gonna hafta sit again. This is almost more than muh heart kin take, but in a good way.”

“You sit, my brother. There are a few strings attached. You may not sell, trade, or give her away. She is to come back to us when you don’t want her or can’t take care of her.”

“Done.” He was still staring at her husband with an expression of awe on his face.

“And… she is gentle… but not broke. You will have to train her to white man’s ways.”

"I'll do my best an' of course, I understand. What a beauty!"

"That would be a suiting name!"

"Beauty it is. Kait, I… uh, don't know quite how ter tell yer man thank ya. It ain't enough jus to say them words."

She smiled, "I'll let him know."

While Kaitlin finished cleaning, Spirit Bear set up a camp for the two of them. When they sat around the cheery fire, each lost in their own thoughts, the blonde stood and went to their bedding area. She brought back several bundles.

"Oh, Bobby, here are your furs and such to help you buy my dress and things you need."

Kaitlin brought the goods before him, and again, her brother's eyes were large orbs in his face. He stood shakily as he perused the items.

"I ain't never seen quality like this, Kait! You did this?" he breathed.

"I had help," she said, smiling with the praise. "Like I said, I learned under the best. They are close to perfection, but the process is *dis-gust-ing*."

"I almost feel like I should say no to all this, but I cain't get yuh no dress unless'n I take 'm."

"We don't need them."

"Yer shore?"

"Yes."

"I kin buy waaay more than a dress an' some food with these!" Bobby trailed off as he saw the chief stand. Spirit Bear went to retrieve something as well.

Upon his return, the leader said, "Tell him that this bison robe is for him. I do not want him to sell this but it is his to keep. It can be used as bedding, a blanket, a coat, or…" her husband nodded meaningfully toward the shabby blankets, "as a cover to ward off the wind."

Kaitlin translated as her *hingnaku* gave him the gift.

"Uh, Kait? I don' know how ter act. I almost
wanna hug the man, but he scares me too much.
How kin 'thank ya' be enough?"

Kaitlin spoke to her husband in Lakota. Spirit
Bear thumped his chest once and said, "It is an
honor to help the brother of my wife."

Bobby took the supplies to his sleeping area and
turned toward the couple. "I need ter… go an'
take care of some needs. I won' be too long."

After he'd gone, Kaitlin said, "I think we have
overwhelmed him." She gave a short laugh.
"It's a good thing, but he doesn't know to
handle it with all that he feels guilty over."

"*Tos*, I agree. *Mazaska Zi Ista*, I have decided
to let you go, but I am still concerned. Do not
think I have forgotten the threats to you. Some
in town will know you were with our band, and
they may be cruel or try to do you harm."

"I have been thinking about this, too, *Woniya
Mato*. I think I may tell them I was rescued by a
white man, and he is now my *hingnaku*. All
who were witnesses otherwise are dead. This
explanation will protect us both."

Spirit Bear considered this. "How will you explain your *hingnaku's* absence when you go into town?"

"I can say he is away hunting so I came to stay with my brother?"

"*Tos*. This should work."

"I would like to see him more than once, if I can."

Spirit Bear's heavy black gaze settled on her. Kaitlin shifted uncomfortably.

"I have not approved this. You are very fortunate I have agreed to let you go at all. It is a gift, *Mazaska Zi Ista*."

"It is one I am very thankful for, *mita hingnaku*," she said with a gentle kiss. "I was only thinking. If my father is in as poor of health as Bobby says, I would like to see Papa as often as I can due to our closeness in location, as he may not live much longer."

"*Mita wastelaka*, need I remind you that you carry our child? You cannot risk it."

"I would never do that, *Woniya Mato*. I would only do this if it were safe."

"This is a discussion for another time. Let us see how the first visit goes and if there is any need for concern."

"That is more than I can ask for."

***

Bobby returned shortly after their conversation had died. He was very humble and subdued around Spirit Bear and was unsure of how to act. The younger man was beginning to really look up to the warrior. Respect and awe were drowning the fear.

"Bobby, I'm tired. I think I'm going to go to bed," Kaitlin announced after a sleepy yawn. "Besides, it's getting too cold."

"I, too, am a goin' ter sleep. I cain't wait to crawl under this warm looking bison cape!"

Spirit Bear stood first and helped his wife to her feet. "*Hanhepi Waste*," he said to Bobby.

"He's telling you goodnight," Kaitlin called to her brother as they walked to their bedding.

"Uh, goodnight, yeh both."

Kaitlin settled in next to her husband. Each of their bodies provided heat for the other. They were lying on bison fur covered with the same. They didn't have the tent that Bobby did, but although cold, Kaitlin preferred the open sky. She loved to look at the beautiful mystery that surrounded the many stars and let her thoughts wander.

"*Mazaska Zi Ista,* I have a question."

"*Tos*?"

"Why do you and your *wicowe* speak so differently? It is difficult for me to understand him where you are easier to comprehend."

"It is because my mother taught me proper English. Papa hoped I could marry into wealth, so when we lived back East, I had to take classes that taught me to be a cultured lady.

That meant I had to know how to walk, how to talk, and how to behave like a lady of class. My brother did not have to worry about the same."

"I am not sure I understand what you mean by 'proper' or 'cultured', but I know that there is a perceived difference with *wasicu* based on the things they own."

"Isn't there, to a degree, with our community as well? I mean, I know we make sure all are provided for, but there is a definite distinction between who is more blessed with wealth and who is not."

"*Tos*, it is true. Some have more than others. Some are more thankful, and some do not thank *Wankantanka* as they should. But we do care for our own much more than the *wasicu*."

"I totally agree, *Woniya Mato*. White people *are* judgmental where the Lakota do not seem to be."

Kaitlin snuggled down into the thick, comfortable robe and deeper into her husband's arms. Spirit Bear smiled into her golden hair as her breathing deepened. Her ability to sleep in an instant was nearly alarming, but he knew the growing *wakanheja* zapped her strength quickly.

The next morning, a glittery blanket quilted the scenery. It sparkled dazzlingly from every blade and branch. Kaitlin could see her breath. It danced in frozen pirouettes as it hung in the icy air above her.

Spirit Bear's absence from their bed was noticeable not because he'd made noise from rising but from the missing warmth his body had provided. The Indian princess was grateful to see he'd already started a fire blazing. She looked into his midnight eyes and was impressed with his smile. His bright teeth against his bronzed skin were more brilliant than the scenery.

"*Mazaska Zi Ista*, I have made you a tea. I have also made your *wicowe* the dandelion root in case he likes what your family would call 'coofee'."

"Oh, *Woniya Mato*! You truly are a blessing to me! I love you so much!"

CHAPTER FIFTY-SEVEN

Brotherly fun

Spirit Bear laughed. "Not as much as I love you, *mita wastelaka*."

"Oh, yes I do!" Kaitlin giggled as she wrapped her body with her wintery goods. "I will drink my tea upon my return." Her husband nodded in acknowledgement as his wife left to take care of her needs.

Spirit Bear took out the bags for storing meat. The hanging venison was not totally dried, but Bobby would have to complete that upon his return to the *wasicu* community. It was frozen and there would be no drying it today unless they nearly cooked the meat over the open flame.

When Kaitlin returned, she swung close to her brother's shelter. "Bobby?"

A groan came from within.

"Bobby?" she called again.

"Whatda yeh want?"

"Rise and shine!"

"Yeh always were a early riser." Bobby
grumbled, but he rolled out of his tent and faced
the glittery world in astonishment.

"You have a hot drink at the fire."

"Kait, I cain't believe meh eyes! I slept like a
baby with muh warm blanket from yer chief! I
cain't even believe it's so cold out and it's a
already time ter get up!"

"Come, brother. I am warm, too, but I would
like a nice hot drink to sooth my throat."

"Tell yer hubby again, thank ya fer my
blanket… and everythin', Kait. Thank yuh too
fer mah deer meat."

Kaitlin nodded as she pulled her brother to the
fire to sit. She gratefully took the tea from her
husband and then handed Bobby his cup. The

young woman sat for a few minutes, sipping her tea, before rising to make *aguyapi*. Her brother just watched in silence. He'd never seen the flat bread bake on clean rocks before. Soon a pleasant aroma was rising off the cooking pones. The blonde passed out pemmican in addition to the warm Indian biscuits.

"What's this stuff?" Bobby asked. He looked with interest at the dried fatty meat as well as the *aguyapi*.

"It's Indian bread and traveling food. Eat it. It's good."

Bobby nibbled the items to taste, then ate with appreciation. "Kait, yuns shore are God sends. Yeh kin make anythin' and everythin' taste good! All this stuff is better than anythin' I've had to eat in a long time." After taking a swallow of his hot drink, her brother's eyes bugged. "Yeh kin even make coffee!" he nearly dropped his cup.

"Boy, you're easy to please," Kaitlin said with a bubble of giggles. "Bobby, I am so glad you're back. It's actually dandelion root not coffee, but it works! Isn't the native knowledge vast? I am glad you can see just a fraction of what these people know. When you're done eating, I'll clean up. Then we need to pack up your meat."

"I'm too impressed fer words, Kait. I woulda never imagined all this stuff!"

"Me, either. We are taught to fear and distrust these people. We think the Oglala and other natives are savages and unrefined, when in reality, we are!" Kaitlin was almost vehement. She took a breath to calm herself. "They *are* fierce when provoked, Bobby, but otherwise, they are the gentlest community one could imagine. If I had to pick monsters, it would be our people."

"I agree that some of our kind are monsters," Bobby said, grabbing another biscuit, "but there are good 'uns, too."

"True. I mean, look at us!" Kaitlin laughed to lighten the mood.

= = =

Spirit Bear just quietly observed the two. He rather enjoyed watching his wife interact with the brother that had been lost to her. She seemed so happy and carefree! So far the *wasicun* man had impressed him as well. The white male was infantile in his skills, but his heart was there and his pride was not an obstacle. There *was* hope.

When his wife gathered up the breakfast mess to clean, Spirit Bear handed the storage skins to Bobby. The warrior took one and showed the white man how to pack his meat.

"*Woniya Mato* wishes you to know that your meat will need to continue drying when you get in your shelter. It will take some warmth to dry the venison to the point where it will not mold."

"Okay. I shore will do like yuns say. I wish yeh had time ter teach meh to make that stuff we had this mornin'."

"I will teach you how someday. Deal?"

"Deal."

"If you want to pack up, I think my husband is ready to go."

"Shore!" Bobby rushed to his make-shift tent and began to pack his meager belongings. He thought about throwing out his ratty blankets, but decided against it. Although not much, it was a minor barrier to the cold. Perhaps his father would want to use them. If nothing else, they would suffice for a pillow. For the time being, they made decent 'bags' to pack his things in. He tied twine around the top so that the blanket-bag stayed secure.

"Bobby, if you don't have any more clothes than what is packed, I insist on you doing something for me."

"What's that, sis?"

"I want you to buy yourself some new clothes. You could use a haircut and shave while you're at it. Okay?"

Bobby started, "But, Kait – "

"No 'but Kaits'! You need these things, and we can help. Will you promise?"

"I don' think it's right."

"Promise!"

"Oh, alright. I promise."

Kaitlin wrapped her arms around her brother.
"Thank you."

"It don' feel right."

"Well, like it or not, it's a done deal!"

Spirit Bear whistled for his horse. *Runs with the
Wind* appeared with two gorgeously made mares
following him.

"That stallion's so purty, it's no wonder them
two girls are a followerin' him!" Bobby stated,
chuckling.

Kaitlin's laughter joined his. "Yes, they are
nice. All three are just stunning horses!"

Soon, all people were mounted on the animals.
Kaitlin rode with her husband on the big
stallion's back while Bobby rode Kaitlin's mare.
Beauty was asked to carry Bobby's blanket bags

and a few other small items as a testimony to her first training steps.

"It's a gonna be cold in the next three day's a ridin'." Bobby was stating the obvious.

"It's true. I'll be fine with my husband to warm me."

"Kait! I don' need to be a hearin' things like tha!"

Both Spirit Bear and Kaitlin laughed. He made an easy target with his animated exaggerations.

"Bobby! I am appalled! I mean that he was like sitting next to a fire. What did *you* think I meant?"

"Uh… um, I thought… that… um, I mean, I thought yeh were…" Fiery cheeks gave away exactly where his thoughts had gone.

"Bobby! You know me better than that!"

"Yeah, sis. I guess I do." Bobby was hanging his head sheepishly. "I didn' mean no insult."

"Hey, straighten up. I'm only making fun of you. I can tease my brother, right?"

"Shore… but yeh were right… now I'm ashamed."

Kaitlin laughed some more. "I love you, Bobby. Chin up. We're all good. Now let's take off. We've got a long while to ride."

CHAPTER FIFTY-EIGHT

Welcome Home

Three days of travel in the cold, South Dakota winds went fairly quickly. Kaitlin was with two of her most favorite people in the world, so time was relative. She grew restless when they were getting close to the white settlement. The conversation died and a feeling of mild sadness settled over the trio.

"We will go no farther," Spirit Bear said, stopping his horse when they were close to where white men dominated. "It is not wise for you to be seen with me," he motioned to the siblings. Kaitlin translated for her brother.

"Bobby, *Woniya Mato* wants you to speak to Papa. Tell him that I will be visiting, but he needs to not mention the circumstances in which I disappeared. Tell him I was rescued by a white man and am now married. I am coming to visit you for a bit because my husband is on a hunting expedition, and I didn't want to be alone. We feel it is safer to tell this tale because I am sure a few will remember the rumors about me being abducted by 'savages' when I only was trying to escape one."

"I shore will, Kait. Thank ya so much fer everythin'. It may take meh a week or two ter get everythin' squared away."

"How will we know when you're ready?"

"Yer man is always out and about. I kin leave a sign fer him, somehow?"

Kaitlin continued to be the liaison between the two.

"Spirit Bear says that will be fine. He will return in two weeks to see if you have left a handkerchief in the crook of that tree over there," she said pointing.

"Tha' should be a plenty a time. If'n there ain't no handkerchief, then tha' means it ain't safe or I ain't quite ready and come check back again."

"It sounds like a plan, my dear brother! I'm so happy I get to see you again… under much better circumstances."

"I'm a sorry fer the way I was, Kait. I love yeh and am so happy I getta second chance."

The siblings hugged. Bobby went to Spirit Bear and held out his hand.

"Bobby, hold up your hand at an angle."

Spirit Bear smiled, and the men clasped hands tightly. It was a handshake of sorts, Native style.

"Please tell him that I ain't never gonna ferget all y'uve done fer me. I'll do muh best to see that I kin repay yeh."

"He knows," but Kaitlin strung some Lakota and tossed it her husband's way.

Spirit Bear nodded once to Bobby, then he motionlessly turned his horse.

"Good bye," Kaitlin said. *Woniya Mato* echoed her words in Lakota.

* * *

When they arrived back at the Sioux village, Wonder Worker greeted them with a few young braves. Spirit Bear handed his wife down to his friend and the young men took the horses to care for them. After entering into their tipi, the couple noticed a cheery fire in their hearth and a warmed soup with fresh *aguyapi*.

"You really are a wonder worker!" Kaitlin exclaimed. "How did you know to prepare for our arrival so precisely?"

"A shaman never reveals his secrets," he said with a laugh. "I had my mother prepare your hut, but I could not stay away." He beamed a handsome smile. "What happened?"

"You mean you do not know already?" Kaitlin asked, nearly exasperated.

Wonder Worker laughed again. He sat by his friend as Kaitlin handed soup, bread, and drink to the men and prepared some food for herself.

"It went well so far, my *kola*," Spirit Bear said.

Wonder Worker cocked a questioning brow.

The war chief continued, "The *wasicun wicowe's* actions were unexpected. His name is now *Tahca KatA*. He is an infant in a man's body, learning to hunt, skin, and preserve meat." He chuckled with the memory.

"You named him Deer Slayer when he is an *ojilaka* in his skills? This is a story I must hear."

The married couple relayed the information about Bobby when they'd happened upon him. Wonder Worker was chuckling along with them at the picture painted by their words.

"You do believe he has healed from his past with the drink?" The medicine man asked.

"*Tos, Wawakankan,* for now, he is genuine. More time must pass for one to know if he is truly healed. He must be tempted many

times to know if he can continue to resist."
Spirit Bear turned to his wife. "I do not say this
to be cruel, but I have seen what that drink can
do if left for consumption at free will."

"I know, *Woniya Mato*. I have
witnessed first-hand from Papa. He has failing
health because of it! I know you mean no
insult."

"What decision was made?" Wonder
Worker prompted.

"I have decided, against my better
judgement, to let her see her father. I am not
happy about this. We gave *Tahca KatA* some
things to help him obtain a dress for Golden
Eyes, and we created a tale for her safety. He
will say that *Mazaska Zi Ista* was rescued by a
white man whom she married. He is off hunting
for a few days, so she came to stay with her
brother. It should protect her while she is
there."

Wonder Worker nodded his head in
consideration. "I think this will work. Does she
plan on just a few hours or a few suns in this
community?"

"We have not discussed this."

"Oh, *Woniya Mato*! Could I stay a few suns?"
Hopeful golden eyes flashed with excitement at
the thought. Her mouth opened slightly,
drawing her husband's attention to her pink lips
and rosy wind-burned cheeks.

= = =

Spirit Bear groaned inwardly. *How could he let
her go, but how could he not?* Finally, he said,
"Let me think upon this." It was going to be all
the commitment Kaitlin was going to get at the
moment.

It was quiet while the three finished eating.
When Kaitlin left to clean dishes, the men began
more discussion.

"You are my *kola* and person I trust most. What
do you say about this deal?" The weight of the
leader's gaze settled on Wonder Worker's
shoulders.

"I can meditate further on this. Normally, I can only predict short durations. I feel that she is protected for a few suns by what the spirits have revealed to me so far. I do not know if *Mazaska Zi Ista* were to continue visiting if she would remain safe. It is something I will have to continuously communicate with the spirits on."

Spirit Bear nodded. "It will be a few weeks before I have to say what she can do. Let me know if your feelings change. At this point, with what you have said, I will let her stay with her *wicowe* for a few suns. I do not plan to tell her so yet. I will wait to hear from my spiritual advisor closer to the time."

Both men nodded in agreement.

Changing the subject, Wonder Worker asked, "When is our next ceremony?"

"Let us meet in the council lodge to speak about this. I say we do it soon."

"*Tos*, I agree. It is time to rest now, my *kola*. I will go now and let you have a respite after your suns of travel.

= = =

When Kaitlin reentered their home, Spirit Bear
was lying in the furs with the cover turned down.
A stoked fire had a cozy temperature waltzing
around the structure. The firelight played on
Woniya Mato's bare chest. The blonde watched
and the golden silhouette faded into bronze as it
licked and played along his muscular physique.

Spirit Bear's vivid smile commanded her
attention to trail back up to his striking face. He
patted the covers with meaning. Kaitlin found
she could barely seal the entrance flap. Her
fingers were shaking slightly.

*What is the matter with me? I'm not an
innocent girl who has never lain with her
handsome husband! Yes, it's bitter outside, but
my hands don't quiver with cold...*

Spirit Bear watched his becoming wife settle in
next to him. Her skin was cold, and a fresh
layer of goosebumps pricked her flesh. Without

a word, the warrior lowered his head and began to work enchantments upon her inviting lips. Her body was pliant; it molded and yielded to his every demand.

The afternoon was spent with many lazy yet sensation-filled sharing of love. Both gave and received. Finally, the couple snuggled down into the downy softness of the bison fur.

 "How can our experiences always stay new and fresh?" Kaitlin murmured against his warmth. "That was magical!"

"You are a gift of love from *Wankantanka*." Spirit Bear said simply.

"I think you are."

Kaitlin giggled as her husband turned her over and began a new wave of attacks on her senses. She gasped, "Oh, *Woniya Mato*! *You* are the gift to *me*!" Love-filled laughter echoed throughout the structure.

CHAPTER FIFTY-NINE

Emotional

That evening, Spirit Bear ate a quick meal with his wife before heading to the counsel lodge.

"Do not wait up for me. We will be discussing plans for the new ceremony."

"Tos, Woniya Mato."

Kaitlin was still weary even though they had napped about an hour. It was nearly dark already. The blonde felt she hadn't done anything useful for the day but was so tired, she didn't really care. Absently, the white woman took out a basket to finish weaving. The golden one intended to fill it with some gifts for her family. By the time she would get to see them, it would be December. Kaitlin always thought of festivities at that time of year. There were lots of scrumptious foods that were limited to winter months. Gifts were given as Christmas time approached.

A tear escaped from golden eyes. Kaitlin never really let herself mourn for her mother. Now her father's health was going downhill quickly. Kaitlin forgave her pa for what he'd attempted to do because it'd led to the love of her life. However, she still held a little resentment. The sympathetic woman would force herself to let it go. Kaitlin reckoned Pa was paying for his choices.

Oh, Mama, I wish you could see me now. I am so happy. I know being married to a Native is not really what you would have pictured for me, but you would have wanted my happiness. I am going to have a baby! I am going to make you a grandma! I only wish you could meet him... or her. Please help Papa when his time comes. He will have a rough go, so if you could be there for his transition, I would feel better.

Kaitlin wiped at the tears freely flowing from her eyes. Suddenly she was overcome with goosebumps that she didn't feel had anything to do with the temperature. It was if the spirits were telling her that her prayers would be answered. The blonde looked up and whispered, "Thank you, Mama!"

Glancing down at her belly, she softly asked, "Warrior Bear or Sunflower, is it you in there that's making me so emotional?" The newly expectant mother tenderly rubbed her tummy. A surge of protectiveness barreled through her nearly taking her off guard.

Kaitlin gasped, "Oh my! You *must* be responsible for all these reactions!" Then, just as suddenly, the blonde was amused at her mood change snaps.

I need to do something to distract myself from my emotions! The golden-skinned woman decided to complete her husband's boots and try her hand at a pair of house shoes with wool lining for her father's Christmas present.

***

When Spirit Bear entered their home, he saw that Kaitlin was sleeping soundly. He stoked the fire and removed his clothing. Inaudibly, he settled next to her. His wife had on her cape dress she loved so dearly. The man of war was a gentle breeze as his hand found the way to her stomach. He protectively placed his hand on her abdomen and beamed.

"Sleep, little *wakanheja*. Soon it will be time for you to meet us. I want you to take care of your mama when she goes to see her papa. I want nothing more than your safe return."

Soon, the warrior willed himself to relax and finally sleep.

***

The next morning, a cool dawn greeted the community. Spirit Bear sounded a drum midday to signify that there would be a gathering celebration in a handful of days. The beat was a signal to start preparing for a feast and to approach the counsel for anything needing addressing.

Kaitlin went to Gentle Rabbit's tipi and called to enter.

"*Hau*, come in, *Mazaska Zi Ista*! *Hokahe*."

"Thank you, *Wawat'ecaka*. What are you going to make for the feast?"

"I will prepare some fresh meat. I've asked *Wawakankan* to get me a nice buck. They are still healthy this time of year. It will make many savory dishes."

"That is too much preparation for one person. Would you like some help?"

"You do not need to cook now, *Mazaska Zi Ista*. You are wife of a chief."

"And I need to keep busy. I can't stand to watch others work. It is an honor to serve my people."

"How did I know you would say this?" Gentle Rabbit teased. "Yes, of course you may help me prepare. But I really like your desserts you arrange as well."

Kaitlin grinned. "Is this a hint? And which flavors do you like best?"

Gentle Rabbit gave her a partial wink, "Hum… surprise me! They are all so good!"

"I will make something new, and I will surprise you! That can wait a bit as it is better fresh and warm. Meat can cook in advance. When is *Wawakankan* going hunting?"

"In the morning."

"I want to make something special, not just food, but a gift for *Haspa Nableca*. I know she is treated very well now, but if you are a *wayaka*, that thought never leaves you. Everyone knows you are nothing. If she is to be inducted as Oglala, then she needs a special gift with her birth."

"You are right. That is why I made her a winter robe to help keep her warm. I think the rest of your women friends have the same idea in mind – to make gifts."

"What should I make her, *Wawat'ecaka*? I have some baskets I can give her that she's admired, but I want something more special than that."

"I think you could construct a special hat to keep her warm. It could go with the cape, and we can decorate them to make them special."

"Oh, that is a perfect idea! May I see your construction?"

"I thought you'd never ask!"

Gentle Rabbit unfolded the ultra-soft bison cloak. It was lined with rabbit fur on the inside, and the outside collar was made, at the top, of more rabbit fur; however, the rodent's fur blended into the softer part of the bison's mane where it would not touch Apple Blossom's skin to irritate. The coarser neck fur lined the bottom. The mahogany leather was pliant and glowed with a fresh coat of oil to sustain the suppleness.

"This is one of the nicest pieces I've seen!" breathed Kaitlin. "How can I ever expect to match this in quality?"

"*Mazaska Zi Ista,* you helped to make this."

"I – I – I did?"

"*Tos*, child. Tell me what you have in mind to compliment the cape."

"Oh, well, I – I think a nice rabbit fur hat would be agreeable. Maybe the inside could be the leather instead of the fur to help cut a little down on static?"

"I think that would complement the cape wonderfully! Now let's get started."

The women worked for several hours on the hat construction. The leather was very easy to mold, cut, and sew the basic pattern with. Tacking on the rabbit fur would take much more time. Kaitlin planned to use braided leather strips for ties and little rabbit balls of fur to decorate the ends. Apple Blossom would look so adorable!

"I also want to make my father a nice robe or blanket when I go to see him."

"That is nice, *Mazaska Zi Ista*. You are too sweet. I hope you do not get your heart broken by him again."

"I have forgiven him, for the most part. I just want to make peace with him before he gets too ill to know what is going on. I love my pa even if he wouldn't win a father award. He's the only one I have."

"*Tos*, this is true. But Kaitlin, how will you feel if you put all your efforts and hard work into pleasing him, and he sells it for drink?"

"I know of this possibility. I hope Bobby can intervene. I will feel good because I tried to make amends, and not just through a gift. I will feel badly, though, if he does get more drink because of my gift."

"Can you live with it?"

Kaitlin nodded through the sudden lump in her throat. "*Tos*," She managed to croak.

"I am not trying to hurt you, daughter. I want to be a factual person. You should know all angles when you do something nice for someone. This way if they let you down, you already anticipated it of a sort. You also expect the good outcomes, so most of the time, one is pleasantly surprised."

"Thank you, *Wawat'ecaka*! You're the best mother anyone could ask for." Kaitlin's tears sprung back to life with the mention of 'mother'.

"What is it, child?" asked Gentle Rabbit, concerned.

"I think the *wakanheja* is wreaking havoc on my emotions," Kaitlin sniffed.

"*Tos*?"

"Yes, one second, I am very sad over my mother I lost years ago, then next I am laughing over how many people I am thankful for!"

"I will see if I can come up with something to help your emotions," Gentle Rabbit stated, "and yes, the *wakanheja* is the cause. Think of how many mood swings you can experience at the Tipis of Isolation. This is a mega version of the hormones. Forgive yourself and recognize it for what it is."

"*Tos, Wawat'ecaka*. Thank you. Your talk helped."

CHAPTER SIXTY

More Time for Relaxation

The next day, Kaitlin arose to another warm, cheery fire. She smiled sleepily at her husband and ran a hand through her tousled hair. It gleamed like gold in the light.

"*Woniya Mato*, I am so thankful to you for always having a fire blazing. I really appreciate it."

"I always rise before you, and it is my pleasure. I am honored to keep my family warm."

"Family?" Kaitlin giggled. "We are working on that but I don't know if we are at that status yet."

Her *hingnaku* cocked a brow.

"I mean, I have enough love for all of us to be a family," she snickered, backtracking.

Her husband prowled over to her and leaped lightly on her. "I have more love."

Kaitlin tittered and whispered, "I do not think so."

"Do you care to repeat that?" Spirit Bear growled, looming up, capturing her attention fully. He'd trapped his wife under his body. He did not put his full weight on her, but she could not have moved if she tried.

"I. Do. Not. Think. So!" she challenged.

"Pregnancy has made you feisty, I see. I have a way to take some energy out of you!" The chief made a playful snarl deep in his throat. Then he teased her by nearly tantalizing her skin in the air above her body. The warrior would make her skin anticipate his touch, then refrain. Kaitlin was arching and making little noises. The warrior used all of his determination to resist.

"Who loves who more?" he asked, his lips hovering inches above her breast.

She panted, "I – I love *you* more!"

"Are you sure?" Spirit Bear asked huskily. His hands ran smoothly up and down her frame. Strong fingers would linger in places designed to ignite passions more deeply. Kaitlin began breathing more shallowly and quickly, and her body writhed in the bedding with need.

Spirit Bear's deep growl was now more insistent but still, he did not take. He continued to torture his wife with his tongue and hands. "I will ask again, *Mazaska Zi Ista*. Who loves whom more?"

Playfully, Kaitlin panted, "Before you said, 'who loves who more' not 'who loves whom more'."

Riled, Spirit Bear lightly nibbled a nipple and flicked it once with his tongue. He ignored Kaitlin's plea for more. "You deliberately ignored my question."

"Do not make me lie to get what I want. If you torture me, my confession will not ring true."

Spirit Bear laughed. "You just do not want to admit what you know to be accurate!"

Kaitlin wriggled free and her hand sought out the part of him that yearned for pressure. Massaging his length, she whispered, "I love you more, chief."

Spirit Bear flipped his wife over and dove into her. He stated hoarsely, "I love you more, *mita wastelaka*. I have proven it many times."

***

"I also have proven my love for you," Kaitlin said as she basked in the wake of the moment. She lay her head on his warm chest.

"*Tos, mita wastelaka*, you have, as have I. We may have to call a draw."

"Agreed. A draw it is."

Spirit Bear chuckled sympathetically as though his suggestion was just to let her think it was a tie, so Kaitlin hit his chest playfully.

***

A short while later, Kaitlin was headed to Gentle Rabbit's house. Of course, her mother figure had already begun to flay the carcass. The fire, also, was blazing.

"Did *Wawakankan* skin this deer for you?"

"*Tos*. He is a good man. He will make *Skeca Ecaca* a good provider someday."

Kaitlin laughed. "You are such a matchmaker, *Wawat'ecaka*."

The blonde grabbed a knife and helped to filet all the meat off the skeleton. When they were finished, the protein was rubbed with spices and salt brush solution. The roasts were wrapped in leaves and put in the embers to slow roast.

Gentle Rabbit fried the tenderloin in its own fat. Other meats were skewered and basted. The smell made Kaitlin's mouth water.

The day was spent cooking to make sure the delectable turned out perfect. Cooking too long or too high of heat would produce dry or burnt pieces. If the fire died, then the meat would be too raw. It was a process that wasn't super difficult, but one did have to be diligent.

The afternoon breeze rattled the remaining leaves around the campsite. A few fluttered past-like brown moths. Kaitlin looked up and noticed the whole village was a flurry of activity, working like bees in a hive.

The chieftain's wife wiped golden tendrils from her face. The venison was nearly complete. The only pieces left were the slow roasting ones. She stooped and moved the embers back to check it.

Only a little blood seeped, so Kaitlin knew by evening, the pieces would be ready. In between checking the deer, Kaitlin worked on Apple Blossom's hat. It was coming together nicely.

"Go ask your man to join me tonight," Gentle Rabbit said. "The tenderloin is excellent. We shall dine on that!"

"Okay! I will not disagree!"

"I am also asking *Wawakankan* and *Skeca Ecaca*."

"I figured so, *Wawat'ecaka*."

The elder woman's head swivel and look made Kaitlin smile.

"You are the Matchmaker, which should be part of your name," Kailin chuckled. "When you said your son would make a good provider, I knew right then and there, you would be inviting them. It is the perfect setup since *Wawakankan* made the kill!"

Gentle Rabbit's beamed. "You're pretty smart, young lady!"

"I try," Kaitlin smiled back. "I will go home now," she stated. "I need to clean up, ask my man, and get ready to return."

***

Gentle Rabbit kept the fire's hungry flames well-fed. Her family and guests were seated on logs and large rocks around the pit. Although it was cold, everyone was appropriately dressed for the weather. Warm gear with warmer robes were worn.

The women passed out plates of venison tenderloin, *Aguyapi* flavored with dehydrated strawberries, and boiled poke. Kaitlin poured water into cups for consumption. After filling their own plates, the women joined in.

"What are you making *Haspa Nableca* as her birth present into the Sioux band?" Kaitlin asked Playful Otter.

"I am actually making her a decorated celebration dress. I believe *Unjinjintka Can Koica* is making her matching boots."

"Oh, that is perfect! Have you seen *Wawat'ecaka's* robe?"

"*Tos*, I have. What are you constructing?"

"I am making her a matching hat. I also will give her some baskets and some decorations for her hair."

"She will enjoy that," Playful Otter commented.

Although more comfortable and less shy in her blooming relationship with Wonder Worker, she subtly watched him from under her lashes.

Kaitlin reached over and whispered, "It is never enough looking, huh?" she smiled at her friend's answering blush.

"I, too, watch *mita hingnaku*. I know he returns the favor," she revealed.

"He is just so handsome. I can't believe that he is still interested in me!"

"*Skeca Ecaca*, you are a very beautiful woman. He sees more than just your beauty and youth! I have never seen that man so into someone as he is in you."

"Really?"

"*Tos.* Can *you* ever recall a time he has dated the same person for more than a moon?"

"*Hiya.*"

"See? Relax. He is into you!"

Playful Otter brightened then looked a little insecure again.

"What?" the blonde asked.

"I just know he will get bored with me eventually."

"Not if *Wawat'ecaka* has anything to say about it!"

Playful Otter's eyes got wider, and then she beamed. Kaitlin nodded in her silent revelation.

CHAPTER SIXTY-ONE

Matchmaker

"Her name is really 'Matchmaker'," Kaitlin whispered.

Playful Otter giggled and everyone looked in her direction. Faintly blushing, the Oglala maiden bowed her head and took another bite of the meat.

Wonder Worker smirked as if he was aware of what was going on. Kaitlin was unsure about him. *Did he really know, or was he guessing?* Her mind was never reasonably sure. The white woman vowed that the shaman really did have communion with the spirits.

Kaitlin patted Playful Otter's back and took another bite of the meat herself.

"*Wawat'ecaka,* you've outdone yourself with the tenderloin," Wonder Worker complimented.

"It is due to the hunter who knows which deer may taste the best," she countered with a meaningful look at Playful Otter. Both Kaitlin and her friend sniggered quietly.

"She does not have to try so hard to get me to agree!" Playful Otter lowered her voice.

"I know. I think *Wawakankan* also wants you to notice," Kaitlin responded.

"How shall I ever eat this food, no matter how flavorful?" her friend asked. "I feel too on-the-spot with everyone looking at me!"

"It is because we all love you!" the blonde reassured.

After the meal, the women cleaned up and sat by their men at the fire. Gentle Rabbit was in heaven as she watched the couples enjoying each other's company. She continued to mill around, preparing things for the feast.

Spirit Bear was seated in front of the fire, and to his left was his wife. The war chief was positioned so that he could see his hearth brother and converse easily. The women were side by side and could also hold a conversation if they chose it.

"What type of winter do you foresee, *Wawakankan*?" Spirit Bear asked conversationally.

"It will be a rough winter, my friend," Wonder Worker responded. A seriousness was evidenced about his brows. "We may have a few casualties, but not so numerous because of our many blessings from *Wakantanka*."

Kaitlin couldn't help but to interrupt, "You think we will lose some people?"

"*Tos*. With the winter I believe is coming, we will. It will mostly affect the really old and really young."

"But can't we *do* something? I mean, if we *know* it's going to happen?" All Kaitlin could think about was Gentle Rabbit.

"We will do everything we can, *mita wastelaka*," her husband soothed. "We help all that ask for it or all that we see who could use help. Sometimes it is just time for the Bird of Death to call. None wants it to be so, yet it happens regardless."

Kaitlin's eyes wandered to where Gentle Rabbit was checking the meat. Her eyes grew watery but did not spill over.

Spirit Bear pulled his wife into his embrace. Speaking in a lowered tone, he said, "Do not worry, *Mazaska Zi Ista*. Mother has many years left. Do you think she would leave her son before she sees him married?" He smiled into her hair, for he anticipated her reaction.

"*Hiya*! She would never leave this world until those two are married!"

Wonder Worker and Playful Otter swiveled their heads to stare at the blonde woman.

"Um… oops… did I say that… out loud?"

Three heads nodded.

Blushing, Kaitlin lowered her head. She could see through the curtain of gold separating her from the others that Playful Otter also was a hue of pink. Wonder Worker's smirk had settled back on his full lips. His eyes twinkled with mischief.

"What is all this talk of marriage?" the spiritual advisor asked as his eyes looked pointedly at the chief's wife.

"Don't look at *me*!" Kaitlin said. "I am just glad *Wawat'ecaka* will be fine this winter!"

Wonder Worker barreled out laughter. "Ah, I see the issue now," he said, still chuckling. "I plan to make my mother happy as she grows older."

All three turned to stare at him. Smiles erupted from every face.

"Whoa, wait a minute," Wonder Worker said with a huge grin. "I did not ask anyone anything yet. It does not mean I will not, but I have not yet… so save the congratulations for a later date. Besides, I want my mother around for a while."

Not one person stopped grinning at his revelation. Teeth nearly glowed in the fading light. Playful Otter seemed to be stained a pink tone but could not wipe the huge beam from her face.

Gentle Rabbit was carrying meat back to her tipi as it finished cooking so she could store it in preparation for the feast. She stopped in front of the crazily smiling crowd with a questioning look.

"What is so amusing?" the respected older woman asked, wiping a graying strand back from her face.

"We love you, mother, and plan to have you around for quite some time!" Wonder Worker revealed.

"This is what makes you all smile like a pack of mad dogs?" she asked, her tone suspicious.

"This is exactly why we are smiling," Spirit Bear intervened. "We know what your life's goal is, and we want you to see it realized, but we also want you to have a long life and longevity. There is enough time for all."

Gentle Rabbit murmured, "This is an odd conversation," shook her head softly, and continued with her chore of putting the venison up. Laughter followed the hard-working woman.

= = =

Playful Otter was unsure of quite how to act. *Had Wawakankan really just admitted that he desired her as a future wife?* The young woman nearly swooned. No matter how hard she tried, the smile would not come unglued from her face.

= = =

Wonder Worker was entertained by his woman's bashfulness and her attempts of trying to play it cool. The maiden kept trying to hide her grin behind her hand or hair. It was precious to watch.

The shaman draped an arm around the Oglala girl and pulled her closer to him.

"*Skeca Ecaca*, have I told you how pretty you are tonight?" he asked huskily.

Playful Otter could not keep from looking into his mesmerizing eyes and watching his full lips as he spoke. They descended and lightly kissed hers.

= = =

Suddenly, a loud noise from the background startled the couples. Gentle Rabbit was standing behind them. Several plates had spilled around her like shattered glass. However, the motherly figure had the happiest glitter in her eye and her face was nearly splitting with her ear-to-ear smile.

"Oh, no," Wonder Worker groaned.

Giggles burst forth from around him. No one was empathetic.

"I'll *never* hear the end of this."

Spirit Bear slapped his back sympathetically. "You can handle this, Brother," he said.

Playful Otter was happy, still smiling, but she nervously twisted her robe as she sat beside him.

Amused, he said, "It matters not," The medicine man lowered his head once more to pass a light but sweet kiss over her pretty mouth.

"It is about time to head home," Spirit Bear announced, clearing his throat. "I'm sure you'll want to walk *Skeca Ecaca* home. I will take my **thawícu** home."

"*Tos*, it is time," Wonder Worker Agreed.

 "Have a good evening, both of you," Spirit Bear called to them as they headed home.

"You also, my *kola*," his brother replied.

CHAPTER SIXTY-TWO

Nearly Oglala

The next morning after breakfast, Kaitlin asked, "*Woniya Mato*, do you think we could invite *Wawakte Towanjila* and *Haspa Nableca* over tonight for dinner? Tomorrow is the celebration, and I want to spend some time with her. I am sure my friend's nerves are jumping even if this is what she wants."

"*Tos*, of course, *mita wastelaka*. It is as you wish!"

Kaitlin and Apple Blossom shared a special bond. The chief's wife had an exceptional tie with *all* of her friends, but it was different with Apple Blossom. The escape they both had made from the encampment when they were slaves connected them in a way that was altered.

Kaitlin felt the closest to Desert Rose of all of her friends, but she loved them equally. Desert Rose was the person who began to break the language barrier for her. The blonde couldn't wait to see her as well, but she wanted a little more one-on-one time with the soon-to-be-freed slave.

Changing her mind on the spur of the moment, Kaitlin interjected, "Actually, my *hingnaku*, would you care if I invite all of our friends over? I want to spend some time with her first, then surprise her with our group. I wish to give her the gifts before her celebration so she can feel extraordinary as she stands in front of the community."

"*Mazaska Zi Ista*, you are a very special lady." The bronze warrior's firm eyes had softened unbelievably for his wife.

"I must be… only because I was the fortunate one who captured your heart!" she replied. When golden eyes met onyx ones, she whispered, "My soul is only complete with you, *Woniya Mato*."

"Our friends will have to wait for a time," Spirit Bear said. "I have more important plans right now." Kaitlin watched his panther like grace as he prowled closer to her. Although he was all predator, she was unafraid. The blonde beckoned him with a welcoming look. Her lips parted seductively, and he pounced.

Their tongues met and danced like long lost lovers. The chief's lips explored the white woman's mouth, face, and neck before returning for recapture. His strong fingers found her curves and massaged them.

"They will definitely have to wait…" she breathed.

***

Kaitlin was excited when she saw her Sky Warrior and Apple Blossom approaching. She jumped up from her food preparation to greet them. Her husband stood by her side.

"*Hokahe*, my friends," Spirit Bear opened the tipi flap before they could call.

The men clasped forearms while the women hugged loosely.

"I have prepared fried squirrel and vegetable soup. I hope you have not yet eaten."

"This is wonderful, *Mazaska Zi Ista*," Apple Blossom said. She lowered her voice to disclose her joy at having been invited over before her big event. "Thank you for the summons. It will help me relax."

Wawakte Towanjila said, "We have brought an appetite as well as *Aguyapi*, drink, and prickly pears for your enjoyment." The warrior's eyes twinkled with amusement.

Taking the items from the couple, Kaitlin thanked them both. The women prepared the plates and served the men. Then they prepared their own plates and joined their loved ones.

"I know you are nervous, but are you excited for the ceremony?" Kaitlin began as she gave her friend a wink.

"*Tos*, I am very thrilled. I am nervous, too."

"You do not seem to be the uneasy type," Kaitlin praised. "You are always so calm even when you're anxious."

"This situation is different. I am sure I will be calm on the outside, but on the inside,

I'm a wreck." The temporary-slave woman laughed nervously, "I will be rejecting my ancestry to join the Sioux. I will no longer be lower than a newborn baby in status, and I live with a powerful chief," Apple Blossom laughed. "I am sure you can understand my anxiety, more than anyone."

"*Tos*, I sure can, *Haspa Nableca*! I am sorry for your dilemma."

"I am sure this is what I want. It is just a death in my mind of who I was. Now I am someone new although I am really the same."

Kaitlin laughed. "That's almost confusing, but I totally got you!"

"We might as well go clean up," Apple Blossom suggested.

"We are going to go now," Kaitlin announced loudly to her husband. "We plan to clean up."

Spirit Bear's grin split his face, and he cocked a brow. "*Tos*. Thank you for letting us know."

Sky Warrior still wore amusement on his face while Apple Blossom looked strangely at the blonde.

"Are you alright?" the still-Pawnee woman asked her friend.

"*Tos.* Why?"

"You are acting a little strangely."

Kaitlin minutely shrugged as she gathered the dinnerware. "I am fine, I promise."

"Sometimes pregnancy makes women act a little odd," Spirit Bear prodded.

Kaitlin gave him a subtle look that pleaded for cooperation. Sky Warrior just smirked in good nature. He had figured out the whole drama.

After the women had left, Apple Blossom asked Kaitlin, "Are you sure you want to help? I can clean up if you need to rest. You did cook the meal."

"I am fine, my *kola*. I... don't know what came over me. Let us go to the area of privacy before our return. I think I shall feel more myself after that."

***

"SURPRISE!" everyone yelled upon the women's reentrance into the tipi.

The blonde was nearly jumping with excitement. "Now do you know what was 'wrong' with me?"

Apple Blossom was so overwhelmed by all of her close friends' attempt to welcome her, all she could do was stand for a few minutes. Finally, Sky Warrior rescued her by draping his arm over her shoulders and leading her back to their spot to sit.

"I – I don't know what to say! I am so honored to have such friends as you!" she finally cried.

"We love you, *Haspa Nableca*!" they all responded.

Spirit Bear and Sky Warrior said in unison, "Welcome to the Bear Claw Clan of the Oglala. We are so glad to have you join our band!"

Apple Blossom nodded with integrity. "I am honored. More than I can say. *Wakantanka* has given me more than I could ever dream!"

"We are just as blessed," her friends responded. "In fact, we want to give you gifts to show how much we appreciate you and your presence within our band and hearts."

Apple Blossom wiped a tear away just as Gentle Rabbit called for permission to enter.

"I will give my gift first," the motherly woman stated. It was wrapped in a warm blanket of many colors.

"This blanket is of the finest quality! Thank you, *Wawat'ecaka*!"

"You are not finished yet. Open up the blanket, young lady."

Apple Blossom sucked in a happy breath. "It is beautiful! How do you construct such magnificent garments? This robe is nearly too pretty to wear!"

"You can wear it all the time or just for special occasions, but my dear, it will be warm. You may choose to cover it continuously this winter!"

"Thank you, *Wawat'ecaka*. You are so amazing! I am so pleased!"

"*Tos*, this is good. You are very welcome."

"I will go next," said the comely blonde. "My gift kind of goes with that one."

Kaitlin handed Apple Blossom an exquisitely constructed basket of grasses of different colors and weaves. It was a larger basket with a tight lid. Apple Blossom opened it and found several smaller, matching baskets inside.

"*Mazaska Zi Ista*, these are baskets like I can only dream of! I have wanted ones like these for a long time, and I *love* the blankets as well!"

"Open the small two, *Haspa Nableca*."

Wide eyed, she did as she was instructed.

Apple Blossom held the exquisite hat up in wonder. She could no longer just look. She put on the cap and cape and did a twirl for her audience. All friends made appropriate noises.

"Now the other small basket."

"Oh, my goodness, *Mazaska Zi Ista*! You have outdone yourself!" She held up the tiny hair combs made with bones and decorated with beads and sparkly stones. "Thank you!!!"

"You are our sister. You are welcome."

Both Playful Otter and Desert Rose laid their gifts at Apple Blossom's feet.

"These two gifts are from us. They match and go together like *Wawat'ecaka's* and *Mazaska Zi Ista's*.

Another wonderfully marked basket of tight, waterproof weave was the wrapping for the final gifts.

"What beautiful baskets," began the overwhelmed woman. "But the dress and boots! I just don't know what to say with all this finery!"

Her friends could see the way the born Pawnee woman was trembling. Everyone got up and hugged her. Soon she was so over-inundated that she no longer felt her nerves.

"Now, let us play some fun games."

"We shall show no mercy," Sky Warrior warned. "Prepare for defeat!"

Chapter Sixty-Three

Time to Celebrate!

Finally, the day of the ceremony had arrived. Normally, festivities were reserved for the evening, but the general merriments were scheduled in the heat of the day due to declining temperatures. For adults wanting to prolong the revelries, gatherings around fires would still be arranged after children went to bed.

The drum tempo had changed from the original beat. It gave subtle messages to the community about how close the opening ceremony was.

Kaitlin was getting nervous. She rushed around her tipi gathering cooking supplies.

"What it is, *mita wastelaka*? What has you flying around like a hummingbird?"

"It is preparing this desert for our friends. I hope I have time because the ceremony begins early," she replied. Her blonde hair curled around her face, surrounding her in a golden halo.

"You do not need to prepare anything, *Mazaska Zi Ista*. There is plenty of food."

"I want to make a desert for our friends. I promised *Wawat'ecaka* that I would. It would mean so much, especially for *Haspa Nableca*."

The chief turned his ebony eyes upon hers. He asked seriously, "Is there something I can do to help?"

Kaitlin stopped and stared at him, her mouth in an O. "You would do woman's work?"

"Why not? You are doing things you do not have to."

"But you're the head chief! You do not have time!"

"I always have time to help my *thawicu*."

Kaitlin took a few deep, calming breaths and went to her husband. She settled in his lap. She grasped his face then kissed his full lips gently. "I am the luckiest woman alive, *mita hingnaku.*"

"We both are lucky. Now, *mita wiwasteka,* what is it you need done?" His hard muscles bulged as he lifted her. Then with feline elegance, he sprang to his feet.

"If – if you would start a cooking fire…"

"Of course!"

Spirit Bear prepared the fire and her special pan. He melted fat to use in the cast iron to keep the pastries from sticking. In the white man's vessel, Kaitlin rehydrated apples and made a thick syrup laden with the fruit. Honey married other spices and a mouth-watering aroma saturated the hut. Kaitlin put the sauce in a different container and took the pan to clean.

Next Kaitlin mixed together flour from nuts and other ground meals. She added more fat and patted down the fatty flour mixture.

Gradually, the concoction began to bubble and rise.

"*Woniya Mato*, will you please hand me the syrup?"

Spirit Bear brought the pot to his wife. He watched as she carefully plopped dollops into the cooking batter. In the spots she'd dropped the syrup, a deeper pocket of flavor simmered into the cooking cake. After a time, the mixture had risen, and the pastry was complete. Kaitlin added a thin layer of the syrup to coat and set it to the side to cool. Then she washed her pan and restarted the process.

When the last cake was cooling, the couple walked to the river to clean up. The chief would begin mixing up his paint for the ceremonies as well.

"I must go prepare with the Tribal Counsel now, *mita wastelaka*. I am sure you wish to help prepare *Haspa Nableca* with your friends."

"*Tos*, my chief. It is so."

                    ***

        All of her friends and Gentle Rabbit had
already begun preparing the young woman. It
wasn't as elaborate as readying one for a
wedding ceremony, Kaitlin decided, but it was
entailed enough. Apple Blossom nearly
implored her for a rescue. Kaitlin simply
grinned and nodded her head once. Then she
joined in on the torture.

        A few hours later, a beautiful, blushing
Apple Blossom stood before her friends in her
new finery.

        "Once *Wawakte Towanjila* sees you, he
will not be able to move!" Desert Rose declared.

        "I agree," said Gentle Rabbit.

        Right on cue, the drum beat changed,
signaling the beginning of the ritual. When
Kaitlin peeked out of the tipi, most of the
congregation had already gathered near the
ceremonial grounds.

"We should go," the only white skinned woman in the village announced.

"What should I do?" asked Apple Blossom nervously.

"You stay here," Gentle Rabbit commanded. "I will stay with you. The rest of you, go!"

After *Wawat'ecaka* shooed them all out, the women went to their reserved spots in the clearing. The men would be joining them periodically during the celebration.

The drum beat stopped suddenly, and *Woniya Mato*, in full war paint and chieftain dress stood before his people. He was not alone; the entire tribal council, decked out in formal wear, flanked his sides. Complete silence was unusual, but for the formidable four, it was a sign of honor.

"We are about to begin our fall celebration," Chief Spirit Bear began. "Here we honor *Wakantanka* and his many blessings to our people."

The gathering cheered.

The distinguished shaman took the floor, "First we welcome the new women to our tribe." Wonder Worker did not have on the war bonnets of the other chiefs; his dress was fine clothing, paint, and a mask made of bone and hide. A few feathers were attached. His head gear shaded the upper part of his face; nevertheless, he had almond-shaped holes fashioned so that he could see.

A group of elegantly dressed young women gracefully approached in winter finery. In a summer ceremony, the young ladies would wear mostly jewelry, paint, and skirts. In the frigid temperatures, this tradition was overlooked.

The silence of the village ended when a lone flute's melody mourned the loss of childhood. The coming-of-age teens bowed to the council members and then to the gathering. Slowly, they began to move with the flute's song. Soon, a rattle whispered, joining in to keep time, accented by a ceremonial drum. A lonely singer began a haunting melody that made a tear leak from Kaitlin's eye.

The young women began to move faster
as the tempo increased. They twirled and
moved in a flowing, graceful circle. When the
music's crescendo ended, the women resumed
their group and swayed in front of the prominent
men.

Wawakankan began a dance that took
the villagers through infancy into childhood and
blurred the growth into one of puberty. His
dancing imagery had his audience experiencing
parenthood with him. When the music stopped,
the silence returned with a vengeance.

Wawakankan bowed deeply to the newly
recognized women. As he called each maiden's
name, she would step forward and bow to the
council and crowd. All acknowledged the
woman's newly announced name. The
multitude would repeat it back, and then she
would walk off the stage. Each status was now
one of woman, not girl. The next girl's name
was called and the events would be repeated.
When none were left, cries of cheer filled the air.

"Now we thank *Wakantanka* by rejoicing in the
lives given in honor to prolong ours," Lone
Wolf stated. "It is time to eat!"

The crowd cheered as masses of food were
brought forth by the women of the community.
Platters steaming with the fruits of their labors
for an entire year was spread before the throng.
Aromatic scents wafted into the air, drenching
the atmosphere. There were so many vast food
choices, one couldn't hope to sample them all.

The new women picked the most luscious and
tempting of choices to fill plates for the counsel.
Then they served their leaders.

Gentle Rabbit has secured a plate for herself as
well as the slave trembling in her hut. Apple
Blossom did not want to appear until she was
summoned.

***

"Look at Singing Cicada!" announced Fresh
Water to Desert Rose. "She kept her name! It
makes me so proud of her, seeing her now as a
woman!" The women conversed as they began
filling their plates with pleasing fare.

"I see Silver Fox is also admiring her new status," Desert Rose replied with a smile. "I am glad for her."

"When she joins us, we will have to tease her!" Playful Otter said. "It will be nice to have the focus on someone new." She giggled.

After the majority of the Bear Claw Clan had eaten their fill and the trays were removed, the crowd quieted. More was to come! Kaitlin watched with anticipation. She saw that Apple Blossom changed into an old tattered dress that had grayed and was brittle.

Wawakankan stepped forward and began a slow rhythmic dance to the slow beat of a drum around the young woman. He began to lightly chant and shake a gourd. Then the spiritual advisor stopped perfectly with the drum beat. Sky Warrior walked proudly to stand beside this lowly statured woman. Resuming his dance, the shaman made about five passes around the couple.

Wawakankan placed his gourd rattle on the ground and picked up a bunch of dried horsetails. He began to waive them over the

man and woman. He waved them back and
forth. Then *Wawakankan* gave half of the
horsetails to Sky Warrior, and the other half
went to Apple Blossom. They began moving
the plants over each other.

When the drum began to beat again, the three
stood quietly while the other members of the
tribal council joined *Wawakankan*. They
formed a happy and smiling circle around the
beaming duo. Apple Blossom looked so radiant!
It was a joyous sight!

Suddenly, Apple Blossom ran off the central
spot but returned a short while later wearing the
beautifully decorated dress given to her as a
present. It was very flattering. The leaders
melted back away to resume their seats while
the community waited in quiet anticipation. The
young woman held up the grayed dress she'd
been wearing.

Woniya Mato materialized. His long, deadly
hunting knife gleamed with power reflected in
the dancing fiery light. He took the dress from
her and held it up for the crowd to see. Then
Spirit Bear gave a mighty war cry and sliced the
dress to ribbons. He turned to Apple Blossom

and Sky Warrior and waived the horsetails over
them. Then he presented the new couple to the
village.

Spirit Bear's rich tenor voice declared, "This
woman, as well as the settlement, will no longer
recognize her Pawnee ancestry; this ceremony
has severed that part of her!"

The gathering went wild with cheering and
clapping, welcoming the new *Oglala* woman
into their midst. The couple in the center of
attention hugged and kissed each other with
love and pride. Then the woman of Sky Warrior
went to join her longtime friends. They were
ecstatic to see the new Oglala was coming to
join them!

CHAPTER SIXTY-FOUR

Silver Fox's Celebration Coup

The group of friends rose as the Oglala's newest member approached. They walked in happy contentment to meet and lead Apple Blossom back to the place of honor for the leader's women.

"You are very beautiful!" Playful Otter breathed.

"I am very nervous!" Apple Blossom countered, "but thank you, *Skeca Ecaca*. It is, in part, due to you!"

"Come, sit!" Gentle Rabbit commanded gently so the ceremony could resume.

The women settled and their attention returned to the men of their hearts.

Lone Wolf came to the center of the ceremonial grounds. "My people," he began, "let us take a few moments to offer a prayer chant to *Wankantanka*. At meal time, were we not blessed with more food than we could possibly eat?"

The crowd roared in agreement.

"We have more than enough to last us through winter, even if the Bird of Death tries to defeat us. We must honor the Great Spirit. He has allowed many animal and plant spirits to be sacrificed so that ours could continue. Our spiritual brother, *Wawakankan*, will lead us in prayer."

Wonder Workers's amazing voice began a sing-song chant. He lifted his arms in praise. The community joined in softly. Then, as the prayer matured in intensity, the population's voice grew as well. It was a very powerful sight to behold.

Soon a dance by the leaders ensued. A lone man offered the traditional song as well as an accompanying drum for the performers. The influential men twirled, dipped, and danced in a circle. Their feet stomped in time. When they paused to lend their voices in sing-song fashion, each of the four sacred directions were honored. Every eye watched the preeminent men.

Their dance resumed and the tempo increased. The men whirled and stomped, shaking their headdresses in cadence. At the end of the dramatic and strangely beautiful honoring, the beat ended simultaneously as the men stopped, in a circle, with their heads bowed. The communal gathering when wild!

After the spiritual appreciation, the assembly knew the formal part of the celebration was coming to a close. The time for little competitions and friendly rivalry challenges were about to occur.

"That was such a meaningful thanksgiving," Desert Rose stated in awe.

"I love how we honor everything that promotes our life and health," Kaitlin agreed.

The women's attention was captured by the striking men who approached with hunter's poise. The leaders' masculine smiles warmly greeted the pretty girl who captured his eye. Soon each woman was sitting cozily with her match.

Young men now took the natural stage for mock fighting. Dramatic drumming accompanied.

"Why don't you go challenge one of those young men, *Isnala Sungmanitu*?" Spirit Bear asked with a laugh.

"Because I would embarrass them too badly, *Woniya Mato*," he responded.

"Why not give them a real show?" Sky Warrior suggested with a wide, mocking grin. "We could fight each other."

Both men chuckled good-naturedly. "Because we are equal and the fight would last all night," Spirit Bear returned. His leader-brother nodded, keeping his wide smile that showed off his white teeth.

The circle of friends noticed a dramatic young man competing.

"Look!" Desert Rose exclaimed. "Is that Silver Fox? I believe he is trying very hard for a certain someone's attention!" She giggled.

"I sure hope Singing Cicada notices! If I know Fresh Water, she will tell her all about it then protect her!"

Desert Rose snickered in agreement then snorted; immediately afterwards, she blushed. Lone Wolf grinned but said nothing.

"What was that?" Apple Blossom asked pointedly.

"N – NOTHING!" Desert Rose responded, mortified.

"I don't believe I've ever seen *Unjinjintka Can Koica* at a loss for words before," Kaitlin teased.

Suddenly, the young men on stage captured the group's attention. The first round of matches had just ended. The competitions would continue until just one man was left. Kaitlin was happy to note that Silver Fox would be going on to the next competition.

Kaitlin smiled at Brave Elk. He was supervising the matches. She would always have a warm spot in her heart for him.

The drum beat tempo increased and then was silent to announce the start of the new round of matches. Silver Fox was paired with Thin Elk. Thin Elk was a wiry young man who was quick on his feet. Although he was the thinner of the two, Thin Elk had more speed. It would be an entertaining match.

"Look!" whispered Playful Otter. "See who is watching?"

The leader group saw a raptly attending Singing Cicada. Fresh Water was hovering close by.

"Call them over!" Desert Rose suggested.

Spirit Bear motioned to a nearby brave and asked him to invite the two young women into their circle. A short while later, the two friends joined them.

"Thank you for having us in your circle," Fresh Water said.

"Yes! Thank you very much!" Singing Cicada agreed. "We have a much better view, now."

"View of what?" an ornery Desert Rose teased.

Singing Cicada blushed but lifted her chin proudly. "I am watching Silver Fox."

Just then, Silver Fox managed to trip his competitor and sent him rolling. However, the fleet footed man turned the roll into a nimble move to land gracefully back on his feet. The crowd *aaahed*. Other matches were on-going at the same time, but most appeared to be watching Silver Fox and Thin Elk.

Thin Elk then took offense and stalked his competitor. Silver Fox beckoned him. At the last moment, however, Silver Fox chanced a look at his woman of interest. It was that moment Thin Elk chose to strike. Silver Fox was very nearly pinned. He managed a quick twist and scarcely escaped the sinewy grasp of the other man.

Singing Cicada gasped and leaned forward. Silver Fox, in a moment of magic, immobilized the other and won the match. Singing Cicada had a wide grin on her face right when Silver Fox's eyes found hers. He pointedly nodded to her. The new woman looked down demurely.

Kaitlin whispered to Fresh Water, "Have you *ever* seen her so quiet, so passive?"

Fresh water admitted that she had not.

The drum beat began again in earnest, announcing the time in-between matches. Fresh Water was more subdued than normal. She kept a watchful eye on her adopted sister-friend but also allowed freedom. The protective woman was simply there to honor and protect.

Singing Cicada was so involved in watching Silver Fox that she did not pay attention to Kaitlin speaking with her motherly *kola*.

"Are you worried about Singing Cicada?" Kaitlin asked.

"No, I truly am not. Sometimes she is so zealous that it can be misunderstood. I don't want to see her in a bad situation in which she had no idea that she may have helped to create."

"*Tos*, I understand."

Singing Cicada was a buxomly young woman who did not really have social boundaries. She spoke what was on her mind whether it was appropriate or not. The young woman cared about what others thought but did not usually think before she spoke.

Singing Cicada's chocolate doe eyes were watching Silver Fox's every move.

Kaitlin began, "Have they been talking? She seems more interested in him than just a maiden watching a man."

Fresh Water gave a quick laugh of amusement. "Have you ever known my friend to *not* break boundaries?"

"True. Does she realize what she is doing by watching him intensely?

"*Hiya,* she does not realize that she is telling every other man she is taken."

"Will you tell her?"

"*Tos*, but it will do little good. It seems that Singing Cicada does not take advice well. It's like she doesn't believe what I say."

"That girl does seem to do what she wants."

Conversation died as the third round of matches began. Several more rounds of matches were completed before the final two men were left standing quietly in the clearing.

Brave Elk announced the dual at the beginning of the final match.

"My friends, these two worthy men now fight for the honor of a coup. We will congratulate all, because it takes courage to fight in front of everyone.

Silver Fox was preparing to fight Broken Arrow. The talking quieted down as the men encircled each other, assessing the other's strengths and weaknesses. The drums had silenced, indicating the match had begun.

Silver Fox made the first move by inspiring an attack. Not only did the fighter miss his mark, but he found himself pushed forward. The young man nearly stumbled and fell. Turning around nimbly, he avoided an early pin by his strategic opponent.

Silver Fox's surprise was still reflected in his eyes, and his friend mockingly smiled. The first "coup" in the battle was won by Broken Arrow. More carefully now, Silver Fox prowled, watching for minute traces as a foreshadowing of his opponent's next move.

Broken Arrow was a few years older than Silver Fox, and he was earning quite a reputation as a warrior to contend with. He was a broader man than Silver Fox, but one still could not call him thick. He was a good strategist and he could read behavior well. It would be a strong challenge for the fox to outwit the arrow.

Both men circled the other, hands down, loose, at their sides. Their eyes hungrily

watched the other for an indication. It was
Broken Arrow who made the next move.

Broken Arrow ran in a zig-zag at his
adversary and feigned at the last moment, very
nearly tricking Silver Fox. However, realizing
the trap before he fell in is what won him the
match. The broader of the men thought his ruse
had succeeded when it actually lent to his own
demise.

After the match, the two men honored
each other. They grasped forearms then faced
the crowd with big smiles.

"My band brother has earned his coup
well, this time. Next time we take the stage, I
will be the victor!"

Silver Fox responded, "Thank you, my
kola. It was a good fight. We are well-matched.
It is true, I barely beat you; however, Next time
you will *not* be the victor. I will continue to
vanquish!"

Both laughed good-heartedly and made
room for Brave Elk. The member of the Brave
Heart Warrior Society wore his honorable

feathers and coups to show his importance in the realm of fighting.

"My band," he announced, "As you can see, we have two new noble men who will be joining the ranks of the *Cante Tinza* in our spring celebration. Throughout the winter months, they will continue to compete and earn coups within the boundaries of our own troop. The winner of the highest number of coups will be the higher-ranking warrior of the two. Good luck and congratulations!"

The ensemble cheered madly.

"I will honor both by giving each a coup feather." Broken Arrow's smile was disbelieving. "But Silver Fox earns two."

Both men expressed their happiness at the blessing before leaving the stage.

CHAPTER SIXTY-FIVE

Disapproval

Singing Cicada jumped up with joy once the announcement had been made. Then, remembering herself, she looked around with slightly pink cheeks. Fresh Water smiled and saw Silver Fox making his way toward them.

"Look who comes to speak with you," she suggested.

Singing Cicada's blush deepened, but she grinned happily.

"Tell him to join us," Spirit Bear instructed.

Soon, the warrior-in-training was seated in the chieftain's circle with many friends.

"Good show, young man," Sky Warrior complimented.

Silver Fox smiled his thanks. "I am honored to be noticed by the chieftains!"

"There is no doubt that you will be joining our ranks soon," Spirit Bear congratulated.

"I hope that is so," he responded. Silver Fox turned his grayish silver eyes to Apple Blossom. "Congratulations to you, also! We are honored to have you be one with our band!" *Haspa Nableca* grinned and nodded.

Wawakankan got Silver Fox's attention. He confided, "A new rite of joining the *Cante Tinza* is that you have to pin the war chief."

Silver Fox's head swiveled toward the spiritual advisor and did a double take, then looked apprehensively at Spirit Bear.

"Do not take him seriously," the superior warrior said with a grin that flashed white, even teeth. "He is messing with you."

The relief etched on Silver Fox's face had Spirit Bear throwing back his head in laughter. Kaitlin lightly elbowed him in the ribs.

"This is all in good fun, my friend," Lone Wolf said to take the heat off of the young man.

"It is a good thing, or I would need to go to visit the area of privacy," Silver Fox stated, his laughter joining the others.

"This young man has a sense of humor. He is likeable, and he is worthy of future warrior status. We approve," Sky Warrior nodded at Singing Cicada.

The young woman bowed her head as her cheeks burned with a fiery light.

Soon, the attention faded off the young couple.

"What are you going to do with your first day of freedom, *Haspa Nableca*?" Kaitlin asked.

"The same I do every day," she responded. "I will cook and clean, carry wood and water, and do other needed chores."

The friends laughed. They knew each person's agenda held similar tasks. After more small talk, Kaitlin decided to share her exciting update.

"I have some news to share," Kaitlin said in a conspirator's whisper. That got her friends' attention. Those close to the Golden One's heart leaned in to hear her news.

"What is it, *Mazaska Zi Ista*?" All eyes waited with impatients.

"My *hingnaku* has begrudgingly lent me his permission to see my father."

No one said a word.

Finally, Apple Blossom said seriously, "Surely, you jest."

"Oh, I do not. He did not want me to go, but my father is very ill."

"And… how do you know this?" Desert Rose inquired.

"Because… I ran into my brother… or rather, he ran into me."

"What?"

"Um… you know when we were gathering wood, and I had to go to the canopy of trees?"

"You mean when you took forever?" Desert Rose's eyes narrowed slightly.

"Yes. Please don't be angry, but my brother was going to 'rescue' me from you. I reassured him I wasn't a captive – that I was married to a chief. He was okay with that as long as I was happy and safe, but he told me about father."

"I can't believe *Woniya Mato* actually agreed to this?" stammered a shocked Apple Blossom. "He knows of the white man's untrustworthy ways."

"Well, it did take some persuading," Kaitlin responded.

"It must have been some major enticing!" Apple Blossom gasped, "He's going to let you walk into a white man's village while you are carrying his child? What will you wear? Your clothing will reveal who you are, and they will know you immediately for siding with the 'enemy'!"

"My brother is going to get me a dress made by the whites. I will say I'm married to a white man, and I've come to visit my brother and father while my *hingnaku* is away on a hunting trip."

"I just don't like it," Desert Rose stated pointedly.

"Me, either," both Apple Blossom and Playful Otter said in unison.

"Nor I," agreed Gentle Rabbit.

All of her friends were of a similar consensus.

"What if those in the village of wood remember everything that happened where you are concerned?"

"*Wankantanka* protects me."

"You know that *Woniya Mato* cannot take on a whole village to protect you," stated Desert Rose. "I am not trying to upset you, but I want you to consider all pieces."

"I really believe he will not need to."

"Are you certain?" asked Gentle Rabbit quietly.

"I would ask my brother to see me at our old home if my father could make the trip. I believe he does not have long to live. My brother won't let any white man harm me."

Her friends looked doubtful.

Kaitlin felt her elation ebbing with her friends' disapproval. Her face fell.

"*Mazaska Zi Ista*, it is because we love you and care about you that we do not want you to do this," Desert Rose tried to console.

"I know. But I do not think that my *hingnaku* would have agreed if he hadn't met with my brother himself and gotten reassurance from him."

More silence met her words.

"*Woniya Mato* actually met with a white man?" asked Desert Rose.

"And the white man walked away?" breathed Apple Blossom.

"Yes. He is my brother. He is well on the path to becoming a strong man on his own. I think my *hingnaku* actually liked him."

Playful Otter said, "I am glad. That does put a slightly different spin on it, but I still don't trust the white men overall, and it makes me nervous."

"Agreed. We will support you, but we don't have to like it."

All of her close friends agreed.

"I respect that. I just really want to see my father, especially if he is so ill."

"When does this all take place?" asked Gentle Rabbit.

"Hopefully soon. I'd say in a week or so if all goes to plan."

About then, Silver Fox and Singing Cicada rose to walk around a bit.

Shortly after they'd gone, Playful Otter asked Fresh Water, "Does she know the statement she is making?"

Fresh Water nodded. Then she grinned. "I approve."

"Yes, I think we all do!"

After things had lightened back up, the friends conversed and joked for another hour before the cold drove them all back to their own dwellings.

***

"Did you enjoy yourself this evening, *mita wastelaka*?"

"*Tos*, only…" she trailed off.

"Only what?"

"My *kolas* gave me a hard time about going to see my father."

Spirit Bear walked over to the bedding after the fire was stoked. He squatted down in front of her and lifted her chin gently with his strong fingers.

"*Wastelaka*, do you understand why?"

She nodded but her eyes were liquid pools of gold.

"They are not only concerned for you, but for me as well."

"They almost acted mad at me, *Woniya Mato*."

"They are not, but they will not understand the risk of danger you will be putting us in by seeing your father. They only understand that he betrayed you, so how could you risk all to see him, even if for the last time."

"Now I really do feel selfish."

"I understand, Golden One. Let your feelings go. I have meditated many times to *Wankantanka*. I feel you will be protected. Otherwise, I would not approve."

"I love you, *mita hingnaku*. I truly feel you do this just for me. How could you approve?"

"I approve out of love for you."

The fire cackled a merry tune in the fire pit, and began to fight with the chill in the air.

"Come, *mita wasetlaka*. Let me warm you in our furs."

Husband and wife snuggled under their bedding robes and shared gentle passions until Kaitlin allowed her mind to relax and finally, sleep overtook them.

CHAPTER SIXTY-SIX

Getting Ready

The day had finally arrived for Spirit Bear to check the location of the tree. Kaitlin was beside herself. She buzzed around the tepee like an angry hornet as she watched him prepare to leave.

"*Mazaska Zi Ista*, calm yourself," her spouse ordered. "Do not fret so, or I will have to stay in order to ensure you and the baby are fine."

Kaitlin took a steadying breath and forced her nervous legs to relax.

"It is just that I want to go, but I do not want to put you in any danger, my love. I'm a nervous wreck."

"Trust me, *mita wastelaka*. I will not put myself in harm's way."

"I do honor you. You are the most notorious war chief! I just love you so much, and all these emotions the baby has brought with him makes it where I cannot control my worries."

Spirit Bear chuckled. "Would you like company while I am gone? I am sure *Wawat'ecaka* would enjoy your companionship."

"If I get too lonely, I will certainly go to Mother's. It will be a long week waiting."

"A week worth the wait, *mita thawicu*."

"*Tos*, but hurry home!"

"You can be sure I will!"

Kaitlin packed up a bag of food and filled his traveling skins with water. Her husband prepared the rest. He did not paint himself but did load his war weapons. Before he left, Spirit Bear pulled his wife in closely for a deep and gentle kiss. Slowly, their lips parted. Spirit Bear's dark eyes watched her lips as they remained parted from his kiss. Finally, he jumped on his painted stallion and like the wind, they quickly blew into the distance. Kaitlin could not rip her eyes from her husband's silhouette until it was no longer visible on the horizon.

Sighing, the Indian princess began to carry out her normal daily chores. She felt alone as she prepared a solitary meal at noon. Kaitlin settled down before the hearth fire and nibbled on some pones made with honey and berries. She had a hot raspberry tea to sip and also some leftover squirrel soup.

Once her tummy was satisfied, Kaitlin settled into the sleeping mats to rest. She was deliciously tired, but it was still some time before slumber overtook her. The dream spirit left her with troubled considerations as well as hopeful ones. Night found her at Gentle Rabbit's fire.

"I am glad you decided to join me, *Mazaska Zi Ista*."

"*Tos,* as am I, *Wawat'ecaka*. Too many worries crowd my mind along with shivers of excitement. I will never sleep by myself."

"I understand."

The evening discussion focused around baby items that needed to be made as well as clothing and shoe construction.

"*Wawat'ecaka*, thank you so much for choosing me to learn your amazing way of making leather. I could not be more honored."

"I am the one who is honored! *Wakantanka* blessed us in many ways by giving you to us."

Kaitlin rose and gave the elder woman a heart-felt hug. The fair-skinned girl wondered if she could ever make the mother figure understand how deep her appreciation was.

"I will stoke the fire while you make your pallet," Gentle Rabbit instructed.

"*Tos, Wawat'ecaka.*"

"*Wakantanka* protects your *hingnaku* like none other. Do not worry."

"I know, my mother, but still, I fear."

"Such is the life of a wife… or mother… especially of a war chief."

Kaitlin giggled then settled into the warm fur blankets. Gentle Rabbit also made settling sounds. Soon, the night was whisked away and replaced by bright sunlight.

Kaitlin arose and quietly stoked the fire. She began a tea just as Gentle Rabbit donned her clothes. The women went to the women's area of privacy together, then made quick work of preparing breakfast.

"What shall we do today, mother?" the blonde asked.

"We will sew more items for your child," the elder said with a tender smile.

Most of the day was spent inside except for the necessary trips to gather wood and water. It was a blustery day, and the wind played violently with the well-constructed homes.

"For our evening meal, I wish to prepare a soup. I will thicken it with cacti, but we will also use tubers and carrots."

"And onion? Maybe a few mushrooms?"

"Sure! What kind of meat do you desire?"

Just then they heard a tapping on the entrance flap.

"*Hau*," called a masculine voice.

"*Hau,* come in, my son! *Hokahe!*"

"I have brought you some fresh rabbit for your dinner," Wonder Worker announced. "Hello, *Mazaska Zi Ista*." He grinned.

"Hello, *Wawakankan.* Mother, how does rabbit in our stew sound?"

"Wonderful!" Gentle Rabbit winked at the younger woman. "Son, you must join us!"

The shaman laughed and said, "Oh, I planned on it!" Wonder Worker handed his mother the skinned meat and sat back to watch the women prepare the food.

"What is Playful Otter up to tonight?" Kaitlin asked.

"She has decided to make me a pair of moccasins. I had to be fitted." He chuckled. "She was very nervous about it. I, however, was nervous about the sharp pins in her hands."

Kaitlin giggled. She could picture her friend's mortified expression. "I hope you did not show your concern."

"Definitely not. I would not dishonor her." Wonder Worker lifted his brows to show he was playing with her.

Kaitlin nodded and prepared strawberry *aguyapi*. She filled the horn cups with water. Finally, the women handed Wonder Worker a plate filled with bread and a roasted drumstick as well as a piping hot bowl of delicious soup. After he began eating, the ladies then prepared their own plates.

"Very good!" Wonder Worker complimented. "It is a perfect meal for such a cold day!"

"Thank you," the two responded. They began to eat as well.

After more conversation and teasing, Wonder Worker stoked their fire and returned to his own dwelling. It was a little early, but the warmth of the hut as well as their happy stomachs led to a delightful feeling of tiredness. It wasn't long before both women were asleep.

                    ***

The next week followed in a similar manner. The frigid temperatures kept most inside the protected walls. Finally, just before the last meal of the day, the beloved voice of her husband called from Gentle Rabbit's entrance flap.

Kaitlin squealed and jumped on Spirit Bear nearly before he had time to enter the dwelling. The chief swung her up into his strong arms and kissed her zealously.

"I have missed you, Golden One."

"I have missed you more, *mita hingnaku!*"

Spirit Bear's throaty laugh was very sexy to his wife. "I doubt that, *mita wastelaka.*"

"Doubt not, my handsome warrior!"

Finally, Gentle Rabbit's Cheshire grin brought them back to their surroundings. A few seconds later, Wonder Worker was also present.

"Well?" his deep voice asked.

"It went well," the chief said as he accepted his meal.

Wonder Worker also received his food.

"So you will leave soon?"

"*Tos*. Not tomorrow, but the following sun upon the breaking morning light."

"I will pray on this tomorrow, brother."

"*Tos*, thank you."

Kaitlin was grinning too much to be able to eat. She was ecstatically excited.

Spirit Bear patted the spot beside him as she received her plate. Kaitlin could hardly obey. She was brimming with nervous exhilaration. Finally, her husband cocked a brow and said, "You must eat before I will discuss plans with you."

This threat did calm the blonde enough so that she was able to manage to get a mediocre amount into her pallet.

Spirit Bear had never noticed the intensity of her stare before. Finally, the chief put down his drink, grabbed her plate, and sat both on the ground. The chief held out his arms, and Kaitlin gladly settled into his lap. Spirit Bear took time to just hold her. The leader's strong but gentle hand caressed her hair.

Spirit Bear softly spoke into her golden tresses, "I have missed you, *mita wastelaka*. I do not know what I will do when you are in the village of the *toka*."

"You will pray for my safe return. You know that *Wankantanka* protects us both and wants us to be together. He will not let any evil befall me."

"He may want to test me," came her husband's soft reply.

"I think he has tested you many times, *mita hingnaku*."

"*Tos,* this is true, but one never knows when the Great Spirit will lay a new challenge at one's feet."

Kaitlin turned to look deeply into her husband's eyes. "*Woniya Mato*, call it women's intuition. This visit *will* go well. I can feel it in my bones. You have nothing to worry about." Then she intertwined her fingers into his and leaned forward for a kiss.

CHAPTER SIXTY-SEVEN

The Final Chapter

Spirit Bear met her half way. Her husband's lips were firm and soft at the same time. They were warm silk as her mouth meshed against his.

Wonder Worker noisily cleared his throat with a smirk encompassing his entire face. "Save it for later," his deep voice demanded.

The couple slowly withdrew, and although Kaitlin's face didn't flame as much as normal, her cheeks had become rosier.

"Time to breathe, you two," their close friend continued to tease.

"My son, would you not have a similar reaction if another pretty female I know was

here, and you had been gone?" asked Gentle
Rabbit.

Wonder Worker's hearty laugh filled the tepee.
"I am sure, Mother, that it would make you very
happy if I were to say yes."

"*Tos*. It would," she said expectantly, her dark
eyes seeking his.

With three eager faces staring at him, waiting
for an affirmation, the shaman finally grinned
and said, "You bet I'd lay one on her!"

The playful tension was severed, and everyone
laughed with good cheer.

"Let us hear your plans, brother," Wonder
Worker encouraged, purposefully changing the
subject away from his romantic interest.

"Basically, I will be taking my wife to see her
brother in two suns. I will wait in the woods
during the time she shares with her blood family.
Then I will bring her back home."

"That *is* basic-but-to-the-point plans," Wonder
Worker chuckled. "Are you going to take
anyone along with you?"

Spirit Bear grinned and said, "*Mazaska Zi Ista.*"

His friend made a face and said, "I believe you know what I mean."

"*Hiya,* my *kola,*" Spirit Bear said chuckling, "I am not willing to risk any others on this endeavor. The less that go, the less likely we are to be discovered, and the safer we will be."

"As always, you are wise, my chief."

After a bit more conversation, the married couple made their way back to their own home. Spirit Bear carried her fur bedding and stoked the fire.   Kaitlin was still full of nervous energy.

"I have something for you, *mita wastelaka.*"

"What is it, *mita hingnaku?*"

"Your brother gave me the *wasicun* dress for you to try. He is afraid it may be a little too big."

"Mother can help me hem it."

"*Tos.* That was also my thoughts."

Spirit Bear retrieved a bundle and unwrapped the brown paper and string so typical to white man society. Kailin was happy to see a day dress of pale pink calico. It had clusters of brown reeds sprinkled in a pattern across the fabric. A second surprise fell out, too. A fancier sky blue gown made of some shiny material spilled out of the package. It had a delicate lace trim on the bodice and sleeves. Kaitlin couldn't help the gasp of surprise that fell from her lips.

"You like?"

"They *are* beautiful," Kaitlin breathed. Every white girl dreamed of a dress like the blue one. "But *Woniya Mato*," she reassured, "I would not return to *wasicu* society, even for a wardrobe of dresses like this!"

Spirit Bear smiled, and his eyes crinkled at the edges. He said, "This is good to hear."

"I will try them on tomorrow."

"That is also good to hear," he said with a suggestive brow wiggle.

Kaitlin giggled and said, "How did you know what I was already thinking?"

The lovers met on the bedding furs and snuggled into the warmth. It wasn't long before hands moved to flesh to help ignite the heating process.

"I love the way you smell, *mita wastlaka.*"

"I also love your scent, my husband!"

Spirit Bear nibbled on Kaitlin's tender neck and breathed on her until she squirmed and goosebumps erupted on her entire body. When she could take no more, she squealed loudly.

The warrior whispered, "Ssshhhh, do you want to wake the village?" Chuckling, he dove back in to bite her neck lightly. His actions resulted in another pearly shriek.

The blonde woman said, "If you do not stop that, the *Cante Tinza* will all be here, ready to fight the menace!"

"Let them come. I do not intend to stop anytime soon!" her husband challenged.

***

As soon as her morning chores were done, Kaitlin was off to see Gentle Rabbit. The young woman was more excited than she should be for the dresses, a touch of the old civilization that was once a part of her past, but the renounced white couldn't help herself. Kiatlin was like a child with a piece of candy. At first, the candy is all the child can think of, but soon it would be out of sight and out of mind.

"*Hau, Wawat'ecaka*!" the young woman called at the entrance flap.

"Come in, *Mazaska Zi Ista!* I am pouring some tea for you now!"

"Thank you so much! What kind did you make?"

"Blackberry and honey!"

"Yum!"

Gentle Rabbit looked up out of curiosity when she heard the *wisping* sound the blue dress made as the blonde placed it on some furs.

"What do you have there, young lady?"

"*Woniya Mato* retrieved these from my brother in preparation for my visit into the village of the *Wasicu*."

"Did you want to show me what kind of dresses you used to wear because you know how clothing interests me?"

"*Tos*, and for another reason. My brother tried to get close to my size, but I was not there to be fitted. They are a little too large…"

"Ah, hah! You would like some assistance with helping them fit better?"

"*Tos, Wawat'ecaka*, if you please."

"*Tos*, child. Let us enjoy our tea, first. Then you can try them on for me."

"Sounds like a great plan. Did you have something else that you wanted to do today?"

"No. I wanted to see if I could help you or your *hingnaku* prepare for your trip."

"Good. This is helping!"

Both ladies laughed as they drank the warmed beverage.

Kaitlin tried on the dresses while Gentle Rabbit tacked them up.

"I will only put in temporary stitching, *Mazaska Zi Ista*. That way, if you should have need of them again, we can let them out or keep it as is. If you were further along in your pregnancy, you would need them as they are now."

"You are very wise, mother. Thank you."

"This blue-silver fabric is interesting," Gentle Rabbit noted. "It is slippery and will be more difficult to work with."

"Will it be okay?"

"Oh, yes, it shouldn't be that big of a deal. It only offers a minor challenge."

Kaitlin breathed a sigh of relief.

"You must have as much faith in me as you do your husband, *Mazaska Zi Ista*."

"I meant no insult, *Wawat'ecaka*. I just know you have probably never sewn on this cloth before. It would be difficult, I would think."

The motherly figure laughed and said, "I am not offended, daughter. I tease only."

After taking the gowns down, Kaitlin found that Gentle Rabbit was every bit the seamstress that the town had to offer. One could not tell it had been taken in and that the seams weren't permanent.

"Oh, thank you, *Wawat'ecaka*! Look at how beautiful this dress is!" Kaitlin gave it a whirl.

"You do look amazing in it," Spirit Bear voiced floated to her from the flap.

"*Tos*. Very *gopeca*!" Gentle Rabbit agreed.

Kaitlin felt a little embarrassed that she'd been caught admiring the dress, but from the gleam in her husband's eye, she wasn't shy long.

"I am not sure I will allow you to take that dress along," Spirit Bear said. "I do not want to have to fight off men for what is mine."

Kaitlin giggled. "You will not have to, *mita hingnaku*."

"Let us hope not," he said, but his eyes still hungrily engulfed her. "Mother, as always, you did a wonderful job."

"I am glad you like!" the mother figure returned, smiling with pleasure.

Spirit Bear turned to his wife. "*Mazaska Zi Ista, uwa yo.* Let us rest before our long travel suns in his cold. You will need it."

"My son, is there anything more I can help you do?" Gentle Rabbit asked.

"Thank you, mother, but *hiya*. I have already prepared our food satchels, supplies, and my weapons. *Mazaska Zi Ista* will fill our water skins in the morning."

"I will take care of the wine tent and anything else you need during your absence."

"*Tos*, thank you."

"I will also prepare a supper tonight so that you can just rest," Gentle Rabbit continued. "Come back when you are ready to eat."

"We will."

After a nap in the deliciously warm bed furs, the happy couple made love leisurely. It was a time of gentle passions, of giving and taking, and of showing the other how much they cared. After a final meal with *Wawakankan* and *Wawat'ecaka*, the pair returned to their dwelling for a night of good sleep. On the morrow, Kaitlin would be leaving for another exciting journey in her life!

Author's note:

I anticipate a third book to the Passion series. Please be
patient as I also work a lot, so the writing process is slower
for me than for some other authors.

With deep appreciation,

Sheri

<u>**Dictionary of Lakota words**</u> (as I understand
them to be)<u>**:**</u>

Reference:

<u>**The Lakota Dictionary,**</u> *New Comprehensive
Edition*

*Compiled and edited by Eugene Buechel and
Paul Manhart*

University of Nebraska Press, 2002

<u>**Single words:**</u>

1.　　*Ableza* - to notice, observe, be aware of,
perceive

2.　　　　*Abuhingia* – to make a sudden
charge/attack

3.　　*Ahiyunka* – lie down & sleep

4.　　*Aglihunni* – rest

5.　　*Aguyapi* – Indian bread

6.　　*Anakiciksin* – to come to one's aid

7.　　*Asniya* – rest (to heal)

8.	*Ayucoya* – well done

9.	*Canmihce* – I trust or believe; I want it very badly

10. *Cante* – heart

11. *Gopeca* – beautiful

12.	*Hanhepi Waste* – good night (on-line translator)

13. *Hau* – Hello

14. *Hingnaku* – husband (on-line translator)

15. *Hiya* - No

16. *Hehaka* – Elk

17. *Hokahe* – Welcome! (greeting after "Hi")

18. *Hoksicala* – baby or child

19. *Hota* – rock

20. *Inyan* – gold

21. *Isnatipi* – Tipis in isolation

22. *Istinma* – Sleep

23. *Itazipe* – bow

24. *Iyotake / Iyotaka* – Sit down (or up)

25. *Iyunka* – Lay down

26. *Isica* – hurt

27. *KatA* – To kill or stun by striking/shooting, strike dead, knock unconscious, knock out (online translator)

28. *Kinyan* – to come or fly by

29. *Kola* – friend

30. *Mato ova* – bear claw

31. *Mitawa; mita* - my

32. *Miye* – I or me

33. *Mni* – water

34. *Mniapahta* – Water skin

35. *Nita* - your

36. *Ojilaka* – baby or young

37. *Oslohankel* – slowly

38. *Pataka* – come to a stop; stop!

39. *Pejuta* - medicine

40. *Peslete* – the top or crown of the head

41. *Pikila* – to be thankful, glad

42. *Ska* – white

43. *Sunka* – dog

44. *Tahca* – the common deer

45. *Tatonka* – bison

46. *Thawicu* – wife   (on-line translator)

47. *Tinpsila* – sweet radishes

48. *Toka* – enemy

49. *Tos* – Yes

50. *Wahinkpe* – arrow

51. *Wakanheja* – baby

52. *Wanapin* – beaded necklace

53. *Wanna* – now

54. *Wahpaka* – dress

55. *Wasicun/wasicu* – white man / men

56. *Wastelaka* – love

57. *Wayaka* – slave

58. *Wi; wiiyayuh* – sun

59. *Wica / wicasa* – man

60. *Wicowe* – relationship as in brother or sister

61. *Wikiskata* –– making love

62. *Winyan; Wiya* – woman

63. *Wiwasteka* – beautiful woman

64. *Wota; Wate* – eat

65.   *Wozan* - to stun or cause pain by impact from a distance (arrow shot)

66. *Yaskepa* – drink

67. *Yazan* – Do you feel pain? (to feel pain)

68. *Yucoya* – Ready

Phrases:

1.   *Ahan iwahwayela* – Stand quietly; Be still

2.   *Ayustankiya ye* – Please stop!

3.   *Lila wiya waste* – Very pretty woman

4.   *Mitawa ogligle wakan* – My good angel

5.   *Miye ahikte* – I will kill you!

6.   *Miye canzeka sni* - I am not angry

7.   *Nimitawa ktelo* – You are mine

8.   *Oyuhlagan sni* – STAY!

9.   *Tiwahe wiconi* – family life

10. *Wistelkiya* – Bashful (Are you bashful?)

11. *Uwa yo* – come here

Names of People:

BOOK I characters:

1.   *Woniya Mato* – Spirit Bear – War chief (main chief) – First kill at 12 winters (Night Hawk); (SC was 8) then his induction into warrior society – parents "disappeared" at age 9. I have it in my mind he became chief at 18 and is now 22.

2.   *Mazaska Zi Ista* – Golden Eyes (Kaitlin) - 18

3.   *Wawakankan* – Wonder Worker – shaman also on tribal council

4.   *Wawat'ecaka* – Gentle Rabbit – master curer – Wonder Worker's mother

5.   *Isnala Sungmanitu* – Lone Wolf – hunting chief

6.   *Wawakte Towanjila* – Sky Warrior – chief of village affairs

7.   *Haspa Nableca* – Apple Blossom – slave woman with Sky Warrior

a. *Nakpa Ihli* – Sore Ear (Snake Strike) – Apple Blossom's first name

8. *Unjinjintka Can Koica* – Desert Rose (likes Lone Wolf) – basket weaver

9. *Skeca Ecaca* – Playful Otter (likes Wonder Worker) – drills holes in stones

10. *Ohitika Hehaka* – Young Elk – young man who watches over Kaitlin

11. *Watila Hehaka* – Brave Elk – Young Elk's warrior name

12. *Zuzeca Pazan* – Snake Strike

13. – Yellow Feather – member of the *Cante Tinza*

a. Quiet Deer – Yellow Feather's wife

i. Red Squirrel – Yellow Feather & Quiet Deer's first child

ii.

14. – Moon Eyes (helped catch fish)

15. – Fresh Water – shares teepee with Kaitlin in teepees apart – motherly to Singing Cicada

16. – New Moon – shares teepee with Kaitlin in teepees apart

17. – Singing Cicada

18. – Morning Dove

19. – Opossum Eyes – girl who is mean to Kaitlin and desires Spirit Bear

20. – Stormy Night – girl who shares teepee with Opossum Eyes in the Teepees apart

21. – Eagle Talon (Yankton Sioux – *future* husband to Opossum Eyes) shared mothers with Sly Coyote

22. – Wise Owl – Yankton chief

BOOK II characters:

23. – Hawk Eyes – Cheyenne chief

24. – Midnight Star – Crow main chief

25. – Bloody Knife – Crow war chief

26. – Bright Sky – female Crow leader

27. – Black Bird – Crow warrior; ½ brother to Sly Coyote (son of Night Hawk)

28. – Raven's Wing – Crow warrior

29. – Falling Rock – Crow warrior

30. – Dark Horse – Crow warrior

31. – Sneaky Weasel – Crow warrior

32. *Sunmanitu Wacitusni* – Sly Coyote –½ Yankton Sioux (½ brother to Eagle Talon) and ½ Crow (son of Night Hawk)

33. *Tahca KatA* – Deer Slayer - Sioux name for Bobby (Kaitlin's brother)

Names of Things:

1. Cante Tinza – Brave Heart (warrior society)

2.   *Wakantanka* – The Great Spirit (God)

3.   Bear Claw Clan of the Lakota (Oglala Sioux) – Spirit Bear's branch of the mighty Sioux Nation

TIME PASSAGES:

1.   Winter – year

2.   Moon – month

3.   Sun – day

Author Bio

Sheri Chapman loves to laugh frequently and enjoys life. She loves to write in multiple genres. From memoirs to paranormal, horror, and romance, she always has a computer nearby to write whatever inspires her. Being an author and Director of Human Resources for Trient Press is a dream-come-true for her.

Sheri has a few books on the Read-it-Before-You-See-It list. Wild Passion renamed "Captive Heart" will be filmed soon. "A Killer, Revisited" is also on the list.

Sheri recently retired from teaching in Missouri Public schools with thirty years of experience. She received her bachelor's degree and first master's in special education from Missouri State University. Later, she pursued administration and got a second master's and a specialist degree from Lindenwood University in educational leadership. Instead of working as a principal or in a district office, she decided to raise her favorite animal: Pomeranian dogs. Sheri raises exotic-colored fluffy babies and sells them to those who genuinely appreciate their little princess or prince. She is licensed and inspected by Missouri State, USDA, her vet, and AKC. Someday, when she has less on her plate, Sheri would love to show her dogs.

Sheri is the mother of four beautiful daughters. She and their father enjoy spending time with each other, family, and friends. Aside from reading and writing, Sheri loves animals and being outdoors. She likes going for walks, fishing, scuba diving, kayaking, playing games, and watching movies. She is a big Harry Potter fan.

More from Sheri Chapman:

My website:
https://prayerpawpuppies.wixsite.com/authorsherichapman

Wild Passion *(Book 1 of the Passion series – historical romance)*

Wild Passion is COMING TO THE MOVIE SCREEN!!!

(It will be PG13 and renamed "Captive Heart")

*filming begins after 2020

Passions of the Heart *(Book 2 of the Passion series)*

Chief Spirit Bear: Rise to Power *(A Passion series story)*

<><><>

"Eyes with No Soul" (YA paranormal suspense)

COMING SOON:

A Killer, Revisited (Futuristic Detective, sci fi thriller)

To stay up to date with Sheri Chapman, you can follow her at any, or all, of these sites:

Facebook Page (author):
https://www.facebook.com/AuthorSheriChapman/

Amazon: https://www.amazon.com/-/e/B07HMHB4BK

Goodreads:
https://www.goodreads.com/author/show/8332075.Sheri_Chapman

Wattpad: http://wattpad.com/user/SheriChapman

Linked-In: https://www.linkedin.com/in/sheri-chapman-a256276a/

Twitter: https://twitter.com/Sheri7303